Catharine Maria Sedgwick, Mary Elizabeth Dewey

Life and Letters of Catherine M. Sedgwick

Edited by Mary E. Dewey

Catharine Maria Sedgwick, Mary Elizabeth Dewey

Life and Letters of Catherine M. Sedgwick
Edited by Mary E. Dewey

ISBN/EAN: 9783337015671

Printed in Europe, USA, Canada, Australia, Japan

Cover: Foto ©Raphael Reischuk / pixelio.de

More available books at **www.hansebooks.com**

THE SEDGWICK HOUSE AT STOCKBRIDGE.

OF

CATHARINE M. SEDGWICK.

EDITED BY

MARY E. DEWEY.

NEW YORK:

HARPER & BROTHERS, PUBLISHERS,

FRANKLIN SQUARE.

1871.

EVER since Miss Sedgwick's death, now a little more than three years ago, those who knew and loved her best have been desirous that some printed memorial should exist of a life so beautiful and delightful in itself, and so beneficent in its influence on others. Many besides must join in this wish; for, although few remain of the generation in which she was a shining light, yet they, and those who were still young enough when her books appeared to feel their characters distinctly moulded by her words of tender wisdom, will rejoice, both for their own sakes and that of younger people who "knew her not," that there should be placed on record a fuller sketch of her life than any that has yet appeared. The volume now offered to satisfy this desire is chiefly made up of such extracts from her letters and journals as can be given to the public, and are also enriched by papers from the hands of Mrs. Fanny Kemble, Mrs. Abby H. Gibbons, the Rev. Dr. Dewey, and William Cullen Bryant, Esq.

The letters are used in chronological order, and inevitably lack connection, except such as is given by their emanation from one character. They are like photographs taken from a hundred points of the same person, and, as in the curious stereoscopic instrument which produces a rounded and life-like image by the convergence of rays from a multitude of such likenesses, so in the mind of the sympathetic reader will arise, it is hoped, from the perusal of these let-

ters, a truer and more vivid portrait of their writer than could
be formed from any merely outside description.

The story of her life is a simple tale as regards outward
circumstances. No striking incidents, no remarkable oc-
currences will be found in it, but the gradual unfolding and
ripening amid congenial surroundings of a true and beautiful soul, a clear and refined intellect, and a singularly sympathetic social nature.

She was born eighty years ago, when the atmosphere was
still electric with the storm in which we took our place
among the nations, and passing her childhood in the seclusion of a New England valley, while yet her family was
linked to the great world without by ties both political and
social, early and deep foundations were laid in her character of patriotism, religious feeling, love of nature, and strong
attachment to home, and to those who made it what it was.
And when, later in life, she took her place among the acknowledged leaders of literature and society, these remained
the central features of her character, and around them gathered all the graceful culture, the active philanthropy, the social accomplishment which made her presence a joy wherever it came.

In the latter part of her life she was fortunately induced
to pen some recollections of her earlier years for the child
of the beloved niece who was to her as a daughter. They
are written with all her accustomed ease and grace of style,
and with a simplicity and freedom which show that the idea
of their being read beyond the family circle never entered
her mind, and, recorded as they were at long intervals, they
are without regular continuity ; but, apart from their chief
interest as an account of circumstances influencing the formation of her own character, they contain so much wise and
delicate reflection, such nice character-painting, and such
charming sketches of life and manners, that in reading them

we regret only that they close so soon, bringing their writer but to her fourteenth year.

Miss Sedgwick's time was mostly spent between Stockbridge and Lenox (villages in Berkshire County, Massachusetts), and New York. She was born in Stockbridge; and when she died, her body was laid among those of her kindred in the burial-ground of her native valley.

St. David's, *January 28th*, 1871.

LIFE AND LETTERS

OF

CATHARINE M. SEDGWICK.

RECOLLECTIONS OF CHILDHOOD.

May 5th, 1853.

MY DEAR LITTLE ALICE,—About two years since your father wrote me an eloquent note persuading me to write for you some memorial of my life, and what I knew of your forbears and mine. If you live to be an old woman, as I now am, you may like to rake in the ashes of the past, and if, perchance, you find some fire still smouldering there, you may feel a glow from it. It is not till we get deep into age that we feel by how slight a tenure we hold on to the memories of those that come after us, and not till then that we are conscious of an earnest desire to brighten the links of the chain that binds us to those who have gone before, and to keep it fast and strong.

The first of our Sedgwick ancestors of whom I have any tradition was Robert Sedgwick, who was sent by Oliver Cromwell as governor or commissioner (I am not sure by which title) to the island of Jamaica. As I am a full believer in the transmission of qualities peculiar to a race, it pleases me to recognize in "the governor," as we have always called him, a Puritan and an Independent, for to none other would Cromwell have given a trust so important. A love of freedom, a habit of doing their own thinking, has characterized our clan. Its men have not been trammeled by old usages, but for the most part have stood on those elevations that first catch the light and command a wide horizon. (There, my dear, I have not got over the second page without betraying my point of family pride and family weakness!) Truly I think it a great honor that the head of our house took office from that great man who achieved his own greatness, and not from the King Charleses who were born to it, and lost it by their own unworthiness.

Of my mother's progenitors I know only that, according to the general New England foundation, *three* brothers—Englishmen—came together to the New World; that they were men of character and estate, and that from one of them my mother descended. The riches went, not in our channel, but to that branch from which your kind and dear friends, Mrs. P. and cousin L. D., came. Riches and our name have no affinities, my dear. The wise man's prayer has been granted to us; we have enjoyed fully the advantage and felicity of being neither rich nor poor. My maternal grandfather was a brigadier colonel in the war in the French Provinces in 1745. The family tradition goes that he was at the taking of Cape Breton, and that he served with honor. You see his picture at your "Father Charles's," a handsome, hale man, with ruddy cheeks and most delicately beautiful hands, rather studiously displayed. I am afraid he had a weakness on that point; or perhaps he showed them to prove to his descendants that he had kept "clean hands," a commendable virtue, physically or morally speaking. He was one of the gentlemen *par excellence* of his time, who maintained the highest associations of the province. I have heard an old Irish servant of his, who maintained a feudal reverence for him, and who used to visit this portrait in the best parlor of our old Stockbridge home, say often, as he stood before it with the tears rolling off his cheeks, "Oh, if you could have seen him with his rigimintals, he would have sceared you!"

My grandmother was the widow of Mr. Sergeant, missionary from a Scotch society to the Indians, when my grandfather married her. Her maiden name was Williams. She was the sister of the founder of Williams College, and a woman much celebrated in her day for her intelligence and character. I have not, like you, my dear Alice, ever enjoyed the pleasure of this relation, which extends our being by one generation, and gives us the twilight as well as the dawn. My father's mother died long before I was born ; my mother's mother, I think, about eighteen months after. I have always heard her spoken of as a remarkable woman in her time, but my most vivid impression of her is from the record of Mrs. Quincy, who, when she was Susan Morton and a young girl, had an enthusiastic love for her mother's old friend, "Madam Dwight," and twice made a pilgrimage to Stockbridge to see her. I shall copy her account for your benefit. "Madam Dwight" spent her last years with a son of her first marriage, Dr. Sergeant, who lived at the old house still standing on Sergeant's Hill. In those days she had four children established in Stockbridge : Mr. John Sergeant, at that lonely point known as the "Wells House ;" Mrs. Hopkins, a mile and a half from the village ; and my mother, mistress of the then new mansion where your Aunt Susan* now lives. The old lady said her first look-out in

---

* Mrs. Theodore Sedgwick, widow of Miss Sedgwick's eldest brother. She died in 1867.

the morning was to see the smoke rise from her children's
chimneys, and with her "second sight" she saw them gathering their little flocks around their breakfast tables.   The
parents have all long ago fulfilled their earthly mission and
gone.   The children, most of them, have followed.   A few
yet linger on, and " Father Charles" and " Aunt Catharine"
may perhaps live in your memory when you read this.

My maternal grandfather died in Barrington, and was
there buried.   There is a monument to him in the old bury-
ing-ground there, and a lovely living monument in the old
elm-trees in the middle of the village, near the house, still
standing, in which he lived.   My mother had but few recollections of him.   He died when she was thirteen.

Here follows Mrs. Quincy's notice of his widow.   A brown
tabular monument marks her burying-place in Stockbridge.

" Madam Dwight, of Stockbridge, came to visit us in
1786.   The daughter of Colonel Williams, of Williamstown,
she married Mr. Sergeant, of Stockbridge, who died in early
life, leaving two sons ; and his widow became the wife of
Colonel Dwight, one of the leading men of Massachusetts in
his day.   Their children were Henry Dwight, and Pamela,
afterward Mrs. Theodore Sedgwick.   Madam Dwight was
again left a widow, and in 1786 was upward of sixty years
of age, tall and erect, dignified, precise in manner, yet benevolent and pleasing.   Her dress, of rich silk, a high-crowned
cap, with plaited border, and a watch, then so seldom worn
as to be a distinction, all marked the gentlewoman, and inspired respect.   She was a new study to me, and realized
my ideas of Mrs. Shirley in ' Sir Charles Grandison,' and
other characters I had read of in works of fiction.   When
she returned home she asked me to accompany her, and, to
my great joy, her request was complied with.   We went up
the Hudson in a sloop, in which we were the only passengers.

"We staid at Kinderhook till the wagon came for us from Stockbridge. I was seated by Madam Dwight, and we were driven by her grandson, a son of Dr. Sergeant. The distance was thirty or forty miles—a day's journey. It was twilight when we reached Stockbridge. The first thing that attracted my attention was a fish for a vane, on the steeple of the church. I said to Madam Dwight, 'How could they put up a poor fish, so much out of its own element? It ought at least to have been a flying fish.' She seemed much diverted at my remark, and repeated it to her friends, confessing that she had never thought of this absurdity herself, or heard it observed by others. Dr. Sergeant, Madam Dwight's son by her first marriage, resided in her mansion-house, where she retained the best parlor and chamber for her own use. He was an excellent man, and the most distinguished physician in that part of the country. We were joyfully received by him and his family. As I was fatigued, Madam Dwight took me to her room, and again expressed her pleasure at having me with her. I can never forget her affection and kindness. Her precepts and example made an indelible impression in favor of virtue and true piety. Her temper and character formed a living mirror, which reflected an image of such loveliness that my heart was truly bound to her. She made me her companion, read to me, and talked to me with the confidence of a friend.

"When, on the morning after our arrival, the window-shutters were opened, the Valley of the Housatonic, softened by wreaths of vapor rising over the mountains under the beams of the rising sun, seemed to my enchanted vision like fairy-land. I exclaimed, 'O, Madam Dwight! it looks like the Happy Valley of Abyssinia. There is the river, and there are the mountains on every side. Why did you never tell me of this beautiful view?' My friend seemed surprised at my enthusiasm. Long familiar with the scene, she hard-

ly realized its beauty.   I became attached to her grandchil-
dren, and passed several months in Stockbridge.   Her
daughter, Mrs. Sedgwick, lived upon 'the Plain,' as it was
called, in distinction to 'the Hill,' where Dr. Sergeant resided.

"When I was recalled home, I parted from Madam Dwight
with great reluctance, and she expressed equal sensibility.
She endeavored to comfort me by saying that she would
visit New York the next spring, and that I should return
with her.   But she was prevented from executing this intention ; and when I revisited Stockbridge in 1792, my friend
was no more."

My mother and Henry Dwight, who occupied the house
at the west end of "the Plain," were the only children of
the marriage of my grandmother with Colonel Dwight.
They had both been previously married.   My grandmother
had three children by the first marriage—Erastus, John, and
Electa.   Erastus was our "Uncle Doctor," a distinguished
physician in Berkshire for nearly fifty years.   He was a
mild, faithful man, and patient as the best of Christians are
with the severest domestic afflictions.   John succeeded his
father as missionary to the Indians.   I believe he worked
faithfully in the field, but I never could hear that the poor
man reaped any harvest.   His Indians had lost the masculine savage quality, the wild flavor, and had imbibed the
dreg-vices of civilization, without in the least profiting by its
advantages.   Electa became "Aunt Hopkins," and was the
ancestor of the present President and Professor of Williams
College.   The President is one of our best moral writers.

There was a traditionary story of my mother's childhood
which used to affect my imagination, for in my youth, dear
Alice, the dark shadows of the Indians had hardly passed
off our valleys, and tales about them made the stock terrors
of our nurseries.   The Indians of New England were at

that time—about 1750—friendly to the white people, but
the Mohawks were a terror to the whites, and to their red
friends. My mother was about two years old when my
grandmother was on a visit with her to her son Erastus (Dr.
Sergeant) in Stockbridge. The servant-men only were at
home—a black man and Lynch, the Irish servant whom I
have already mentioned. There was an alarm—the hideous
cry, "The Indians are coming!" There were no horses in
the stable, and the women decided at once to set off on foot.
My grandmother gave her little girl Pamela (my mother) to
the black servant, and dispatched him. Lynch followed
soon after, and, descending the hill, heard a faint cry from
a thick copse by the road-side. The cry came from the
poor little girl, whom the terrified man had relieved himself
of as soon as out of sight. Lynch took her up and carried
her to a place of safety. The Indians did not come, but
Lynch ever after looked upon himself as a hero in our family annals, and, in truth, pretty much as its founder. Poor
old man! It was a proud day for him when "the Judge"
(my dear father) and all "the family" went in "the old
coachee" to dine with him. His tremulous voice and shaking hands were almost firm again as he stood at his door
in *Larrywang* to welcome us. His name was Lawrence,
and "wang" is Indian for a cluster of houses, so the little
hamlet at the west end of Stockbridge was named for him.
I do not know if it has yet lost the designation.

Through all my childhood, Larry Lynch was the only Irish
inhabitant of Stockbridge! I do not believe there were
then half a dozen in the county. I think their influx did
not begin before 1830—and now there are two thronged
churches in Berkshire, and occasional mass in all the villages where they swarm. What would dear old Dr. West
our sixty years Defender of the Puritan Faith (the Doric pillar of Hopkinsianism), what would he say to these multitu-

dinous children of Antichrist! One of the oldest members of his Church, Mrs. Ingersoll, the deacon's wife, after the departure of her meek helpmate (he was the weaker vessel), rented the deacon's old hat-shop—he was hat manufacturer to the village—to Billy Brogan. It was a little, unpainted, one-story building, in the same inclosure with her house—none but an Irish family would have gathered there. When the Irish became numerous enough, mass was to be celebrated in the village, and Billy Brogan's habitation was selected as the largest domicil among them, and therefore fittest for the purpose. Nothing could exceed the indignation of the deacon's widow—a Yankee Mause*—nor the energy of her invectives, necessarily restrained within the decencies of Puritan objurgation. To have mass on her premises—a Catholic priest within her gates—"mass in the deacon's shop! the shop turned into a *Cathedral!* No, she had rather burn it!"

The result of this new experiment in the world of a distinct race, with marked characteristics and a religion of their own, living among us with the full benefit of equal rights and privileges, you, my dear Alice, may live to see. But, as ignorance can not compete with knowledge, nor get the mastery of it till there is an immense odds of brute force, as a despotic religion has neither sanction nor security in the midst of free institutions, I trust, my dear child, that the Irish, by the infusion of an element of warmth and generosity into our national character, will have done us more good than evil. I am inclined to think they have already done this for us. I have so lively a recollection of the time when we were in the transitive state—when the old well-trained slaves had disappeared—when the few black servants to be hired were shiftless, lazy, and unfaithful, and our own people scarcely to be obtained, or, if obtained, coming "to ac-

* Mause Headrigg, in "Old Mortality."

commodate you," and staying only till they could accommo-
date themselves better, that I feel grateful for Irish servants,
with all their Celtic infirmities on their heads—their half
savage ways—their blunders—their imaginativeness—indefiniteness—and *curve-lines* every way. They desire employment—they are willing servants—they are sympathetic and
progressive, and I have at this moment, June, 1853, a girl in
my service, Margaret Pollock, a pearl of great price. She
is a Protestant, to be sure, but she was born and bred in
Ireland, and I would not exchange her for all the service I
could distill in Yankeedom.

I have sore recollections of the time when I rode the
country round to get, for love and money, girls to do the
family work. Unwilling they were to come, and incompetent when they came. My father's house was one of the
few where the domestics were restricted to the kitchen table.
"Oh," said a woman to me, whose daughter I was begging
for, "now Catharine, we are all made out of the same clay,
we have got one Maker and one Judge, and we've got to
lay down in the grave side by side—why can't you sit down
to the table together?" We were vexed and fretted, and
thought the people presuming, impertinent, and stupid; but
stupid they were not, and we were not philosophers. They
used their power; they had something better before them than
domestic subordination and household service. *Their* time
had come, their harness was thrown off, fresh pastures were
before them. They did not, perhaps, use their freedom
gracefully, but they enjoyed it, and it was theirs. The West
and the factories have absorbed all this population, and
Providence has sent the starving hewers of wood and drawers of water from other lands to us, to be taught in our
kitchens, and to be borne on by the mighty wave of progress
that is steadily tending onward and upward here. It is not
left to our choice—Providence makes of our homes Irish

school-houses, **of our mothers and** daughters involuntary missionaries! **Thus, if you will but** observe it, dear Alice, you will see **that God works** more effectively than man, in a wider field, and with greater means. **He** sets the sun in **the sky, and it lights** the world; we are proud of the gas-**lights that** dispel the darkness of a city, just enabling us to **know a** friend from a stranger. God sends rain over our vast tracts of land, refreshing harvest-fields, ripening the fruits of the earth, nourishing our gardens, and filling rivers as well as cisterns; we take a watering-pot and save a few plants from perishing. A few good men and women of the land go forth to teach **the** heathen; God, when **the** time came to deliver the Irish people from their oppressors, sent them forth to the plentiful land reserved for them here, where they till and *are tilled*. Their children will melt into **our** population, in which there must be an amalgamation **of va-**rious elements, the calculating, cold, intellectual Saxon, the metaphysical, patient German, the vivacious, imaginative, in-**definite,** changeful, uncertain **Celt,** the superstitious North-man, the fervent children **of the** South. A strange com-pound **must** come out of this. There is support for **all** living nature—the "finest of the wheat" for the basis, **and** sour and sweet, and spice and spirit—a " De'il**'s bro' "** it **will** be—or ambrosia **for** the gods, a perfecting **and** consum-mation of the species.

But **I am** far enough off from our family history, or rather my **own** story, which I began **with; but** fearing, dear Alice, that **you would never** know **how I** came here, I have, and shall transmit **to** you all that **I know** of my progenitors. My father, Theodore Sedgwick, **was** educated at Yale College, **New** Haven. **He was** supported there by the generous ef-**forts** and **sacrifices of his** older brother John. **The** family fortunes **seem to** have run out pretty **much after** the death of the commissioner or governor sent **by** Cromwell to the island of Jamaica, and after being fixed at West Hartford, Connecticut, for two generations, my grandfather, one, I believe, of a large family, removed to Cornwall, and purchased a large farm on its bleak hills.   He opened a "store" there, and, just arrived *in mezzo cammino*, he died of apoplexy and left three sons and three daughters.   Uncle John was head of the house, and at once resolving, with my grandmother's earnest and ready co-operation, to maintain my father at college, he opened a tavern to obtain money which could not be worked out of the stony land of Cornwall.   My father pursued his studies to the last year, when, being a party in some boyish gayeties quite outside of the Puritan tolerance of the times, he was expelled by the president, of whom I received the impression, I can not say with what accuracy, that he was a compound of pedagogue and granny.   My father, sobered by this cloud, took to divinity, and went to Dr. Bellamy's to study theology.   The doctor, I rather think, from the current anecdotes of the time, had considerable sympathy with the secular side of my father's character.   At any rate, with his entire sympathy and approbation, my father turned from divinity to law, and began and finished his legal studies with Mark Hopkins, of Great Barrington, Massachusetts, a distinguished lawyer of his time, and grandfather of the present President of Williams College.*

* My father used to tell with much gusto of Dr. Bellamy that one of his parishioners, who was a notorious scamp, came to him, saying, in the parlance of the divinity that pervaded this part of New England at that period, "I feel that I have obtained a hope!"   The doctor looked surprised.   "I realize that I am the chief of sinners," continued the hypocritical canter.   "Your neighbors have long been of that opinion," rejoined the doctor.   The man went on to say out the lesson—"I feel willing to be damned for the glory of God."   "Well, my friend, I don't know any one who has the slightest objection!"

I heard yesterday, while on a visit to my dear friend, Dr. Dewey, at Sheffield, another equally characteristic story of this old friend of my fa-

My father appreciated highly Mr. Hopkins's talents and virtues, and always spoke of him as a man *" comme il y en a peu."* Like other patriotic civilians, Mr. Hopkins took up arms during the Revolutionary War. An old man, a soldier of that time—a pensioner of ours—told me the following anecdote : Mr. H. had a command at White Plains, or in that vicinity, when the British were in great force near them. News came that he was ill (I believe of the disease of which he afterward prematurely died). My father went to him at great personal risk, for the British were advancing, and our people retreating. He procured a litter and soldiers—my informant was one of them—and Mr. H. was placed on the litter and hastily carried off. They heard firing ; Mr. H., weakened by illness, was terrified, sure he should be taken prisoner, or they should all be shot ; he implored my father with tears to leave him to his fate, and save himself. My father of course resisted, cheered and sustained him, and conveyed him to a place of safety. My father afterward married the young half-sister of Mark Hopkins's wife, Pamela Dwight, my beloved and tenderly remembered mother.

My father first opened an office in Barrington (Bryant, the poet, occupied it afterward), and I have heard him say that for six weeks he sat looking up and down the street, like poor Dennis Bulgruddery, for a client, but no client came, and he took down his sign and moved off to Sheffield, where he began his honorable legal career. He married, before he was twenty-one, Eliza Mason, a relative of the late

---

ther. One of his Church was up before that solemn tribunal for some profane words spoken in wrath. He was a man liable to be provoked to a sudden gust of passion by a scamp, but tender and cherishing as a June dew to the widow and fatherless. After hearing the evidence of his accusers, Dr. B. said, " The poor man is a grievous sinner on one side, but, my friends, I think he has more of the milk of human kindness in his heart than all the rest of my Church together !"

celebrated Jeremiah Mason. She died within the year of their marriage, of small-pox, which she caught from my father. It was the practice of those times in our rural districts to shut patients ill with this hideous disease in a hospital (some little shanty set apart, out of the village, and called the pock-house) till they were pronounced beyond the possibility of communicating it. My father, thus certified, went home to his young wife. She was in a condition that made it imprudent to take inoculation. It was believed that she caught the disease from combing my father's hair, which he wore long and tied in a cue, according to the fashion of the times.

My father, through life, cherished the most tender recollections of this poor lady. Not long after her death, he was lying upon the bed he had shared with her (a "field bedstead," with a bar across the two foot-posts), and unable to sleep; he said to himself, "If I could but see her as she was, in her every-day dress—see her once more, I should be comforted." (Oh, how many of us, Alice, would give the world for that one sight more, one look, one word!) Well, he pondered on this thought till suddenly the room filled with a light—not like the light of lamp, not like a thousand, the brightest—not like the light of the sun, but a heavenly radiance, and his wife—his young wife, her face lit with love and happiness, stood leaning over the bar at the foot of his bed, looking on him. He raised himself on his elbow; he, wondering, surveyed her from head to foot, and fantastically, as we sometimes do in our strongest emotions observe trifles, remarked the buckles in her shoes; he sprang forward to embrace her—she was gone—the light was gone—it was a dream. "If I had one particle of superstition," he would say, "I should believe that my wife had appeared to me!" And yet I think my dear father had that particle of superstition, for through his whole life he had once a year a dream

that was like a visitation of this girl-wife. She always came
to restore to him those days of young romantic love—the
passages of after life vanished. I can well remember the
sweet, tender expression of his face when he used to say, " I
have had my dream !"

I do not know precisely the period that elapsed between
my father's first marriage and his second one to my mother.
It was not long—not much more, I think, than the canonized
" year and a day." In that time marriage was essential to
a man's life ; there were no arrangements independent of it,
no substitutions for it ; and, besides, my father was domestic
in his disposition, out-and-out social ; he could not endure
solitude unless he were intensely absorbed in business, and
he married. My mother was the only daughter of Brigadier
Colonel Dwight and my grandmother, who had been the
widow of the excellent missionary Sergeant. My mother's
family (of this I have rather an indefinite impression than
any knowledge) objected to my father on the score of family, they priding themselves on their gentle blood ; but as
he afterward rose far beyond their highest water-mark, the
objection was cast into oblivion by those who made it.
Their union was a very perfect one : reverence, devotion,
with infinite tenderness on her side ; respect, confidence,
and unswerving love on his. Their eldest child was called,
at my mother's request, Eliza Mason, after the first wife—a
proof of how generous and *unjealous* she was.
I have just (October 6th, 1853) come into possession of
some old letters which have carried me back deep into the
interests of my parents' lives, and to give you, my dear child,
some notion of my mother's character, her wisdom, her con-
jugal devotion, and self-negation, I copy a letter she wrote
to my father at a time when he was to decide whether to
continue in public life or retire from it. His continuance

involved his absence from her during the winter, when, with very delicate health and a nervous temperament, she must be left for many months in this cold northern country, with young children, a large household, complicated concerns, and the necessity of economy. A distance of two hundred and eighty miles—hence to Philadelphia—was a very different affair from what it would be now. The winter journey, if most prosperous, would occupy five or six days, and might twice or thrice that time, so that it was nearly as grave a question as it would be now whether a husband were to pass his winters in London. N.B.—There is in the style a deference not common in these days, and you will observe, too, an old-fashioned form of expression.

"Pardon me, my dearest Mr. Sedgwick, if I beg you once more to think over the matter before you embark in public business.

"I grant that the 'call of our country,' 'the voice of Fame,' and 'the Honble,' 'right Honble,' are high-sounding words. 'They play around the head, but come not near the heart.' A wish to serve the true interests of our country is certainly a laudable ambition, but the intention brings many cares with it. You best know what they are, as you have had a large share of them already.

"The new government is yet untried. If I mistake not, the success of it depends more on the virtue and economy of the people than on the wisdom of those who govern, or the uncommon excellency that is supposed to attend the form.

"Should the people find they are not happy under it, the fault will all be in their rulers. They will be subjected to the envy of some, the reproach of others, and the remarks of all. The interest of your family deserves some attention. Men in public life are generally dependent in more senses than one. Should you find your circumstances straitened at a future day, I **know, from the** tender affection you have for your **children, it would give** you great pain.   **A re-** turn to Congress would then be painful, and would be thought degrading.   **On my** own account I will say nothing but that **I have no**t a distant wish that you should sacrifice your hap- **piness to** mine, or your inclination to my opinion.   If, **on the whole, you think** a public line of life will be most conducive **to** your interest and happiness, I will pray that He who is alone the author of all good will strew peace in all your paths.   Submission is my duty, and, however hard, I will try to practice what reason teaches **me I am** under obligation to do."

My father decided for public life, and I believe my mother **never** again expressed one word of remonstrance or dissat- isfaction.   She, no doubt, was gratified with his honorable public **career, inasmuch as it** proved his worth, but I think **she had no sympathy** with what is called honor and distinc- tion ; she was essentially modest and humble, and she *looked beyond.*

She was oppressed with cares and responsibilities ; her health **failed** ; she made no claims, she uttered no **com-** plaints **; she** knew she was most tenderly beloved, and held in the very highest respect by my father, but her physical strength was not equal to the demands upon her, and her **reason** gave way.   She had two or three turns of insanity, **which** lasted each, I believe, some months ; I know not how long, **for I was too young to** remember any thing but being told **that my "mamma was** sick, and **sent** away to a good doctor."   **This** physician, I **have** since learned, was a Dr. Waldo, of Richmond, who took my mother to his house, **and** was supposed to treat her judiciously and most kindly.   **But** oh ! I can not bear to think—it has been one of the **saddest** sorrows of my life to think how much aggravated misery **my** dear, gentle, patient mother must have suffered from the ignorance of the right mode of treating mental diseases which then existed.*

My mother may have had a constitutional tendency to insanity, but I believe the delicate construction of a sensitive and reserved temperament, a constitution originally fragile, and roughly handled by the medical treatment of the times, and the terrible weight of domestic cares, will sufficiently account for her mental illness without supposing a cerebral tendency which her descendants may have inherited. But this fear may be wholesome to them, if it lead them to a careful physical training, to guarding against nervous susceptibilities and weakness, and to avoiding the stimulants and excitements so unfavorable to nervous constitutions. I firmly believe that people may be educated out of a hereditary tendency to insanity more surely than one can eradicate a liability to consumption, or any other scrofulous poison.

I am sure my father felt throughout his public career a harassing sense of the suffering it occasioned my mother. In a letter to my sisters, then young girls, dated 1791, three years after the letter I have quoted from, he says, " You can imagine how much the conflict between a sense of public duty and private inclination affected my spirits and temper while I was at home. I most sincerely endeavored to weigh all circumstances, and to discover what I ought to do. This I believed I did, but the struggle was severe and painful."

* * * * * *

" The description you give of her patience and resignation

---

* Mumbet was the only person who could tranquillize my mother when her mind was disordered—the only one of her friends whom she liked to have about her—and why? She treated her with the same respect she did when she was sane. As far as was possible, she obeyed her commands and humored her caprices ; in short, her superior instincts hit upon the mode of treatment that science has since adopted.

is precisely such as I should have expected. You know not, my dear children, the blessing of having such a parent. While she possesses all the softness and tenderness which renders woman so amiable, she has a greatness and nobleness of mind which I have hardly known equaled by her sex. How dignified, how exemplary in all her sufferings!"

In the same letter he says, "This life is a checkered scene. I myself have been what is called a prosperous man. I have reason to bless God I have been less unfortunate, even in my own opinion, than many others. To the view of the world, I have been, I doubt not, an object of envy. Connected with one of the best of women, blessed with many children,* all hopeful, and those who have become more advanced of good characters and deserving them, in easy circumstances, respectable in my profession, honored in my own country, and known and respected in others, yet I feel that this life is far from affording felicity. How important is it, then, that our hopes should not rest in these things!

" May, my dear children, that gracious Being, whose goodness has done better for me than I deserved, be the kind protector and guardian of my beloved offspring, most fervently prays your ever affectionate papa,

                              "THEODORE SEDGWICK."

I had in my hand yesterday another of my father's letters, which may entertain you at the distance of time you live from the dynasty of Washington, for it is "sixty years since."

"*Philadelphia,* 1794. I dined yesterday at the President's, where I was treated with a distinguished partiality very grateful to my feelings. The President, you know, never sits at the head of his table. That place he particularly re-

---

* Judge Sedgwick was at this time forty-six years old, and his children were seven in number : Eliza, Theodore, Frances, Harry, Robert, Catharine, and Charles.

quested me to take ; Mr. Dandridge, as usual, sat at the other end. When Mrs. Washington retired, she stopped and desired me not to go away until I had been entertained by *Nelly's** playing. Accordingly, I went up stairs, and the good lady requested me to take a seat on the sofa by her. She then asked if I had any particular tune which was a favorite with me, and added, '*For Nelly can play any thing.*' Submitting myself to her taste, to prevent discovering that I had none, Nelly played several grave and solemn tunes, and accompanied them inimitably with her voice. Mrs. Washington, perceiving me unusually solemn, turned to Miss Custis and said, with her usual amiable simplicity, ' Nelly, play for Mr. Sedgwick "Chase dull care away ;" don't you see he wants to be enlivened?' After spending with the good family an hour, I accompanied them to a concert for the benefit of a French family."

These were victims of the Revolution, and he goes on to detail particulars of several then in Philadelphia, among others the Duc de Liancourt and the Bishop of Autun. But we, in our day, are more familiar with the reception of exiles than my father was, and you and your contemporaries, dear Alice, are like to have the opportunity of a similar hospitality.†

* Miss Eleanor Custis, Mrs. Washington's daughter.

† *From Reminiscences dated July,* 1812.

In the year 1782, just at the close of our Revolutionary War, my father dined with the officers of our army at Verplanck's Point. The illustrious Washington was there. Just before the sun set, Gen. Washington was called out. My father then rose to take his leave, but was deterred by the general requesting him to stay, and telling him that he would show him something which he was sure would be very gratifying to him. The roll was then called, and all the troops paraded. Gen. Washington then, pointing to two objects, told my father that all the men between them were from Massachusetts, and made one hundred and fifty more than one half of his whole army.

I copy for you a little letter written by my father to his eldest child when she was a little girl of ten years. It is a fair sample of the fond, tender letters he was in the habit of writing periodically and punctually to his children while he was immersed in the most important national affairs.

"Accept my thanks, my kind and good child, for your

When my father was first elected to Congress, which was not till after a very sharp contest, he had a very slight acquaintance with Washington. The first evening he arrived at the seat of government he went with a friend to be presented at the President's levee. The President immediately recognized him, stepped out of the drawing-room, gave his hand to my father, and told him he was very glad that he was elected at last.

This was a most gracious reception from a man characterized by a deportment reserved almost to severity. To my father, who knew how to appreciate even a look from the greatest man of any age or country, it was a mark of distinction and kindness peculiarly grateful.

I have heard my father relate an instance of the repelling dignity of Washington's manner on an occasion when it was proper for him to repress familiarity. Gardoqui, the Spanish minister, at one of the general's levees, advanced from the crowd, and, with an air perfectly easy and familiar, slipped his arm within the general's, and began to whisper to him. He only began, for Washington shook him off with a look that would have awed temerity itself. Gardoqui shrunk back into the crowd, and paid the penalty of his forwardness in silence and shame.

On the last day of Washington's administration, he invited my father, with Mr. Ames and Mr. Goodhue, to take a family dinner with him. When the gentlemen were retiring, he begged my father to remain, as he said he had a great deal to say to him. * * * * The President spoke of his successor as a man of science and integrity, but he said no man would be the worse for wise counselors. He had heard that my father, Mr. Ross, and some others purposed withdrawing from the government, and he had heard it, he said, with deep concern, as he wished that such men should give all their talents and influence to aid this last experiment of a republic. For himself, he retired that he might be a spectator, as it was a common remark that a by-stander was a better judge of a game than one of the parties could be. Thus he modestly expressed his desire to see how our chariot of state would move when he who had so long guided it in safety should have relinquished the reins.

kind and pretty letter by Mr. E——. Believe me, my sweet prattler, that you can not, more than I do, regret our separation. Should it so happen that my duty will permit, I will fly on the wings of Love to see and embrace my lovely, sweet children. If you knew how happy I was made by the information that you are a good child, you would not fail to continue to be so. I do not believe you will. I should be miserable if I did. Remember, my love, that our happiness or our misery depends chiefly on our good conduct, and you will not fail to endeavor to be good. Be kind to your mamma. She is good. She deserves all your attention. Remember that you are the oldest child, and that you can reward your parents' care by a good example.

"Farewell. I heartily pray God to make you virtuous and happy."

In all his letters he expressed the most thoughtful love for my mother, and the highest appreciation of her character. When fearing a recurrence of her mental malady, he says, "Read to her, or persuade her to read diverting books. Every other object must submit to an attention to her. Is company diverting, she must be indulged with it. Does it increase her gloom, it must be kept from her. She is the best of human beings, and every circumstance of business or of pleasure must be made to submit to her restoration."

I have been reading a mass of my father's letters from 1784 to 1789, addressed to my sister Eliza and to my mother. My sister Eliza resembled my mother much more than Frances or myself. She had her modesty, her self-diffidence, her humility. This was a constitutional quality, but so authorized and enforced by their religion that to them both it took the potent form of a duty.

I rather think that my mother was intellectually superior to my sister; if not originally, by the long partnership with a superior mind occupied in great affairs. Her long separations from my father seem to have been almost cruel to her. He continually laments over them, and, but that his compunction is tempered by the conviction of an overruling duty to his country, he would have been miserable. Her sufferings are past, and, I doubt not, prepared her to enjoy more keenly the rest and felicities of heaven. The good done by my father in trying to establish the government, and to swell the amount of that political virtue which makes the history of the Federal party the record of the purest patriotism the world has known—*that remains.*

You do not seem now, my dear little Alice, like one who will ever be curious to inquire into the shades of political virtue ; but who knows but one of the boys may one day be prying into his ancestors' history, whose pulses will beat quicker for the testimony I give to my father's earnest devotion to his country.

I was a child at the period of the great ferment occasioned by the decline of the Federal party and the growth of the Democratic party. My father had the habit of having his children always about him, and we had so strong a sympathy with him that there was no part of his life which we did not partake. I remember well looking upon a Democrat as an enemy to his country, and at the party as sure, if it prevailed, to work its destruction. I heard my father's conversation with his political friends, and in the spontaneous expressions of domestic privacy, and I received the impression then (and, looking back with a riper judgment, I feel assured of its correctness) that the Federal party loved their country, and were devoted to it, as virtuous parents are to their children. It was to my father what selfish men's private affairs are to them, of deep and ever-present interest. It was not the success of men, or the acquisition of office, but the maintenance of principles on which, as it appeared to them, the sound health and true life of their country depended. They dreaded French influence—they believed Jefferson to be false, the type of all evil—they were a good deal influenced by old prestiges—they retained their predilections for Great Britain. They hoped a republic might exist and prosper, and be the happiest government in the world, but not without a strong aristocratic element; and that the constitutional monarchy of Britain was the safest and happiest government on earth, I am sure they believed.

But, firm to the experiment of the Republic, they had no treasonable thought of introducing a monarchy here. Their misfortune, and perhaps the inevitable consequence of having been educated loyal subjects of a monarchical government, was a thorough distrust of "the people." I remember my father, one of the kindest-hearted of men, and most observant of the rights of all beneath him, habitually spoke politically of the people as "Jacobins," "sans-culottes," and "miscreants." He—and in this I speak of him as the type of the Federal party—dreaded every upward step they made, regarding their elevation as a depression, in proportion to their ascension, of the intelligence and virtue of the country. The upward tendencies from education, and improvements in the arts of life, were unknown to them. They judged of the "people" as they had been, as were the "greasy, unwashen multitude" of Rome and of Shakspeare's time—as they are now for the most part in Europe, utterly inexperienced in government, incapable of attaining to its abstractions, or feeling its moralities.

My father felt it to be his duty to remain in public life at every private sacrifice—at the expense of his domestic happiness, his home-love, which was his ruling passion. I know he must have felt the craving that all men conscious of power feel for enlarging the bounds of their horizon. The Miltons are not content to be "inglorious," nor the Hampdens to be mere "villagers."

Still I am sure that nothing short of a self-devotion to his country's good would have induced him to leave my mother, winter after winter, tottering under her burden of care, and so far separate himself from his little children, whose lisping voices seemed to follow him, and whose loved images were ever about him. Nothing can exceed the unintermitting tenderness of his letters to my mother. He never failed, in any pressure of business, to write to her and to his children. How well do I remember the arrival of those packets! The mail came but once a week, and then we all gathered about our mother, each expecting, and very often each receiving, a letter "from papa!" I can see them now—the form of the letters—the directions, as they looked then. I *do* see them now, time-worn and discolored, but still imbued with the essence of my father's soul. No man was in his affections a truer image of Him "who is love."

My mother, after years of decline from a life of ill health, died in 1807, at the age of fifty-four.

The portrait I have of her was as faithful a likeness as so wretched a painting could be. Bad as it is, it will give you an impression of her personal dignity, and of the sweetness and sensibility of her character, and of her temperament, which, if not originally a sad one, became melancholy from her tragic personal trials.*

I will copy here a character of her, written, I think, by my brother Harry. It has a little of the stiffness of an unaccustomed pen, and the formality of an obituary, but it was true to the letter, which few obituaries are.

"*Mrs. Pamela Sedgwick.*—In attempting to offer a tribute

* A good engraving from this picture is published in Griswold's "Republican Court," printed in 1855.

to her memory, the author feels the most trembling solici-
tude. That eulogium, which ought to have been kept sacred to eminent merit, has been so prostituted to vulgar use
and on unworthy occasions, that there remain no terms by
which to distinguish such virtue as was that of this most excellent woman.

"Through a whole lifetime she never once expressed a
feeling of impatience. Such was the strength of her submissive piety; but, from the sensibility of her temper, she
was often afflicted with the severest anguish, from an appre-
hension that her life was useless.

"She seemed sweetly to repose on the pillow of Faith,
and, when tortured by pain and debilitated by disease, she
not only sustained herself, but was the comfort, support, and
delight of her family.

"Her sufferings, in degree and duration, have been perhaps without a parallel, but they reached not the measure
of her faith and her patience. Had she endured less, she
would never have exhibited, and her friends could never
have estimated, the invincible meekness and the gentleness
of her heavenly temper. It may not be profane or irrever-
ent to suppose that, with some distant resemblance to our
Redeemer, she did not suffer solely for herself—that her
trials and her piety were in some measure designed for the
instruction of others; and we may be permitted to hope
that her example and her memory, by their influence on the
heart and the conduct, will contribute to the eternal welfare
of those she most loved. Many whom she has instructed in
the spirit and practice of the holy religion she professed,
and many whose wants and pains have been relieved by her
bounty and soothed by her attention, will gratefully acknowledge that this is but a faint delineation of her virtue,
and their tears will confess that, though the sketch is imperfect, it is not false.

" What her friends, and, above all, what her husband and
children have suffered, must be left to the conception of the
reader—*it can not be told.*   But it is hoped that they will try
to dismiss all selfish regards, and to rejoice that she is now
where the righteous have their reward, and the weary are at
rest.

" Stockbridge, Sept., 1807."

Beloved mother !   Even at this distance of time, the
thought of what I suffered when you died thrills my soul !

My father felt the solitariness of his home.   He married,
a little more than a year after my mother's death, Penelope
Russell, a Boston woman, of a highly-respectable family, an
agreeable exterior, and an attractive vivacity.   My father
was flattered into this marriage by some good-natured friends
who believed he would be the happier for it, and knew she
would.   Like most second marriages where there are children, it was disastrous.   The poor lady was put into a life
for which she was totally unfitted.   She knew nothing of
the business of country domestic life, and her ambition to
shine in it was simply ludicrous to us, and onerous to her.
She fluttered gracefully enough through the inanities of town
drawing-rooms, but the reality and simplicity of our country
life was insupportable to her.   We were all matured ; I was
eighteen, Charles sixteen, the rest all married or away from
home—but I forget, dear Alice, that I began with telling you
the story of my own life, and that I shall come, in due time,
to this chapter of its experience.*

* As, unfortunately, this autobiography was never completed, and
breaks off with the close of its writer's childhood, this painful subject
may be closed here in a few words.

During the four years that passed between Judge Sedgwick's last
marriage and his death, his children, though bitterly grieved at seeing a

I was born, then, in 1789, December 28th, in a bitter cold night, as I have heard my Aunt Dwight say, who was present on the occasion. It was in the southwest room of the dear old house, that which your Aunt Susan now occupies as her parlor, and in which your "father Charles" was born two years after, in December, 1791. I came into the world two months before I was due. It was owing to this, probably, that I had the delicacy of complexion which made my good uncle, Dr. Sergeant, and "Mumbet" remember me as "fair and handsome as a London doll." I know nothing memorable of my infancy except that my sister Eliza, through all that severe winter, slept in the room with my mother, and got up in the cold watches of the night to feed me, my mother being unable to nurse me. What such a love-service was those only can estimate who remember our houses before the winter atmosphere was tempered by stoves.

How faint and few are the recollections of a childhood that flowed smoothly on the current of love! I remember my first attempt to say "Theodore" and "Philadelphia," and I remember a trick I had of biting the glass from which I was drinking, and, from a comparison of dates, this was within the first two years of my life. Now, my darling, don't think I am superannuated because I think it worth while to record this. It is associated with my first impression of my father. I remember that there was company at table—Miss Susan Morton, from New York.* I remember where she

woman of so superficial a character in their mother's place, never failed in deference and attention to the companion he had chosen, and so unchanged was their reverential love for him that he probably never suspected their unhappiness on this account.

Within a month after her husband's death, Mrs. Sedgwick returned to her friends, and it is enough to say of her that she left a family all possessing quick sensibility, and governed by sincere and practical religious feeling, without having inspired either respect or affection.

* Afterward Mrs. Quincy, from whose Reminiscences a passage is given above (*ante*, p. 16.)

sat, where my **father sat, and where I sat.** I recall *perfectly* the feeling with which **I turned my eye** to him, expecting to see that brow (which **all his life long marked to** me the state of his **feelings as distinctly** as the degrees **on** a thermometer do the state of the weather) cloud with displeasure, but it was smooth as love could make it. That consciousness, that glance, that assurance remained stamped indelibly— and I think I have never known a greater fear than to see a cloud on that brow.

How trivial, too, are the recollections of childhood! The next notch **on** my memory **is of being sent over** to Mrs. Caroline Dwight, to borrow a **boy's** dress of Frank Dwight's, which **was to be the** model of your "**father Charles's**" first **male** attire. Then **come** thronging recollections of my childhood, its joys **and** sorrows—"Papa's going away," and "Papa's coming home;" the dreadful clouds that came over our sunny **home when mamma was** sick—my love of Mumbet, **that** noble woman, the main pillar of our household— distinctly the faces of the favorite servants, *Grippy*, Sampson Derby, Sampson the cook, a runaway slave, "Lady Prime," and various others who, to my mind's eye, are **still** young, vigorous, and alert! Not Agrippa, for him **I** saw through the various stages of manhood to decrepit old age. Grippy is one of the few who will be **immortal in our** village **annals.** He enlisted in the army of **the** Revolution, and, **being a** very well-trained and adroit servant, he was taken into the personal service of the noble Pole, Kosciusko. Unlike most heroes, he always remained a hero to his valet Grippy, who **many a time has charmed our** childhood with stories **of his soldier-master.** One I remember, of which **the** catastrophe moved my **childish** indignation. Kosciusko **was absent** from camp, and Agrippa, to amuse his fellow-servants, **dressed in** his master's most showy uniform, and **blacked** with shining black-ball **his** legs and **feet** to resemble boots.

Just as he was in full exhibition, his master returned, and, resolved to have his own fun out of the joke, he bade "Grip" follow him, and took him to the tents of several officers, introducing him as an African prince. Poor Grippy, who had as mortal an aversion practically as our preachers of temperance have theoretically to every species of spirituous liquor, was received at each new introduction by a soldier's hospitality, and compelled, by a nod from his master, to taste each abhorrent cup, brandy, or wine, or "Hollands," or whatever (to Grippy poisonous) potion it might chance to be, till, when his master was sated with the joke, he gave him a kick, and sent him staggering away. I think Grippy was fully compensated by the joke for the ignominy of its termination. He had a fund of humor and mother-wit, and was a sort of Sancho Panza in the village, always trimming other men's follies with a keen perception, and the biting wit of wisdom. Grippy was a capital subaltern, but a very poor officer. As a servant he was faultless, but in his own domain at home a tyrant. Mumbet (mamma Bet), on the contrary, though absolutely perfect in service, was never servile. Her judgment and will were never subordinated by mere authority; but when she went to her own little home, like old Eli, she was the victim of her affections, and was weakly indulgent to her riotous and ruinous descendants.

I believe, my dear Alice, that the people who surround us in our childhood, whose atmosphere infolds us, as it were, have more to do with the formation of our characters than all our didactic and preceptive education. Mumbet had a clear and nice perception of justice, and a stern love of it, an uncompromising honesty in word and deed, and conduct of high intelligence, that made her the unconscious moral teacher of the children she tenderly nursed. She was a remarkable exception to the general character of her race. Injustice and oppression have confounded their moral sense;

cheated as they have been of their liberty, defrauded at whole-
sale of time and strength, what wonder that they allow themselves petty reprisals—a sort of predatory warfare in the
households of their masters and employers—for, though
they now among us be free, they retain the vices of a degraded and subjected people.

I do not believe that any amount of temptation could have
induced Mumbet to swerve from truth. She knew nothing
of the compromises of timidity, or the overwrought consci-
entiousness of bigotry. Truth was her nature—the offspring
of courage and loyalty. In my childhood I clung to her
with instinctive love and faith, and the more I know and
observe of human nature, the higher does she rise above others, whatever may have been their instruction or accomplishment. In her the image of her Maker was cast in material
so hard and pure that circumstances could not alter its out-
line or cloud its lustre. This may seem rhodomontade to
you, my child. "Why," you may exclaim, "my aunt could
say nothing more of Washington, and this woman was once
a slave, born a slave, and always a servant!" Yes, so she
was, and yet I well remember that during her last sickness,
when I daily visited her in her little hut—her then independent home—I said then, and my sober after judgment
ratified it, that I felt awed as if I had entered the presence
of Washington. Even protracted suffering and mortal sickness, with old age, could not break down her spirit. When
Dr. F. said to her, with the proud assurance of his spiritual
office, "Are you not afraid to meet your God?" "No, sir,"
she replied, "I am not afeard. I have tried to do my duty,
and I am *not* afeard!" This was truth, and she spoke it
with calm dignity. Creeds crumble before such a faith.

Speaking to me of the mortal nature of her disease, she
said, "It is the last stroke, and it is the best stroke."

Her expressions of feeling were simple and comprehensive. When she suddenly lost a beloved grandchild, the only descendant of whom she had much hope—she was a young mother, and died without an instant's warning—I remember Mumbet walking up and down the room with her hands knit together and great tears rolling down her cheeks, repeating, as if to send back into her soul its swelling sorrow, " Don't say a word ; it's God's will !" And when I was sobbing over my dead mother, she said, "We must be quiet. Don't you think I am grieved? Our hair has grown white together." Even at this distance of time I remember the effect on me of her still, solemn sadness. Elsewhere, my dear, you will see notices of the memorable things in her life, and I need not here repeat them.* Her virtues are recorded, with a truth that few epitaphs can boast, on the stone we placed over her grave. Your "father Charles" wrote the inscription.

My dear Alice, I wish I could give you a true picture, and a vivid one, of my *fragmentary* childhood—how different from the thoughtful, careful (whether judicious or injudicious) education of the present day.

Education in the common sense I had next to none, but there was much chance seed dropped in the fresh furrow, and some of it was good seed, and some of it, I may say, fell on good ground. My father was absorbed in political life, but his affections were at home. My mother's life was eaten up with calamitous sicknesses. My sisters were just at that period when girls' eyes are dazzled with their own glowing future. I had constantly before me examples of goodness, and from all sides admonitions to virtue, but no regular instruction. I went to the district schools, or, if any other school a little more select or better chanced, I went to

* Miss S. refers to an article on Mumbet which she wrote for some periodical, whose name I can not ascertain.

that. But no one dictated my studies or overlooked my progress. I remember feeling an intense ambition to be at the head of my class, and generally being there. Our minds were not weakened by too much study; reading, spelling, and Dwight's Geography were the only paths of knowledge into which we were led. Yes, I did go in a slovenly way through the first four rules of arithmetic, and learned the names of the several parts of speech, and could parse glibly. But my life in Stockbridge was a most happy one. I enjoyed unrestrained the pleasures of a rural childhood; I went with herds of school-girls nutting, and berrying, and bathing by moonlight, and wading by daylight in the lovely Housatonic that flows through my father's meadows. I saw its beauty then; I loved it as a playfellow; I loved the hills and mountains that I roved over. My father was an observer and lover of nature, my sister Frances a romantic, passionate devotee to it, and if I had no natural perception or relish of its loveliness, I caught it from them, so that my heart was early knit to it, and I at least early studied and early learned this picture language, so rich and universal.

From my earliest recollection to this day of our Lord, 13th October, 1853, nature has been an ever fresh and growing beauty and enjoyment to me; and now, when so many of my dearest friends are gone, when few, even of my contemporaries, are left, when new social pleasures have lost their excitement, the sun coming up over these hills and sinking behind them—the springing and the dying year—all changes and aspects of nature are more beautiful to me than ever. They have more solemnity, perhaps, but it is because they have more meaning. .If they speak in a lower tone to my dimmed eye-sight, it is a gentler and tenderer one.

What would the children now, who are steeped to the lips in "ologies," think of a girl of eight spending a whole summer working a wretched sampler which was not even a tolerable **specimen** of its species! But **even** as early as that, my father, whenever he was at home, kept me **up and at his** side till nine o'clock in the evening, **to listen to him while** he read aloud to **the** family Hume, or Shakspeare, or **Don** Quixote, or Hudibras! Certainly I did not understand them, but some glances **of** celestial light reached my soul, and I caught from his magnetic **sympathy some** elevation of feeling, **and that** love of reading **which has been to me "**education."

I remember a remark of Gibbon's which corresponds **with my** own experience. He says that the love of reading with which an aunt inspired him was worth all the rest of his education, and what must that "rest" have been in the balance against the pauperism of **my** instruction!

I was not more than twelve years old—I think but ten— when, during one winter, I read Rollin's Ancient History. The walking to our school-house was often bad, and I took my lunch (how well I remember the bread and butter, **and** "nut-cakes," **and** cold sausage, and nuts, and apples, that made **the** miscellaneous contents of that enchanting lunch-basket!), and **in the** interim between the morning and afternoon school I crept under my desk (the desks were so made as to afford little close recesses under them) and read, and munched, and forgot myself in Cyrus's **greatness!**

It was in those pleasant winters **that** Crocker brought, at the close of the afternoon school, "old Rover" to the school-house door for me to ride home. The gallant, majestic **old** veteran was then superannuated, and treated with all **the** respect that waits on age. I believe this was the hardest service he rendered, but this made his life **not quite a** sinecure, for it was my **custom and** delight to take up my favorite school friends, one after **another, and** "ride" them home, putting old Rover to his **utmost speed, and** I think the poor

old horse caught something of our youthful spirits, for he
galloped over the plain with us, distancing the boys, who
were fond of running at his heels, hurraing and throwing up
their hats.

I was a favorite with my school-mates, partly, I fear, because I had what the phrenologists term an excessive love
of approbation, and partly that I had, more than the rest,
the means of gratifying them.   On Saturday it was usual to
appoint two of the girls to sweep the school-house and set
it in order, and these two chose a third.   I was usually distinguished by the joint vote of my compatriots, and why?
I had unlimited credit at the "store," where my father kept
an open account, and, while the girls swept, I provided a
lunch of Malaga wine and raisins, or whatever was to be had
that suited the "sweet tooth" of childhood.   I well remember my father's consternation when he looked over the semi-
annual bill, and found it dotted with these charges, "per
daughter Catharine," in country fashion.   He was much
more amazed than displeased, but I remember he cut me
off from thereafter being in that mode "glorious" by a "my
dear little girl, this must not be in future."   What would our
Temperance zealots say to so slight a rebuke on such an
occasion!   But it was effectual, and left no stinging sense
of wrong, which a harsher visitation of an unconscious error
would have done.

Oh, how different was my miscellaneous childhood from
the driving study and the elaborate accomplishments of
children of my class of the present day!   I have all my life
felt the want of more systematic training, but there were peculiar circumstances in my condition that in some degree
supplied these great deficiencies, and these were blessings
ever to be remembered with gratitude.   I was reared in
an atmosphere of high intelligence.   My father had uncommon mental vigor.   So had my brothers.   Their daily hab-

its, and pursuits, and pleasures were intellectual, and I naturally imbibed from them a kindred taste.* Their "talk was *not* of beeves," nor of making money ; that now universal passion had not entered into men and possessed them as it does now, or, if it had, it was not in the sanctuary of our home—there the money-changers did not come. My father was richer than his neighbors. His income supplied abundantly the wants of a very careless family and an unmeasured hospitality, but nothing was ever given to mere style, and nothing was wasted on vices. I know we were all impressed with a law that no prodigalities were to be permitted, and that we were all to spend conscientiously ; but our consciences were not very tender, I think, and when I look back upon the freedom of our expenditures, I wonder that the whole concern was not ruined. I don't remember that I had a silk frock before I was fourteen years old. I wore stuffs in winter (such fabrics as in the present advanced condition of manufactures a factory-girl would scarcely wear ; one villainous stuff I particularly recall for school wear, called "bird's-eye"), and calicoes, and muslinets, and muslins for summer ; but, thus limited in quality and variety, I was allowed any number ; and I remember one winter, when

---

* My brother Robert says in a letter to my father, written when he was between twelve and thirteen, in a school vacation, "We have followed your directions, which were, that the leisure time we could have we should study Horace, which we have read through, and expect to begin Cicero de Oratore next term. We enjoyed ourselves at Williamstown. I think myself quite happy when I am reviewing the sublime works of Virgil. His works are incomparable, and the beauty of almost all his descriptions is inexpressible."

Then follows a rapturous exclamation at Cicero's eloquence, and a long quotation from him. In the same letter there is a long philippic against the "Jacobins" and their proceedings at Williamstown. The letter is written in a hand such as few sons of gentlemen, even of that early age, would now write, but the subjects intimate mental habits and sympathies not common to boys of twelve.

I was about nine or ten, being particularly unfortunate in scorching my "bird's-eye," I bought, at my own discretion, three or four new dresses in the course of the winter. And in the article of shoes, the town-bought morocco slippers were few and far between, but I was permitted to order a pair of calf-skin shoes as often as I fancied I wanted them, and our village shoemaker told me in after life that his books showed fifteen pairs made for me in one year! No disrespect either to his fabrication or his leather; the shoes were burnt, or water-soaked, or run down at the heel—sad habits occasioned by the want of female supervision. My dear mother, most neat and orderly, was often ill or absent, my sisters were married, my father took no cognizance of such matters, and I had a natural carelessness which a lifetime of consciousness of its inconvenience and struggle against it has not overcome. You, dear Alice, are brought up with all the advantages of order in both your parents. But, missing this, I look back with satisfaction to the perfect freedom that set no limit to expansion.

No bickering or dissension was ever permitted. Love was the habit, the life of the household rather than the law, or rather it was the law of our nature. Neither the power of despots nor the universal legislation of our republic can touch this element, for as God is love, so love is God, is life, is light. We were born with it—it was our inheritance. But the duty and the virtue of guarding all its manifestations, of never failing in its demonstrations, of preserving its interchanges and smaller duties, was most vigilantly watched, most peremptorily insisted on. A querulous tone, a complaint, a slight word of dissension, was met by that awful frown of my father's. Jove's thunder was to a pagan believer but as a summer day's drifting cloud to it. It was not so dreadful because it portended punishment—it was punishment; it was a token of a suspension of the approbation and love that were our life.

Have I given you an idea of the circumstances and education that made a family of seven children all honorable men and women—all, I think I may say without exaggeration, having noble aspirations and strong affections, with the fixed principle that these were holy and inviolable?

I have always considered country life with outlets to the great world as an essential advantage in education. Besides all the teaching and inspiration of Nature, and the development of the faculties from the necessity of using them for daily exigencies, one is brought into close social relations with all conditions of people. There are no barriers between you and your neighbors. There are grades and classes in our democratic community seen and acknowledged. These must be everywhere, as Scott truly says, "except among the Hottentots," but with us one sees one's neighbor's private life unveiled. The highest and the lowest meet in their joys and sorrows, at weddings and funerals, in sicknesses and distresses of all sorts. Not merely as alms-bearers, but the richest and highest go to the poorest to "watch" with them in sickness, and perform the most menial offices for them; and though your occupations, your mode of life may be very different from the artisan's, your neighbor, you meet him on an apparent equality, and talk with him as members of one family. In my youth there was something more of the old valuation than now. My mother's family was of the old established gentry of Western Massachusetts, connected by blood and friendship with the families of the "River-gods," as the Hawleys, Worthingtons, and Dwights of Connecticut River were then designated. My father had attained an elevated position in political life, and his income was ample and liberally expended. He was born too soon to relish the freedoms of democracy, and I have seen his brow lower when a free-and-easy mechanic came to the *front* door, and upon one occasion I remember his turning off the "east

C

steps" (I am *sure* not kicking, but the demonstration was unequivocal) a grown-up lad who kept his hat on after being told to take it off (would the President of the United States dare do as much now!); but, with all this tenacious adherence to the habits of the elder time, no man in life was kindlier than my father. One of my contemporaries, now a venerable missionary, told me last summer an anecdote, perhaps worth preserving, as characterizing the times and individuals. He was a gentle boy, the son of a shoemaker, and then clerk to the clerk of the court. The boy had driven his master to Lenox, and all the way this gentleman, conscious that his dignity must be preserved by vigilance, had maintained silence. When they came to their destination, he ordered the boy to take his trunk into the house. As he set it down in the entry, my father, then judge of the Supreme Judicial Court, was coming down stairs, bringing his trunk himself. He set it down, accosted the boy most kindly, and gave him his cordial hand. The lad's feelings, chilled by his master's haughtiness, at once melted, and took an impression of my father's kindness that was never effaced.

There were upon the Bench, at the time my father was placed on it, some men of crusty, oppressive manners. The Bar were not treated as *gentlemen*, and were in a state of antagonism, and some of them had even determined to leave their profession. My father's kind, courteous, considerate manners were said by his contemporaries to have produced an entire change in the relation of the Bench and Bar. His children, from instinct, from the example of their parents, and the principles of their home, had that teaching whose value Scott so well expressed in the "Fortunes of Nigel." "For ourselves," he says (and what does he not say better than another man—not to say any other!), "we can assure the reader—and perhaps, if we have ever been able to afford him amusement, it is owing in a great degree to this cause—that we never found ourselves in company with the stupidest of all possible companions in a post-chaise, or with the most arrant cumber-corner that ever occupied a place in a mail-coach, without finding that, in the course of our conversation with him, we had some ideas suggested to us, either grave or gay, or some information communicated in the course of our journey which we should have regretted not to have learned, and which we should have been sorry to have immediately forgotten."

It was the same principle by which Napoleon made himself the focus of every man's light ; and in our humble, obscure village life, we profited by this " free-trade" school of ideas. There were no sacrifices made of personal dignity or purity ; nor, if there was in condition or character a little elevation above the community we lived in, was it preserved by arrogant vigilance or jealous proscription.

Three of my brothers were my seniors. I have no recollections of the eldest during my childhood ; he was away at school and at college, but with Harry and Robert I had intimate companionship, and I think as true and loving a friendship as ever existed between brothers and sister. Charles was the youngest of the family, and so held a peculiar relation to us all as junior, and in some sort dependent, and the natural depositary of our petting affections. I hardly know why, but I believe it was because my father could not bear to send him away from him, that his means of education were far inferior to his brothers'. He did not go to college, and, except a year or two's residence at Dr. Backus's, in Connecticut, I think he had no teaching beyond that of our common schools. He had extreme modesty, and a habit of self-sacrifice and self-negation that I fear we all selfishly accepted. I do not think it ever occurred to him that he was quite equal to his brothers in mental gifts, and it was not till we had all got fairly into life that we recognized in him rare intellectual qualities. His *heart* was always to us the image of God.

But all my brothers were beloved, and I can conceive of no truer image of the purity and happiness of the equal loves of Heaven than that which unites brothers and sisters. It has been my chiefest blessing in life, and, but that I look to its continuance hereafter, I should indeed be wretched.

My brother Harry was, I think, intellectually superior to any of us. He had a wider horizon, more mental action, and I think he was the only one of us that had the elements of greatness. But he had great defects of mind, which, co-operating with the almost total loss of his eyesight, led to the great calamity of his life.* He had that absence of mind and fixidity of thought so dangerous where the tendencies are all to what the Germans call subjectivity. Never was there a more loving, generous disposition than his, nor tenderer domestic affections.

But my particular and paramount love in childhood was for your uncle Robert. We were bound together from our infancy, and I remember instances of tenderness while he was yet a little boy that are still bright as diamonds when so much has faded from my memory, or is dim to its eye.

Once, when ransacking the barn with my brothers for eggs, I somehow slipped under a mass of hay, and was so oppressed by it, and so scared, that I could scarcely make a sound. Robert heard my faint cries, but could not find me, and he ran to call my father, who, with some friends who happened to be with him, soon extricated me. From their caresses and conversation I inferred that my danger of suffocation had been imminent, and I looked henceforward upon my favorite brother as my preserver. How brightly

* Mr. Harry Sedgwick was insane during the last few years of his life.

are some points in our childhood's path illuminated, while all along, before and behind, the track is dim or lost in utter darkness! We can not always recall the feeling that fixed these bright passages in our memory. They are the shrines for our hearts' saints, and there the light never goes out.

Robert was, more than any other, my protector and companion. Charles was as near my own age, but he was younger, and a feeling of dependence—of most loving dependence—on Robert began then, which lasted through his life. I remember once when I was ill, and not more than five years old, his refusing to go out and play with "the boys," and lying down by me to soothe and amuse me. How early we are impressed by love and disinterestedness! These are small matters, my dear child, but they are the cement of household loves.

Manners are now so changed, and education so pressed, that you would be surprised by the various rustic duties then performed by the sons of a man in my father's position. In the progress of civilization, offices and exercises similar to these will come to be considered a healthy part of a high education. They do the mind and heart good—the mind by forming and developing observation, the first faculty Nature unfolds, and the heart by awakening and cultivating sympathies with the laboring classes.

It was the duty of our boys to drive the cows to pasture in the morning, and to fetch them at night, and our pastures being a mile distant, this was rather onerous. Errands were never-ending, and well do I remember being very early impressed with Robert's fidelity and good humor in discharging these ever-recurring offices. He from the first manifested a keen perception of the ludicrous, and a most innocent love of it. A short time before my sister Frances's confinement with her first child, and while I was staying with her, my father came to New York in midwinter, then a formidable journey, to **bring Mumbet to** nurse her. Robert came with them. **My dear** mother, before this, had the attack **of paralysis which cut her off from** the **care** of her family. **My father had** employed as housekeeper and general **family** directress my aunt, the widow of my mother's **half-brother.** She had the strictest integrity and the **kindest** intentions, with strong sense, and a love of intellectual pleasures. She had been bred in a large family, which owed its preservation **and** advancement to habits of the strictest economy. With **principles** and habits engendered by education, and **made firm as a rock** by stern necessity, she came **into an** affluent **family, unaccustomed to** restriction, **with streams of expense** flowing **out on every** side, **which** she felt bound in conscience to **stop.** My father honored her intentions *en masse*, and laughed at the details, **and his children caught the** laugh without imbibing the reverence. **She fitted Robert out for** this first visit to **New York with a pair of pantaloons** of home-made cloth, **and** dyed **with butternut-bark, which** made a sort of motley brown. For fête occasions he had a pair remodeled from his brother Theodore's, **blue** broadcloth worn to fragility, **so** thin that Robert said he could **not** look at them without making a rent, nor at the butternuts without the dye coming **off.** Whether this absurd infliction of **economy was** relieved **by a resort to** New York tailors I do not remember, but I **rather think** not, as a recourse to so **expensive** a mode of supply **for a country boy** of thirteen **was scarcely to** be thought **of in those days** of severe **simplicity.** Certainly the *sixty* pantaloons **that one** of **the New** York coxcombs is said to **have brought home from** Paris never afforded half the pleasure that **these rustic** garments did to us.

Robert always maintained that when, walking with **him, I** saw in the distance a city acquaintance, **I played** the Levite, **darted across the street,** and walked **on the** other side.

When at home, and dressed in his gossamers (he never ventured out in them), he scared a rigidly decorous maiden sister of Mr. Watson half out of her wits by every now and then exclaiming, "There they go!" the poor lady's imagination painting the catastrophe.

What changes in our domestic modes since then, when vestiges of patriarchal life lingered among us! My father had flocks of sheep, and after shearing-time women came and took the fleeces, and spun and wove them at their homes. All the servants' clothing was of this home-made cloth, as well as the overcoats of "the boys," and, I believe, all their common winter clothes. Carpets perdurable and well-looking were made in this way, and rugs, and woolen sheets, essential when our houses had no stoves, and fires out of the parlor, kitchen, and "mamma's room" were an unknown luxury.

This, my first winter in New York, when I was eleven years old, was an era to me, though I do not remember much of it. I had the best teaching of an eminent professor—of dancing, M. Lalliet,* and had a French master who came three times a week, and who, to my brother Robert's infinite amusement, complimented my "grande appréhension," but who, as far as I can recollect, taught me nothing, because, as I imagine, I preferred reading pleasant books, and being petted by pleasant people, to the task of learning lessons.

It was at this early period of our lives that your Aunt Susan and I first met. Could it have been foreseen by any cast of our horoscopes how lovingly our destinies were to mingle? In that pleasant dancing-room in Broad Street we

---

* When I think that then there was but one accepted French dancing-master in New York where now there are nearly a million inhabitants, I feel as if I had been on the earth as long as the Wandering Jew!

two country-girls met. She had been sent to her uncle, Brockholst Livingston, then an eminent judge in the United States Court, to be perfected in the arts and graces of young ladies. Her rare intelligence had been developed by rare opportunities. She had led a romantic life for three or four years on our frontier, living partly in a fort with Gen. Harrison, afterward President of the United States. She had that rare gift, refinement, cultivated by high breeding, and she revolted from the rantipole manners of the undisciplined crew of girls around her. Susan Ridley was my senior by eighteen months. She remembered noticing a quiet little girl, whose behavior was rather a contrast to that of the rabble rout ; she was, she said, interested by her demeanor, and her face, and her abundant curling hair ; she longed for her companionship ; she did not even know her name till one day she picked up a pocket-handkerchief the girl dropped, and found marked on it with hair—no indelible ink in those days!—C. M. *Sedgwick*, the name she was to bear, and enrich, and transmit. But we were yet to remain strangers. My less fastidious sympathies soon bound me up with the romping girls, and my future sister remained apart.

About two years after, we met at Mrs. Bell's boarding-school in Albany. She was just finishing a term of two years when I entered as a day-scholar. This school had enjoyed great reputation, and was sustained by the first families in the land. Mrs. Bell was a decayed gentlewoman, of Irish descent (indeed, I rather think born in Ireland), who had been much in the society of clever men, had a very cheerful disposition, and various social talents. But alas! I had already too much social taste and facility, and the bane of my life—a want of order and system—found no antidote there. Mrs. Bell was a serious invalid, and had become a regular valetudinarian in all her habits. She rose late, was half the

time out of her school, and did very little when in it. But
she was always ready to throw out poetic riddles and co-
nundrums that charmed us, and all the more that they generally involved some little love-preference or romantic incident of the school-girls' life. She had decided leanings toward those pupils who were cleverest and socially most attractive, and connected with her friends out of school bounds.
She liked to have us with her in the evening, and to attract
to her circle the intelligent people within her reach.

Susan Ridley was about leaving the school, a full-grown,
very elegant, and, according to the standard of those times,
a very accomplished young woman. My brother Theodore
introduced me at the school. I was received by Miss Bax-
ter, the niece and assistant of Mrs. Bell, with a practiced,
easy air, and a sweeping courtesy that daunted the poor little rustic. It was the peacock spreading his tail before a
poor little straggler from the coop ; and when my brother afterward reproved my "little dot of a courtesy," I was ready
to sink into the ground.

I remained at the noon recess, and a beautiful girl, An-
gelica Gilbert, afterward a belle in New York, with a sweet
and graceful courtesy that made a lasting impression on me,
offered to teach me (an unknown art to me then) rope-
jumping. When I was fairly inducted, and tying on my hat
to go home, one of the mannerless girls shouted out to me,
"Give Miss Ridley's love to your brother !" I turned, and
saw a delicate, fair, and elegant girl overpowered with confusion, and blushing up to the roots of her soft brown hair,
who cried out to me, "Oh don't, don't !" In fact, some
months before this time, a mutual interest between her and
my brother Theodore had begun, which continued through
their most happy marriage with a purity, strength, and mutual confidence and joint blessing to others that might au-
thorize and confirm the belief that "marriages are made in

heaven." From that hour she was my dear friend, without variableness or shadow of turning, I may say without irreverence, for she has intensely struggled to conform to the admonition, "Be ye perfect as your Father in heaven is perfect," and has succeeded as far as human infirmity admits.

She was naturally drawn to me. I can take little credit for this; I loved her enthusiastically, and never, I am sure, desired any good for myself more earnestly than her hand for my brother. She remained but a short time at school, but even then we began a correspondence that has continued to this time. We had a mail-bag hanging in the school, which was each day filled and discharged. Of course, as you may suppose, dear Alice, I was a large contributor to this daily literature.

There was another gifted girl at the school, Mary North. She became a *lover* of mine, and was jealous of every schoolgirl that I liked. She had been much flattered by her elders, she was conscious of superiority, and thought the first place was her right. To me she was affectionate and true. She was handsome too, which is not reckoned a secondary gift to a woman. She disappointed expectation by her early death—I think she was not more than seventeen when she died. I have retained to this day a grateful recollection of her—grateful, because she once honestly and kindly told me of a besetting infirmity of mine, and made me earnestly desire to eradicate it. It is not her fault that I have not. You will see, my dear Alice, that I had, if not the legitimate means of instruction, at least some rare advantages in my school-days—the elevating society and friendship of a superior woman, and cultivated companions and friends who enriched my mind, though it was not laid out, planted, and tilled quite in the right way.

Lenox, Aug., 1854.—Another year is gone, and I am admonished that few *can* remain to me, and this day, at 12 M., alone in my little parlor, your dear father and mother here on their annual visit, having just finished telling a fairy tale to you, and Will, and Lucy Pike, I have taken my pen to note some changes in the condition of our village since I was young. I remember the making of the turnpike through Stockbridge—I think it must have been about forty years ago—and that was a great event then, for it enabled us to have a stage-coach three days in the week from Boston to Albany, and three from Albany to Boston. In due time came the daily coach, arriving, after driving the greater part of the night, the middle of the second day from Boston.

It then seemed there could be nothing in advance of this. Your uncle Theodore has the honor of being the first person who conceived the possibility of a railroad over the mountains to Connecticut River. He proposed it in the Legislature, and argued so earnestly for it, that it became a very common reproach to him that he was crazy. Basil Hall, when he was in Stockbridge, ridiculed the idea, and said to your uncle, "If you had it, what would you carry over it?" He did not live to be confuted, nor your uncle to witness the triumph of his opinion, but I have lived this very summer to travel to the Mississippi by rail!

The daily coach was a great advance on my earliest experience, when a mongrel vehicle, half wagon, half coach, drawn by horses that seemed to me like Time to the Lover, came once a week from New York, letting the light from the outer world into our little valley, and bringing us letters from "papa." Now, at 3 P.M., we read the paper issued the same morning at New York.

We had one clergyman in Stockbridge, of sound New England orthodoxy, a Hopkinsian Calvinist. Heaven forbid, dear Alice, that you should ever inquire into the splitting of these theological hairs! Sixty years he preached to us, and

in all that time, though there may have been at some obscure dwelling a Methodist or Baptist ranter, the "pious"
of the town all stood by the Doric faith.   The law then required each town to support a clergyman, and his salary
was paid by taxation.   The conscience was left free ; he
who preferred to dissent from the prevailing religion could,
on assigning his reasons, "sign off ;" but I believe he was
required to transfer his allegiance to some other ministry.
Now the clergy are supported by the voluntary system, and
a man may revert to heathenism (some do !), and no man
call him to account.   I have elsewhere and repeatedly described our good pastor of sixty years—stern as an old Isra-
elite in his faith, gentle and kindly in his life as "my Uncle
Toby."   I dreaded him, and certainly did not understand
him in my youth.   He was then only the dry, sapless em-
bodiment of polemical divinity.   It was in my mature age
and his old age that I discovered his Christian features, and
found his unsophisticated nature as pure and gentle as a
good little child's.   He stood up in the pulpit for sixty
years, and logically proved the whole moral creation of God
(for this he thought limited to earth, and the stars made to
adorn man's firmament) left by him to suffer eternally for
Adam's transgression, except a handful *elected* to salvation,
and yet no scape-grace, no desperate wretch within his ken
died without some hope for his eternal state springing up
in the little doctor's merciful heart.   Some contrite word,
some faint aspiration, a last slight expression of faith on the
death-bed, a look, was enough to save this kind heart from
despair of any fellow-creature.

Dr. West belonged to other times than ours.   His three-
cornered beaver, and Henry Ward Beecher's Cavalier hat,
fitly denote the past and present clerical dynasties ; the
first formal, elaborate, fixed ; the last easy, comfortable,
flexible, and assuming nothing superior to the mass.

I will try to sketch the doctor's outward man for you. He was not, I think, above five feet in height. His person was remarkably well-made and erect, and I think the good little polemic was slightly vain of it, for I remember his garments fitted accurately, and nice hose (in summer always of black silk) displayed a handsome calf and ankle, and his shining black shoes and silver buckles impressed even my careless eye. He had good teeth, then a rare beauty, even to his greatest age, but all his features were graceless, and there was nothing approaching comeliness of form or expression, but an eye ever ready to flow with gentle pity and tender sympathy. His hair was cut à la Cromwell, as if a bowl had been inverted on his head, and his foretop cut by its rim. His knock at the "east door" was as recognizable as his voice; that opened to him, he came in, and, taking off his hat, saluted each member of the family, down to the youngest, with the exact ceremony, and something of the grace of a French courtier; he then walked up to the table between the two front windows, deposited the three-cornered beaver, put his gloves in his hat, and his silver-headed cane in the corner, and then, taking a little comb from his pocket, he smoothed down his thin locks, so that every numbered hair on his head lay in its appointed place. Then the dear little gentleman sat down, and compressed the geniality of his nature into the social hour that followed, being, during that hour, uniformly served with the fitting type of that geniality—a good glass of wine. These visits occurred always once a week; and, if any temporalities in the Church required confidence or consultation, as much oftener as he felt the want of my father's sympathy or advice, for it was rather noticeable that, for these purposes, he preferred my father to any or all of the "elect."

Poor old gentleman! his last days were not his best days. He had a colleague who was a sneaking fellow, frequenting

men and women **gossips, and** fabricating scandal against
the little doctor **and his second** help-meet, and endeavoring
thereby to monopolize to himself the **favor of the** parish and
the whole **salary.**   The doctor's age had imposed seclusion ;
he was personally almost a stranger to the generation **just
grown, and** suddenly it was discovered that the greater **part
of his** people were alienated from him, and that many believed that he and his wife lived in a drunken companionship.   Those who knew the **almost** Judaical regularity and
strictness of his life and **the truth of** hers earnestly adhered
to them.   Council **after council was called,** the town was
divided into factions.   **Mrs. W——, a feeble,** trembling, timid old lady, was barbarously put upon trial, **as cruel** as the
"putting to the question," and no satisfactory evidence appeared against her.   Then the doctor's life and habits were
put **to proof** ; after numerous hearsays were detailed, and
rags of gossip, that had been manufactured by the colleague,
S——, and passed from hand to hand, were disposed **of,**
Parson Kinne was called up.   He was an old polemic, **a**
man of stanch honesty, whose truth no man believed could
be shaken.   He **had resided** in Dr. W——'s family **six**
months **at** a time.   He had been so scrupulously reserved
that no one knew what he would testify ; S—— believed it
would be full against the doctor, **and we, his friends,** shiv-
ered lest the good old man might have been perverted from
a right judgment by the crafty communications and insinu-
ations of **S——,** and might have misinterpreted the doctor's
habit **of taking a** single cheerful **glass** during the day.
Kinne was as grotesque **in** looks and manners as Dominie
Sampson, **and** to some of **us** it seemed that Scott must have
been gifted with second sight, and drawn "little Harry's"
tutor after the pattern of our Puritan.   I shall never **forget
when he** was called on, and stood up within the semicircle
—an awful halo—of clergymen around **him.**   He said that,

during a ride with Mr. S—— two or three years before, that gentleman had told him that "Dr. W—— and lady" were guilty of gross drinking—that they consumed such an amount of rum (specifying it) in a month—that the doctor set a mug of rum by his bedside at night, and rose repeatedly to drink it—etc., etc., etc. And all this while Mr. Kinne was living in the family.

"Did you believe this, sir?" asked one of the council.

The old man shook his faded yellowish wig, smiled with a most comical mixture of contempt, triumph, and simplicity, and replied, "Not—one—word—of—it—sir!"

A low murmur of shame and disappointment ran over the assembly, while a sort of *feu de joie* broke from the few devoted friends and allies of the good old man. Mean, vulgar, cruel as the persecution was, it never touched within the holy circle of the doctor's charities, never invaded his peace, nor clouded his serenity. He even, through the whole of S——'s crawling through his slimy way, "hoped that now Mr. S—— meant to do better," and not one bitter word or shadow of resentment escaped him, so that after sixty years of utterly useless polemical preaching, he closed his career with "practical observations" on love, charity, forgiveness, and self-negation, that sunk deep into some of our hearts.

I remember one anecdote rather illustrative of his preaching. He held the Hopkinsian doctrine that Christ died to manifest God's wrath against sin, repudiating the strictly Calvinistic creed of Christ's vicarious atonement. Upon one occasion, Dr. Mason, of New York, who then was the most conspicuous pulpit orator in the country—a man confident in his faith, and bold to audacity—preached for Dr. W——. Mason was a tall, burly, fair man, in the heart and vigor of life. I can not forget the figures of the two men, as they stood together, for our pastor was perfect in the ceremonials of courtesy, which he would not violate by sitting down in his own pulpit. **Dr. Mason** thundered away in a sermon of an hour and **a half upon the** doctrine of substitution, every eye fixed on him in the deepest attention. The next **day** the "little doctor" (so my father always styled him) **came** as usual, and, in talking over the sermon, said, "The **people did** not understand one word that he said;" **and then** added with a sigh, and oh! with what mournful truth, "and I am afraid they have never understood me either."

One of the periods **most marked in my** childhood, and best remembered, because it was out of the general current of my life, was a summer when I was seven or eight years old, passed under the care of my cousin Sabrina Parsons, in Bennington, Vermont, at the house of the Rev. Mr. Swift, **the** husband of my father's eldest sister. There were a **dozen children,** more or less, some grown, some still young —the kindest and cheerfulest people in the world. I was an object of general affection and indulgence. I remember distinctly, and I see it now with my mind's eye, a cherry-tree of fantastic shape that my cousin Persis, my contemporary, and I were in the habit of running up like kittens, **to** the dismay of my tender, sickly aunt, who would invariably raise her bedroom window and call out, "Girls, come down! **you'**ll break your necks!" I am now the old crone, and, **alas!** I now should **probably** mar the sport of idle, fearless **girls in the** same way. No, dear Alice, I don't honestly **think I** should. I should be more like to try to climb the cherry-tree **with them.**

When I **lived at my** uncle's was **the period** of the most bitter hostility between the Federalists and Democrats. The whole nation, from Maine **to** Georgia, was then divided **into these two** great parties. The Federalists stood upright, **and** with their feet firmly planted on the rock of aristocracy, but that rock itself was bedded in sands, or rather was a boulder from the Old World, and the tide of democracy was surely and swiftly undermining it. The Federalists believed that all sound principles, truth, justice, and patriotism, were identified with the upper classes. They were sincere Republicans, but I think they began to fear a republic could only continue to exist in Utopia. They were honest and noble men. The Democrats had among them much native sagacity; they believed in themselves, some from conceit, some from just conviction; they had less education, intellectual and moral, than their opponents—little refinement, intense desire to grasp the power and place that had been denied to them, and a determination to work out the theories of the government. All this, my dear Alice, as you may suppose, is an after-thought with me. Then I entered fully, and with the faith and ignorance of childhood, into the prejudices of the time. I thought every Democrat was grasping, dishonest, and vulgar, and would have in good faith adopted the creed of a stanch old parson, who, in a Fast-day sermon, said, "I don't say that every Democrat is a horse-thief, but I do say that every horse-thief is a Democrat!"

While I was at Bennington, I know not to commemorate what occasion, small gold eagles were struck, and presented to the ladies of conspicuous Federal families. My grown-up cousins had them. They were sewn into the centre of large bows they wore on their bonnets. I remember well pining in my secret soul that one was not given to me, and thinking that my father's position entitled me, though a child, to the distinction. One memorable Sunday, while my uncle was making the "long prayer," and I was standing on the bench in the clergyman's great square pew, my cousin Sally's bow got awry; the eagle "stooped" under its folds; and I, to save her from the ignominy of not showing her colors, walked around three sides of the pew, and disturbed not only my pious cousin's devotions, but many others', by the

pother I made in rectifying the bow. I remember my good
uncle, on being **told of the exploit,** instead of reproving me
for my misdemeanor, **heartily joined in the** laugh.

After all, I believe there was a deal **of** good humor and
village fun mingled in with the animosities. **The** village
street, according to my recollection, extended a long way,
some mile and a half, from a hill at one end to a plain at
the other. There was a superannuated, parti-colored horse,
that had been turned out **to find** his own living by wayside
grazing, with now and **then a chance** handful of oats from
charity, who was used as a walking **advertiser.** He came
regularly from **the hill, the Democratic quarter,** placarded
over with jibes and **jokes** on **the** Federalists of the plain,
and returned with such missives as their **wit could** furnish.

My pleasant sojourn there was concluded by a bilious fever, through **which I was** tenderly attended by one of **my
cousins, a young physician.** I **suffered** in my convalescence
from the pangs of hunger, and one Sunday morning, having
been left alone, and supposing **all** the family to be at church,
I crept (I could not even **stand alone) out** of my bed, and
down stairs to the buttery ; but, on opening its door, there
were two of my cousins regaling themselves with a lunch of
cold chicken ! I burst into tears at my discomfiture. They
gave me a chicken-bone, and carried me back to my bed.
The intense delight with which I gnawed that bone to its
last fibre might enlighten the medical faculty.

I remember, while at Bennington, receiving from my father **a morocco** thread-case and pocket-book, with a silver
crown in it, and how enchanted I was. My father, generous
without limit to his children, never would associate his com-
ings home with gifts—he would have no craving but that **of
the** affections. On **one** occasion, when I was a lisping child,
some **one** asked me what papa brought me from Philadelphia. "Nothing," I replied, "but he called me his dear lit-

tle lamb, and his sweet little bird." This charmed my father, and confirmed his theory.

My dear Alice, would you like to know what were the
books of my childhood? You, of the present time, for whom
the press daily turns out its novelties, for whom Miss Edgeworth has written her charming stories, and Scott has sim-
plified history, will look upon my condition as absolute in-
anition.

The books that I remember (there were, perhaps, besides,
a dozen little story-books) are Berquin's "Children's Friend,"
translated from the French, I think, in four volumes—I know
I can remember the form and shade of color of the book,
the green edges of the leaves, the look of my favorite pages.
Then there was the "Looking-glass," an eclectic, which contained that most pathetic story of "Little Jack." Then
there was a little thin book called "Economy of Human
Life," made up of some small pieces of Mrs. Barbauld's.
That was quite above my comprehension, and I thought it
very unmeaning and tedious. There was a volume of
Rowe's "Letters from the Dead to the Living," which had
a strange charm for me. I do not think that I believed them
to have been actually written by the departed, but there was
a little mystification about it that excited my imagination.
And last and most delightful were the fables, tales, and ballads in a large volume of "Elegant Extracts." I have sometimes questioned whether the keen relish which this scarcity
of juvenile reading kept up, and the sound digestion it promoted, did not overbalance your advantage in the abundance and variety that certainly extinguishes some minds,
and debilitates others with over-excitement.

All books but such as had an infusion of religion were
proscribed on Sunday, and of course the literature for that
day was rather circumscribed. We were happily exempted

•

from such confections as Mrs. Sherwood's—sweetened slops
and water-gruels that impair the mental digestion. We
lived as people in a new country live—on bread and meat
—the Bible and good old sermons, reading these over and
over again. I remember, when very young, a device by
which I extended my Sunday horizon ; I would turn over
the leaves of a book, and if I found " God" or " Lord," no
matter in what connection, I considered the book sanctified
—the *taboo* removed !

Both my sisters were very religious. They were educated
when the demonstration of religion and its offices made
much more a part of life than now—when almost all of
women's intellectual life took that tinge. They were both
born with tendencies to the elevated and unseen ; their religion was their pursuit, their daily responsibility, their aim,
and end, and crowning affection.

They both began with the strict faith. Sister Eliza suffered from the horrors of Calvinism. She was so true, so
practical, that she could not evade its realities ; she believed
its monstrous doctrines, and they made her gloomy ; but for
the last fifteen years of her life she was redeemed from this
incubus ; her faith softened into a true comprehension of
the filial relation to God, and I have often heard her say
that it was impossible for her to describe the happiness of
her redemption from the cruel doctrines of Geneva.

Sister Frances's imagination saved her from a like suffering. However deep the slough into which she was cast, she
would spread her wings and rise up into a pure atmosphere,
bright with God's presence. She was one of those who believe without believing ; her faith was governed by her
moods ; when she was bilious and unhappy—very rarely—
she sank down again into the slough.

Thank God, their sweet spirits are now both expatiating
in truth which is light !

My sisters were both married when I was still a child. I was but seven when my sister Eliza was married, and I remember that wedding evening as the first tragedy of my life. She was my mother-sister. I had always slept with her, and been her assigned charge. The wedding was in our "west room." I remember where the bride and groom stood, and how he looked to me like some cruel usurper. I remember my father's place, and the rest is a confused impression of a room full of friends and servants—I think Mumbet stood by me. When the long consecrating prayer was half through, I distinctly remember the consciousness that my sister was going away from me struck me with the force of a blow, and I burst into loud sobs and crying. After the service, my father took me in his arms, and tried to quiet and soothe me, but I could be neither comforted nor quieted, so I stole out into the "east room," where Mumbet, Grippy, all the servants did their best to suggest consolations. Then came my new brother-in-law—how well I remember recoiling from him and hating him when he said, "I'll let your sister stay with you this summer." He let her! I was undressed and put into bed, and I cried myself to sleep and waked crying the next morning, and so, from that time to this, weddings in my family have been to me days of sadness, and yet, by some of them, I have gained treasures that no earthly balance or calculation can weigh or estimate!

One of the finest passages in **Fanny** Kemble's "English Tragedy" was, as she told me, suggested by this passage between me and Dr. Pomeroy, which I had related to her.

Oh dear sister! what a life of toil, of patient endurance, of sweet hopes, heavenly affections, keen disappointments, harsh trials, acute sorrows, and acute joys then opened upon you! What a life of truth, fidelity, faith, labor, and love you lived! And just when you seemed to have come to a station of rest—when the children to whom you had so long been the mother-minister began to minister to you, you were stricken down! God's will be done! You have been saved many, many sorrows, and, I trust, see the purpose, unknown to us, of many afflictions that have since fallen on your house!

Through my sister Eliza's life, the tenderest union, the most unwavering confidence subsisted between us. A few days since, I saw a letter from her in which she calls me her "sister—mother—child—friend."

I have said nothing of the personal appearance of my sisters. Eliza was short, in her girlhood perfectly symmetrical in her form, with pretty arms, and little hands and feet—very dark, with pretty, dark eyes and hair, and a very gentle, modest, retiring manner, but with great decision in her affections and opinions. She and Frances were as unlike in appearance as in character. Frances was above the common stature, with a fair skin, and blooming cheeks, that continued blooming all her life; hazel eyes—one of them particolored—beautiful bright chestnut hair, a Roman nose, and a very handsome mouth. She was a great reader in her youth of poetry and romances. Eliza was occupied with household duties, first in her father's house, and then in her own; first nursing her mother, and supplying a mother's place to the children, and in her married life having twelve children of her own to care for. Frances was excitable, irritable, enthusiastic, imaginative; Eliza calm, patient, quiet, reserved, and sternly, scrupulously true. Frances was sympathetic and diffusive beyond any one I have ever known; Eliza's affections were within the range of her duties, and strictly governed by them. No sphere could bound or contain Frances's interests or affections; Eliza was the steady light of her home; dear sister Frances shone widely and irregularly, but, if ever a soul was kindled with holy fires, hers was. She loved her friends with the faith and enthusiasm of devotees—but she sometimes changed her faith.

Her marriage was not a congenial one. She endured much and heroically, and through her sweet benevolence and wide sympathies she enjoyed a great deal, though, to a superficial eye, her life seemed an utter failure. Never was any portion of it so complete a barren but she could find some flower to cherish, some fruit for refreshment. She never took a day's drive in a stage-coach, or a night's sail on a steamer, but she found some wayfarer to whom she listened with faith, whom she remembered with interest. She loved my father with a passionate filial devotion, and all her family with enthusiastic affection.

A permanent member of our household, who might have had some influence in the formation of our characters, was a cousin of my mother, Mr. W——; his familiar sobriquet, by which he was known to all the children of the village as well as to our household, was " Uncle Bob."

He was my father's partner in business for more than twenty years, and was esteemed a sound lawyer—a man, I believe, of more acuteness than enlargement, of remarkable memory, and of incorruptible integrity. Something of a Monkbarns in his scoffings at womankind, he covered, under a privileged ridicule of the sex, a real liking for them. I have heard hints of his strong attachment to my sister Eliza, of his having been withheld by a proud fear of refusal from declaring it, and of his vexed disappointment at her engagement to another. He lived till he was fifty-four in Benedict railings at the sex, and then—married. His attachments were strong, though he was utterly undemonstrative ; his prejudices inveterate and proclaimed. He made no demands and gave no trouble. He had an unlimited respect for my mother, and regard for my father. He

loved the children, and laughed at us all. He was so unob-
trusive of his society that he seemed unsocial. He preferred
the smallest room, into which no one ever intruded, and a
corner seat at table, where he had elbow-room without an-
noying or being annoyed. He was abstemious in eating
and drinking, played an excellent hand at whist, and piquet
and backgammon better than any body else, but he never
could be slidden in to make up a wanted party to a game.
He was not one of those convenient single people who are
used as we use straw and cotton in packing—to fill up vacant places. His claims were always attended to and his
rights respected. Profanity was the habit of the times, and
he carried it to the most extravagant lengths ; his taste was
corrupted by the coarse and gross modes of Swift, and Smol-
lett, and Sterne ; the stream of a sensual literature had not
yet run far enough to deposit its filth ; still his life was honest and pure ; the world would not have bribed him to take
God's name in vain in the sense of the Decalogue, and his
manners were so disinfected by the admonitions of my
mother and the example of my father, that my brothers,
though they held constant vivacious intercourse with him,
never caught his bad habits of speech.

He had jocular characteristic salutations for us all. How
often have I heard him say to Robert,

> " Master Bobby's married.
>   Pray what says St. Paul ?
> If I'm not mistaken,
>   ' Marry not at all !' "

And I was " Kate the curst," or " Kate of my consolation," etc., etc., as his humor was.

The family modes of hospitality have something to do
with the formation of character. That open-hearted, open-
doored hospitality which has characterized the disposition

of every member of our family was imbibed in our child-hood.

My father's public station and frequent residences in town gave him a very extensive acquaintance, and his affec-tionate temper warmed acquaintance into friendship. There were then no steamers, no railroads, and a stage-coach through our valley but once a week. Gentlemen made their journeys in their private carriages, and, as a matter of course, put up at their friends' houses. My father's house was a general *dépôt,* and when I remember how often the great gate swung open for the entrance of traveling vehicles, the old mansion seems to me to have resembled much more an hostelrie of the olden time than the quiet house it now is. My father's hospitality was unbounded. It extended from the gentleman in his coach, chaise, or on horseback, accord-ing to his means and necessities, to the poor lame beggar that would sit half the night roasting at the kitchen fire* with the negro servants. It embraced within its wide girth a multitude of relations. My father was in some sort the chieftain of his family, and his home was their resort and resting-place. Uncles and aunts always found a welcome there ; cousins summered and wintered with us. Thus hos-pitality was an element in our education. It elicited our faculties of doing and suffering. It smothered the love and habit of minor comforts and petty physical indulgences that

---

* Oh that blazing fire ! There may be such in Western homes, but they will never again be seen on this side the Alleghanies. As the short winter day closed in, a chain was attached to a log, and that drawn by a horse to the door-step, and then rolled into the fireplace, shaking the house at every turn. Then came the magnificent "fore-stick," then piles on piles of wood—and round the crackling fire what images appear ! Mumbet, queen of the domain ; Grippy, how loved in those days ; Sam-son, the runaway slave, a faithful servant of many years ; Lady Prime, Betty, "little Bet," rather impish, and old "Tip-Top," the Gaberlunzie, the jest and the terror of my childhood !

D

belong to a higher state of civilization and generate selfishness, and it made regard for others, and small sacrifices to them, a **habit**.   Hospitality was not formally inculcated as a virtue, **but it** was an inevitable circumstance—a part of **our social** condition.   The table was as cheerfully spread **for others as** for ourselves.   We never heard that hospitality was a *duty*, nor did we ever see it extended grudgingly or with stinted measure to any guest of any condition.   This gathering into our ark of divers kinds of human creatures had a tendency to enlarge our horizon, and to save us from the rusticity, the ignorance of the world, and the prejudice incident to an isolated country residence.   The evils of this state of things were the increased burden to **my** mother, already overladen with care, and latterly the complete frittering of my time, for in our last years *at home* our old family servants were dispersed—it was the transition period **between** black servants and Irish—and the imperfect domestic service had to be made out by the members of the family.

It was during the winter in New York I have already mentioned that I first went to the theatre, an epoch in a child's life.   It was in the time of the Hodgkinsons, charming performers, and in the beginning of Cooper's career. He was the first of second-rate tragedians.   My **first** play was Macbeth.   Hodgkinson played Macbeth, Cooper Macduff.   **When** they came to the final fight, I entreated my brother to take me out of the house.   He laughed at me.   I said, "I know it is not real, but **they are** really enraged!" How much delight I had from the few plays I saw that winter!   What an exquisite portion of the pleasures of imagination come, or have come, **to** the young through the drama! **To** this day, the drying **at** the fire of a wet newspaper recalls the eagerness with which I dried the daily paper to read **the** play-bill, and truly it is now a sweet odor to me!

I did not at that period form any girlish friendships, or any acquaintance out of my dancing-school. There was an old lady who lived opposite to my sister whom I was very fond of visiting, and to this day I recall her kindly aspect, her florid complexion, her pots of beautiful artemisias, and her pleasant tales about the Revolution, in which I believe her husband had played a conspicuous part as commissary. How well I remember those flowers! Flowers I have always loved next to *dear* living creatures, and I can recall the look and odor of the particular friends of my early childhood, the damask and cinnamon roses under our front windows and in the garden, the large plant of old-fashioned, honest peonies that stood near the little garden, the bluebells, and, above all, the pinks, my mother's favorite, and till now the memorial I wear through all the summer months for her.

I remember little of that winter, but I went once to a large family dinner at Jacob Morton's with my brother Theodore. Our host asked me, the only stranger guest, which part of a huge turkey, in which he had put his carving-fork, I would take. I knew only one point of manners for such occasions, dear Alice—that I must specify some part, and, as ill luck would have it, the side-bone came first into my head, and "Side-bone, sir," I said. Oh, what a lecture I got when we went home! the wretched "little chit that compelled a gentleman to cut up a whole turkey to serve her!" I cried myself to sleep that night. My brother, then a student at law in Mr. Riggs's office, was very ambitious that his sister should be an adept in the polite arts. From that time till I was sixteen or seventeen I had an inexpressible dread of his observation and criticism. My manners were frank, confiding, and artless, but not conventional— and neither my brother nor my long social life has taught me to be so.

April 24th, 1860.—I go on, dear Alice, with my narrative. I was thirteen years old when I went to Albany. My brother Theodore had just opened an office there, and formed his partnership with Harmanus Bleecker, a gentleman of the pure old Holland stock—a gentleman in his education, association, and tastes. He had a ruling taste for mental pursuits, and was loyal to them all his life. He was silent and laconic, but delighted in a social atmosphere. He was all his life compared to such old Romans as have illustrated the sterner virtues.

The circumstance most exciting to me in this part of my life was my father's coming to Albany and taking me to Canandaigua, then a weekly journey, now scarcely eight hours! But oh, the pleasant vicissitudes of that long travel —the disastrous chances of bad taverns, and the felicity of good ones—the unexpected meeting with old friends and the making new ones, and the delightful novelty of the every day of a first journey! We traveled in a charming easy carriage (probably English-built), a phaeton which my father had already possessed many years. It was so high that, as I recall it, it seems as if, like Homer's divinities, we had made a halt in mid-air. We had excellent horses, and a house-servant, Cato. (Poor fellow! he ended his life in our state's prison.) We were the first half day toiling through the sands between Albany and Schenectady. There an old gentleman, Glen, my father's comrade in Congress, came to the inn and dined with us, and my father and he sat over their cigars and wine till the heat of the summer's day subsided, when we mounted into our phaeton and proceeded to a little Dutch inn on the Mohawk, a few miles' drive. I think it is not common for young persons at thirteen to receive positive happiness and ineffaceable impressions from Nature, but pictures were then daguerreotyped upon my memory that have never faded. Our first evening, sitting out on the back "stoop" of our inn, overlooking a meadow sloping down to the Mohawk—a new moon, and the leaves just quivering in its light—hundreds of fire-flies glancing through the air and sparkling in the grass—the firmament clear and bright with stars, and my dear father sitting by me with his cigar, in a serene obliviousness of all mortal ill, and an effusion of affection that was his "magnetism"— this may be the heavenly state before we make acquaintance with the faculties and conditions of a more expanded life.

In my fifteenth year I was sent to Mr. Payne's boarding-school in Boston, and was there for six months. I was at the most susceptible age. My father's numerous friends in Boston opened their doors to me. I was attractive in my appearance, and, from always associating on equal terms with those much older than myself, I had a mental maturity rather striking, and with an ignorance of the world, a romantic enthusiasm, an aptitude at admiring and loving that altogether made me an object of general interest. I was admired and flattered. Harry and Robert were then resident graduates at Cambridge. They were too inexperienced to perceive the mistake I was making ; they were naturally pleased with the attentions I was receiving. The winter passed away in a series of bewildering gayeties. I had talent enough to be liked by my teachers, and good nature to secure their good will. I gave them very little trouble in any way.

Mr. and Mrs. T——, old friends of both our parents, made their house our home. Entire indulgence and open-door hospitality were the law and habit of their house. They had five daughters growing up in savage ignorance. There I met my brothers, and there we were all petted and flattered. * * * * * When I came home from Boston I felt the deepest mortification at my waste of time and money,

though my father never said **one word to** me on the subject.
For the only time in **my** life I rose early to read French,
and in a few weeks learned by myself more than I had acquired all winter.   But, alas ! what irretrievable opportunities gone !

Here all direct narrative ceases, although fragments be-
longing to the same general **plan of** Recollections, and addressed to the same person, will occasionally be met with in
a later part of this memoir.

A few childish letters have been preserved, which may be
presented here, as showing a characteristic warmth of feel-
ing, and freedom, as well as carefulness in expression.   The
first is written at the age of ten.

Miss Sedgwick to her *Father.*

"Stockbridge, Jan. 12, 1800.

"MY DEAR PAPA,—Last week I received a letter from
you which gave me inexpressible pleasure.   You said you
supposed that I had enjoyed the pleasure of sister Eliza's
and the children's company, but I had not when I received
your letter ; it was such very poor sleighing we did not ex-
pect them ; but, my dear papa, can you conceive of the
pleasure we felt when hearing a sleigh drive up, and, going
out, **we** perceived that sister Eliza **and her dear** children
were in it ?   We were almost too happy.   Theodore had arrived two or three days before, Mr. Watson that afternoon.
Judge of our pleasure.   I thought if you, Henry, and Robert were here, and mamma was well, our happiness would **be**
complete.   You said that we should derive more pleasure
from their company in two hours than you would this whole
winter.   **My** dear papa, I can easily believe you.   **I** should

be willing to impart to you my happiness on this occasion, but it is impossible. I see—indeed I think I see in **Mr. Watson** every thing that **is** amiable. I am very much **pleased** with him ; indeed we are all of us. Mamma sends her **love** to you. She sleeps **better than ever** she did, I think. Theodore sends his love **to you.** Your affectionate, dutiful daughter,   **CATHARINE MARIA** SEDGWICK."

The next, a year later, illustrates **the tenderness of her relations** with her father, and **her early and enthusiastic** sympathy with him in his public career.

Miss Sedgwick to her Father.

"Stockbridge, February 1, 1801.

* * * * "You say in one of your last letters that the time will soon come when you shall take leave of Congress forever. **That day shall I,** in my own mind, celebrate forever ; **yes, as long as I live I shall** reflect on that dear **time** when my dear papa left a public life to live in a retired one with his **dear wife and** children ; then you **will have the** pleasure **to think,** when **you** quit the door of the House, **that** you are going to join your family forever ; but, my dear papa, I can not feel what you will when looking back on **your** past life in Congress. You will remember how much **you** have exerted yourself in order to save your country. **What** a blessed reflection that will be ! * * * * * * You say in old age, when almost all our friends leave us, and we have little more in this world to enjoy, our friends ought to be resigned **to our** leaving them. Do you think, my dear papa, that **I could** leave my dear parents in their old **age?** No ; I should **be happy** in reflecting that I could in a measure reward them **for all their** kind care **to** me when I was young. I do not **think that we can have** any reasons for leaving our friends when **they grow old.** I think the longer we live with them **on earth the** more we are endeared to them—at least any body who has ever entertained any affection for their **parents."**

In the following, the style of the girl of fourteen **has become more** ambitious, but even the formality then fashion-**able can** not quite overpower its native grace.

Miss Sedgwick to her **Father.**

"Stockbridge, April 1, 1804.

* * * * "**We are all looking for the** time, and anticipating the pleasure which **your arrival will give** us, and indeed it is almost the only topic we have for conversation. Stock-**bridge is barren** of incidents to call forth **either wonder,** admiration, or disgust. I sincerely believe there has nothing **happened since** your departure that has affected us as much, **or appeared of half the importance,** as some wounds which **old Bose** has received ; and, **though** we feared they **might prove** mortal, **he is** apparently in **a state of** convalescence ; but I yet have my doubts **whether the** poor animal will survive **to see** his dear master.

"*April* 2. The town-meeting is over ; the Jacobins have carried the day ; they have a majority of seven for governor, **ten** for lieutenant governor and senator. Mr. Williams says there were at least thirty people there whose faces he never **saw before, and who,** he verily believes, if they were turned out **of the house, and the** doors had been shut upon them, never would **have found** the way home, for they were led there by our *wise* and *great* men. * * * * * But their most diabolical act was endeavoring to lessen Dr. West's salary ; fortunately they did **not succeed.** Thus you see, my dear **papa, I** have become quite a politician ; but I have written **this merely** for your information. Yours affectionately,

"**C. M.** SEDGWICK."

Miss Sedgwick's fame was, of course, a literary one, but to those who had the happiness of knowing her, the charm and interest of her personal character far outweighed her merely intellectual gifts, and in the selections from her letters and journals, by which it is now attempted to give a picture of her, incomplete indeed, but yet faithful, it will be found that the larger number have reference to her domestic life. Moreover, her existence was, from first to last, so intertwined with that of a large and singularly interesting family, that it would be impossible to present it as a single thread, removed from the rich web of which it made a shining part; and this must be the excuse, if excuse is needed, for the introduction of many passages from her own letters, and fragments of those addressed to her, illustrating the strong and peculiar tie which united her to her brothers and sisters, and to their children and children's children.

The following letter, written to her niece, Mrs. Minot, the eldest daughter of her brother Charles, concerning a collection of his letters which was printed for private circulation, bears so directly on this point, that I insert it here as preface and key to all the subsequent family letters. It is true, she is speaking only of the interest felt by his descendants in the writings of an ancestor, but it has a much larger application in the great and blessed brotherhood of humanity, which she, of all women, would have been the first to appreciate.

Miss Sedgwick to Mrs. K. S. Minot.

"Lenox, June 24, 1860.

* * * * "Before I proceed farther I will answer your inquiry about your father's letters. As to personality, you can judge in respect to your own letters better than I. But I would caution you against suppressing expressions of tender love and favor from motives of delicacy. They, above all others, characterize him, and will be of inestimable use and value to your children and children's children. Think, my dear Kate, what it will be to them to have the freedom of the sanctuary of such a heart! After that, I think every little thing involving family life and local history should be preserved. How we should like to have such records of our parents—our grandparents! Now we live but in one generation. In reading over your father's letters to your uncle Robert, I am more than ever struck with the heavenliness of his character, the simplicity and modesty of his boyhood, the confidingness, self-negation, and humility of his youth, the delicacy, disinterestedness, and self-denial of his early manhood, and the wisdom, wit, nice discrimination, dignity, independence of his manhood ; and above all, directing, inspiring, controlling all, his angelic love. In looking back upon our family life from a position that is like that of a retrospect from another life, and in comparing it with any other that I have intimately observed, the love and harmony, kept aglow by a constitutional enthusiasm, seems to me unparalleled ; and I look upon my parents, the source of it all, with an admiration and gratitude that I have no words to express."

Miss Sedgwick spent the winter of 1805–6 in New York with her sister, Mrs. Watson, whose increasing family gave exceeding pleasure to their young aunt, and the children were put under her care for the summer of the next year.

Miss Sedgwick to her Mother.

"New York, Jan. 17, 1806.

"To me, my beloved mother, is allotted the delightful task of informing you that our dear Frances has this morning given us a lovely daughter. Teach us, mamma, to be grateful to that bountiful Providence, who is continually pouring down upon us unmerited blessings. Mr. Watson and Frances wish me to say every thing affectionate for them to you and the family, but you can better conceive the feelings Frances has toward the best parents in the world, at such a time, than I can describe them. Our dear little boys are both well. They are taught every day to drink their grandpapa's and grandmamma's health, looking at their pictures."

Miss Sedgwick to Mr. Watson.

"Stockbridge, July 15, 1807.

"I have just completed my daily task by lulling my little Kate to sleep, and giving my 'good-nighty' kiss to my sturdy boys, who are just now fast locked in the arms of their hugging friend Morpheus. To an absent and affectionate father no picture of his children in any point of view can be presented that is not interesting. Whether they are painted climbing the trees, driving their hoops, or 'with shining morning face, creeping like snails unwillingly to school' (the latter, we must all confess, would not be a very unfair representation of your tardy sons), is a matter of indifference. But to those who are blessed in their dear society, and consequently condemned all day to the clattering of their heels, and the more intolerable clattering of their tongues, their sleeping are their pre-eminently charming moments. However, my dear Mr. Watson, to square my conduct by the golden rule of 'doing as I would be done by,' in justice to my dear little charges, I should tell you that, in the absence of their legal protector, they are the best children in the world, obedient and quiet, which, by the way, are the two first virtues I should inculcate. You charged me most particularly with regard to the boys' attending school; they apparently have lost their truant disposition, although I must confess they do not evince much ardor in literary pursuits.

Catharine **does not yet articulate any words.** I hope she is not to be denied **the privilege of her sex.**"

The **following autumn, the** beloved mother, **to** whom the first **of these two** letters was addressed, died, and the next year **Judge** Sedgwick, to whose genial and affectionate **nature** widowhood was intolerable, married again. From this time **till** his death in 1813, five years later, Miss Sedgwick **was** either **at** home, or in Albany **with** her brother Theodore, now married **to Miss** Ridley, or with Mrs. Watson.

Mr. Harry Sedgwick to Miss Sedgwick.

"Stockbridge, 4th April, 1809.

"**My** friends in Boston received me **with the** utmost cordiality, but I was much mortified (personally) in finding that **a very considerable part of** my importance was derived from **a certain female relative, a** little chit of a thing, about nineteen **years old. How derogatory to the** dignity of a man! Acuteness **in** special pleading, **skill in the** languages, fourth of July orations, all disregarded, and **to be** noticed for a little thing in petticoats, called a sister, merely because *it* happens **to be** pretty, amiable, and accomplished! I told **the** people over and **over** again that I wished they would not **make** so much of you, and take **a** little **more** cognizance of **me. But** all would not do; the conversation still fastened **on the** principal and disregarded the adjunct."

Mr. Theodore Sedgwick to Miss Sedgwick.

"Albany, 1808.

* * * ***** "**Robert is the delight of our** society. His character as a wit is established. His fun flies like grape-shot; **nobody** escapes entirely unhurt. His absence will make **a chasm which nothing can fill up.**"

Mr. Theodore Sedgwick to Miss Sedgwick.

"Albany, October, 1809.

* * * * "Oh, that I were rich! All Stockbridge should be transferred here, or all Albany there. You should all and every one of you have a suite of apartments in my house. * * * * As it is, I must be contented with my cob-house in Steuben Street, and make myself as happy with one or two of you at a time as the absence of the remainder will permit me to be."

Miss Sedgwick to Mrs. Watson.

"Stockbridge, December 11, 1809.

* * * * "We have looked and listened for papa, in vain, for a week past. The roads are intolerably bad. You, whose eyes are accustomed only to the variety of round stones and flags, can hardly conceive of the mud one day and the elevation of the hubs the next. This is the first day that the smiles of the sun have greeted us for a week. I am sure Jaques's promise of no enemies but 'winter and rough weather' would never have tempted me to a country life. However, I must do it the justice to say that I have never passed three months more peacefully and happily than the last. Our fireside, if not brilliant, has been uniformly animated with good humor. Laura has quietly pursued the devious windings of her needle ; Mary (who is emphatically 'meek nature's child') and I have alternately sewed and read, till Harry has joined us to enrich us with his flow of intellect. You know our dear Charles has gone to Bethlem ; his situation is a very advantageous one ; this consideration alone could reconcile us to the deprivation of his delightful society."

"New York, February 22, 1810.

* * * * " Mr. Watson, in a letter which we received yesterday, mentions his determination of spending a night with you before his return. We are rejoiced at it, for his sake, for yours, and for ours. You will not, perhaps, think that *we* can have any particular interest in any thing which can protract his return. But if you will recollect for a moment the worship of images and relics, you will not wonder that we shall have no small addition of happiness from Mr. Watson's having *seen you and heard you.* * * * * Have you seen Walsh's Review? If you have, you no doubt think it an honor to American literature. I hope you are a subscriber for that or the Edinborough Review. The latter, I think, is the most valuable as a literary journal, the former for the high integrity of its political principles."

"Albany, March 23, 1810.

" I am sorry, my dearest sister, to repress your tenderness by a confession, mortifying and humiliating to me, but nevertheless due to truth. On no subject would I voluntarily be guilty of hypocrisy, and on that which involves all the importance of our existence I should shrink from the slightest insincerity. You misunderstood my last letter. I exposed to you a state of mind and feeling produced, not by religious impressions, but by the convictions of reason. I do, my dear Frances, feel my utter destitution of any 'claim to reward,' my entire helplessness as it regards any merit of my own, and entire dependence on mercy, mediation, and atonement. I should be unworthy the tenderness that dictated your letter if I did not acknowledge that my heart is not filled with that entire reverence and love for the Supreme

Being which he *requires* from his creatures. **I am utterly
destitute** of those holy affections which should **be so com-**
pletely incorporated with our being as to become a **part of
it.** I have not a fixed belief on some of the most material
points of our religion. There have been moments of my
life when **I have had a** lively, importunate, though, alas!
transient **interest awakened in serious things,** but the cares
and the **pleasures of this world have operated** on these sudden **impulses as the 'thorns' in the parable.** Change of
scene or society has induced me to shake off **these impres-**
sions as fetters that constrained **my vivacity, and to venture**
forward again, forgetful of the precious anchor I had **so**
lightly thrown away."

Miss Sedgwick to Mrs. Watson.

"Albany, April 20, 1810.

* * * * "Harry will be here to-morrow, but not a word
of my **darling boy, so I must relinquish the hope of seeing**
him. I wonder, **my dear Frances, if you love him more**
than I do. **Is it your** habit and **your delight to** think of
him every night, **to wish** for him every day? You **have**
other children, I have but *one;* do not be alarmed at my
claiming him. My power **over** him is that of affection ex-
clusively, and it must yield to the deadening influence of
separation ; yours can not.

" Susan has heard that there is an India ship arrived, and
she wishes you to select from its cargo cambric of the quality you sent me, enough for two coat-dresses, made to wrap,
with trimmings of the same. She does not care how cheap
you get it, provided it is as fine as mine. **One yard and a**
half of fine book-muslin, for handkerchiefs. **In addition to**
what she **wants for** the dresses, trimmings, etc., **she** wants a
yard for **I don't know what.** I wish there was some philosophy in vogue that would free us from the slavery of these

petty wants. Nothing less than the 'genius of universal emancipation' will effect it, and I am afraid that even this wonder-working genius has no microscopic eye to discern the pigmy chains that bind us in this debasing dependence. These aspirations to heroic indifference are nothing more nor less than the consequence of a provoking disappointment of my mantua-maker; so you see I am not free from, but irritated by my chains."

Miss Sedgwick to Charles Sedgwick.

"New York, December 17, 1810.

"I could not resist a certain impulsive motion toward my pen when I heard that General W—— was going this evening, and I involuntarily began to address my dear Charles. I can not say that I should not have done it with malice prepense, but the fact is I did it without any prepense at all. If I do not write more than ten lines, and those not worth the reading, forgive me, dear Charles, in consideration of an intolerable headache and stupidity. I am no philosopher; I deny the doctrine that pain is no evil, and hold that an effect must follow a cause, and that if I have a headache I must have a heart-ache too. I presume our friend, Mrs. F——, has long before this dispelled the 'dark clouds' that shrouded her purpose, and made you all stare and gape with amazement. I think we shall soon get so accustomed at Stockbridge to the most 'wonderful wonders that the world ever wondered at,' that they will be no more strange to us than the rising and setting of the sun. We will write a new play, which shall annihilate the reputation of The Rival Mothers and The Rival Queens, and call it The Rival Strangers. And, if you please, dear Charles, we will have an *under-plot*. There shall be a young man, in all the pride of self-confidence, conquered at the very moment that he is boasting his security against the whole artillery of a young lady's charms. You must supply me with the *detail of incidents*, and I will furnish the denouement.

"We often wish, my dear brother, that you were here to partake in some of our pleasures, and to confer a great deal of happiness. But, after all, there is no place like that home that is adorned and blessed with the presence of our beloved parent.

"I am extremely concerned to hear of Mrs. Sedgwick's indisposition. Tell my dearest papa and tell her that I am sure I could be of service and comfort to them, and that, if they wish it, I will come home at any time. There are persons constantly going to Albany with whom I would willingly trust myself, and with whom I think I could go comfortably. My dearest papa must not withhold the expression of his wishes from any consideration of the difficulty of traveling at this season, for I do not fear it at all; and even if I did, I hope I could conquer trifles for them."

Mr. Robert Sedgwick to Miss Sedgwick.

"New York, October, 1811, just as he was about to be admitted to the bar.

* * * * "Your letters lie open before me, and, as often as I cast a look at them, I thank Heaven that I have such a sister, and my heart swells with a pride which, I am sure, would not bring a blush upon the cheek of the purest saint above. I have often thought it almost a miracle that, in the providence of God, I have such sisters and brothers—that we have still such a father, and that we have had such a mother. Our mother is in heaven: God grant that we may meet her, as a family, there. But, while we remain on earth, let us never waste a particle of that invaluable treasure which we have in each other's affections."

Miss Sedgwick to Mr. Charles Sedgwick.

"New York, February 20, 1812.

"Your letters, dear Charley, are like angels' visits in more than this point of resemblance—that 'they are few and far between.' I am afraid, if an angel was to vouchsafe me the honor of a visit, she would not come with words so sweetly soothing as those dictated by a brother's partial kindness. I should hear a very different story when the words came to be weighed in the balance of truth. Indeed, my dear Charles, all the sermons I hear in a month, and all the writers on human depravity, with Hopkins at their head, and all the misanthropic sayings of all the old bachelors and cynics that have ever lived can not counteract—the 'sweet morsel' I can not call it, but—the mass of flattery you have so elegantly served up in your letter. It has been said by some great and wise man, and by a thousand that are neither wise nor great, that *habit* is second nature ; now, by the aid of this wonderful operator, I had just begun to be reconciled to the sight of my own features in the mirror of truth (and a picture more delightfully horrible no trafficker in human woes could desire), when your letter arrived and turned me as impulsively from the hateful reality to the sweet illusion it presented, as I would shut my eyes upon a spectacle of misery to dream of happiness. The next letter that you write, by way of unraveling this web of mischief, I desire may be filled with extracts from Hopkins's Diary, Edward's Meditations, and Uncle West's Sermons."

Mr. Harry Sedgwick to Miss Sedgwick.

"Boston, June 22, 1812.

"In looking over my letters, I found a delightful scrap of yours on the sacred character of a pastor. I believe that I shall insert it in the Messenger, that you may enjoy the novel pleasure of seeing yourself in print. I have, my dear sister and dearest muse, the pleasure to inform you that, by the appointment of the superior powers, for one third portion of the time I guide the public taste and direct the public mind, viz., one week in three I superintend the Messenger by request of proprietors. Now, unlike the Turk, I *can* bear a sister near the throne. I proffer to you the fairest portion of my dominions, nay, the royal palace—the imperial seat itself. You shall reign sole empress of the POET'S CORNER."

Miss Sedgwick to her Father.

"New York, March 1, **1812.**

"I am startled at the date of my letter. Except when I think of you, my dear father, and of some others that my heart aches to see, this winter seems to have flown like the vision of sleep. Your observation that your life appeared to you a long one, has often impressed me as the most striking proof of the *profitable* employment of your time. I have regarded your life to find some rules of action to apply to my own, but I have relinquished the scrutiny with the same feeling of disappointment that the humble architect of a cottage would have, turning from the survey of a lofty palace, in which he had almost absurdly hoped to find a model for his little dwelling. A life dignified by usefulness, in which it has been the object and the delight to do good, and the happiness to do it in an extended sphere, does, however, furnish some points of imitation for the most limited routine of domestic life. Wisdom and virtue are never at a loss for occasions and time for their exercise, and the same light that lightens the world is applied to individual use and gratification. You may benefit a nation, my dear papa, and I may improve the condition of a fellow-being. I know I am not ungrateful for the blessing of your example, and I trust that I am not without some ardent desires to benefit by it.

"The Doctor's letter was written in such a jesting mood, that I thought the account of your attack of the gout was a figure of speech, to decorate his epistle. Charles's letter, however, informed us that you had in sober earnest a *genuine* attack. I am almost afraid that you will suspect me, as you have formerly, of a malicious satisfaction in your pain. I am certainly bound to speak the truth in so honorable a presence, and therefore I must confess to you that I was not sorry that the disorders which threatened your health had found this termination. I hope, my dear papa, that you have not been very persevering in your efforts to counteract the kind purpose of nature. I know very well that it would take more than all the sophistry of the Stoics to convince you that 'pain is no evil;' but I hope it enters into your system of practice, if not of philosophy, to submit to a lesser evil (though it be even as severe as the gout) to escape an alarming danger. You will not think, my dear father, that I am regardless of your suffering; so far from it, that, were my prayers effectual, every moment of your life would be filled with ease and enjoyment."

Judge Sedgwick was on a visit to Boston with his wife and daughter when he was seized with his last illness, and died January 24, 1813. Miss Sedgwick's first acquaintance with Dr. Channing was during his ministrations at the death-bed of her father, and his doctrines must have been strongly recommended to her mind by the acceptance they found with the person she loved and revered most on earth. It was years, indeed, before she was able to receive them fully, but his lofty spirituality, and clear, calm intelligence, drew her on, as she came to know him better, and the intimacy which began within a short time between her and his sister, Mrs. William Russel, and his sister-in-law, Mrs. Frank Channing, aided powerfully in freeing her from the dark and dreary dogmas of Geneva. It would be giving, however, a false impression to say that she was ever heavily enthralled by the Calvinistic theology. One of her sisters, Mrs. Pomeroy, was, and suffered all that a tender spirit can from such cruel perversion of its best instincts ; but her own orthodoxy, though sincere, had always a very liberal tendency, and, as appears from a letter quoted previously (March 23, 1810), and expressing much of the morbid and unnatural sense of helplessness, and alienation from divine things, inculcated by that creed, she was unable to believe some of its "most material points." When she joined Dr. Mason's Church, at the age of twenty, it probably appeared to her, from her previous observation and training, the only way of expressing the deep sense of religious obligation which underlay her whole nature, yet she early revolted from the harshness and irrationality of the belief. Dr. Mason's eloquence charmed her, and his fervency interested her, but the degrading nature of his views concerning God, and their stern cruelty toward man, together with his fierce intolerance of opposite opinions, repelled her more and more. In 1820 the first Unitarian Society was gathered in New York, and in 1821 she formally separated herself from the Calvinistic Church, and soon after, with her brother Henry and his wife, joined the new communion.

But this belongs to a later period. The next letters refer to her father's illness and death.

Miss Sedgwick to Mrs. Watson.

"Boston, January 5, 1813.

"MY DEAR SISTER,—Our fears have been calmed by the favorable appearance that our father's disorder put on, but for a few days past he has not gained, and for two days I think he has lost ground. He has been uniformly silent as to his feelings and apprehensions till yesterday. Yesterday

Mrs. Sedgwick walked out for the first time, and while she was gone I was alone with him. He said to me (without my introducing the **subject)** that he had for many years been extremely desirous of making a public profession of religion **(here he was** so much agitated as to be obliged to stop for some time). He had been deterred from very unworthy motives—he had feared giving pain to Dr. West and many good people in Stockbridge by joining any other than their Church, and he could not bring his feelings to joining that. He was so much overcome that I made every effort to sustain and assure him. I told him that Mr. Channing had been desirous to see him. He said that if he understood Mr. Channing's belief, it agreed with his **better** than any **other** clergyman's in Boston, and, should it please God to restore him to sufficient health, it should be his first act to devote himself **to** Him. I suggested that, should he wish it, Mr. C. could administer the sacrament to him here. 'Not at present, my love,' said he, 'for if it should please God, I wish to do it in the face of the world.' My dear Frances, I know you will be overwhelmed with gratitude that we have so much to console us in any event. How shall we evince our sense of the tender mercies of our God, and, above **all,** this last surpassing kindness?"

Miss Sedgwick to her Sister, Mrs. Pomeroy.

"Boston, January 15, 1813.

"**Saturday Mr.** Channing visited papa. Papa imparted to him **his** earnest desire to unite himself to the visible Church, and his reluctance **to** defer it. Mr. C., who indeed is a minister of consolation from the throne of mercy, readily acquiesced in his wishes. He explained to him his understanding of this holy sacrament, which agreed entirely with papa's. He then proceeded to administer it in the most solemn and affecting manner. Papa expressed, in re-

ceiving it, his desire to repose himself entirely on the merits
and **atonement of our** Savior. The performance **of this**
duty seemed to remove the bar of reserve that opposed the
flowing out of papa's heart, and he now shows that he feels
his tenure of life **to be** very slight, and that his affections
dwell on heavenly things ; the Word of God, that precious
gift to men, whose **worth** I believe is most felt in the sick-
chamber, he listens to with unremitting interest. Oh, may I
never be ungrateful for the blessed privilege of being allowed
to watch the varying looks, and hear the tender accents **of
our** beloved parent. Our excellent **brothers are devoted,
and** I sometimes feel, when we are all assembled around **our**
father, as if our sainted mother watched and **approved us.**"

Miss Sedgwick to Mrs. Watson.

"Stockbridge, February 15, 1813.

" Every day's experience teaches me better what we have
lost, and **enables me, I** hope, in some degree, to improve this
rebuke of our heavenly Father. Still, when I review the
few last years, I forget the bitterness that has been infused
into our cup of **joy, the** corrosion of our cares, and we seem
to have closed a day of happiness, whose brightness was
never shaded by a single cloud, or sullied with a single spot."

Miss Sedgwick to Mr. Robert Sedgwick.

"Albany, March 11, 1813.

" **You** need not fear to give me pain by recurring to the
scenes we have passed through this winter. No, my dear
brother, the recollection of them fills all my solitary **moments** with cherished and elevating thoughts. **I am most**
solicitous that the impression they have made should never
be weakened—that **we may** remember **that we** have seen
and felt the triumph of that mercy which rescues mortality
from the taint of sin and the curse of death. And may our

experience of the loving kindness of our heavenly Father
strengthen our devotion to him, and make us to seek more
earnestly that salvation which is the free gift of Infinite
Mercy!

"We have a treasury of sweet and consoling reflections in
the remembrance of the lives of both our parents, and all
rendered ineffably precious by the hope that they have passed from earth to heaven; that they are now reaping the fullness of that joy which can not be impaired, though it was
purchased by suffering."

Miss Sedgwick to Mr. Robert Sedgwick.

"Stockbridge, June 7, 1813.

"I have just finished, my dear brother, the second perusal
of your kind letter which I received to-day. I often think
that, if our hearts were elevated and tempered as they should
be, our prayers would be filled with gratitude and praise.
The current of our affections to our friends is in a propor-
tionate degree sweetened with those qualities. There is an
activity in the principle of love that, like the impetuous element of fire, brightens and purifies every object it touches.
A necessary humility, my dear brother, compels me to see,
in the operation of your own mind, some of the causes of
those expressions of partiality which have dilated my heart
with gratitude to Him who hath been pleased to give me
such value in the eyes of those whose favor I covet above
every earthly good. I do love my brothers with perfect devotedness, and they are such brothers as may put gladness
into a sister's spirit. I look to you as the representatives
of my father, and I bless my God that counsel, protection,
and love, parental in its disinterestedness and its tenderness,
blesseth my life. Never, my dear Robert, did brother and
sister have more ample experience of the purity of love, and
the sweet exchange of offices of kindness that binds hearts

indissolubly together. Indissolubly I say, for that tie on which the acceptance and the blessing of God rests can not be sundered. There is a sacredness in the love of orphan children that none can comprehend so well, or feel so intensely as we do, for to whose lot hath it fallen to possess such parents as we have, or to feel such pangs in severance from them? * * * * Have I almost concluded my letter and not thanked you for the Corsair? If you had seen my pleasure in reading it, it would have been the best thank-offering. Byron ought to be ashamed of wasting his noble genius upon Giaours and Corsairs. He might as well hide the ugliness of states-prison convicts with pearls and diamonds as veil the deformity of his heroes."

After Judge Sedgwick's death, Mrs. Sedgwick returned to her own family, and Catharine became housekeeper for her brothers in the old home, endeared to them the more through sorrow. The few letters that my limits permit me to select from those of this period show the quiet happiness of her life, varied by an occasional journey or visit, a winter in Albany with her brother Theodore, and the quartering in Stockbridge of some French officers in the British service, prisoners in the War of 1812. Among these were some clever and accomplished men, whose society was a delightful acquisition in the tranquil country winter, and always looked back upon with keen interest and pleasure.

Miss Sedgwick to Mr. Robert Sedgwick.

"Stockbridge, July 2, 1813.

"There is hardly a joy or sorrow passes before me, dear Robert, that I do not bear it on my mind to you, and yet how seldom have you the record of it! I suppose that you will think that affection, like the Frenchman's pity, should have some visible effect, and would rather say 'love me a

E

letter,' than that I should love you with 'a love passing that of woman.' I am not myself an admirer of love in the abstract, or a believer in the passions agitating and swelling the fountain of love, the heart, unless I can see the evidence flowing from it in streams of benevolence and kindness.

"I rejoice, my beloved brother, that you feel the importance and efficacy of that religion which alone can give us grace in this world and life in the next, and I long to see you give your testimony of your acceptance of the forgiving love of your Master. Our souls are his, and shall we not freely sacrifice to him the best affections and services of our hearts, showing forth our love, and proving by our confidence and obedience that we are no longer outcasts from his family? God grant, in his infinite mercy, that we may all touch the garment of our Savior's righteousness and be made whole."

Miss Sedgwick to Mr. Robert Sedgwick.

"Stockbridge, August 15, 1813.

* * * * "I am satisfied, by long and delightful experience, that I can never love any body better than my brothers. I have no expectation of ever finding their equal in worth and attraction, therefore—do not be alarmed ; I am not on the verge of a vow of celibacy, nor have I the slightest intentions of adding any rash resolutions to the ghosts of those that have been frightened to death by the terrors of maiden life ; but, therefore—I shall never change my condition until I change my mind. You will acknowledge, dear Robert, that, notwithstanding the proverbial mutability of a woman's inclination, the probability is in favor of my continuing to stamp all the coin of my kindness with a *sister's* impress, particularly when you consider that every year depreciates the coin in the market of matrimony."

Mr. Robert Sedgwick to Miss Sedgwick.

"New York, August, 1813.

"My VERY DEAR SISTER KATE,—Your letter of Wednesday has just reached me ; my very soul thanks you for it. * * * * I can never be sufficiently grateful to my Maker for having given me such a sister. If I had no other sin to answer for than that of being so unworthy of her as I am, it would be more than I could bear, and yet, when I read your letters, I almost think I am what I should be. I know I feel a strong aspiration to be such, and I am sure they make me better as well as happier. Lamentable, indeed, would be the degradation of any being who would not make any effort to merit such affection, who would not find fresh strength and fresh spirit in wielding the armor of virtue from the consideration of its value and from the fear of its forfeiture."

Miss Sedgwick to Mrs. Pomeroy.

"New York, March 12, 1814.

" My spirits were refreshed with your kind letter, dear Eliza, soon after our return from Philadelphia. In consequence of the extreme fatigue of the journey, and a cold which I caught, I have been confined to the house, and chiefly to my bed, until yesterday. This will excuse to you my apparent neglect in not before giving you an account of our return. We were so continually in company while there that we were fairly *tired out* before we left. Just on the eve of our departure I took care to excite your sympathy by communicating to you my horrid fears. I was several times on the point of deciding to remain there until the traveling should be better, but *that* there was so little reason to hope for at this season of the year, that I thought I might as well take my chance ; for, as Robert very sagely observed, the worst that could happen was breaking our necks. How-

ever, the roads were, in fact, more tedious than dangerous,
and, though my foolish heart was hardly out of my mouth
all the way, there was more cowardice than wisdom in it.
In our mountainous regions we have no idea of the capacity
of the earth for making mud in this flat and clayey country.
Robert often amused himself with imagining your misery in
the like situation. I am sure our fellow-travelers must have
often wondered who the 'little lady' was. However, dear
Eliza, your sweet and welcome image always soothed me
into silence and tranquillity. I never, in any situation, felt
more lively emotions of confidence in the protection of
Heaven, nor more animated sensations of gratitude for it.
I am convinced that if we lived more spiritually, more under
the impression of a particular providence, we should find in-
calculable comfort resulting from it—that simplicity of confidence that a little child feels in the presence of a parent
where he is assured nothing will harm him. I am very anxious to hear again from your little boy. I fear you have
suffered a great deal of fatigue and anxiety for him. He
was but a delicate little plant at best, but so lovely and interesting that I thought him worth great pains in the rear-
ing. You always have some trouble among your children
when I am away from you. The absence of my *maternal
care*, I suppose. The other day, when I was sick—would you
believe it, dear Eliza?—I was so babyish as actually to cry
because I could not see you. I thought my rheumatism
would have vanished if I could but have felt the healing
touch of your little hand."

Mrs. Pomeroy to Miss Sedgwick (1814).

"And have you been sick without affording me the comfort of nursing you? * * * * Oh, my dear sister, may God
in great mercy long spare your precious life. It is precious
to many, but I can tell no one how dear it is to me. Strange,

but most true, you are to me mother, child, friend, and sister, and I have long known that you are held too closely."

Miss Sedgwick to Mr. Robert Sedgwick.

"Stockbridge, September 10, 1814.

"I think, my dear brother, we shall find, in the different conditions of life, a more impartial distribution of blessings than we are at first apt to believe. I mean to apply this to the different advantages for religious improvement in the city and country. The city is the theatre for great men. The energy of one powerful mind is diffused through a great number; the magic touch of eloquence awakens them to life and action; the dry bones are shaken; a living soul is breathed into them, and they are thus quickened in the paths of pleasantness and peace. The country is condemned to the ministration of inferior men, but it presents every facility for moral refinement and religious improvement. As you once said to me, dear Robert, 'the impress of God's bounty is upon all his works.' Every object proclaims a present Deity. 'Day unto day uttereth speech, and night unto night showeth knowledge;' and the heart must be insensible, or the spirit rebellious, if we do not with fervency join in the exclamation of the Psalmist, 'Let every thing that hath breath praise the Lord.'"

Miss Sedgwick to R. S. Watson.

"Stockbridge, November 30, 1815.

"Only think of it, dear, but you have been gone several weeks, and have not written one word to your aunt, who loves you better than all the boys of your size in Christendom. No doubt you have been attending to some great affairs, and have forgotten your poor old aunt. No, my dearest boy, I don't believe a word of it. I dare to say you think every day of Stockbridge and of your friends, and never for-

get there is nobody in the wide world that loves you better
than your own true 'aunty.' To-day is Thanksgiving. You
do not know what that is. Well, I will tell you. At the close
of the year, the governor of the state tells all the people that
they must go to church and give thanks to God for all his
goodness to us, particularly for making the sun to shine
upon the earth, and the showers to fall upon it, so that the
things that grow upon it are ripened. Last summer you
saw the apples on the trees. Now they are picked, and part
of them made into cider, and part of them laid into our cellars to eat. You saw the wheat, and the rye, and corn growing. It is now all gathered, and prepared for us and for our
cattle to eat. Well, dear Bob, to make a long story short,
after church we have a noble dinner of fat turkeys, geese,
ducks, fowls, etc., besides mince-pies, and apple-pies, and the
Yankee's glory, pumpkin-pies, and are all as happy as possible, remembering who it is that has given us all these good
things."

Miss Sedgwick to Mrs. Watson.

"Albany, March 25, 1816.

"I look forward to a very happy summer at S. Have
we not always been happy there? I esteem it the greatest
privilege of my life that I have been enabled in some humble measure to fill the place of our departed friends by contributing my efforts to preserve the attractions and enjoy-
ments of that home. And now, dear Frances, more than
ever, I discern the wisdom and goodness of Providence in
so ordering my life that I shall have it in my power to add
to the quiet and happiness of yours. The great disadvan-
tage and the only reproach of a single life is, that we poor
spinsters are generally condemned to uselessness, and Satan, availing himself of his prerogative, 'finds mischief still
for idle hands to do.' It has always, and I pray it may ever
be my happy destiny to have employment enough to keep

me out of danger of falling into the folly of repining or the meanness of envying."

Mr. Robert **Sedgwick** *to Miss Sedgwick.*

"New York, March 28, 1816.

* * * * "Nevertheless, my dearest sister, I would not have you love me any less than you do, because your affection has an irresistible power to improve and to elevate, to lift above low attachments, to separate from unworthy associations, to cheer me when I am sad, to rouse me when I am inefficient, to rescue both me and the world from that sort of morbid quarrel into which we are apt to get with each other, when it seems as if there were nothing here worth living for, and to pour a golden light on every object that skirts the path of my pilgrimage."

Mr. Robert **Sedgwick** *to Miss Sedgwick.*

"New York, September, 1816.

"Thanks, thanks—how cold a word, my dearest Kate, in return for your heart-cheering letter! It came to me in the midst of my Nol Pros., special verdicts, depositions, protests, business correspondence, etc., like a visitant from the skies. Indeed, my dear Kate, you may laugh at me, if you will, for saying so, either for my affectation or my romance; there is something about your influence over me which seems to have 'shuffled off all mortal coil' of earthliness; to be unmixed with any thing that remains to be perfected; to be perfectly spiritualized, and yet to retain its power of contact with every part of its subject; in short, to be that with regard to which I hardly know whether I have any distinct conceptions, or whether I want language to express them. Lest I should talk foolishly on this subject, I will dismiss it, only begging you not to forget how your letters cheer, rejoice, elevate, renovate me."

In 1817 Harry Sedgwick married Miss Jane Minot, of Boston, a union by which the happiness of the whole family was increased as much, if possible, as his own, and which gave to Miss Sedgwick, in particular, a sister whose rare sweetness and strength of character, and piquant originality of mind, excited her admiration and love in a degree that was only heightened by an unbroken intimacy of more than forty years.

Mr. and Mrs. Harry Sedgwick at once established themselves in New York, and their house, at first in Greenwich, and afterward in Warren Street (places now unknown in social life, and connected in the minds of the rising generation only with bales of merchandise or lumbering drays, but pleasant with friendly dwellings and cheerful firesides in the memories of those who still see them in the quiet sunshine of fifty years since), became a new centre of quickening life and warmth, not only for the family, but for a large circle of friends.

Mr. Robert Sedgwick to Miss Sedgwick.

"New York, June 11, 1817.

* * * * "We could learn nothing of Harry and Jane at New Haven, and the mystery was not solved till we found that they had been the melancholy sport of the winds from Wednesday last, when they embarked from Providence in a packet, till Sunday evening."*

Mr. Robert Sedgwick to Miss Sedgwick.

"New York, July 7, 1817.

* * * * "I have just come from passing a very cosy evening with Harry and Jane ; * * * * one which may reasonably confirm our conviction that we have rational resources for enjoyment even within ourselves. * * * * I love Jane

* This "voyage" is now made by steam in six or seven hours.

more and more every day. Harry is indeed much blessed. Such a wife as he has never can get out of fashion—that is to say, grow old, to the humor of a sensible man's fancy. She is not merely lovely, but ever active in goodness ; every day exhibits, if not a new grace, at least some more favorable and winning form of one you knew before."

Miss Sedgwick to Mr. Robert Sedgwick.

"Albany, February 11, 1818.

" Here I am at last, dear Robert. I returned with Susan on Friday last. She passed a few days with us, and we went together to visit our good old uncle John. The Genius of the Cornwall Hills arrayed himself in all his fury to greet the delicate nerves of his city visitors. Snows and wind did greatly prevail against us, but we made our way safely through the drifts, and returned with a renewed impression of our excellent uncle's patriarchal wisdom and goodness. It is delightful to perform a duty in relation to such a man —to throw it upon such a soil. I want very much to have our dear Jane see uncle before the effacing hand of Time has impaired the strong features of his character. Jane is so perfectly inartificial herself that I am sure she would admire such a noble *chef d'œuvre* of Nature's canny hand as Uncle John."

Miss Sedgwick to Mrs. Watson.

"Albany, March 30, 1818.

" I am glad you receive and impart so much pleasure to 'my friend Mr. Ashburner.' I am sure he has the claim of a 'wayfaring man in a weary land.' All the people here lumped together are not so much *society* as he can furnish from his unassisted powers."

Miss Sedgwick to Mr. Robert Sedgwick.

"Stockbridge, July 8, 1818.

"My dear Robert, I received your letter yesterday morning just as my hands were immersed in a pan of cake, and all my faculties employed in the various work of a preparation of dinner for a brace of clergymen and their wives, who had just come in upon us. You may imagine it produced some confusion of ideas. The roar of the cataract of Niagara and the stirring of a custard; the sweet image of *les belles sœurs* and the heaven-forsaken visage of my chief cook and bottle-washer; the rush of thoughts occasioned by the arrival of the fair foreigner, and the sedative of Cousin Mary White's monotonous looks and voice; the glowing image of Margaret; the sweet, maternal tones of our dear Jenny's sweet voice; Harry's 'cooing noises,' and the ringing of plates, and the dire clash of pots and kettles—all, altogether, almost unsettled my poor brains."

The next event of importance in the family record was Charles's engagement, early in 1819, to Miss Elizabeth Dwight, of Northampton, Massachusetts. It was probably in anticipation of this that Miss Sedgwick wrote under date of

"January 7, 1819.

* * * * "Our dear Charles—our youngest brother—claims a portion of our kindness, and deserves it. Our hearts yearn toward him as did Joseph's to *his* younger brother, and we can join in that emphatic benediction, 'God be gracious to thee, my son.' Oh that we could also 'put the money in the sack's mouth!'"

Mr. Robert Sedgwick to Miss Sedgwick.

"March, 1819.

* * * * "Charles! Charles! I have hardly been able, since his exchange of vows, to think of any thing else. It does appear to me that there has hardly ever been any thing so bright and soft in moral beauty as that which this union presents. I received a letter from Charles yesterday expressing the overflowing of his heart toward us all. I do not think that we shall any of us lose any of his love. Tell me whether you feel your possessions there less because a new dominion is established? I should not be ashamed of being still a bachelor if I thought that the acknowledgment of a new allegiance would in the least degree impoverish the revenues which are sacred to you."

Mrs. Jane Sedgwick to Miss Sedgwick.

* * * * "I have never read so interesting and so beautiful a tale as Charles's love-story. His passion is too tender, too elevated, and too true for any silly expressions; it has in it all that is exquisite in poetry and all that is enchanting in reality. There is a moral lesson conveyed by their happiness, for, had they been less virtuous, they would have been incapable of such affection."

Miss Sedgwick to Mr. Robert Sedgwick.

"Albany, March 24, 1819.

* * * * "Charles has fixed his marriage for the 1st of September, I believe. I presume you have heard from him. He seems determined 'to prove his faith by his works,' and I am so old-fashioned as to believe that He who provided the offering for Abraham will take care of these two beings who have lived in conformity to His laws. This may not be orthodox, but I am very much given to such heresies.

Love certainly does cast out all fear, or we should not feel willing to expose our infirmities to those we love best, when we conceal them from all the rest of the world. To you alone, my dear Robert, would I confess that the thought of resigning my place in Charles's heart has cost me some bitter tears. But I am conscious this is a selfish weakness. I know it is ingratitude to my God—ingratitude to my brother —whose heart is expansive enough for all our claims upon its tenderness. The sorrow has been almost as transient as it was unworthy. I shall be made happier by every event that augments the happiness of my brothers, and I desire, with all humility, to take the place they may appropriate to me. * * * * * You may love another better, you must not love me less."

The first paragraph of the next letter displays some of the homely cares of a country housekeeper fifty years ago.

Miss Sedgwick to Mrs. Watson.

"Albany, March 28, 1819.

* * * * "As to the candles, I think, on the whole, Maria had better make some. I believe there is some cotton-wick in my closet. If not, you can get Tamor to spin some. Candles are 22 cents per lb.; that, with the additional charge of the box and the transportation, would make them come a good deal higher than our domestic manufacture. * * * *

"I find that Mr. B———* has written to you. He deserves, my dear sister, and he needs, all the tenderness of your friendship. I hope, if you have not already, you will soon write to him. Say every thing you can to stimulate his mind to exertion and activity. If you were not a miserable agent for such a purpose, I would beg you to persuade

* A rejected lover of Miss Sedgwick.

him that the object of his pursuit was not worth the regret of such a noble mind as his. * * * * * My love to all the dear children of both houses. Tell them I shall answer their charming letters by the first private conveyance. Tell Mr. Charles that I have just sent off a long letter to the East, to convince Elizabeth that I have not forgotten her. It behooves me not to provoke the wrath of a smart young sister-in-law. Some kindlier feeling might have helped to make me write. Good-night, my dear sister. My eyes are almost out of my head, and my hand stiff. Tell dear little Bob and Fan that I would fain have had a letter from them."

Miss Sedgwick to **Mr. Robert Sedgwick.**

"Albany, November 21, 1819.

* * * * "I wonder if you have entirely put away the childish feeling of home-sickness. I fell into what, in your college days, you used to call a reverie, just at sunset this evening. I was awakened from it by the lowing of one of Rockwell's cows under the window. For a moment I thought I was at Stockbridge ; and, when I fairly opened my eyes, and saw the beautiful new moon shining on these brick houses, I could have cried because I could not see her silver beams playing on our own little stream, and shining through the naked branches of dear Charles's trees. I sometimes think my love for that spot is, for these philosophic, enlightened times, too much like that of the savage, who thinks his heaven is to be one great hunting-ground. There I have located my heaven. I doubt not that if we are, through the mercy of God, permitted to attain a state of felicity, we shall look back with gratitude and delight to that spot where immortal hopes first expanded our hearts, where those frames of mind and habits of character were formed which inspired the first desires for the love and goodness that are finally to constitute our happiness. How

shall we then look **upon that sacred** place which is now sealed with the **sad signet of** mortality, brightened by the resurrection **and the life!** **And shall we** then, **do** you think,
my dear **brother,** be permitted to rejoice **in** the unbroken
union **of our** hearts in the growth of our **immortal** existence?
How grateful, how faithful should we be to our Redeemer!
'He hath brought life and immortality to light.' **All the**
hopes that sustain and **cheer** existence here are the **fruits**
of his love, his compassion, and his sufferings."

*Miss Sedgwick to **Mrs. Watson, on the** Death of her oldest Son.*
                                    "**New York,** March 15, 1820.

"My **dear, dear sister, what** shall I say **to** you? What
can I say but that I mourn with you your heavy sorrow!
Oh, my dear Frances, you know my heart, and you know
that it **is** wounded and grieved with yours. The Holy Spirit
is your comforter, **and let us** acknowledge the ineffable consolation with which he has softened your calamity. **Truly**
our God **is** a God of tender mercies, a compassionate **Fa-**
ther; and his compassions were most manifest **in his deal-**
ings with our dear Theodore. My dear Frances, his **spirit**
has been prepared for this great change, and who that knows
the tumult, the temptations, the miseries of this world, would
bring a spirit back from **its rest, its glory?** Oh, my dear
sister, I know how many hopes have been cherished, what
strong affections wounded. But your child is not lost. He
has **gone to** a safe and happy **place.** Do not let your
thoughts dwell on the last scenes of suffering, on the triumphs of mortality, or, if still busy, busy thought *will* return
there, think of them as subjects of thankfulness and praise;
for were not the peacefulness, the submission, the patience
of your dear child assurances that the good work was **done**
—that he had prepared to meet his God—that the **world**
had passed away, and a better life dawned in his soul?

"My first impulse was to go immediately to you, but our brothers thought that you had all you could now derive from human aid and comfort, and that the difficulty of the journey would be such that I had better delay it for the present. I hope to-morrow's mail will bring us particulars from you. Do, my dear sister, if you can, write to me. My love to Mr. Watson and the dear children."

Miss Sedgwick to Mr. Robert Sedgwick.

"Stockbridge, May 17, 1820.

"I was not disappointed yesterday in my expectations, my dearest Robert. Charles came in, when the winds howled and the rains beat violently, with your letter; and its sweet influences shut my senses, for a little while, on all outward things. If any body wants to know the worth of a letter, let them *wait* for one ten days in the country in an easterly storm, with some sick and some sorrowful friends, with the chain of their interest in those they have left unbroken, the influence of the habit of seeing them and of hearing them every day unabated, and, above all, the habit of loving them with a sort of dependence that makes you careless of other sources of happiness and other means of pleasure. * * * * I wish you would give my best regards to Mr. Sewall, and tell him that I have had great success in my agency. I sent for Mr. Bryant last week, and he called to see me on his return from court. I told him Mr. Sewall had commissioned me to request some contributions from him to a collection of Hymns, and he said, without any hesitation, that he was obliged to Mr. Sewall, and would, with great pleasure, comply with his request. He has a charming countenance, and very modest, but not bashful manners. I made him promise to come and see us shortly. He seemed gratified; and, if Mr. Sewall has reason to be obliged to me (which I certainly think he has), I am doubly obliged by an opportunity of securing the acquaintance of so interesting a man. I suppose Jenny will, as usual, amuse herself with my enterprise, but 'nothing venture, nothing have.' I mean my next letter shall be to Harry, for, though he is a silent partner, it is no reason why he should not be spoken to.

"If there is any fresh tea arrived, do send and charge to me 6 lbs. That which I brought tastes just like Windsor soap-suds."

Mr. Theodore Sedgwick to Miss Sedgwick.

"Albany, June 6, 1820.

* * * * "Having this moment perused your letter the third time, I could not help giving you an answer to it, though there be nothing in it interrogative. Nor was it meant to be tender, or sentimental, or learned, but, like all your letters, it is so sweet, so excellent, so natural, so much without art, and yet so much beyond art, that, old, cold, selfish, unthankful as I am, the tears are in my eyes, and I thank my God that I have such a sister."

Mr. Robert Sedgwick to Miss Sedgwick.

"New York, September 26, 1820.

* * * * "It is well that it is not in the nature of things that those joys which seem to have taken up their most blessed abode at Stockbridge should provoke envy. If it *were* possible, I should be afraid of the contrast between my rueful countenance at breakfast and its rueful respondent in the looking-glass, and the group of faces which I can see gathered round the goodly board in the east room, or drawing up to the evening fire. Oh, what is good, if it be not to dwell upon all we have loved, and to cherish all we still love, in that, to me, sacred mansion! I had, on Sunday, a charming letter from dear Jenny*—what a pearl she is !"

* Mrs. Harry Sedgwick.

Miss Sedgwick to Mrs. Frank Channing.

"Albany, August 10, 1820.

* * * * "Our letters have as few circumstances as lovers', and therefore there is no need of a business-like, vulgar reference to your last in order to reply to it. *That* is at Stockbridge, but its record, as well as that of every other kindness you have done me, is on my heart. You know enough of my sister Susan to believe that I have not renounced, without a 'hope to be forgiven,' the charms of the country at this beautiful season for her society ; and if, as the best philosophy teaches, the happiness we derive from the beauty of Nature is from its bearing the signs of intelligence, and thus appealing to our moral and intellectual principles, why should we place the 'pomp of groves and garniture of field' in competition with the most perfect image of the Creator. I certainly do not ; and, though I love our green meadows, and morning melody, and setting sun, and the sacred evening stillness, and the 'holy peace of the broad expanse,' and all the sweetnesses and liberty of the country, I am willing to leave them all for those I love. I can not wonder at your regret at leaving the country. My happiest days have been spent there, and I am still so spell-bound by its charms that I often forget that the stream of time has carried me far beyond the period of *justifiable* romance, as questionable a term, probably, in the ears of the Rationalists as 'justifiable homicide' would be in those of a literal Quaker. This city is perfectly thronged with travelers to and from the Springs. Saratoga was never so full or so fashionable. The North and the South have given up, and the East and the West have not kept back. There are rival belles of all degrees, kinds, and *colors*, from our fair Northern beauties to the questionable hues of the West Indies. Wealth, you know, is the grand leveling principle, and every body nowadays

understands the **philosophy of colors too** well to give in **to** a vulgar prejudice **against a** dark complexion. * * * * * I am catholic **enough to be** very much **gratified to** hear of the **growing** prosperity of your *mission* in New **York.** I hope **this little** Church may prove a burning and a shining light, **and live** to have its claims acknowledged **by those whose ignorance** I hope, more than their malice, leads ţhem to oppose it." * * * *

Miss **Sedgwick to Mrs.** *Charles Sedgwick, at Stockbridge.*

"Albany, November 19, 1820.

" I hoped before **this, my dear** Elizabeth, to have had a letter **to** answer from you ; **but, if I accuse you** of negligence, you will interpose your baby for **a shield,** and then I **can** not strike. She is a little usurper ; **but it is** always the luck **of usurpers to** be treated with more deference than the legitimates. The line I received from Charles on Friday was **a good deal better** than nothing, though somewhat **to** my hungry appetite like the mustard without **beef that Pe**truchio tendered to poor Kate. When **you write, dear Eliz**abeth, do tell me how he **is—whether he is recovering his col**or, his flesh, and his hardiness. **I shall not** indulge the ab**surd hope** of getting any information from him on these top**ics ;** and let me **know, my dear sister,** every particular of all your healths and happiness ; your smallest pleasures will interest me more than the gayest scenes I can mingle in, and **are, indeed, in** comparison to them, what the household gods were to **the** statues of the temple. * * * * I **have** been almost **incessantly occupied** since **I have been** here, and I can scarcely think **of a thing** I have done. **Oh** yes ! I have **been to one very smart party** at the Governor's, where I **saw** nothing, **my** dear Elizabeth, half so enviable as a **seat by your stove,** with your cheerful face on one side of **me, and** your mother on the other, trotting her little pet **nursling, and**

Charles (for he must be in every happy grouping—to me)
hovering somewhere about, I care not where, if he is not flat
on his back—*un pauvre rheumatique*—and Kate* just coming in from school, and the cradle, and the little horse, and
'all appliances and means' appertaining to a nursery. However, you may like the vision of my eyes better than that of
my imagination, and therefore I will present to you the Lady
Governess—a lady of dignified, youthful presence (youthful
for forty), dressed in white poplin, receiving her guests gra-
ciously, with a mouth the corners of which incline a little
upward, as if her sarcasms *would* where her courtesies *must.*
The Governor, looking somewhat as a lion does when his
keeper beats him into good nature—poor man, quite as
thoroughly convinced that 'all is vanity' as ever Solomon
was. If you fill up the picture with all the fashion and gayety Albany can furnish—several pretty girls, one or two old
and half a dozen young dandies, one figurante from New
York, dancing and music, very little good cheer, and plenty
of nothing but ice-cream, you will have all that I remember,
to which I had no thought of devoting two lines in this hasty
letter."

*Miss Sedgwick to Mrs. Channing, in reference to the Unita-
rian Church in New York.*

"New York, February 19, 1821.

* * * * "Great events have occurred among your people
in this place of their captivity since our last communication.
Lucy R—— has no doubt given you the particulars. As
she has 'sown in tears,' she is now one of the most joyful
of all the reapers in this portion of the vineyard. 'The
sparrow hath found a nest,' and sings as sweetly as if she
were perched on her native boughs. I am a little surprised
that your good people of Boston do not feel more interest in

* Miss Sedgwick's niece, Catharine Watson.

this scion from their stock, and *you* will not impute to me
prejudice or bigotry if I venture to say to you that their indifference seems to me to indicate a want of that zeal which
should always be the fruit and aid of a good cause.   Devotedness to religion can not be abstracted from that mode
of it which we believe true and best.   While those of the
orthodox faith are traversing sea and land, forsaking brethren and sisters, and houses and lands, and penetrating the
untrodden wilderness, those of a 'purer and more rational
faith' seem neither to lift their hands or breathe their prayers for its propagation.   Now, my dear Mrs. Channing, I
confess this lukewarmness is a stumbling-block to me, and,
if you can remove it, you will (if my vision is not in fault)
remove a blot from your escutcheon.   I go very often to
the chapel, but as Lucy says she shall cease to admire my
candor if I become a convert, I shall probably remain as I
am—a *borderer.* * * * *

"I hope you have enjoyed the pleasure of seeing the unrivaled Kean.   Do not fail to see Lear.   It is by far his
greatest character.   I can not conceive that any dramatic
representation should excel it." * * * *

Miss Sedgwick to **Mrs. Channing.**

"New York, March 12, 1821.

"DEAR MRS. CHANNING,—Never doubt that that is a
'spirit from heaven' which says to you, 'Write,' when I am
to be the subject benefited by the inspiration.   I felt, when
I read your letter, as if it was still warm with the glow that
had sent you to your pen, and I read it with the same eagerness with which I should have drank in your words if my
eye had met the eloquent beam of yours.   My dear friend,
has any presumptuous creature of this doubting generation
ever suspected your zeal?   I should as soon suspect the
sun of counterfeiting light as to dream you were lukewarm

in any thing. No, my dear Mrs. Channing, it is not your ardor, nor your brother's and Mr. Ware's devotion and fidelity that I doubt, but it is a general indifferency, which I hear complained of by your own friends. I thank you for opening your fold to me, though I yet remain within the straitened inclosures of orthodoxy, or even should choose to wander in open pastures. However, as hopes are not the easiest mode of conveying facts, I will say to you, in all plainness, that I have not yet made up my mind to adopt the new faith. I think you are nearer the truth, by a very great deal, than the orthodox, and yet there are some of your *articles of unbelief* that I am not Protestant enough to subscribe to. I have many dear friends, who never will change their opinions, who would be shocked and deeply wounded by what they would consider my apostasy. My own family are all joined with, or approximating to you, and they are all sufficiently enlightened, rational, and liberal not to condemn those views of religion which they know are directed and controlled by a supreme reverence for God, and a sincere and zealous love of that truth which He has revealed in the Bible. If the new Church had such a pastor as your brother or Mr. Ware, I should not hesitate, for I should think the benefit I might derive from them would outweigh every other consideration. My dear Mrs. Channing, I could write a letter full on this subject, for it interests me more than any other at present, but I dislike to talk so much about myself in a way to show that I think my own views and plans of great importance. To you I have said more than to any one else, and, if I have seemed egotistic, you must take some of the blame for the confidence you inspire, and set the rest down to the subject, which certainly transcends all others in interest. I fear I shall not see Boston this spring, though I know not how I shall have philosophy to resist Mary's kind invitation, with the sweet enforcements that accompany it.

Robert and I intend going to Niagara in July. My sister, Mrs. Pomeroy, and Charles are to be here on a visit this spring, so that my time will be all occupied. * * * *

"We have just laid our hands on 'Kenilworth.' I saluted it with as much enthusiasm as a Catholic would a holy relic. It is now lying beside me, looking so fresh and tempting that I think I deserve some credit for having resisted it thus far." * * * *

Miss Sedgwick to Mrs. Watson.

"New York, April, 1821.

"You hint, my dear sister, at some temptation to which you think me particularly liable. I hope I am not so blinded by self-love as to be incapable of discerning a fault when pointed out to me, or so selfish and ungrateful as not to turn from a precipice because I did not first see it. I know it is much more agreeable to profess a general humility than to own a particular fault. After all this, you may think it very inconsistent for me to declare myself unconscious of the danger to which you allude. I am, it is true, in a city where Fashion maintains her empire, and has her willing and unwilling subjects, but if I was with you in your house, or with Charles in his blessed retreat, I should not be more independent of fashion than I am now. We have nothing to do with the fashionable gayeties of the city. Our visiting is all of a familiar and domestic kind, and there is, of necessity, a good deal of time run away with where you have a large circle of acquaintance and must be accessible to all, yet I think we lead, as far as can be under such circumstances, rational and domestic lives. The situation of our family this year has, of course, kept me at home, and, with two or three exceptions, I have not been out of the circle of our intimate friends. I have been a few times to see Kean—not, my dear sister, in conformity to fashion, for nothing is more unfashionable in New York than the theatre. I have not had the satisfaction I should have had from his wonderful exhibition if I had been sure that this was a right indulgence. If I had been sure it was wrong, I think I should not have been tempted to go. Perhaps I am 'fighting the air,' but, my dear sister, I think it is much better to speak plain, 'to speak the truth in love,' than to have any timidity in relation to subjects of such importance. Our heaviest burden is sin, and those who attempt to lighten it for us certainly most efficiently obey that injunction which says, 'Bear ye one another's burdens.'

"I presume you saw the letter I wrote Susan, in which I said that I did not think I should go to Dr. Mason's Church again. I have not been since. This has been a subject of continual anxiety and pain to me. I have done nothing rashly, nor without an anxious consideration of what was my duty. You know, my dear Frances, that I never adopted some of the articles of the creed of that Church, and some of those upon which the doctor is most fond of expatiating, and which appear to me both unscriptural and very unprofitable, and, I think, very demoralizing. On some important points I think the doctor is all wrong. Still, it was so painful to me to give up the privilege and happiness of church-membership, that, until I thought it became an imperative duty to leave it, I remained one of that congregation. My example is hardly any thing in this city, but, as far as it goes, I thought myself bound not to lend its sanction to what seems to me a gross violation of the religion of the Redeemer, and an insult to a large body of Christians entitled to respect and affection. I have not become a member of the Unitarian Society, though I think I should if they had such a clergyman as Mr. Channing or Henry Ware—I mean like them in their religious sentiments. I hope and believe, my dear sister, that you will not disapprove my conduct; if

you do, tell me so frankly.   I know I have risked much and
lost much, for I have many friends whose confidence and
affection constitute a large portion of my happiness, who
have not liberality enough to think there is any religion beyond the pale of orthodoxy.   I do not know but I shall be
debarred communion with the orthodox churches, but, if so,
I must try, and I shall, with the blessing of God, bear the
privation with meekness, trusting that He who is my hope
and my Savior will own me as His disciple.   Any thing is
better than insincerity, than feeling ourselves obliged, from
prudence, to conceal our sentiments.   Such a prudence borders too closely on hypocrisy."

Miss Sedgwick to her brother Robert.

"Stockbridge, June 2, 1821.

* * * * "I admire, dear Robert, the admirable adroitness
with which you insinuate your grief at my departure.   I know
too well the theory and experience of an agreeable succession of ideas to flatter myself that my memory (all that was
painful in it) did not pass away as rapidly as the shadow of
the clouds before the bright sun of that crowd and caravan
of Bostonians.   Even 'Temps le Consolateur' will not get a
monument this time.   I am not so selfish as you may think.
I care not how much those who are as my own soul value
my presence, but I do not desire they should mourn my absence.   Life is quite too short for useless regrets.   Our present duties need all the life they can get from the leaven of
cheerfulness. * * * * * I have been trying for two days to
answer Mr. Channing's letter, but I can not make out any
thing that satisfies me at all.   I know this is very foolish for
a grown-up woman, and one that has been grown up so long,
too, but I am quite incapable of the courage necessary for
such an undertaking.   But I shall write, if I don't make out
better than poor Jeanie Deans did in her literary efforts.   I

had rather submit to **any** intellectual degradation, in **Mr.** Channing's opinion, than to have him **think me insensible** to his great kindness. * * * * * I went to **the school the** other day **to hear** the boys speak off Demosthenes and Cicero, and I **was quite** amused, **for** I had almost forgotten **to** what seeming **torture the human body can be** put without stretching it on the rack. * * * * **Charles is** constantly at . Lenox, **and seldom** comes home **at night.** I have remonstrated **with him, as** Hall is retained **on very high wages** till the Fall. But he says there is a **great deal** of business behindhand, which has been laid aside. **Oh, my dear** Robert, **this** place is dreadfully changed without him. **I have never** felt so oppressed by the **changes** in **our** family. **The house is** so still and solitary. My imagination is continually filled with those looks and **voices** that animated every **part** of the house—that beamed **with** love and rung with joy. Elizabeth is very **pleasant and kind, and** the baby a sweet little creature, but those beloved ones whose hearts responded to mine as 'face answereth **to** face in the water' **are** all gone, or far away. This is not right—a single repining **thought is base** ingratitude—they are unbidden and unwelcome guests, **but** they will **come.** **The** country is *perfectly beautiful.* 'Nature's universal robe' was never more enchanting."

Miss Sedgwick to Mrs. Channing.

"Stockbridge, June 4, 1821.

"My dear Mrs. Channing,—I left on my table at **New** York an unfinished letter to **you,** which should, and **would** have convinced you that I felt my debt to you. At Albany **I received** the kind letter which destined me **the pleasure** of an **introduction** to your cousin, Miss Cabot. **I knew she** was **to be in** New York with **your** brother, and, I assure you, it required all the **effort I am capable of '**in patience to possess my soul' under such **a host of** disappointments.

L

The loss of Dr. Channing's society has been in some degree compensated to me by a letter from him, as kind as unexpected. I shall always preserve it among a few sacred documents that I possess, which have power to refresh the drooping spirit, and stimulate a languid piety. You would have laughed at me if you had seen with what fear and trembling I accomplished a reply, with all the 'contortions of the sibyl,' but, alas! without the inspiration. Ease is absolutely necessary to writing letters with any success. If there is any thing that pervades my whole character, it is a love of freedom that 'leaveneth the whole lump.' When I had accomplished the mighty labor, I could have cried over it—a stupid composition, very like the first awkward attempts of a boarding-school girl of 'pretty talents.' My mortification did not all result from wounded pride, but I am afraid your brother, if his goodness does not avert such an opinion, will think me very impertinent to occupy his time with a long letter, when a simple acknowledgment would have been enough. But, my dear Mrs. Channing, these troubles must be quite uninteresting to you. I have had nobody to pour out my heart to before. Those who inspire confidence must sometimes feel the pain of sympathy. My letters from New York do not in the least console me for my loss of Miss Cabot's acquaintance. She has captivated all my friends there. I try to feel a benevolent pleasure in the happiness they have enjoyed, and to trust that I shall participate it, at some period of my existence, in this world or a better. I look forward to forming a great many agreeable acquaintances when there shall be no such material obstructions as intervening mountains, and we shall no longer be closed in by the limited operation of our present organs—when there shall be a perfect community of light, and joy, and feeling, for all of one heart and one mind. I was not aware, until I received your letter, how strong my hope had been that you would join our Canada party. I do not doubt that you have decided righteously, but I have **been almost tempted to wish** that your conscience was not quite so enlightened. I can not imagine **any** thing that could be so delightful as **to have** you with us. **I would not, even to** accomplish so good an end, taint your **morals with Jesuitry, but,** in the technics of this region, **I do wish you could 'see it to** be your duty' to confer so **much pleasure, and** to recruit, with new and changing scenes, your own health and spirits. The country is as beautiful as Eden could have been when all was pronounced **good.** Youth is always beautiful, and Nature now is a perfect emblem of the morning of life, so bright and unspotted, ➤ **so** full of hope and promise. My dear brother **Charles has entered** upon the **duties of an** office which, for the most part, confines him at Lenox, six miles from us. **This is a** sad privation **to us. There is a sunny** influence in his presence **;** like **the light of heaven, he brightens** every object **around** him. **He is felt in all. The** emolument of his office, though small, **is very necessary to him, and I** *try* **to be thankful and** satisfied. My cousin, Henry Dwight, will carry this letter to you, and, though I do not deserve it, I hope (it is not uncommon for our hopes to outstrip our deserts) he will bring me one in return."

Mr. Charles Sedgwick brought his wife, on their marriage, **to the old** Stockbridge home, where they lived for two years, when his business relations with the neighboring town of **Lenox** became so close that he found it necessary to **make** it his residence. This was a bitter grief to his sister ; **and** to explain, in some degree, a distress which, in **the present** easy **connection** of the two villages, might appear **unreasonable,** it **must be remembered that Lenox was then** a bare and ugly **little village, perched upon** a desolate hill, at the end of six miles' rough and steep driving. It is true, the

natural beauty which has since assisted in giving it celebrity existed then ; but we all know how much habit, association, and cultivation do in enhancing natural beauty, and
making it precious to us, and, to a native and lover of the
rich valley of Stockbridge, with its soft and graceful varia-
tions of meadow and wood, its gentle river, and its shelter-
ing mountains, and the appearance of refinement even then
given to its dwellings, Lenox must have seemed dismally
bleak and uncouth. Besides, Miss Sedgwick's affections
were so gathered about her paternal home, that life in any
other spot in the country would have seemed to her like
exile and banishment ; but she may have smiled in after
years, when her prediction was fulfilled, and Lenox *had* become, next to Stockbridge, " the dearest spot on all this
earth" to her, at the unmitigated repulsion with which she
at first contemplated it.

Miss Sedgwick to her brother Charles, on the occasion of his
proposing to remove permanently to Lenox.

" MY DEAREST CHARLES,—I need not tell you, for you
know already, how I feel the contemplated change. Your
presence here has been to me like the spirits of our parents,
and it never seems home to me when you are gone. I had
made up my mind with some composure to your residence
at Lenox for three years, but the thought of your living there
permanently is like dissolution to me. Still I know, my
dear Charles, all evils are worse in the anticipation than the
reality, and *if* it is best that you should go, I will do what I
can to be resigned—to be cheerful. Wherever you are I
must have a home, and Lenox must be to me, when you and
yours are there, the dearest spot on all this earth."

This removal involved other changes. Mr. Theodore
Sedgwick henceforth took possession of the family mansion,

which has ever since been delightfully associated with his
name and that of his admirable and lovely wife. His sister's summers were for many years passed with him under
the roof so dear to her, and her winters with one of her brothers in New York, for Robert's marriage in 1822 gave her a
second home in town.

Meanwhile, in the summer of 1821, she made an excursion to Niagara and Canada with her brother Robert, Mr.
and Mrs. Theodore and their son, and Mrs. B——. The
following extracts are from the full journal she kept for the
sake of her friends at home, and are charmingly characteristic :

"Palatine, 52 miles from Albany, June 22, 1821.

"MY DEAREST JEANIE,—This day we have begun the
'grand tour.' Is it not a singular coincidence, considering
the uncontrollable nature of human affairs, that we should
have commenced the undertaking on the very day Robert
appointed last year? We were drinking tea together last
August (1820) at Sister Susan's. A jaunt to Niagara was
discussed, and R. concluded the talk by saying, 'Well, Kitty,
at any rate, you and I will start the 20th of next June.' He
left New York on the 20th. Many a man's reputation for
prophecy has been established upon a less striking verifica-
tion than this. My conscience did not need 'jogging,' for
the intention of communicating my pleasures to you and
Harry as I went along has constantly been one of my most
delightful anticipations. I have been so long in the habit
of sharing all my booty with you, that now, when I expect
so rich a spoil, do you think I will deprive myself of his beatitude who giveth? It would be a shame to keep any social pleasure from Harry, who never yet had a *solitary* enjoyment. We left Albany this morning all well and in fine
glee. We have engaged extra post-coaches to go as far as
Utica at the very moderate price of $30. A fairer day

never invited to 'Nature's high festival.' You must remember the ride on the borders of the Mohawk. I do not care, as our friend E. C. says, to 'harangue about scenery,' but, dear Jane, it would be treason against nature if the heart did not dilate at the sight of this beautiful stream, as full, from the late rains, as the 'brimful Clyde,' reflecting the verdant banks, the overhanging trees, the richly wooded hills, and the clear heavens. * * *

"While our breakfast was preparing at Schenectady, we walked through its dirty streets to the high ground which Dr. Nott has tastefully selected for his *university*. His pupils might learn some lessons in theology from the fair volume of Nature open before them that should soften the influence of some of the severest dogmas of the strictest systems. We saw all along the opposite bank of the river a multitude of men at work on the canal. We are told more than one thousand are between this place and Albany. * * *

"*Utica*, 24*th*.—Here we arrived last evening, after a day of pleasure, mingled with a little vexation—enough to secure us from the insipidity of a draught of uniform sweetness. In the morning, at Palatine, our driver, offended at our having selected a house he did not patronize, and, like his betters, choosing to use his 'little brief authority' in tyranny, did not come for us till 6 o'clock. This worried brother T., who, you know, does not like to be imposed on, and he gave the fellow quite an edifying lecture upon the natural rights of man. We, at least, were touched with its justice, and the man, if he did not repent of the wrong he had done us, was mortified at it. * * * *

"The canal, when completed, must be one of the most stupendous monuments of the enterprise, industry, resolution, and art of man. The scenery was enchanting, and, in spite of a melting sun, we all agreed to wipe out 'a' scores' with Fortune thus far. We went also to see the little canal,

which was made here more than twenty years since. During
the operation of a boat's passage through the locks, which
happened just at the moment we arrived at them, a poor
blackey fell from the bank into the water ; he was not hurt,
and his accident produced a burst of merriment from the
vulgar fellows about him. 'You ain't white yet !' said they,
as the poor fellow shook the water from his woolly head.
How hard it is to belong to a degraded caste—to be born to
the inheritance of jibes and jokes ! My interest in this
place was doubled by the recollections associated with it.
At my first emancipation from childhood, I had visited it
with my beloved father. I recollected with gratitude the
patience and interest with which he explained to me the
construction and operation of the locks. * * * *

"(P.S. by R., preserved, not for its justice, but its characteristic humor.)—'I crowed !' said a scene-shifter, 'when
Garrick played Hamlet ;' and 'I rung the bell !' said another
of the children of humble ambition, 'when Whitfield preached ;' and I, says I, put a P.S. to Kit's letter, and thus, as it
were, ride on a pillion, on her Pegasus, to immortality, etc.
* * * *

"Brutus, on the Canal, 85 miles from Utica, Tuesday, 26th.

"The boat is drawn by two fine horses : the hindermost
has a rider. They go on a very fast walk, at the rate of four
miles an hour, including stops, which recur every eight miles.
The canal is forty feet wide and four deep. We passed six
locks during the night, and we all joyfully left our hot little
cabin, where I had spent all my time in fanning away the
musquitoes, to enjoy the novelty of mechanical rising and
falling. Sue sat near the bow of the boat. She reminded
me of some of the heroines of song as we awaited, in these
walled inclosures, the opening of the immense gates, which,
without much aid from fancy, at 1 o'clock in the morning,
by the feeble light of the lamps, looked like a portcullis to

an ancient castle, or any thing else your imagination might
choose to liken it to.   Just at nightfall we met the Murray
family, and stopped long enough to go on board their boat,
where we saw an Indian chief of the Sac tribe thirty inches
long! a sort of a stump of a man ; like to the three wise
men of Gotham in the respect that his lower extremities
were placed in a *bowl*, to facilitate his traveling.   The Mur-
rays told us he spoke five Indian languages and the French,
but we had no opportunity to try his 'prodigious erudition,'
as the poor creature had more delicacy than we manifested,
and averted his head from us.   I must confess myself tired
of the canal, though, as *you* may guess, its safety commends
it to my coward heart.   R. says we are much in the condition of a tea-cup swimming about in a slop-bowl. * * * *

"*Buffalo, June* 29*th.*—After we left Batavia the face of
the country changed.   It has quite a new look—here and
there log houses, and fields full of stumps, but every where
abundance and comfortable abodes.   I find all the people
are our country people, and, true to my love of 'finding out
folks,' for which you so often laugh at me, I have some clish-
maclaver with the landlady or some of her household wherever we stop.   To-day I brightened the faded eye of a withered 'octogenarian,' who was breaking up the curds for her
granddaughter's cheese, by telling her that I came from the
land from whence she emigrated some forty or fifty years
ago.   She said she 'set more store by one from New England than by all the town of Clarence.'   She was struck
with admiration at T.'s beautiful face, and said, ' Whoever he
belonged to, he was a perfect beauty.'   The modest blush
her remark spread upon his full cheek justified her expression.   Dear boy, he has been the delight of all our hearts.
I am not disposed to allow that ' Life's enchanted cup but
sparkles at the brim,' yet his glad innocent face does indicate that to him it is a sweeter draught than to those that

have tasted the bitter drops that sometimes mingle with its waters. * * * *

"This beautiful country stimulates my patriotism. That passion which is inspired by the peaceful triumphs of man over Nature, if it is not as romantic, is certainly more innocent than that which is kindled by battle-grounds, and I should even venture to put our cheerful dwellings, and fruitful fields, and blooming gardens against the ivy-mantled towers and blasted oaks of older regions, and busy hands and active minds against the 'spectres that sit and sigh' amid their ruins. You saw this place immediately after the devastation of the last war, during which every habitation save one was burnt. You would be surprised at its phœnix resurrection. There are 1200 inhabitants, three congregations, a beautiful Episcopal church, a bank, court-house, and several fine brick houses, some of them quite as large as any in Albany." * * * *

To L., S., and E.

"*Mouth of the Niagara.*—There were two subjects of curiosity in Oneida, and I was very sorry that the arrangement we had made with the canal-boat did not allow us to stop there at all. The one was the clergyman who presides over the spiritual interests of the poor natives. He is a far-away cousin of ours. Do not be startled, my dear girls, though some Indian blood is mingled in his veins with a fairer current. He is descended from a daughter of a Parson Williams, of Deerfield. She was taken by the savages during one of their incursions into the newly-formed settlement of our pious ancestors. She was so young that she soon lost all recollection of her parents. Many years after, when peace was established with our wild neighbors (but not till after the bear's claws and teeth had been taken out), her friends made a fruitless effort to recover her. She had mar-

F 2

ried an Indian, and chosen his country for her country, and
his God for her God ; and, like the tender and true-hearted
Ruth, she has been the mother of a servant of the Lord.
Mr. Williams (for he bears the name of his maternal ancestors) is said to labor with great zeal and some success among
the remnant of his tribe.

"Here, on the margin of the river, were encamped seven
families of Irish emigrants, making in all fifty. They had
entered the country at Quebec, and expressed great satisfaction at having arrived within our territory. One poor
woman, with John Rogers's complement of children, and one
sick one in her arms, *hoped* to find her husband in Mercer,
in Ohio. In another tent was a poor man with ten children, whose wife had fallen a victim to the hardships of the
passage. He looked quite dispirited. I asked him how
they liked our country. 'Och, ma'am, and we could not
miss liking it,' said he, 'we find the people so free and hos-
pitable.' One sweet pretty girl, niece to the woman who
had died, had, like Abraham, come out from her country,
and kindred, and friends, and without, I believe, the incite-
ment of a special call so to do. I asked her how she could
leave them all. 'Sure it is, ma'am,' said she, 'if it thrive
well with me, they will all come after.' The poor Irishers !
they do all come first or last. This pretty girl was a Protestant, so I thought I could not give a better 'God-speed'
to her pilgrimage than by bestowing on her my Testament.
She received it as if she had some notion of its value." * * * *

"*Niagara Falls, July 1st.*—We arrived at the Falls yesterday at 1 o'clock, or, as they call the place here, at Stam-
ford. We immediately obtained a guide, and all, with one
heart and one mind, with the most impatient curiosity, descended to take our first view of the Falls. I know it is
impossible to give an idea of the beauty and sublimity of

the scene. If I fail to do it, I may impress my memory so strongly as to be able at some future time to recall the images that are before me at this moment. From Forsyth's the walk toward the Falls is for some distance through a level and shaded road ; then you descend a deep pathway, with steep banks on each side, covered with a verdure that resembles the new-mown grass, fresh and sparkling from a recent shower—a beautiful peculiarity that it always preserves, and owes to the continual humidity of the atmosphere. These banks are overhung with butternut and beech trees, elms and lindens. Under a beautiful linden we first caught the view of the American Fall, which is directly in front of you as you approach the bank. This is one straight sheet of water, with a single interruption from a small intervening island, covered with evergreen. You see the rapids beyond it, the bridge Judge Porter has thrown over them to Goat Island, his fine house, almost hid by the majestic trees around it, and two little islands on the brink of the fall. They look, amidst the commotion, like the ships of some woodland nymph gayly sailing onward, or you might imagine the wish of the Persian girl realized, 'Oh, that this little isle had wings !' At the termination of this road, and near the bank of the river (which is one half mile from Forsyth's), is an old stone house, inhabited by a Yorkshireman and his wife. Sue and I called to see them while we were resting our weary limbs (for with all this regale of the spirit there is weariness of the flesh). The old man gave us a piteous account of his trials : he said when he laid in his bed he could never tell when it rained nor when it thundered, for there was always a dripping from the dampness, and the deafening roar of the fall ; and then his poor cattle, in winter, were always covered with icicles. It was a mighty fine thing to come and see, but we should be sick enough of it if we had as much of it as he had. 'Il n'y a rien de beau que l'utile' is a fair maxim for a poor laborer. We expressed our sympathy, which was certainly more appropriate than our contempt would have been. * * * *

"3d *July. On board the steam-boat Ontario, Niagara River, Youngstown.*—We left the Falls yesterday morning. The morning was rainy (the first rain we have had since we left home), but, notwithstanding, we all went through showers above and mud below to take our farewell of the Falls. Dear Robert, whose benevolence is indefatigable, was not willing to have me come away without going under Table Rock. We descended the steps once more together, and scrambled over the rocks, which in some places are so soft that you can break off pieces and crumble them to powder in your hands. We walked under the tremendous projection of rock, which here forms a considerable arc of a circle, the summit, as you stand in the depths of the excavations, projecting many yards beyond you, with trees hanging over the extreme point. Every thing is so vast that you seem introduced to a new state of being, and almost doubt your identity. The heights and the depths, the moisture of the atmosphere, which gives to every leaf and spear of grass in the crevices of the rocks a tender green ; the fishermen below, who seem dwindled to children, all combine to form a scene as new as it is imposing. But it is not these banks of rock ('qui semblent en harmonie avec le torrent solitaire, image du temps, qui les a fait ce qu'elles sont'), it is not that solitary and eternal torrent that produces the awe you feel, inspiring devotion amidst these objects, but it is the 'Spirit of God moving on the waters.' It is the vastness of every object, expressing the infinity of the Creator, and thus bringing you into his visible presence. * * * * We took our leave of the Falls with a mixture of sadness and gratitude. 'Glory had been at one entrance quite *let in*,' new images of the power and the glory of the Creator had been conveyed to our minds through this avenue, and our hearts united in a Te Deum for all that we had enjoyed from this marvelous work. * * * *

"I forgot to mention to you a party of Greenwich Street shopkeepers we met at Niagara. They have come into this picturesque world for what, unless 'Peter Domer's Riddle' will help us to a solution, I can not tell. Well, here they have come to spend all the profits of their patient labor in measuring tape and dealing out pins and needles for the last twenty years. Yesterday I heard them say they had been dreadfully disappointed in their journey—they had not seen a broiled chicken nor a roast pig since they left New York! Remember the philosophic maxim, dear Charles, 'de gustibus,' etc. If we have the Falls, why should not they have chickens? Is not it difficult sometimes to abstain from the pharisaic thanksgiving? * * * *

"*5th July. On board the Ontario.*—We passed a delightful day with our kind friends at Rochester. It was a refreshment that we needed, for even our short privation of faces and objects that were familiar to us had caused those unpleasant sensations of travelers that Madame de Staël has so well described : 'Voir des visages humains, sans relation avec votre passé, ni avec votre avenir, c'est de la solitude et de l'isolement, sans repos et sans dignité, car cet empressement, cette hâte pour arriver là on personne ne vous attend, cette agitation dont curiosité est la seule cause, vous inspire peu d'estime pour vous-même.' You may smile at my attempting to apply language which belongs to the traveler 'solitaire et isolé' to our merry, happy party. I will not contend for the aptness of the quotation, though I might for its eloquence. * * * *

"Descending the steep bank to the river, Mr. E. pointed us to a railway made to facilitate the conveyance of freight up and down the bank. Captain Vaughan has a son on board, a sprightly **boy of** twelve, who last year was descending this **railway in the box (like** a wagon-box fixed on rollers). The **rope broke the** moment **they began** their descent. Young Vaughan seized a child **who** was with him —a *stranger*—and jumped over. The child was quite uninjured; and the boy, whose instinctive benevolence and self-possession you will admire as much as I do, sustained very little injury. The box acquired immense velocity in the descent, and, of the two other persons with them, one was shockingly mangled and the other instantly killed. * * * * * When **we** had got ourselves quietly re-established in the boat, I went to inquire after a poor woman—a steerage **passenger**—who had been suffering from a paroxysm of **toothache, and** for whom I had procured some laudanum **and** camphor before I left the boat. In reply to my inquiries, **she said,** 'I am quite easy; but it was not your trade, (*sic*) ma'am, that cured me. The captain is a seventh son of a seventh son, and he said he could cure **me with** stroking my face. **I know** it is a simple **thing to tell, but it** did cure me.' Who will quarrel **with a superstition that** cures the toothache?

"We have been sitting on the roof of the ladies' cabin, **and, by** the light of this beautiful crescent, which now 'seems **to shine** just to pleasure us,' watching our winding path through the 'Thousand Isles.' The heavens are yet bright-**ened** by the parting smiles of day. The verdant islands are of every size and form—some stretching for miles in length, and some **so small** that they seem destined for a **race** of fairies; some **in** clusters, like the 'solitary set **in** families,' and some like **beautiful vestals in** single loveliness. The **last** streak of daylight **has faded from** the west, and the **blush on the waters is followed by** the reflection of the 'far **blue arch' and its starry** host. The fishermen's lights **are** kindling along the margin of the river; our **mate** says we are having a 'most righteous time.' Captain **Vaughan**, whose simplicity and unostentatious kindness have won **their way to all** our hearts, has fired his signal-gun for us **several times,** that we might hear the reverberations amidst these islands. The mate says, ' Don't they hollow well ?' They do indeed, as if we wakened **the spirits of their deep** solitudes to send us back our **greeting. The captain has just** ordered the signal to be **given to** his fisherman, who immediately answered it by kindling a bright light on the shore—a pine **torch, I** believe, for by its bright flame I perfectly discerned a little hut on the brink of the water, the element on which **he** lives, for there does not appear to have been a tree **fell-** ed from the deep woods that surround him. **He put off in** his little canoe freighted with fish, and in **a few minutes** completed his exchange with our steward, who, in return for the fish, furnished him with gunpowder and whisky, which our pleasant **little mate gave** him, saying, ' Here is your *tea*, fisherman.' **He looked as** wild as poor Effie's boy, Whistler. Robert (dear Robert, who has been my kind angel thus far on my journey of life) said to me, as I sat snugged **up in** his cloak, ' **Kate, we** shall remember this a great **while.'** Dear Jane, may not these beautiful scenes, that seem now like ' glimpses of heaven,' be among our pleasures of mem**ory** if ever we enter into the blessed inheritance of the saints ? * * * * * We are seated vis-à-vis **in** our little boat, **with one** small sail. The boat has freight enough to keep **it steady,** and, though this is very little, it occupies a great portion of our room, so that we are obliged to sit on boards without the amelioration of a cushion, almost as **compactly** as we should in a stage-coach. The St. Lawrence **presents an** appearance quite novel to us. **It resembles one of our** rivers when brimful from a freshet. We have already pass- ed two **of the Rapids. The river usually** descends so much **as** to give great velocity to the current before you come **to**

the Rapids.   You find yourself suddenly impelled forward
as if by an unseen and invisible hand ; the banks seem flying from you ; still your passage, though almost as fleet, is as
noiseless as that of the planets in their orbits.   Suddenly
you pass into the waters that are foaming over their hidden
bed of rocks.   The boatmen throw themselves prostrate in
the bottom of the boat to avoid the dashing billows, their
oars being useless in these agitated waters.   The skillful
steersman strains every nerve at the helm to guide the boat
in its difficult path.   It seems very perilous to my cowardly
nerves, but it is not so, as is proved by the rare occurrence
of accidents.   I am not so quiet as I could wish, but the
rest of the party are more reasonable, or have stouter hearts,
and are as merry as possible.   We have just passed Crist-
laer's Town, another war-scene ; but these theatres for 'ambition's honored fools' are quite common in this country.
* * * *

"*Montreal, 9th.*—We disembarked at Coteau before the
storm had arrived at the poetic height requisite for description.   Be thankful that you are spared that.   We sought
refuge in the Boatman's Inn, which, upon inquiry, I found
was kept by a Mr. T——, a man who had emigrated from
Barrington.   His wife, too, was from the Bay State, but they
seemed not to have retained any of the thrifty habits and
getting-along faculties of our home-land.   The only Yankee
symptom I observed was the expression of regret from the
woman that her children had neither the privilege of schools
or meetings.   She could get no spiritual refreshment but by
crossing the river and going thirty miles into the States.
She had Catholic churches in her neighborhood, but, according to her view of things, partaking from their board would
reverse the Scripture rule.   It would be giving the dogs'
meat to the children.   We regretted that we had not brought
some tracts for distribution in this land of spiritual ignorance

and famine. This wretched inn resembled nothing I have ever seen or heard of so much as the 'Clachan of Aberfoil,' and, bating the dirks and the Baillie, I think it was in no whit superior to that. Besides Indians, emigrants, Canadians, and boatmen who had taken shelter from the storm, there were numbers of those people that we call tavern-haunters, who not only find their 'kindest,' but their *only* 'welcome at an inn.' These were stupefied or noisy from the revels of the preceding night, and were either lounging on the beds, or swearing and drinking. The house was tapestried with spiders' webs, and blackened with smoke and all manner of defilement. The storm continued so long that the captain of our boat and the pilot decided that it would not be prudent to proceed that night. We were determined to seek some better fortune than that of Mrs. T——'s inn, and after dinner Robert and I sallied forth to a French village a little distance from the shore. To our great joy, we saw a sign with 'Auberge et Laugement' on it. The bad French was not our affair, but the neat tavern was ; and, after having engaged three decent apartments, which were then occupied by some milords, but were to be vacated before night, we proceeded, in high spirits, to explore some other habitations in the neighborhood, which on some pretext we entered. We found no difficulty in gratifying our curiosity. The Canadians are noted for their civility. This quality is woven into the texture of French character. The Canadians seem to have lost the enterprise, the activity, gayety, and ingenuity of their ancestors, but politeness is still as easy to them as if it were instinctive. We entered a house where the family were occupied as in our farmers' houses. The mother was spinning, and the eldest daughter weaving. We inquired why they did not teach English to their children. They said they did not love the language— the English had done them too much wrong. They complained of their oppression during the last war. The old woman said **the militia** officers would take from them 'des veaux, **des moutons,** des *dar*dons, des poulets, tous, tous, tous.'' We inquired if the children **were taught to read,** and **found** that two of the younger ones had been sent to a boarding-school some miles distant. A modest little girl **was** called up to exhibit her acquirements. Her school-book **was a** collection of morceaux from the Fathers. She read **a** prayer of St. Augustine's, while the old people stared at her with wonder and delight, as if they had seen a successful experiment in chemistry. I have acknowledged to you that the Rapids **terrified me.** 'Le Galop' and 'Le long Saut' had quite satiated my curiosity, and I had no anxiety **to** see 'Les Cedres,' 'Les Cascades,' and the 'Split Rock.' **A fine post-coach,** which was to return in the morning to Montreal, offered me a tempting opportunity, and Robert, ever kind, and perhaps too indulgent, was willing to accompany me. Mrs. B—— was as glad **as I** was to back out **of** the boat. Brother Theodore looked upon me as **quite dis**graced by my cowardice, and urged **this as a fair occasion** to discipline my coward nature. He was right, I believe ; but I have of late been so accustomed to delicacies that I **had** not resolution to swallow so disagreeable a draught, **and** without fear, but *with* reproach, I took most ingloriously to my '*land paddles.*'

"River St. Lawrence, July 11.

"MY DEAR JANE,—You are not obliged to read, but I must **write, and** write to you, for I have so accustomed myself to the stimulant which the hope of giving you pleasure affords me that I **can** not do without it. This has often **sent** me to my **pen when tired nature** would have sent me to my bed. * * * *

"We stopped at **the** wall which incloses La Maison **des Prêtres.** This is a beautiful place to which the priests of the Seminary of St. Sulpice resort once a week, with their pupils, for recreation. We had no passport, and we were at our wits' end for the means of gratifying our curiosity; but is a Yankee ever at his wit's end? We determined to pass the barrier, and trust to our own cleverness for the rest. The house is an ancient fortress, erected by the French government as a defense against the incursions of the savages. It is inclosed by a stone wall twelve feet in height, and with two round towers at the entrance of the court. Robert led us up the court, and, as he entered the door, a round-faced, jolly-looking priest, who sat sleeping by the open door of another apartment (where the young priests were playing at billiards!), advanced toward us. Robert told him we wished to see their establishment. He replied that it would be difficult to grant our request, as it was their day of recreation, when, according to the rules of the house, they admitted no visitors. However, he called an elder brother, whom Robert addressed as 'Reverend Père.' He told him we were strangers from the United States with a courtesy of manners that would have been quite *au fait* at the court of Versailles. The old man, a complete Abbot Boniface, waived his scruples, bowed politely, and led us on. He said to Robert, 'You must be from France, dear sir, as you speak French like a Parisian.' So much for his having had the manners to call him Reverend Père. He might have said, with more propriety, 'Your politeness is Parisian.' He led us through a beautiful flower-garden to a spacious inclosure, partly below the hill and partly on its brow, through which is a canal, with a fountain and a bark canoe, and on each side of the canal fine butternut and linden trees. We met the superior, a man of very elegant appearance, and, as we are informed, of great accomplishments. He advanced toward us, and said it was contrary to their rules to permit ladies to enter the grounds when the priests were there. Robert pleaded our ignorance, which he with a benignant smile admitted as an apology, saying, 'You were not obliged to divine,' and begged us to proceed.   One of the reverends was reposing under the protecting shadow of a noble tree, with a book in his hand.   Others were sauntering on the bank of the canal, and all presented a scene of contentment and indulgence not strictly compatible with their self-denying system.   It is pleasant to see an open and fearless relaxation of their slave service.   It must be far easier to be good, under this fair sky, where, though 'deep the silence, yet how loud the praise,' than in the sullen gloom of a cloister. * * * *

"The evening before we had spent with a New England party at our friend Mrs. Day's.   Her pleasing family and cordial kindness made us feel quite at home, and that is one of the 'feelings to mortals given' worth almost all the rest. Last evening at 10 o'clock, Robert and I, whose weirds seem destined to be dree'd together, took leave of our dear friends. Few parties have ever been composed of more harmonious materials.   Much as I wished to see Quebec, Robert and I felt at the moment of parting as if we would rather share the fortunes of the rest to the end of the jaunt. * * * *

"We arrived under the steep battle-heights of Quebec a few minutes after nine, just as the twilight had faded away, having accomplished our sail of 180 miles in a little more than eighteen hours. * * * *

"After breakfast we hired the *only carriage* in Quebec and a gig, and went with the F——s to see the Falls of Montmorenci.   The road is intolerably bad, and though the distance is not more than eight miles, we did not get back until three. * * * *

"Montmorenci is not more than twenty yards in breadth, and falls about 180 feet, some say 250, but it looked to me but very little higher than Niagara.   The fall is about fifty rods from the mouth of the river, and has evidently re-ceded from the banks of the St. Lawrence to its present tumbling-place. Thanks to my country bringing up, I descended the bank the nearest way without difficulty, while our town-bred companions were obliged to go a circuitous path. It was ebb tide, and Robert and I walked along the margin, passed the projection of the rock a few feet from the fall, and got near enough to the foot of it to have the best view of it, and to get thoroughly drenched with the spray. The water makes a single graceful leap from the summit of the rocks to the foaming bed below. All waterfalls are beautiful objects, and this is distinguished among its species, but in my eyes did not quite deserve its celebrity, which it may perhaps in part owe to the historic interest of the spot. You and I, dear Jane, should deem it a profane presumption for the soldier to mingle the harsh dissonance of war with Nature's musical voice, as it steals upon the sense in the murmuring of the stream, or swells to sublimity in the roaring of the fall. * * * *

"After dinner we had the good fortune to obtain the guidance of some of the officers of the 37th Regiment, who first escorted us to the parade-ground, where we saw the soldiers go through their evening exercise. They then conducted us around the fortifications and to Cape Diamond. They were extremely polite and obliging, and did not scruple to show us every thing we wished to see. I shall not undertake to describe these fortifications to you. They did not look quite as formidable as I expected. I felt, like a smart little Yankee boy of whom we had heard, that we might *take* them. This child, a cadet ten years old, who, Captain Hall told us, came with his father in his boat to Quebec last summer, was accidentally separated from his party while walking about the fortifications. He met a common soldier, and requested him to show him the way to the Plains of Abraham, whither the party was destined. He

gave the soldier **some money,** intending it as a requital for
his guidance.   **As** they walked along, he asked the man to
explain **the design of any** part of the fortifications he did
not understand, and the good-natured soldier was delighted
to gratify his intelligent curiosity.   After **a while** the boy
paused, and said, 'Well, it is very strong, that's **certain, but**
I think *we* could take it.'   '*We!* who are *we?*' said the man.
'Why, *we* Americans.'   'You an American!' said the man,
with a terrible oath, dashing away the money the boy had
given him ; "and have I been serving my king four-and-
twenty **years, to** be bribed by an American boy at last!' * * * *

"I had **seen** enough of Quebec. When we first approached it, I felt some risings of envy that a place which seemed
to be one of the natural **portals to our great** country should
be in foreign hands.   But the covetings of national pride
were soon cured by the conviction that the support of such
an expensive military position would make it a very dear
acquisition, and it can not be at all essential to our safety
or defense.   The British are welcome to it.   It must **be an**
odious place of residence, 'altogether inconvenient,' as Dr.
F. said of the ill place.   It is built, you **know, on a** precipitous hill, and the ascent from the lower town (which is a
narrow piece of ground rescued from **the** hill, and bound in
by the water) is almost perpendicular.   The governor's residence (the Chateau) is in such a position as Edgar pictured
to the imagination of poor Gloucester.   Lady Dalhousie's
back windows, from whence she looks **into an** abyss upon
the roofs of the houses **of the** lower town, would afford a
fine situation for 'le diable boiteux.'   We **were** treated with
kindness by every one from whom we had occasion for any
favor, English and Canadian. * * * *

"*Saturday,* 13*th.*—We sailed at 11 last night. The **current of** this racing river runs at the rate of three, four, **and**
in some parts seven miles an hour.   Of course the ascent is

at best twelve hours longer than the descent. We stopped
at Three Rivers, and our polite captain allowed us time to
go on shore, and went with us to the convent. The Sisters
would not admit us without a passport from the Grand Vicaire. The captain, who did not fancy the delay, and did
not esteem the sisterhood a privileged order, called them,
with some emphatic expletive, a parcel of old cats. There
was no evading the rule, and some of the gentlemen went to
the house of the Grand Vicaire, who was kind enough to
grant a permit, notwithstanding they had cut short his afternoon's nap. Among these nuns I found a young woman
who was born and bred in Hanover, New Hampshire—a
Yankee nun! Her countenance was bright and rather
pleasing. The coarse linen band they bind around their
foreheads, and the deep linen collar, make them at first look
old and ugly. We purchased some pretty bark-work here,
and bade adieu to convents, without a sigh of envy at their
seeming security from the storms of life. They, with Rob
Roy, belong to the great class that 'are ower bad for blessing, and ower good for banning.' * * * *

"*Monday*, 16*th. Lake Champlain.*—Here we are, dear sister, making the best of our way home. I begin to snuff my
native air, and feel its inspiration warming my heart with
the anticipated delight of home faces and home scenes. I
begin to suspect that I am quite too national for this philosophic age, but would not, if I could, be cured of my prejudices in favor of my own people." * * * *

Miss *Sedgwick* to Mrs. Channing.

"Stockbridge, September 25, 1821.

"Your prompt and kind letter, my dear friend, in some
small measure made up to me the severe disappointment of
not seeing you. Have you read Miss Wright's book, and
do you not think some of our vulgar editors have abused

her? 'She is not accurate,' I know, as our friend Bleecker gravely said of one of the most outrageous romancers in the world. Alas! that it is so; what woman is? I have but just looked into Miss W.'s book, but she seems to me to have a habit of thinking on subjects that most of her sex know nothing about. At any rate, she is a stranger and a woman, and, as such, entitled to our courtesy and our sympathy. I fear our New York friends will be disappointed in H. No ''prentice hand' is capable of laboring in that vineyard. They want just such a man as Henry Ware—a man wise and skillful, with *some* experience, and full of every gracious affection. I hope to hear that your brother William is going to a kinder climate for the winter. We should need all our confidence in the unfailing wisdom and goodness of Providence to enable us to submit to his removal to the mansions prepared for him. Ware seems to me more like your brother in the spirit of his devotional writings than any other man. The article on 'Love to God' in the last 'Christian Disciple' breathes the spirit of your brother. My devout little sister, Mrs. Pomeroy, who is as pious as the very best of Scripture ladies, has read it twice with tears in her eyes. She relishes such healthful and sweet food, though she is willing now and then to take the medicine of controversy. Her mind has entirely escaped from the thraldom of orthodox despotism, and she rejoices in her freedom. But I beg your pardon, my dear friend; you do not know my sister, and you live beyond the sound of our gloomy polemics, so that you can not even imagine what liberty to such a captive is. Robert is with us, and with his cheering influence, and the charities of home, and the bright new robe Dame Nature has lately arrayed herself in, we are happier than most of our race, and quite as happy 'as is consistent.' My dear Mrs. Channing, I mean, if possible, to see you this winter, and then I shall hope to have some help to this snail's progress in your affections. Do write to me soon ; a letter from you always makes a gala-day, and leaves a long track of light on my path. My love to your children, and believe me, my dear friend, yours truly, C. M. SEDGWICK."

Miss Sedgwick to Mrs. Channing.

"New York, December 5, 1821.

"Your letter, my dear friend, was accidentally delayed at Stockbridge, and I did not receive it till it was five weeks old, so that, if friendship was liable to the rapid decay of matrimonial love, the honey-moon would have been over with it. There are some things, thank Heaven, that do not need the relish of novelty, and your letters are among them. My life is a good deal like that of the Israelites that came up out of Egypt, save that it is not passed in a wilderness. I certainly am but a sojourner, and in that sense have an existence in actual conformity to the apostolic injunction. Your accounts of your brother are delightful ; his restored health is a mercy to be acknowledged with devout and joyful thankfulness, as his removal would be a national calamity. I have felt a superstitious dread of his death. It seemed to me that it would be a frown of Providence upon the cause he has so zealously adopted, and so materially advanced. I should not venture to express such an opinion to many, for some would deride it, but it does seem to me there is a want of seriousness and of holy fervor in your clergymen. I have sometimes felt this very painfully. There is among them a great ardor for intellectual attainments and superiority, but many of them want the holy devotedness that seems to me essential to their high calling. They come, in the name of their Master, to 'heal the sick, and bind up the broken-hearted ;' to seek the lost, and reclaim the wanderer. If the mission is delightful, it is most serious, and requires all the energy of a human being, and that, too, kin-

G

dled by a spark of heavenly flame. But, my dear Mrs. Channing, I did not mean to preach a sermon ; it is not my vocation, nor your duty to listen. You will not be surprised that just now, as the little Church here is so busy, this subject should be uppermost in my mind. If you think as I do, you have so much influence, in the sphere you move in, that a little occasional lay-preaching from you might produce great effect. I heard Dr. Mason's farewell sermon to his people on Sunday last. It was, on all accounts, a lamentable performance, and, as I thought, indicated considerable debility of mind, as well as almost incurable disease of heart. As usual, he gave the 'rational Christians' an anathema. He said 'they had fellowship with the devil : no, he would not slander the devil, they were worse,' etc. Will you not say, as a pious Catholic once did after a furious attack of the doctor's upon the true Church, 'We must pray for Dr. Mason?' * * * * I am quite sorry that your charming domestic circle has been invaded. Matrimony does certainly seem very meddling and impertinent to those that have nothing to do with it. It is very strange the apostle should have deemed it necessary to admonish Christians to possess not, since the mutability of life so constantly teaches and impresses the lesson. To 'possess not' seems to me the sure consequence of possessing. Your home has not at all lost its attractions to me. The hope of passing a few weeks in Boston this winter has been one of my summer dreams, but, as the time approaches, I fear my courage will be frozen up by the cold weather. Can not you, my dear friend, who have so much more resolution than I, be tempted to come here, and let your light shine upon our ordination? You may have scores of ministers to attend you, besides the gallant knight Edward, who, I understand, is coming to New York, as Cogswell goes to Paris, 'to study.' Whether his researches are to be confined to Greek, or to the more dif-

ficult language of a lady's eye, he has not yet announced."
* * * * *

Miss Sedgwick to Mrs. Channing.

"New York, February 21, 1822.

* * * * "I am grieved to hear that your brother William
is suffering, as you prophesied, from the climate of Boston.
I hope you will send him South with the opening of the
spring. I am quite pleased to hear of Mr. Dewey's success
among you. He is a neighbor of ours in the country, and, I
believe, deserves the favor he has found. William Ware is
growing in our hearts very fast. As far as preaching in the
pulpit and the preaching of example goes, he takes excellent care of our spiritual concerns. Do you ever hear Walker? We think him a tremendous great gun—destined to be
one of the first men in the country. He has the vigor of
Bossuet—Bossuet converted to rational Christianity. * * *

"I hope you have read the Pirate with delight as we have.
It certainly is a highly poetical production. Who but Walter Scott could have created such a scene on a barren isle
of the Northern Ocean! The world here is divided into
the followers of Minna and Brenda. They seem to me the
fair representatives of this world and a higher. * * * * I
have written amid female chatterers talking to me and at
me. You must forgive me for sending the letter; but I am
afraid you will think as Dr. Johnson did about the dinner,
which did well enough, but was not a dinner to invite a man
to." * * * *

Miss Sedgwick to her brother Charles.

"New York, Feb. 22, 1822.

"I was much obliged to you, my dear brother and sister,
for your letters, brief as they were. There are no days so
bright as those that bring me letters from home, and when

I think that not one this winter has conveyed any unpleasant intelligence, I rejoice with trembling. This unexampled exemption from the certain evils of life, throughout a large family circle, can not last ; the day of adversity must come, and God grant that we may meet it with unwavering confidence in his goodness, with humble resignation to his will, and with a grateful remembrance of past mercies. We have had a great deal of pleasure from a glimpse of Bryant. I never saw him so happy, nor half so agreeable. I think he is very much animated with his prospects. Heaven grant that they may be more than realized. I sometimes feel some misgivings about it ; but I think it is impossible that, in the increasing demand for native literature, a man of his resources, who has justly the *first* reputation, should not be able to command a competency. He has good sense too, good judgment and moderation, and never was a man blessed with a warmer friend than he has in Harry. This is one sure anchor in all winds and weather ; and besides Harry, there are many persons here who enter warmly into his cause. He seems so modest that every one seems eager to prove to him the merit of which he appears unconscious. I wish you had seen him last evening. Mrs. Nicholas was here, and half a dozen gentlemen. She was ambitious to recite before Bryant. She was very becomingly dressed for the grand ball to which she was going, and, wrought up to her highest pitch of excitement, she recited her favorite pieces better than I ever heard her, and concluded the whole, without request or any note of preparation, by ' The Water-fowl' and ' Thanatopsis.' Bryant's face, ' brightened all over,' was one gleam of light, and, I am certain, at the moment he felt the ecstasy of a poet."

The engagement of her last unmarried brother, Robert, to Miss Elizabeth Ellery, of Newport, Rhode Island, who was at the time a stranger to all his family, was the occasion of the following letter from Miss Sedgwick to her sister :

Miss Sedgwick to Mrs. Watson.

"New York, February, 1822.

"Robert feels his happiness very incomplete till he has the expression of his friends' sympathy, and he was sadly disappointed this morning not to get a letter from you or from Susan on the subject. I trust they are on the way, for you know any want of interest in others when our own feelings are strongly excited is very painful ; and no one knows or feels more than you, my dear sister, the right of this dear brother to all our hearts can feel or our tongues express. Jane and I have made up our minds that you will take a great fancy to Elizabeth. She is certainly a great provocative to the imagination. She is gaining on us all, and I think, from all I can learn of her, she must have a high-principled character. She has a very bright, intelligent face, without being handsome. Allston has selected her eye for a picture of a prophetess, and it has the expression of a seer into futurity. For my own part, my dear sister, I have tasked myself to the duty of resignation with more fortitude than you would expect. I am through the worst of it. Indeed, I have so much cause for gratitude that a repining thought brings the sting of guilt with it."

Mr. Robert Sedgwick to Miss Sedgwick.

"February, 1822.

"You will never know, my beloved sister, so long as the obstructions of sense stand between heart and heart, how mine has been melted by your kind and generous conduct. I know, my dear, that all you have suffered has proceeded from a love of which I am unworthy. * * * * It is a very common sentiment that a sister must give up her place in a

brother's heart when his wife takes possession of it. If this
were so, I should be sorry to see you ever reconciled to my
marriage. But, if I know aught of true love, instead of con-
tracting the heart, it gives new strength to all its best affections. Upon what do all these affections depend for their
cultivation and growth, if not upon the objects of common
sympathy and interest? He who made the heart never
ordained that its empires should be like those which are
marked off on the surface of the earth. He has never appointed that a sister's portion should be taken away to be
given to a wife."

Mr. Robert Sedgwick to Miss Sedgwick on the eve of his Marriage.

"New York, August 9, 1822.
* * * * "Though I am in the greatest possible confusion
and hurry, I can not leave town without telling you that my
heart never turned toward you or leaned upon you with
more pure, faithful, ardent, and confiding affection than at
this moment. God reward you, my beloved sister, for all
you have been to me, and enable me to cherish a tender
and unalterable sense of all I owe you. I know nothing
that would alarm me so much for myself as a consciousness
that I was losing my love for you."

Up to this time Miss Sedgwick appears never to have
thought of writing for the public. She says, in a letter to
one of her friends, so late as February, 1821, "My dear
brother Theodore makes a most extravagant estimate of my
powers. It is one thing to write a spurt of a letter, and another to write a book;" and if her first book had not been
almost as unpremeditated as a letter, it is possible that her
modesty might for some time longer have repressed a talent
as delicate as decided. But now, after her connection with

the Unitarian Society, her recovered intellectual freedom, and the desire to help others to escape from the chains which she had broken, led her to write a short story bearing on these points, which she at first intended for a tract. On showing it to her brother Harry, he advised her to give it a larger form and scope, and print it as a tale, and in this way the " New England Tale" appeared in 1822, and was at once received with such interest and favor as to give its author an immediate position in the world of American literature.

Miss Sedgwick showed her sound judgment and artistic intuition in this her first romance by planting it upon her native soil, where people and incidents could be used with the freedom given only by long familiarity. She struck here the key-note of all her after success. Her dramatic power lay in her thorough knowledge of the strength and weaknesses of the New England character. Though her genuine love of romance sometimes betrayed her into scenes and situations tinged by sentimental moonlight rather than by the honest light of day, she is always natural and discriminative when her foot is on her " native heath ;" and whether it is the country folk of to-day, with their quaint peculiarities, whom she describes, or the same people under Shaker rule, or roused by revolutionary feeling, or, still farther back, as settlers of the forest, Puritan fighters against the wolves, the Indians, the world, and the devil, or whether it is the same stock refined by culture and placed in the midst of modern social elegance, her creations are real and living persons, drawn with a truth and vigor which give them a freehold right in the land of fiction, from the half-witted and whole-hearted Kisel of the " Linwoods" to the lovely, impulsive, and fascinating Hope Leslie, and the excellent and uncompromising Miss Debby in " Redwood."

The New England Tale was received with enthusiastic

pride by her brothers. Mr. Theodore Sedgwick wrote as follows :

"Stockbridge, May 6, 1822.

"DEAR KATE,—I have read 130 pages of the book. It exceeds all my expectations, fond and flattering as they were. I can not express to you with what pride and pleasure my heart is filled. I had no doubt of the result, but hope and anticipation are now converted by the happy reality to fact and knowledge. I shall not rest till I have seen the whole, and beg that you will let me know when I shall also greet the architect of this exquisitely beautiful fabric. Dear Kate, we are in rather a moody state here for the want of your society."

And her brother Harry, in a more business-like letter, expresses no less gratification.

"New York, May 25, 1822.

"Jane had a large packet of letters to-day from Boston, all of them praising the tale. What is much better, Bliss White has increased orders from the booksellers. Bliss told me to-day that the public had just begun to find it out ; that its sale was dull at first, but now it was going off very rapidly, and much beyond his expectations, and would soon be entirely exhausted. In the course of a few days I will send you a draft of the Preface for the second edition for your approbation. Let Theodore also try his hand at it. He has a good knack at such things. Bliss says that the only difficulty with the book is the unfavorable representation of the New England character, and that the writer must bring out something of the same kind in which this mistake shall be corrected. I think he is right.

"I think, dear Kate, that your destiny is now fixed. As you are so much of a Bibleist, I only say, don't put your light under a bushel. Your work came out under the most unfavorable circumstances. The title (though taking) is certainly unlucky; that's my fault. The orthodox do all they can to put it down; Carter's notice casts a damp, and the New-Englanders feel miffed. Still, it has decided success from its own merits; so have done with these womanish fears. I don't know of any thing which now gives me so much excitement as the certain prospect of your future eminence. I wish you to keep me constantly informed of your plans, and how far they get into execution. I think you will find great advantage in writing in disconnected masses, which you can afterward weave together. In this way you may save your bright ideas when they are brightest and most interesting.

Miss Sedgwick to Mrs. Frank Channing.

"New York, Sunday evening, 1822.

"I do not know, my dear Mrs. Channing, but I should call any tolerably Christian, neighbor-like treatment from you better than my deserts, but that which I receive is so much better that I have not words to express my gratitude. Your kind interest in my concerns is a part of your own generous nature, and is so entirely independent of any merit in me, that I feel as humble as Calvinists profess to feel, and as all should feel on this subject of merit. My book! If all poor authors feel as I have felt since obtruding myself upon the notice of the world, I only wonder that the lunatic asylum is not filled with them. I hardly know any treasure I would not exchange to be where I was before my crow-tracks passed into the hands of printer's devils. I began that little story for a tract, and because I wanted some pursuit, and felt spiritless and sad, and thought I might perhaps (at least I was persuaded that I might) lend a helping hand to some of the humbler and unnoticed virtues. I had no plans, and the story took a turn that seemed to render it quite unsuitable for a tract, and after I had finished it I was persuaded to publish it. I claim nothing for it on the score of literary merit. I have some consolation in the conviction that the moral is good, and that to the young and simple in our country-towns, if into the hands of any such it should fall, it may be of some service. I am more anxious than I can express to you to remain unknown, but that, I fear, is impossible now. One source of thankfulness and rightful, honest, joyful pride I have in an eminent degree. Criticism has been disarmed by affection, and from my dearest and nearest friends I have received such expressions of interest and sympathy as I shall never forget, and never cease to be thankful for. * * * *

"I have at last had an opportunity of seeing and admiring your friend Greenwood.* I am sure he must have a delightful character. I mean I should be sure if you had not told me so, though you may upbraid me with my slowness in finding it out. The truth is, that when you hear so much of any person as I had heard of Mr. Greenwood, you expect to be astonished as with a sudden blaze of light, and manners so unostentatious, and conversation so unpretending as his, seem quite commonplace. If you were not too good to be envied, and if I did not try to be too good to envy, I might be in danger of looking with an evil eye upon the privilege you enjoy of his fine society." * * * *

Miss Sedgwick to Mrs. Channing.

"Stockbridge, June 15, 1822.

"I am sorry, my dear Mrs. Channing, that you should ever, in regard to any instance of your interest in me, doubt of my gratitude. I must be constituted strangely if I did not acknowledge and feel your zeal for my happiness and improvement, and if I have ever seemed to disregard it, it

* Rev. Dr. Greenwood, of Boston.

must have been from reasons that you could not know, and therefore could not discreetly weigh as I could. I am not at all prepared for many of the advantages that might be reaped from a voyage to Europe, and as to happiness, I have had such an old-fashioned bringing up, that there is no equivalent to me for the pleasures of home, the voices and the smiles of brothers and sisters, and the caresses of children. I should be ashamed to confess to the learned and the literary that there is nothing distant and foreign that has such charms to my imagination as the haunts about my own home, a chase along the banks of our little stream with the children, breaking willow-sticks for the boys, and helping the girls to get the flowers, and devising and leading their sports. I am perfectly conscious that this is all very rustic and antiquated, but it is my taste, and that word, you know, silences dispute, as the shout of my merry troop of revelers stops pursuit when they cry ' Screw up.' Forgive me ; you can not understand the technics of our sports. It would have given me pure delight to have seen you, my dear friend, and Eliza Cabot at Stockbridge, and if it had not been for a homely but wise adage of my old nurse, who used, on the occurrence of an irremediable evil, to say, ' Don't cry, child, for spilt milk,' I might have bewailed your not coming in a very unsuitable manner for a grown-up woman. I should have delighted to have rambled over our hills, and along the margin of our quiet, modest little river with you, now when Nature has her beautiful garments on, unworn and unsullied, the earth every where sending forth its promise, and fragrance and melody finding their way to the imagination through their appointed paths. Social and animated as you both are, I would not have you think your intercourse would be limited to trees and brooks. My brother and sister are *good company* for any body. Our dear Charles, you know, we look up to as one of Nature's *chefs-d'œuvre;* his

wife is a very fine and charming woman, and their little girl
seems made 'to envelop and contain celestial spirits.' So
much for our family circle (and, from *pure modesty*, I have
omitted three other *wonderful* children, and an old lady, who
has the virtues of the patriarchs, and the improvements of
modern times), and beyond the enchanted precincts where
you may suspect the spell of egotism, we have Col. Dwight,
who is *au fait* in all the arts and graces of the beau-monde,
and an *East Indian* (not a Housatonic) philosopher, a man
of genius, of experience, of observation, highly gifted in the
powers of conversation, in short, quite a study. Besides all
this galaxy, we have just now a wandering luminary from
England, a gentleman of science, who travels with a fine tel-
escope, and all manner of wonderful instruments, and with
whom the family are to sit up all night star-gazing as soon
as the planets mend their ways in so far as to rise a little
earlier. I should be delighted to visit Boston in the course
of the summer, but I should neither go nor stay with any
reference to my little tract. I protest against being supposed to make any pretension as an author ; my production
is a very small affair any way, and only intended for the
young and the humble, and not for you erudite pro-di-gi-ous
Boston folks. I should rejoice to see again my old friends
that I dearly love, and your friends, so worthy of being
loved ; and that I could add any thing to your happiness, my
dear Mrs. Channing, is temptation enough. Some of my
friends here have, as I learn, been a little troubled, but, after the crime of confessed Unitarianism, nothing can surprise them ; these are only the most bigoted ; and, for the
most part, my friends are just as cordial as ever, some more
so, and I do not despair of convincing the most prejudiced
that I am not a Mohammedan, nor an atheist, nor even an
apostate. I love my own people and my own home too well
to resign or abandon either, and I have good hope of living

to laugh with them over our present difference, and if we do not in this world, I am pretty sure we shall in another.* When you see my dear friend Mrs. Minot, do remember me most affectionately to her. It does not seem to me possible that your wing should ever tire, that you should ever need any excitement to the perpetual spring within. Do you know when our countryman Dewey is coming this way? I quite long to look upon a Christian minister who does not regard me as a heathen and a publican. Do write to me soon ; out of the fullness of your generous heart distill upon us some drops. Farewell, my dear friend.

"Ever truly yours,   C. M. SEDGWICK."

Miss Sedgwick to Mrs. Channing.

"Stockbridge, August 17, 1822.

* * * * "Now, while I am on controverted points with you, I wish to set you right in relation to a mistake of yours about the feeling which your letter on the subject of my little book excited. I *was not hurt.* I simply wished to convince you that I neither grounded fears nor claims on that humble production. I could not endure the idea that I had written myself out of the affections of my own people. Here is the home of my heart, and though there is undoubtedly some transient dissatisfaction, my friends here love me better than those who have not been bred up with me can. They think, as they express themselves, that I am in a dreadful error, but I believe they would for the most part concur in an expression I heard reported from the good little wife of our parson, 'I hope you do not love her the less for it.' I do not say this boastingly ; I believe it is right that we

---

* An excellent aunt of Miss Sedgwick, who was very fond of her, said to her one day, as they were parting, after Miss Sedgwick had become an avowed Unitarian, "Come and see me as often as you can, dear, for you know, after this world, we shall never meet again."

should feel more pleasure in the affection of our inferiors
than in the praise of our superiors, and nothing could in-
demnify me for the loss of the kind feeling of my humble
country neighbors." * * * *

Miss Sedgwick to Mrs. Pomeroy.

"New York, January 10, 1823.

"Thank you, dear Eliza, for inquiring after our Church.
Mr. Ware, we think, improves constantly; his sermons have
a more serious, or what is called evangelical character. Religious experience is, I think, the work of time, and you can
not expect a very young man to be as skillful in teaching as
one more mature, who knows from personal observation and
actual experience the wants of human nature and the power
of religion. Mr. Ware's character is an excellent one, and I
doubt not will abide severe scrutiny. He is so modest and
unpretending, his talents so respectable and his application
so steady, that he must command every one's respect; and
then, you know, 'when a man's ways please the Lord, he
maketh even his enemies to be at peace with him.' We are
just now very busy about establishing a charity-school, and
we hope soon to get it in operation. Our plan is to have it
kept in one of the lower rooms of the church by a woman,
and superintended by the ladies. We mean to teach the
children the rudiments of learning, and how to mend and
make their clothes, darn their stockings, etc. Our society
is small, and far from rich, but we hope to accomplish it.
Egbert dined with us on Friday. He enters into our wishes
with considerable zeal, and promises to do every thing we
wish. Is it not good to interest young men in works of benevolence?"

Miss Sedgwick to her niece, Miss Watson.

"New York, January 22, 1823.

"The last, my dear Catharine, has been a year of particular interest to you. It has witnessed your entrance upon a period of life when you begin to feel, more deeply than light-hearted youth can feel, your own responsibility ; it has witnessed the maturing of your principles, and the beginning of purposes of usefulness and generous devotion to the good of others. And it has witnessed the public dedication of yourself to the service of our Lord and Savior. This is a most important and affecting event in your life. It does not, perhaps, create any new duties, but it certainly suggests new motives to exertion and fidelity, that the world, before whom you have done this, may never call in question the laws of the Master because the servant is faithless. What manner of persons, my dear Kate, ought we to be, seeing that the kingdom of our Master must be established in our hearts ; seeing that it is not enough to hear, but we must obey ; not only promise, but do the will of our Lord, who has come, not to save us *in* our sins, but *from* our sins? Heaven must be begun here. We must be watchful not to admit, certainly not to permit or to cherish, any passion or affection which can not enter into those mansions that are prepared for the followers of the Lamb—that can not abide the pure light of the Sun of Righteousness. God grant to us the influences of his Spirit to strengthen every thing that is good and resist every thing that is evil within and without us."

Miss Sedgwick to Mr. Robert Sedgwick.

"Stockbridge, June 11, 1823.

"Thank you, dearest Robert, for your kind, very kind letter. It came unexpectedly, and made my heart dance, like

a sunny ray darting through a cloud. No one knows how
I prize every tender expression from you, nor how necessary
they are to me, nor how much I try to make them less necessary. I am rejoiced to hear that Elizabeth is better. I
have thought of her constantly and with great anxiety since
I left you, and have longed to have her here, where every
thing breathes such a healthful and cheering influence. It
is not the habits of youth, it is not the prejudice of over-
weening partiality that makes this spot so beautiful in our
eyes. It is a paradise—one of Nature's temples, and oh,
how unlike those built by man, where the drowsy worshipers
reason themselves into a languid devotion! Here love and
joy, and peace and praise are the spontaneous language of
the heart, and all in sweet accord with the voice that cometh from the mountains and the meadows, the waving branches and the frolic shadows. But I grow too romantic, and
you, immersed in Cedar Street, will laugh at my rusticity.
I am afraid of furnishing food for Lizzy's and Harriet's merriment. If it had not been for my dread of farewells, I
think I should have gone back with you from the steam-boat.
We were horribly crowded. Pamela and I were obliged
to sit up and snatch what sleep we could with our heads
leaning against a post, and a ' most foul and pestilent congregation of vapors' settling about us ; they were quite too
dense to float. Pamela contrived to find provocation to
laughter, while I was supported by the brevity of the trial.
I found David Ingersoll awaiting me with the colts that had
given his parents a somerset over the meeting-house hill.
They brought me safely home, however, and I found our
dear sister and her family all well and cheery. I went the
next day to Lenox, and staid till Sunday, and I find of our
blessed Charles that 'wherever the Duchess of Gordon is,
there is the Duchess of Gordon.' No matter where his body
is, it envelops and contains the same celestial spirit. Eliza-

beth, too, is as affectionate and charming as possible, and the children, I think, as dear to me as if they were my own. Charles is a princely child. Kitty has not changed in the least, but Charles has improved incredibly, and, I think, is the noblest, sweetest little dog I ever saw. He looks as if he would grace the lion's skin that Richard wore, and is as gentle as his father. Dear little Kit was so glad to see me that she forsook all others and cleaved unto me."

Miss Sedgwick to Mrs. Watson.

"Stockbridge, October 14, 1823.

"I was rejoiced and grateful, my dear Frances, when you were here, to see that you had the enjoyment of a peaceful, and, as it seemed to me, of a beatified spirit ; for the light of your face expressed that most emphatic language of religious resignation and happiness which says 'it is well with me.' Can we doubt that these jubilees of the spirit come from a heavenly ministration ; that He who has provided all his creatures a seventh day of rest, and who commanded that the seventh year should be a year of freedom to the servant, supplies to those who, like you, dear sister, have given their hearts to Him, periods of repose, release, and holy joy that the children of this world know not of? This home, so precious to us all, seems to have been consecrated by the spirit of love. In all the changes that have taken place here, that affection which from our tenderest years presided over us, has still softened and blessed every vicissitude.

"I had like to have forgotten to tell you that I have received a very gratifying letter from Miss Edgeworth. This is quite an epoch in my humble, quiet life. The letter is entirely satisfactory to me, though some of my kind friends would fain believe that she ought to have buttered me up more."

Mr. Harry Sedgwick to Miss Sedgwick.

"New York, June, 1824.

"DEAR CATHARINE,—I have no doubt that you will be ready at once to forego all personal emolument in regard to the New England Tale, and accede to Mr. H.'s request to print a cheap edition of 3000 for circulation. I think there are several objections to this plan. 1st. It is desirable that the new edition be printed under the supervision of a friend. 2d. If brought forward professedly as a controversial article (as I think it would be under Mr. H.'s auspices), it will not be so useful as it would be if considered simply a literary effort. 3d. I have some doubt whether Mr. H.'s application is any thing more than an individual impulse. 4th. You would have the air of a champion for the liberal party. I think that if a second edition is to come out, it should come at once. If people can't get books when they want them, they borrow, or the want goes over. The present edition is more than two thirds disposed of."

Miss Sedgwick to Mr. Robert Sedgwick.

"Lenox, November 1, 1824.

"I have broken off, my dear Robert, from discoursing with the Misses Piety, Prudence, and Charity, in the Pilgrim's Progress, to indite a scroll to you, the which it hath long been in my heart to send you. Poor Charles and Lizzy have trudged up the hill Difficulty to wait on the preaching of Parson S. One sermon a day is quite as much as I have grace to listen to. I have pretty much settled myself in the opinion that the advantages of public worship, the edification of the example, etc., are more than counterbalanced by the apparent sufferance of doctrines dishonorable to Christianity, and by the certain growth of habits of listlessness and indifference, which are the least offensive states of mind induced by such preaching. However, as I am aware that my inclinations are enlisted on one side of the argument, I have some distrust of the result, and so I compromise the matter by going half the day. * * * * I find that, though I have never contemplated Charles's removal here with any resignation, now that the evil has become inevitable, and that he is really fixed here, I perceive many beauties that I have before been quite blind to. And as I stand at the window, and gaze on the hills that stretch before me in every variety of height and position, the sun sends his gleamy smiles along their summits almost as pleasantly as on our own mountains; and the little lake that sparkles in the valley, now that its leafy veil has fallen, is plainly seen from these windows, and is a faint consolation for the absence of our river. Still I fear I shall never look upon Charles here without feeling that he is a stranger and an exile; and I am sure that in my musings I shall always build castles in my *native* air, and people them with *all* those, dear Robert, who were the companions of my childhood."

*Miss **Sedgwick** to Mr. Charles Sedgwick.*

"Steam-boat Kent, November 19, 1824.

"I wrote you a line to-day from the steam-boat office, where we had arrived after hurrying poor little Charles, who was never hurried before, till I believe he thought the world would be turned upside down with the velocity of the wagon-wheels, which moved at the rate of five miles an hour. Well, there we staid *four* hours, which were, in spite of philosophy, both long and tedious, and diversified only by the entrances and exits of half a dozen loiterers, who were engaged in the profitable business of looking out for the steam-boat, with occasional visits from two little idle boys, who, like wharf-rats, infest the docks, and who amused them-

selves with playing 'push-pin.' The steam-boat came at
last, and Theodore appeared at the wharf in a little boat,
and brought me a letter from Frances, in which she said
that there would be a Mrs. Folger on board, daughter of a
Mr. Sampson, who was a clergyman, and finally died a Unitarian ; this lady is (as F. said) a *religieuse*, who exhorts at
meetings, visits the sick, and devotes herself to all Christian
offices. Frances thinks her almost beatified, and begged
me to draw nigh to her without allowing her to suspect my
heresy. I did not know how to select her, but, in the accidental shuffling of the company, we soon fell together, and
into a conversation half sentimental and half religious. She
paused very soon, and asked, 'What Church do you attend?'
It is a test question, you know, and, though an unlucky one,
I answered it boldly, and cut the silver cord at once.
'Oh! I am grieved for you,' she said ; and thereon we proceeded to a long talk, which has been dropped and resumed
at intervals ever since (now 11 o'clock). She has the face
and voice of a saint, and is filled with all Christian grace
and experience but charity for a heretic. She talks sweetly, and, if my reason did not rebel, I should listen to her
with awe. Besides her, we have no characters on board but
a fat, good-natured Canadian lady, with her family, on her
way *home*, as all colonists affect to call the 'mother country.' Good-night. My fancy pictures you all locked in
sweet sleep; and my dear Kitty! would that she were as
near to me as she is to you!

"*Sunday evening, 21st.* I took leave of you on board the
boat. My evangelical friend anxiously awaited the comple-
tion of my writing, and then renewed her expostulations ;
all excepting ourselves and the chambermaid, a colored
woman and a Methodist, had retired to their berths, so that
we occupied the arena alone. The old blackey, on hearing me accused of denying the Lord that bought me, tramp-

ling on the precious blood, accounting it an unholy thing,'
etc., lifted up her voice and besought me no longer to trust
to blind guides, but to read my Bible, and said I might attain to her light!!! But, alas! I loved darkness rather than
that light, and crept into my berth, and, earnestly aspiring
to the zeal and devotedness of the interesting preacher, I
fell asleep."

Miss Sedgwick to Mr. Charles Sedgwick.

"New York, November 21, 1824.

" *Thanksgiving morning.* Never was there a more beautiful morning to be thankful for. We can not make this festival like that in the land of our fathers, but, in humble imitation of it, we are going to have a supper-party, when all
our friends and kin are to be assembled, including our good
cousins Margaret and Roderick. One of my first thanksgiving thoughts takes me to the little cluster at Lenox, which
I can not dwell upon without such emotions of the heart as
are appropriate to the day; and just now, while I was reading some of the fullest strains of David's praise, I could not
help just putting in a little parenthesis of my own.

" *Wednesday.* Dearest Charles, I have just received your
most beautiful letter, and it has sent its sweet savor into my
very heart of hearts. I know that I don't deserve such expressions from you, but, though this consciousness dashes a
few drops of the bitter of humiliation into my cup, still I drain
it to the very dregs—*dregs* it has not; but to the last sparkling drop. Never was a letter more welcome, for I had got
my head as full of nonsense as Kate; and last night, after
our supper, I had a feeling like a warning to prepare for bad
news, and I could not sleep—at least my sleep was broken
by those awful thoughts and shadowy appearances that in-
trude on the imagination the saddest scenes of human experience. But with the morning hath come joy, and I am
very, very thankful.

"I must relate to you an anecdote I heard to-day of a little boy of Mrs. H. C——'s, who is a little more than four. His mother had just put on him a new suit of clothes, and, for some misdemeanor, had punished him and told him to stand in the corner. Soon after she perceived that he had cut his sleeve in several places from the elbow down. She called him to her and asked him what he meant by such behavior. 'Mother,' said he, 'it was excessive grief; the Bible, you know, says "they rent their garments."' The boy's cleverness averted his punishment. What mother could be expected to maintain her gravity in such circumstances? I dare say the Edgeworths, who are so fond of making 'great trees from little acorns grow,' would conclude that the most mischievous associations had been introduced into the boy's mind, who will henceforth think it safe to deviate from the straight path of right, provided he has wit to lend him her pinions to waft him over the pitfalls in his way."

The next two letters are addressed to Mr. Charles Sedgwick's oldest child, the niece who from this time was the object of her aunt's peculiar care and affection, and who repaid it to the last with the tender attention of a daughter. It would be impossible to give a full idea of Miss Sedgwick's life without constant allusion to this close and engrossing tie, which made so large a part of its occupation and happiness, and as, notwithstanding, much of her time was passed in separation from this chosen niece, her letters to her were constant, and I have drawn largely from them, even from those written while their recipient was yet too young to read them for herself. These last are exceedingly sweet in their exquisite and uplifting sympathy, and those in later life delightful as a journal sent to an intimate friend, but those addressed to the girl of twelve and fourteen strike me as the most remarkable of the series. Letters to young people often fail, either in being written too evidently for their improvement, or too much upon their own level. These are written as to an equal in taste and feeling, from a friend with larger opportunities of observation, and must have afforded a stimulus as subtle as powerful.

Miss Sedgwick to her niece, K. M. Sedgwick.

"New York, November, 1824.

"My DARLING LITTLE KITTY,—Here I am in New York, one hundred and fifty miles away from you. It is a great distance. I can't see your pleasant face, nor hear your sweet voice, nor your songs, nor take you in my arms, nor look at the mountains with you, nor walk to the river. But I can remember all the pleasure we have had together, and thank our Father in heaven for it; and I can hope that when summer comes I shall see you again, and I pray God to bless you and to love you. And every night I think of you when you used to kneel down by me and say your prayer, and I hope you will never forget to do that. Kiss dear little brother for me, and tell him it made Aunt Kitty feel very *cryish* to think he went off to Lenox without her bidding him good-by. Little Jane is a very good girl; she says you must come to New York and stay with us. She has got an old rag baby, and you would laugh to see what a fuss she makes with it. To-day she screamed because Fanny pricked it, which she said would make it bleed. Was not that laughable? Jane went to church to-day, and sat up quite like a lady. Good-night, darling.

"Yours, as ever, AUNT KITTY."

To the same.

"New York, December 24, 1824.

"My DARLING KITTY,—When is that next week coming when you are going to write me a letter? I am looking out

for it every day. You know, my beloved Kitty, that nothing pleases me so much as to get a letter from you, and to
hear that you and dear Charley are well and good. You
can't think how pretty little Harry grows ; his little cheeks
are as red as a rose, and his deep blue eyes as bright as the
stars, and he laughs as heartily as a little man. To-morrow
will be Christmas here, and then we shall have merry music
with the ringing of the bells. I wish my beloved Kitty was
here. Good-by, darling.

> "Your own aunt,   C. M. Sedgwick."

Now that Miss Sedgwick's literary powers had received
public and unquestioned acknowledgment, her own tastes
and the eager encouragement of her friends alike persuaded
her to pursue the fair opening before her, and give free rein
to her natural gifts, and in "Redwood," published in 1824,
we see the first result of her deliberate intention. The
same quick and enlivening sympathy followed her through
its composition.

Mrs. Susan Sedgwick to Miss Sedgwick.

> "Stockbridge, March, 1824.

* * * * "Ever since you have carried *Redwood* out of
the house, I have been in a fidget about him. While you
were in my sight, and I knew that your progress was delightful and sure, though from unavoidable interruptions it
was slow, I was contented, but now I am very impatient of
any delays. Do tell me in your next when it will be out."

Mr. Harry Sedgwick to Miss Sedgwick.

> "New York, August 24, 1824.

"Redwood sells very well ; about 1100 are gone. The
sale is constantly increasing, and the booksellers say that it
is now better than Redgauntlet. The difference between

the first and subsequent works of the same writer is immense. I have no doubt that your fourth work will go off as well as any of Cooper's or Irving's—I think better. Professor Everett wrote the article in Hale's paper concerning Redwood."

From the same.

"New York, October 24, 1824.

"The booksellers are all teasing me to know when another work will come from the author of 'Redwood.' They say it will go as well or better than one from Cooper or Irving."

"Redwood" had the honor, rare in those days for an American book, of being immediately reprinted in England, and it was also translated into French, and published on the Continent.

A lady of Philadelphia, a correspondent of Miss Edgeworth, sent Miss Sedgwick the following extract from one of her letters :

"May, 1825.

"'Redwood' has entertained us very much. I am so much flattered by the manner in which my writings are alluded to in this book, that I can hardly suppose I am an unprejudiced judge, but it appears to me a work of superior talent, far greater than even 'The New-England Tale' gave me reason to expect. The character of Aunt Deborah is first rate—in Scott's best manner, yet not an imitation of Scott. It is to America what Scott's characters are to Scotland, valuable as original pictures, with enough of individual peculiarity to be interesting, and to give the feeling of reality and life as portraits, with sufficient also of general characteristics to give them the philosophical merit of portraying a class."

H

Miss Sedgwick to Mrs. Charles Sedgwick.

"New York, January, 1825.

* * * * "I spent last evening at **Robert's, and we** read with delight the memoir of Lafayette in **the last North** American. There is something sublime in the *consistency* of this great man in all the extremes of fortune—steadfast amidst the temptations of unequaled prosperity and (oh, shame to his persecutors!) unparalleled adversity; an enthusiasm governed by reason **and directed by** benevolence. What a delightful example to our **species,** and still shining in its brightness where every **eye may behold it.** * * * * Yesterday **evening** Harry told **me he had sent a copy** of Redwood to Mrs. Barbauld, and **that he had a** letter for me from her. No happiness that did not spring from my own family circle ever produced an emotion of such pure delight and gratitude. I would send the letter to you, that you might see **the** lines **traced by her** own venerable hand, but I can **not bear** to part **with it, or expose it to** any **unnecessary risk.** I therefore copy it:

" 'DEAR MADAM,—The **state** of my eyes, which have been weak and painful for some time, and are by no means well **now,** must plead my **excuse** for not having yet thanked you for the entertaining novel with which you favored me. You Americans tread upon **our** heels in every path of literature, but **we** will not be jealous of you, for you are our children, and it **is the** natural wish of parents that children should outstrip **their parents in every thing good and lovely.** In religious **matters particularly you** are proving to us that much true **devotion, and at least a** *decent* provision for its public exercise, can subsist **without** an establishment. What a field you have **for** description in wastes and woods so **late-** ly trodden by the foot of man, savage life giving way every

where to the social blessings of civilization, and just enough
remaining to show how much has been gained by the exchange. Should you ever come to England, dear madam,
or your brother (which, by the way, you ought to do, this being your mother-country), I shall, if in the land of the living,
be happy to pay my respects to you. Excuse the handwriting of this letter, for in truth I can hardly see to write,
and believe me, madam, your obliged and obedient servant,

"'A. L. BARBAULD.'"

Miss Sedgwick to Mr. Charles Sedgwick.

"New York, January 20, 1825.

* * * * "I went to Mr. Sewall's in one of those horrid
fits of depression when one would cut one's throat if (as Jane
said about killing the chicken) it would not hurt. But when
I got there I found the rooms full of agreeable people, and
before the evening was over I thought this quite a holiday
world. Halleck, alias Croaker, was there. I have never
seen him before. He has a reddish brown complexion, and
a heavy jaw, but an eye so full of the fire and sweetness of
poetry that you at once own him for one of the privileged
order. He does not act as if he had spent his life in groves
and temples, but he has the courtesy of a man of society.
He dances with grace, and talks freely and without parade.

"Robert has just brought me a letter from E., received
by the Howard. He has sent Redwood *à la Français* by
the same ship ; we shall probably get it in the course of a
day or two. Poor Debby will make a more ridiculous figure,
I am afraid, than she did at Lebanon.

"'My DARLING KITTY,—You are certainly coming to
New York, and I think of it every day and every night. Jane
says every day, "Why don't Kate come *this* day ?" We
shall have a great deal to do when you come ; many pleas-

ant walks and rides to take. I hear that Charley is the
sweetest boy that ever was, and my dear Kitty as good as
ever. It would make my heart ache and my eyes cry if you
were not good. Don't forget me, dear, nor forget to love
me. Your own   AUNT KATE.'"

Miss Sedgwick to Mr. Charles Sedgwick.

"New York, 1825.

* * * * "I spent yesterday with little R., devoting myself, to the exclusion of every thing else, to fixing over two
old frocks. In the evening we went to a party at Mrs.
Schuyler's, principally made up of our own congregation,
for, like all the proscribed, we are clannish. I had the
pleasure of sitting for five minutes next Mr. Webster,* and
talking with him for half that space of time, and this morning I have paid the penalty of all my pleasures by a headache and sleepy eyes. * * * * By the way, I don't know
whether you have yet been told that there is a notice, a sort
of advertisement of Redwood, in the Constitutionnel, a Paris
newspaper. Harry was told last evening that there was a
dispute in the Paris newspapers whether it was or was not
written by Cooper. It is to be hoped that Mr. C.'s self-
complacency will not be wounded by this mortifying news.

"*Monday morning.* I was summoned from my letter to see
Mr. Webster, who made us a very agreeable call. He talked
of birds and beasts as well as La Fontaine himself. His
face is the grandest I have ever seen. It has all the sublimity of intellect."

Miss Sedgwick to Mr. Charles Sedgwick.

"New York, February, 1825.

"MY DEAR CHARLES,—There is a gentleman here who is
compiling a biographical account of the distinguished men

* Daniel Webster.

of our country. He has repeatedly applied for some documents in relation to our beloved father. I wish you to furnish every thing you can. If you could give precisely the dates of his efforts for the blacks and his interposition for the Shakers, they would be valuable facts. Whatever is done must be done immediately. I am afraid it is already too late. You had better talk with Susan, who has done more than any of us to preserve the records to be transmitted. Such a document may be most valuable to your children—to us, whose hearts are written full of his virtues, these public memorials must all seem cold and poor."

To the same.

"New York, March 27, 1825.

"The long winter is past, and I begin to count the days and hours till your arrival. I could not but smile at your request, Elizabeth, that I would get something between summer and winter wear for Kate for the last of April. Jane and Fanny have had their calico frocks on for a month, and I have seen ladies walking in the street in bareges, which are mere gossamer, with thin muslin spencers. The blasts of March are blowing furiously to-day, and none but the gifted bard could hear the voice of promise in these rude winds. I doubt not they pass over the Lenox hills with a fell swoop; but still I think by the last of April dear Kate will not need a *demi-saison* frock."

Miss Sedgwick to Mrs. Watson.

"New York, June 5, 1825.

"We have had Eliza Cabot here for a few days, and have enjoyed her sweet society as much as it is possible to enjoy such a blessing in this hurly-burly city. I often wished, my dear sister, that you, whose heart naturally unfolds to such celestial influences, could have shared with us the happiness

that is diffused by a mind so elevated, so full of holy feeling
and benevolent purpose, so purified from the dross of the
world, so above the world. This is not a rhapsody. I feel
with Eliza the presence of a superior spirit, the reality of
what I long and sometimes resolve to be, but what I am far
from attaining."

To the same.

"New York, May 25, 1825.

"It is one of the unsearchable secrets of Providence to
me that, with your capacity for enjoyment, and with the rich
resources of your generous nature, your own happiness
should be so limited, and your means of imparting to others
so circumscribed. It is a dark and impenetrable mystery;
but through the thick clouds there are gleams of light, and I
can perceive, my dear sister, that you are making advances
in spiritual life which are not made by those who lag by the
way to enjoy the flowers and fruits that spring up in their
path, but that perish in the using. Oh, it is good—we must
believe it is good, to be left alone with God; to feel that all
happiness but that into which He breathes his own immortality is transient—that all love but His is variable and imperfect. It is good sometimes to anticipate the hour of
death, to know what manner of persons we shall be when
the flatteries of life and the illusions of the world vanish;
when the vapors of the earth shall be dissipated; when light
shall no longer lend its magic coloring; when the voice of
affection shall be still; when the dim eye can not rest on
looks of kindness; when the arms that sheltered us fall
away, and the strength that supported us is weakness; when
our souls shall be alone with God.

* * * * "Harry and Robert are engaged in a speculation in the Rhode Island coal-mine which is now very promising. Harry is buried deep in it. He scarcely hears you
when you speak to him on any other subject.

* * * * "I have got a bagatelle which I shall publish that I think is much better adapted to children than this.* I meant it for a tract, but Harry thinks I had better print it for profit, as he says people value a great deal more what they pay for."

Miss Sedgwick to Mr. Charles Sedgwick.

"Boston, June 17, 1825.

"The great day has arrived, and is as beautiful as if heaven smiled on our patriotic celebration. The city was never so full—half so full, the people say. There are hundreds vainly inquiring for a lodging. The Common is spread with tents to shelter the militia of the adjacent towns. It is expected that a hundred thousand people will be present. Mr. Webster expects to make 15,000 people hear him. He and his wife sent me an invitation to go in their party, so that I think I shall be sure to be among the hearers—the select few. * * * * I was last evening at a party at Mrs. Quincy's to meet the general ;† was twice introduced to him, and twice shook his well-shaken hand. It is a pleasure certainly to grasp a hand that has been the instrument of so noble a heart, but the pleasure is scarcely individual, for the hand is extended with as little personal feeling as the eyes of a picture are directed.

"*Saturday.* I am 'one of the survivors who fought, bled, and died on Bunker Hill.' I can only give you generals. The oration was in Mr. Webster's best style of manly eloquence. It was all fine, and there were some very fine strokes of genius in it; but you will see it and judge for yourselves. You will find from the papers that all the world was there—some say 75,000, some 100,000. We went at nine, and did not get home till after four, so that, except for

* Referring to some extracts from a journal given to the children.
† Lafayette.

the pleasure of the remembrance, the balance was rather on the painful side ; but when I think of that magnificent man ; of the cloud of witnesses ; of those old weather-beaten survivors, with their palsied limbs and nerveless arms, once strong and raised in their might for us ; of the good Lafayette looking with the benignity of a blessed spirit upon the countless multitude ; of the old man's prayer ; of the union of voices pouring out their praise—when I think of all these things, I am grateful that I was permitted to see and hear."

Miss Sedgwick to Mr. Charles Sedgwick.

"New York, December 28, 1825.

"MY DEAR CHARLES,—You write such beautiful letters up in that Lenox office that I shall begin to think that much-dreaded court-house hill is a sort of modern prose Parnassus, only that I know there is no mount like the inspiration of the spirit, no Helicon like the pure fountain of love.

"We are leading very quiet lives ; no morning calls, dear Lizzy, or next to none, and very few evening parties, and those have been dull enough to save them from all suspicion of gayety.   I have now and then attended the Athenæum lectures.   We had one the other night from one of the lights of the College on Roman literature.   Of Rome he said nothing but that he wished us all to awake from the dream we had too long indulged that Romulus was really suckled by a wolf.   He informed us, also, that letters were brought to Greece by the Pelasgii, and not the Phœnicians ; and then he went on to a very pretty homily all about his private religious feelings ; and then he proved to his own entire satisfaction that *A* and *T* were primeval letters—that *A* was a wonderful symbol of something, and that *T* prefigured the doctrines of man's sin in Adam, the Incarnation, Atonement, Trinity most especially, etc., etc.   And this a lecture on Roman literature !"

Miss Sedgwick to Mr. Charles Sedgwick.

"New York, February 24, 1826.

* * * * "I fancied you sick on the road, sick in Boston. I thought of all the mortal cases of influenza, etc., etc., but I trust, my dear brother, that the same kind Providence that has as yet preserved entire the silken bond with which he bound us as a family together, will for some time to come keep it from that severance which can not be avoided. When I think of the possibility of living in the world without you, Charles, my soul loses all its courage, and I feel as if the same blow must crush us both. If I die first, you have others nearer to you left, and, though I know you would weep bitterly for me, and never forget me, yet, thank God, you would not feel that desolation you would make. Should you be removed first, I promise you, my beloved brother, that yours shall be mine. Elizabeth, and the children, and I would cast our lot together, and my means and efforts should be devoted to them ; this is not much, but it is an exemption from want. Lizzy is dear to me, not only as your wife, but as having been to me a most faithful and affectionate sister ; and your children, Charles, you know I love as if they were a part of my own body and soul. I do not say this from any impulse or sudden feeling. Our own loss the past year,* and the various sudden deaths and reverses in the circle of our acquaintance, have led me to think a great deal of the certain changes that await us, and to form resolutions in the view of various contingencies. And I have thought of the possibility of realizing some of my apprehensions, and that, at any rate, it might relieve you of the anxiety every father must feel to know my determination, though God grant that determination may never be acted on. * * * * I have been

* This refers to the death of Egbert, a much-beloved son of Mrs. Pomeroy.

quite dissipated for the last fortnight—at three large parties ;
at the last we had all the varieties of rival belles, who are
the most beautiful dancers in the country, and who played
on the harp and piano as if the world hung on Cæsar's
fate. We had a Miss ———, who is a perfect 'natamy' (as
Mumbet says), with her sleeves half way down to her elbows,
so that her armpits were perfectly exposed ; her bones
looked as if she would rattle if you touched her. Jane said
she wondered if she ate. Anthony Bleecker said she'd want
a great deal of *dressing* to be eaten."

The next letter is in amusing and (alas !) hopeless contrast to the present state of things at Stockbridge and the
vicinity, where, last summer, a well-advised householder refused to take a boarder at less than $20 a week, and would
as soon have thought of throwing an elephant as a horse
into the bargain.

"Stockbridge, June 14, 1826.

"MY DEAR ROBERT,—I received yesterday your letter
about Mrs. Rogers. I immediately applied to Mrs. W., and
she has agreed to take Mrs. Rogers and her woman for $5
a week. I shall write Mrs. R. by this mail all the particulars of the arrangement. The place, you know, is a most delightful one. The family are very good sort of people. The
board is very high for this *region;* I took care to insinuate that
the price was high, and that for such a consideration it would
be but a reasonable make-weight to throw in the occasional
use of the horse and chaise. To this Mrs. W. assented,
only stipulating that the horse could not be promised for
every day."

Miss Sedgwick to K. M. Sedgwick.

"New York, January 11, 1826.

"MY BELOVED KITTY,—Good-morning to you. I have

been dreaming of you all night, and I thought you and I were walking in a beautiful grove, and the grove was of apple, and pear, and peach trees all in blossom, and here and there was an orange-tree, the boughs loaded with fruit, and hanging so low that you could pick them as we walked along, and some of the trees were nutmeg and cinnamon, and they gave out a delicious perfume, and grape-vines hung in beautiful festoons from tree to tree, and rich bunches of grapes were dangling all about us, and through the grove there winded a bright, clear stream of water, like our own Housatonic, and all along the banks grew flowers of every description, which gracefully bent toward the water, which reflected their beautiful faces like a mirror, and the bottom of the river was covered with pebbles as white and smooth as polished marble, and the fish were frolicking about them, and the birds were flying over our heads, and sometimes they would alight at our feet, and sing their sweet songs to us. They seemed like little friends, they were so tame and gentle, and their nests were in plain sight, so that we could see what nice care they took of their young. And as we walked along, we saw father and mother sitting under a tree, and little Charley was kneeling by them, saying his prayers. And then you looked up at me, and oh, how bright and sweet you looked! and you said, 'Aunt Kitty, is not this Heaven?' and I caught you in my arms, and then I waked."

* * * *

Miss Sedgwick to Mr. Charles Sedgwick.

"Boston, October **27, 1826.**

"MY DEAR CHARLES,—I presume that my letter to Susan has already informed you of our safe arrival. The journey was without any fatigue, and the pleasantest I ever took in a stage-coach. Robert was in fine spirits, and every circumstance concurred to make me enjoy it. One old soldier

I never shall forget. He was not like most of our old pensioners, a subject of pity on account of (perhaps) accidental
virtue, but every thing about him looked like the old age of
humble, frugal, industrious virtue. And then he was so patient under the severest of all physical evils (and I have not
Eliza Cabot's magnanimous contempt of bodily pain), so
cheerful and bright, so confiding in kindness, and so trust-
ful in his fellow-creatures. But you will think me extravagant, for I can't present before you the picture of the old
man, with his hands nicely clad in famous green mittens,
knit, as he said, with a tear in his eye, 'by his youngest *dar-
ter,*' leaning on his cane, the horrid cancer decently dressed
and sheltered, talking with a benign expression of his old
friends, his eye kindling, and his form straightening with a
momentary vigor as he spoke of the heroic deeds of his
youthful companions, and the serenity, and meekness, and
philosophy with which he spoke of his sufferings and the
progress of them."

Miss Sedgwick to Mr. Charles Sedgwick.

"Boston, November 21, 1826.

"MY DEAR CHARLES,—Harry arrived here yesterday, after being delayed at the mine till that time. He is in fine
spirits about the coal. I hope he has ground for his sanguine expectations, but I have no faith in any of our name
becoming rich. We always have something ahead that we
think reasonable to ask, and if I could see you in the possession of a cottage (that is, a nice house) on Stockbridge
Plain, and $1500 a year, and Fanny snugly sheltered in the
valley, I would compound for the rest of the family to remain as they are. We should not be anxious to be placed
in any condition of increased responsibility, and besides,
with money would come some balancing evil, and so, upon
the whole, let us pray for contentment and gratitude.

"The gentlemen here are all expressing their regret that Theodore is not to be here this winter, and I am glad to find that it is a serious feeling of loss. Mr. Quincy said to me the other day, 'We *want* him ; we don't know how to do without him.' By the way, has not Mr. Quincy come out bright with his market ? I dined there last Saturday, and in the evening he ordered the carriage and took us down there. It was beautifully lighted, and we walked through it, and I could not but compare his feelings with the vulgar sentiment of a Roman conqueror passing under his triumphal arch."

Miss Sedgwick to Mr. Charles Sedgwick.

"Boston, November 4, 1826.

"One of the greatest pleasures I have had here, or could have any where, has been seeing Mr. Channing.* I have twice dined and spent the evening in his company, and sat next to him all the time. There is a superior light in his mind that sheds a pure, bright gleam on every thing that comes from it. He talks freely upon common topics, but they seem no longer to be common topics when he speaks of them. There is the influence of the sanctuary, the holy place about him. Such an influence can not be lost, and I perceive a deep seriousness, an energy of religious feeling in the conversation of some of my friends, that seems to me more like what I have read of than any thing I have before seen. Elsewhere I have seen the poor, the sick, and the afflicted detached from the world and turning to communion with the God of their spirits, but here I have met with some who have every thing that the world can give, who feel that it is all very good, and yet their minds are intent on heavenly things. It seems to me that it would be impossible to live within the sphere of Mr. Channing's influence without

* Rev. Dr. Channing.

being in some degree spiritualized by it. * * * * You would all be pleased **at the unanimous** and strong sentiment that prevails **here in relation to the Greek business.** Harry is lauded **as if he were a real Greek hero.** I am afraid he will **sacrifice** his eyes, if not his life, in their cause."

Miss Sedgwick to K. M. Sedgwick.

"Boston, November 12, 1826.

"MY DEAR KITTY,—I am very glad that you are so happy. When I read your little letter, I fancy I can see you and hear you, and see **your little** frolicksome **sister ;** but then, when I feel how **far** I am **away from** you, my heart **is** sad, and the tears will come in my eyes, and I think over and over that I never again will **leave my Berkshire home for such** a long time. I dined the **other** day in company with Miss ———, and we talked a great deal about you and Charley, and your kind father and mother, and she said a great deal about their goodness to her, and then I thought they minded what our Savior says—if we are kind to rich and great people there is not much goodness in it, because we know they can do as much for us as we can do for them, and so we shall get it all paid back ; but if we are kind to those who have nothing to do for us in return, why then we are really kind. God is the father of us all. He loves *all* his children, and **he is** certainly pleased when he sees those that are young, **and** well, and happy **doing** something for the poor, and the sick, and neglected. I went yesterday with Mr. ——— **to** see his mite of a baby, and it is a droll-looking little thing ; its hands are **not a** bit bigger than your wax doll's, and its face is about **as big** as the top of one **of your** china-cups, and when it **cries** it looks like a white mummy. I went to a meeting a few nights ago where there were ladies and gentlemen learning to read—that **is,** to read well, and I heard **so** much said of the importance of reading well, that I determined to beg you, my dear Kitty, never to read aloud without trying to read as well as you can, and to beg your mother to correct the only fault in her reading for your sake, for mothers will do more for their children than they will for themselves. My darling child, remember me, and do not love me less because I am away from you, and kiss dear Charley for me.

"Your own aunt and friend,   C. M. SEDGWICK."

Miss Sedgwick to Mrs. Watson.

"New York, December 3, 1826.

* * * * "I think I have never enjoyed five weeks of my life so much as the last five, or that I can look back upon any period with so much to awaken gratitude to God. I never was sensible of receiving such an impulse to my religious purposes and hopes. I have been much with those who *dwell in light.* I have seen and heard Mr. Channing a great deal in public and private. I have received the emanations from his holy mind—there should be a quickening influence from them. I was continually with my sweet friend Eliza, whose Christian course is brightening, and in the society of those whose intellectual natures are sanctified by an enlightened religion. I should be insensible not to feel these privileges, and if I do not make some improvement of them I shall be indeed an unprofitable servant."

The uneasiness expressed at the close of one of the late letters with regard to Mr. Harry Sedgwick's eyes had a painfully real foundation. They became worse and worse, and for a time he was perfectly blind.

Miss Sedgwick to Mr. Charles Sedgwick.

"New York, February 26, 1827.

"MY DEAR CHARLES AND ELIZABETH,—I have been put-

ting off writing for the last two days in the hope that the
second operation on Harry's eyes would be over. But these
good-for-nothing surgeons have kept us in hot water since
last Thursday, putting it off from day to day on some pretext or other. I don't believe a butcher, jailer, or common
hangman gets his heart so hardened as a doctor—as most
doctors. I am glad that I know such a man as Dr. Jones
or Watts. There are natures that fire melts, but will not
harden. Harry, as Jane says, is a pattern for Job himself,
but still he is severely tried ; and, though he makes very light
of the operation, it can't be pleasant to sit for a week thinking of that crooked wire and knife going into your eyeball !

"*Wednesday evening,* **28th.** I purposely delayed my letter
till to-day. The operation was gone through this morning.
It was a little longer than before, as the doctors were anxious to cut away the substance more, and I think he felt it
more ; but it is really, for the object to be attained, a very
small affair. There seems to be no threatening of inflam-
mation, and Stevens pronounces, with perfect confidence, on
perfect success. The *anxious* meeting is at this moment in
his room, though Jane and I have just been laying our heads
together to request them to adjourn down stairs, lest he
should get too much excited. The manifestation of kind
feelings, the thronging of friends to your house, and, above
all, the sentiment of entire dependence on God and gratitude to him, are, in such events, merciful compensations
for the evil that attends them. I can not think that Harry
will recover his eyes so as with safety to pursue his profession, but all must be left to time to determine."

The eyesight was restored, but a still heavier affliction followed. Miss Sedgwick says, in her " Recollections :"

" My brother Harry was strong, active, capable of any endurance, and of a bold, sanguine, and cheerful temperament —an indomitable spirit, and a mental capacity that never tired.

"In the delightful exercise of all his faculties he was suddenly arrested by failing eyesight. He did not know how to modify his plans or temper his expectations. He wanted the wisdom of patience and resignation—the docile submission to the bit and rein that it had pleased Providence to put upon him. He made the fatal mistake of struggling against the inevitable instead of yielding to it. Just at this epoch came the failure of a speculation that offered to his expectation boundless wealth, which, to his noble disposition, was alluring but as the means of unlimited beneficence. And, direst of all to him, then came on the famous 'Greek cause,' in which the interests of Greece (then struggling for her freedom) were to be supported against the imputed frauds of some New York merchants. Many commercial and mercantile interests were complicated in this cause, and an immense labor was done by my brothers Harry and Robert. Harry brought to it his indignation at violated justice, his enthusiastic love of freedom, and all the ferment of his intense nature. He worked with his impaired eyes all day and far into the night, and when the work was suspended he was sleepless with anxiety as to its issue. The condition of his eyesight deprived him of the diversion of external objects, and increased his natural tendency to concentration. The failure of his business enterprise co-operated to press him on to the tragic end, and thus the clearest and most powerful intellect I have ever intimately known was wrecked!"

Mr. Sedgwick was insane, with lucid intervals, for three or four years, when the prolonged nervous excitement wore out a life which all who knew him agree to have been one of rare nobility, strength, and beauty.

It was the **summer** after his first attack that Miss Sedgwick published **her third novel, "Hope** Leslie," the first which **had been printed without his devoted care** and criticism. **It was** received with even more favor **than its** predecessors, and was indeed, as her note-books show, **the** result / **of** still more careful study, while her style acquired **additional** freedom and grace with each fresh effort.

This was a happy season of her life, notwithstanding the overshadowing cloud of her brother's illness, which, lightened as **it** was by constant hope, did not preclude the enjoyment of her increasing reputation, enlarging circle of friends, **the proud** attachment of her family, and the rich pleasure of intellectual **creation.**

Miss Sedgwick to K. M. Sedgwick.

"New York, March 9, 1827.

* * * * "Mr. Miller dined with us yesterday. He is one of our countrymen who has been fighting for the poor Greeks, and he **has** come home to America, and told so many **sad** stories of their sufferings that he has made many kind hearts feel more for them than **they** did before. To-day he **sails again** for Greece in a ship loaded with provisions for those poor starving people. It must be very pleasant to give meat **and bread** to good people that are ready to perish. He **told** us of a good man, a Mr. Langdon, a rich American merchant who lives in Smyrna. This gentleman bought a beautiful little Grecian girl seven years old. You know the Turks sometimes torture, **sometimes sell,** and sometimes kill their Grecian prisoners, **and death is thought** the greatest mercy by those **who fall into their hands, so** you may think **how** happy this little girl felt to be bought by an American, **who** did not make a slave of her, **but** treated her as his own **beloved child. But she was** not quite happy; her father **had been** killed, **and** her mother and her old grandmother

were in the hands of the Turks. One day some Turks brought a captive to Mr. Langdon. It was the little girl's mother, and the Turks asked a great price for her, because they knew Mr. Langdon was so good that, for the sake of both mother and child, he would certainly redeem the mother, and he did ; and last of all they brought the grandmother to him, and, though she was old, and good for nothing to them, they asked $470 for her, and Mr. Langdon paid it, and now all three live in his house, and all love him dearly. One day he had a very bad toothache in one of his front teeth, and he said he must have it out, and mentioned that in his own country they put in other teeth in the place of decayed ones. 'Then,' said the mother, 'you shall have one of my teeth to supply yours ; with all my heart I would give them all to you.' She had a beautiful set of teeth. He told us many other agreeable anecdotes, and represented the Greeks as a very fine people, inquisitive, improving, very graceful, and courteous."

Miss Sedgwick to Mr. Robert Sedgwick.

"Lenox, July 6, 1827.

* * * * "I hear from all quarters what honestly seems to me very extravagant praise of 'Hope Leslie.' I trust I shall not be elated by it. At present I certainly am not, for I feel too heavily oppressed, too firmly grappled to the earth to mount in the balloon of vanity. It is fair that you should share whatever of praise is bestowed—you, the faithful usher and godfather of my little 'Hope.' Miss Francis* writes me that she had nearly completed a tale, founded on the fortunes of Captain Smith. 'Alas for my Pocahontas !' she says ; and then, after adding that she shall give her up, she says, 'However, I give her up with less reluctance than the artist whose labors of fifteen years were destroyed by the

* Afterward Mrs. L. M. Child.

French troops in their invasion of Italy, for I love my conqueror.' Is not that beautiful? Better to write and to feel
such a sentiment than to indite volumes. * * * * I was
very much gratified, the other day, by a formal note of thanks
from Robbins here, as 'one of the descendants of the Pilgrims,' for the manner in which I had treated them. I
wanted this assurance from one of the leal."

Miss Sedgwick to K. M. Sedgwick.

"New York, December 5, 1827.

* * * * "You can not imagine what a surprise it was to
us to see your father. Aunt Lizzy has a new girl, who, I believe, thinks that she keeps tavern, so many persons have
come here lately. Sunday morning your Aunt Watson arrived, and Monday, when your father came, the girl came
up stairs in the greatest consternation. 'Ma'am,' says she,
'there has another person come, and brought in his baggage, and seated himself, and won't tell his name.' I asked
if he were young or old. 'Very young—he may be a little
older than Mr. Theodore.' So there, in the breakfast-room,
father seated himself, and it was amusing to witness the surprise and delight of the family, as they assembled one by
one. What a delightful thing it is, my Kitty, to possess
such a character as your father's! Whenever he appears he
is welcome, and every face is brightened with smiles; he
produces an effect like the sun when it suddenly glances its
bright beams from behind a cloud, as we have seen it sometimes, when it touched up the mountains, and streamed
athwart the valley. 'House and hole' may be full, but still
there is always room for father." * * * *

On the occasion of a report that Miss Sedgwick was about
to engage herself to a gentleman to whom her brother Theodore thought there were serious objections, he wrote her a

letter, in which, after affectionately but forcibly setting forth his views, he goes on to say :

"Stockbridge, November, 1827.

" In regard to your present situation, it is certainly a singularly happy one ; you must not, upon light grounds, change it. The sincere, tried, devoted affection of all the older members of the family, the tender and filial reverence and attachment of the younger, the admiration and respect of a large circle of friends, serve to bind you to that spot and confine you within that circle in which all these blessings are enjoyed. * * * * To this I can not but add that I look forward to the exertion of your literary talents as a great national blessing, and that I can not willingly anticipate any contingencies which may deprive us of it."

Miss Sedgwick to Mrs. Watson.

"New York, December 23, 1827.

" Brother Theodore is here, on his way to Boston. He is still riding his hobby, the railroad, and I trust his real devotion to the public good will be rewarded by seeing this great state improvement. Men are so generally engrossed with the eager pursuit of wealth or pleasure, some modification of sensual, perishable enjoyment, that it is refreshing to see a man living for more disinterested and generous purposes."

Miss Sedgwick to Mr. Charles Sedgwick.

"New York, February 5, 1828.

* * * * " You know we have had a Mr. Ladd here delivering peace lectures. He certainly is a man of extraordinary talents. He reminds me of Dr. Mason in his best days, but he has a far more enlightened mind. The whole course of his life has shown a strong tendency to enthusiasm in the noblest of all causes, the cause of human happiness. You

will see a little **notice of him in** 'The Post' of to-morrow.   I
don't **know when I have been so much** interested and delighted by any body.   Enthusiasm fed **by reason** is sacred
fire **on a holy** altar. * * * * **Figure to yourself a** man of almost Uncle John's stature, with a face expressive **of** acute-
ness and benevolence, and a voice that sounds like **the spirit of** the north wind, with a Yankee pronunciation, and **an**
energy of manner that expresses the earnestness of the soul.
When **he** came here **he met with** every discouragement.
The clergy said, 'Be ye warmed and be ye fed,' but did not
lift **a** finger.   He was told he would have no audience, but
he replied, 'Give me one candle-snuffer and *one auditor*, and
I will lecture.' "

In **1828 Mrs. Charles** Sedgwick **received into her** house a
few children, to educate with her own, and this was the beginning of the family school, since **so widely known** and **so**
justly celebrated, which closed only with her life **in 1864.**
She **wrote** also several books for children, among them '**The**
Beatitudes,' which many must recollect as among the literary treasures of their childhood ; and she contributed, under
the signature of *Mater,* to the Juvenile Miscellany, a charming little periodical edited for years by Mrs. Child.   The
following letter shows the lively and practical interest taken
by Miss Sedgwick **in** even the smallest details **that** con-
cerned her friends.

Miss Sedgwick to Mrs. Charles **Sedgwick.**

"New York, February 15, 1828.
* * * * "The publishing committee have **paid for** tracts
—perhaps not quite as much as the Miscellany, but decently.   I do not know whether they do now, but I dare say, if
they do not, Bowles and Dearborn would, and Harry, who
is, for his friends, literary broker, would make a bargain for

you. I think you had best copy it again. Make each Beatitude a complete piece in itself. Draw a deep black line at
the conclusion of each, and leave a space, and begin each a
little more formally; have all the explanations and excur-
sive conversation first, and finish each with a little anecdote
or story by way of illustration. You have abundant matter, and all these little arts of arrangement help the effect.
These are suggestions, my dear sister, and not dictates,
though my curt manner of expression may give them the
Basil Hall aspect."

The " Basil Hall aspect" refers to a long letter addressed
by that gentleman (who had then recently been on a visit to
Stockbridge) to Miss Sedgwick, at the suggestion of a mutual friend, criticising the style of her writings in the habitual tone of an Englishman, holding himself entitled *as an
Englishman* to lay down the law on all matters of taste and
precedent. She replied to him with admirable candor and
good temper, and at the same time with a dignified asser-
tion of her right to independence of judgment. He apologized for having displeased her, but they parted rather cold-
ly. When, however, Miss Sedgwick went to England in
1839, Captain Hall was the most kind, cordial, and devoted
of friends, as she has recorded in her journal, and they maintained ever after an occasional correspondence with mutual
pleasure.

Miss Sedgwick's acquaintance with the celebrated historian Sismondi was begun the previous year, by her sending
him, through the persuasion of her brother Harry, a translation which she made of one of his essays, accompanied by
a copy of Hope Leslie. She at once received a warm letter
of thanks, to which the following is the answer, and this was
the opening of a regular correspondence, continued with in-

creasing interest on both sides till his death in 1842, and afterward kept up by his wife.

Miss Sedgwick to M. Sismondi, **Geneva, Switzerland.**

"New York, March 15, 1828.

" MY DEAR SIR,—Licensed by your permission, I venture again to address you, and to attempt to tell you how much pleasure your letter gave me, and diffused through a large circle of your admirers and my friends. I would convey to you a sense of the benefit done me, for, to a benevolent spirit, it must be one of the dearest felicities of high exaltation that its light falls on the distant and the humble. But, after all, you can not estimate the benefit, for you are not aware of the homage your writings have inspired ; and, more than this, you can not know (no one can who is not personally a stranger to you) that you infuse into them a moral life, that you breathe your own soul into them, impart to them—if I may thus express myself—a portion of your own identity. This seems to me to be one of their attractive and attaching peculiarities. It is this that makes us feel them to be the production of a being whose affections and sympathies are kindred to our own ; his happiness becomes a matter of personal interest to us, and his kind notice falls on the heart like the familiar voice of a friend, touching the mysterious springs of the affections.

" The notice you have bestowed on ' Hope Leslie ' has made me anxious to redeem a fault I have unintentionally committed in so delineating the Pilgrims as to degrade them in your estimation. I meant to touch their characters with filial reverence. Their bigotry, their superstition, and, above all, their intolerance, were too apparent on the page of history to be forgotten. But these were the vices of their age, and they were only partially disengaged from the chains that bound their contemporaries. They deserved, in a good degree, the opinion you have entertained of them. They had a most generous and self-devoting zeal to the cause of liberty, so far as they understood it, but they were still in the thraldom of Judaic superstition, and adhered steadfastly, as unhappily a majority of their descendants do, to Calvin's gloomy interpretation of Scripture, even now the popular dogmas in our enlightened country. It is but right that a sweet fountain should be opened at Geneva, whence such bitter streams have flowed.

"Our early history has, I believe, been more accurately and minutely written than that of any other people. Our good fathers maintained an unwavering faith that they were under the special and even visible government of Providence, and this strong conviction gave importance and religious sanctity to the most trifling circumstance. Theirs was, as you say, a family history, and if a lamb strayed beyond its bounds, or an untimely shower fell on the reapers, the mishaps were a common concern, and were carefully recorded. 'Mishaps!' I am but a degenerate child. The greatest as well as the smallest events were shaped by Providence for them; the great agents of nature were made subsidiary to their purposes; the storm that 'curled the monstrous waves' was raised to wreck some profane heretic who had presumed to scoff at the orthodox faith, and the frost that congealed a whole continent was sent to freeze a poor barber's fingers, 'whose tongue was more nimble than his fingers, and who jested withal about the elders' discipline.' Your historical pursuits may inspire you with some curiosity to see a specimen of our early documents, and I have therefore selected an authentic work which has the merit of being characteristic of the times it illustrates. I shall send also an oration by one of our most eminent men, which, as it refers to the same period, and is in itself an eloquent production, may not be unacceptable to you. I shall venture also to inclose to

I

you an essay on the character of Napoleon (that prodigy of
our own times), written by Dr. Channing, of Boston, whose
name has probably reached you, and whose philosophic and
original mind is employed in illustrating topics of high moral interest.

"I need not assure you that I shall esteem it a favor at
any time to send you such literary productions as may be
worthy of your attention, and I should only be restrained by
my ignorance of what communication you may have with
us, and by the fear of being obtrusive.

"Once more M. de Sismondi must permit me to thank
him ; the sunbeams may fall unregarded on the palace, but
the rays that enter the cottage window are felt and enjoyed.
* * * * I was particularly gratified that Madame Sismondi
approved my translation, for I am certain it must be far
more difficult to satisfy the requisitions of her affections than
the demands of your self-esteem. I beg she will accept my
best wishes."

Miss Sedgwick to Rev. Dr. Channing.

"New York, April 28, 1828.

"MY DEAR FRIEND,—My brother Robert promised me
he would himself answer your inquiries relative to the success of the monitorial system of instruction in this city. I
find that the pressure of his office business has as yet prevented his writing, and, though I have nothing to communi-
cate in reply to your request, I can not consent any longer
to appear guilty in your eyes of such gross negligence. The
result of all the observations my brother has been able to
make seems to be that the monitorial system is chiefly recommended by its superior cheapness. I am myself so ignorant on the subject that it would be presumptuous in me to
say any thing—indeed you are so wise in Boston that perhaps uniform silence would be our best discretion. Mr.

Ware gave me sad accounts of your high-school. Is it possible that you have come to the conclusion that knowledge will make your people less useful and less happy? If the servants become wiser than their mistresses, and the ladies have their own labor to perform at last, it will but fall into the hands of the inferior class. But this is horrible democracy—treason against my caste. However, I can not believe that knowledge disqualifies for any thing. It would make the girls more contented and more efficient. It would enable them to perform their labors in half the usual time, and give them grace to submit to all the allotments of Providence. * * * * Are we not to see you here this spring? When I think of all that has been done and suffered to Christianize the earth ; how the ocean has been crossed, and trackless deserts penetrated, to preach to the ends of the world, I can not but wonder that there is not enough zeal to prompt some of our apostles to come to this great missionary field, where there are more to whom the Word might be addressed than could be found in traveling thousands of miles. Here is the grand point for distribution over the continent. There are one or two (and not more) who break down all barriers when they are here ; the rest, as to proselyting, might as well stay at home and preach to their own people. * * * * Mr. Walker gave us two stirring sermons yesterday. He would do infinite good here, and, if the doctrine is worth propagating, it is his paramount duty to come here. It is the duty of your association to send him, and of his friends to give him up, for a glorious cause. At least, to speak more modestly, it is so borne in upon our minds. Will you present me affectionately to Mrs. Channing? Forgive this bold and hasty letter, and believe me yours truly and gratefully, C. M. SEDGWICK."

There are people, and not altogether thoughtless people

either, who, looking upon so bright and cheerful, and, at the
same time, so rich and varied a life as these letters portray,
seeing the atmosphere of refinement, culture, and love in
which it was passed, and the sweet, thoughtful, and sympathetic temper with which its various events were met, would
say, how perfectly happy such a woman must have been!
how complete her satisfaction in life!   They forget that this
very vivacity and sympathy bring their corresponding pains,
and that a nature so finely strung, so delicately sensitive to
happiness, must have equal susceptibility to suffering.   Her
niece, Mrs. Minot, speaking of a time somewhat later than
this, and when she was accustomed to pass her summers in
Lenox with her brother Charles, and to go for the winter to
a home scarcely less dear in New York, says: "One of the
most vivid recollections of my childhood is of her agony of
grief (this is not an exaggerated phrase) as the time of her
leaving us approached.   Before the day of railroads she
went to Hudson by stage, and thence by boat to New York.
She always delayed going till the very last boat, and sometimes staid too long, till the ice had blocked the river, and
she had to make a long, circuitous land journey.   A deep
gloom hung over her spirits, and she used to take leave of
us as if she should never see us again.   To be sure, separation from your friends in the winter, in those days of slow
communication, was a very different thing from what it is
now."

But there are secret shadows on the spirit, gloomy passages through which all tender and sensitive souls must
walk, or they would not be what they are—griefs not betrayed during life to the dearest friends, unspoken sufferings
from which few are exempt, and from which none who know
the rich experience they bring would desire to be free.
From the sacred and touching record of such feelings, unveiled by death for reverent eyes, if the following passage be

presented to assist in producing a living portrait of its writer, it is that she herself would seem, near the close, to au-
thorize it, and to bequeath this shade of experience for use
to others.

Journal. ·

"*New York, May* 18, 1828. Again the spring is here, the
season of life and loveliness, the beautiful emblem of our
resurrection unto life eternal. I have seen the country
again arrayed in its green robe, with its budding honors
thick upon it, the brimful streams, all Nature steeped in
perfume, as if the gates of Paradise were thrown open, and
the air ringing with the wild notes of every bird upon the
wing. Even the poor little prisoners that are hanging beside the walls in our pent-up yards open their throats to
pour out the hymn of the season, and Poll Parrot jabbers,
laughs, and screams a wild note of joy. I will not say, with
the ungracious poet, that I turn from what Spring brings to
what she can not bring, but alas! I find there is no longer
that capacity for swelling, springing, brightening joy that I
once felt. Memory has settled her shadowy curtain over
too much of the space of thought, and Hope, that once to
my imagination tempted me with her arch, and laughing,
and promising face, to snatch away the veil with which she
but half hid the future—Hope now seems to turn from me;
and if I now and then catch some glimpses of her averted
face, she looks so serious, so admonitory, that I almost believe that her sister Experience, with an eye of apprehen-
sion, and lips that never smile, has taken her place. All is
not right with me, I know. I still build on sandy foundations; I still hope for perfection, where perfection is not
given. The best sources of earthly happiness are not within my grasp—those of contentment I have neglected. I
have suffered for the whole winter a sort of mental paraly-

sis, and at times I have feared the disease extended to my affections. It is difficult for one who began life as I did, the primary object of affection to many, to come by degrees to be first to none, and still to have my love remain in its entire strength, and craving such returns as have no substitute. How absurd, how groundless your complaints ! would half a dozen voices exclaim, if I ever ventured to *make* this complaint. I do not. Each one has his own point of sight. Others are not conscious—at least I believe they are not—of any diminution in their affections for me, but others have taken my place, naturally and of right, I allow it. It is the necessity of a solitary condition, an unnatural state. He who gave us our nature has set the solitary in families, and has, by an array of motives, secured this sweet social compact to his children. From my own experience I would not advise any one to remain unmarried, for my experience has been a singularly happy one. My feelings have never been embittered by those slights and taunts that the repulsive and neglected have to endure ; there has been no period of my life to the present moment when I might not have allied myself respectably, and to those sincerely attached to me, if I would. I have always felt myself to be an object of attention, respect, and regard, and, though not *first* to any, I am, like Themistocles, *second* to a great many. My fortune is not adequate to an independent establishment, but it is ample for ease to myself and liberality to others. In the families of all my brothers I have an agreeable home. My sisters are all kind and affectionate to me, my brothers generous and invariably kind ; their children all love me. My dear Kate, my adopted child, is, though far from perfect even in my doting eyes, yet such as to perfectly satisfy me, if I did not crave perfection for one I so tenderly love. I have troops of friends, some devotedly attached to me, and yet the result of all this very happy experience is that there is no equivalent for those blessings which Providence has placed first, and ordained that they should be purchased at the dearest sacrifice. I have not set this down in a spirit of repining, but it is well, I think, honestly to expose our own feelings — they may serve for examples or beacons. While I live I do not mean this shall be read, and after, my individual experience may perhaps benefit some one of all my tribe. I ought, I know, to be grateful and humble, and I do hope, through the grace of God, to rise more above the world, to attain a higher and happier state of feeling, to order my house for that better world where self may lose something of its engrossing power." * * * *

Another extract from the same private journal, referring to Mrs. Follen, may be admitted for its beauty of feeling and description, now that the only person whose modesty could be pained by its appearance has been called with her friend to another, and, as they both believed, a larger and happier sphere.

"*Boston, September* 15, 1828. Eliza Cabot's wedding-day. I have been with her through the week preceding her marriage, and have seen her character come out like thrice-refined gold. Never have I witnessed such a sweet serenity, like the mild and continual shining of the sun on a rugged way, such celestial feeling—devotion, benevolence, charity, sisterly love, friendship, all receiving their dues, and love, that selfish, engrossing passion, only serving to give increased vitality to all the rest." * * * *

Miss Sedgwick to Mrs. Watson.
" Boston, September 20, 1828.

" I went on Thursday to the celebration of the two hundredth anniversary at Salem. It was a beautiful day. This

magnificent bay sprinkled with its islands, and floating on
its bosom the wondrous messengers of every land ; the
shores covered with cheerful dwellings, all manifesting prosperity, activity, and enjoyment ; and then the rocky and sterile land, calling up affecting remembrances of those whose
virtues we were going to celebrate, all prepared us for the
day. The homogeneous population of this part of the country shows off such a scene to great advantage. At New
York there can not be a common sentiment. Here the old
man and the little child, the high and the humble, feel the
same blood stirred by the same thoughts. Judge Story was
very sensible and animated, and did not tire us with a two-
hours' harangue. We dined at his house. Old Dr. Holioke,
a man past his hundredth birthday, walking firmly and erect,
and looking like the representative of far-gone ages, was
present, and gave great interest to the scene. At the dinner Judge Story held up a large pewter platter, a relic which
belonged to the first settlers, filled with an indifferent pear,
called the Endicott pear, planted by the first Governor Endicott. 'Here,' he said, 'is what the Pilgrims had ;' and
then, elevating an elegant silver basket filled with necta-
rines, peaches, and grapes, 'here,' he said, 'is what their
children have.'"

Journal.

"*Lenox, December* 31, 1828. My poor brother! Thanks
to thee, merciful God, that it is not crime, nor the suspicion
of crime, that we bewail. Beset with fear and dread, I have
been made at moments to feel thankful that I knew it was
a sickness of the mind, the greatest physical calamity, and
not a moral derangement. But to see a mind once so powerful, so effective, so luminous, darkened, disordered, a broken instrument—to see him stared at by the vulgar, the
laugh of children—oh, it is too much! and yet his reason

and his affections are struggling with this evil. His love seems an inextinguishable light; it shines through the darkness."

"*January* 25, 1829. My dear Charles returned the 14th of January. The result of his journey was better than we hoped. * * * * If we still retained the ancient and horrible belief in the possession of evil spirits, we might believe that our poor brother's tormentors were rebuked by the Spirit of God which dwelleth in Charles. Harry was yielding and docile as a submissive child in his hands. This was not a supernatural agency, but that admirable sagacity that discerns the most subtle operations of the mind—that tenderness of feeling that enables a person of such exquisite sensibility as Charles to transfuse himself into another, to guard every avenue of feeling, to touch the broken instrument with a master's hand, and bring forth music where others only produce discord. There was always a confidence in his manner to Harry, respect, and tenderness. He was sometimes sportive, and threw a light on the follies of his insanity—not the sudden flash that irritates, but a laughing sunbeam." * * * *

Miss Sedgwick to Mr. Charles Sedgwick.

"New York, February 2, 1829.

"I have taken my pen (would it were a better one), not so much to gratify you, my beloved Charles, as because I feel the necessity of holding some communion with you—a *hankering*, a hungering and thirsting to be near you. I usually come to my room at this hour, the time when Elizabeth sallies forth for her evening walk, and give it to those thoughts and feelings that come unbidden, that press upon us—*come?* they are what constitute our mind and its affections. You know, my dear Charles, that you are with me in these quiet and tender meditations; my brother, more

I 2

than brother. I know nothing of love, of memory, of hope, of which you are not an essential part. If ever I attain to any adequate conception of the purity, and peace, and intensity of heavenly affections, it is from that I feel for you. In all that I have been unfaithful to you, that I have disappointed and afflicted you, I feel that my own forgiveness is far more difficult than yours to be obtained."

Miss Sedgwick to Mr. Robert Sedgwick.

"Stockbridge, August, 1829.

* * * * "Oh, I never shall forget this pleasant visit to you! If I had gone the grand tour in search of pleasure, I should not have found so much. You, my dear Robert, are wiser and better than almost any body I ever knew in seizing and improving those opportunities of happiness that others pass by either churlishly, or ignorantly, or recklessly. How much they lose, and how much you gain! The affections are, like the elements of water, and air, and all the common bounties of Providence, given to all, and in what sad neglect they are permitted to lie!—like waste and barren sands that might be filled with exquisite flowers and fruits. * * * * I had a singular 'compagnon du voyage' in the stage-coach—one of the Geibs, a brother of him of whom we purchased the piano. He, too, is an eminent musician, and was traveling for his health, and to tune Kitty's piano by the way. He has lived in all the quarters of the globe; is an observer and a philosopher; has a good deal of genius, and a good deal of that proud sort of conceit that the original thinkers of an inferior station are apt to get. He and I were the only talkers in the stage, as graduates hold a colloquy on the stage. Our companions dropped off by the way, and we left Barrington *tête-à-tête*. He was aware that I belonged to the Sedgwick concern, and that was all. 'Can you inform me, ma'am,' he said, 'whether I shall see the authoress of Redwood?' and when I pleaded guilty, he complimented me by saying that he concluded by my conversation that I was 'a person of reading and reflection!'"

Miss Sedgwick to Mrs. Watson.

"New York, January 18, 1830.

"MY DEAREST FRANCES,—I found two letters here from you when I returned from Philadelphia. I received civilities enough to turn a younger head than mine; but age has too many sad and heavy realities to permit us to be dazzled by a little sunshine. Philadelphia is a delightful place. I saw probably the very best aspect of its society—the cultivated, enlightened, and accomplished. They are like the Bostonians in giving the honor due to intellectual merit in their estimation and cultivation of the mind, but they have more ease, facility, and grace. They do not seem to be afraid to speak lest they should commit themselves for life. The climate has a more genial influence; they are more mercurial, without being frivolous or flippant. In one respect they appeared to me to be inferior—the judgment of a stranger should be very modest—there is much less religious sentiment in the higher classes, more indifference to the subject, as if it were only fit to interest the vulgar and the weaker sex.

"On my return I passed a day at Burlington at Mrs. Bradford's, the daughter of Elias Boudinot, and once the companion of General Washington and all that coterie. She has the freshness and vigor of middle life with the raciness of the olden time. She had known and admired our dear father, and received me with warmth as the daughter of a friend. She keeps up all the stateliness of the old style, gracefully softened by the comfort and ease of modern times, which is something like the influence of the sweet Southwest in walks of regular and lofty trees."

"New York, January 24, 1830.

"My DEAREST CHILD,—Your sweet letter, so neatly written that it gave me great hopes that, even if your coming to me depends on your carefulness, I shall not be disappointed, arrived some days since. * * * * Letter-writing is one of the accomplishments I hope you will excel in. Letters, if we are social and affectionate as we should be, we must write, and of course they are constantly-recurring opportunities of giving pleasure. Now, dear Kate, it is best to begin life with setting a right value on these small occasions of doing good, for they make up a great sum. Letters should be affectionate, natural, and graceful—almost every body can get as far as that—then make them as witty, or sensible, or in any way agreeable as you can." * * * *

"Clarence" was brought out in 1830, the first, and, with one exception, the only one of Miss Sedgwick's larger works whose scene is New York in the modern time. It is the most romantic, and, at the same time, the wittiest of her novels, and while it fascinated younger readers by its story, it charmed elder minds by its high-bred intelligence, and its sweet and noble humanity.

The letters in "Clarence" are particularly fine, and might serve as models in the art, besides being characterized by strong dramatic individuality.

"New York, March 7, 1830.

* * * * "Of all the labors that I ever have undertaken, copying is the severest. I have now nearly come to the end of my first volume, and hope to finish it on Tuesday, so that that will be completely ready for the printer, and the rest I

shall do without the painful sense of being hurried. I believe I wrote to you, but I am not sure, that R. sold the copyright of an edition of 2000, to be printed uniform with 'Hope
Leslie,' for $1200. I am quite satisfied with this. It in-
sures me that compensation and a good publisher. I believe that is as much as they can afford to give. They say
in their **letter** that the cheap reprints of popular English
novels have reduced the value of copyright productions as
much as Hope Leslie has raised the **reputation** of mine.
I am not satisfied with Clarence, and **never shall be** with
any thing I write. That is the misfortune of a familiarity
with fine works, carrying your taste so far ahead of **your** capacity; but I do think (and perhaps that augurs ill **for** its
real merit—it may be the old story of the mother and the
rickety child over again)—but I do think, **nevertheless, that**
it has a great deal **more in it** than any **thing else I have**
written, and that it is better adapted to the general **taste of**
novel-readers I am **sure,** because it has romantic faults, and
because it has something to do with every-day and present
life. I miss excessively, more than words can tell, the light
and repose of dear Harry's criticisms. I felt a reliance **on**
him that I can never feel on another; a confidence that I
should not expose myself to any severe criticism; and I miss
the sweet excitement of Jane's eager interest. To balance
these, I have more experience, and consequently far more
self-confidence, and I have vastly less fear or care about the
result. I have tasted the pleasure of reputation, and know
what it is worth, and I know it is *not* one of the ministers **of**
the inner sanctuary. Dearest Charles, I should **make an**
apology to almost any one else **for** all this about **myself, but**
I consider that whatever is my concern is **just** about as
much yours."

Miss Sedgwick to Dr. Pomeroy.

"New York, March 13, 1830.

"MY DEAR BROTHER,—I can not bear that my whole winter's campaign should pass away without any communication with you. I am not satisfied with contriving fictitious happiness and fictitious misery. My heart reverts to the real and bitter sorrows that cloud our life, and my thoughts to the happy homes whose goodness, love, and intelligence mock the brightest tints of my pencil. And then my characters! What can my brain manufacture to compare with the father who has the spirit of five-and-twenty, with the virtue of a more advanced age, who, with the resolution of the old Roman and the fire of Bunker Hill, is contentedly caring for his flocks and herds, giving the tenderness of his heart to his little Benjamin, and is the stay and staff of his children, when most men lean on them for support? And what to that excellent aunt and sister, who, truly loving the praise of God more than the praise of men, and loving and serving others more than herself, is still blessing all around her with her kindness and her example, and diffusing a light, full of gentleness and promise, like the serenest setting sun? I say nothing of the vines that, separated from the parent stalk, and flourishing and fruitful, still turn their faces homeward, as plants at a window always turn toward the light; or of that sweet image of her sainted mother's virtue and loveliness, our blessed Sue;* nor of the bright-eyed sisters, full of promise and hope; nor of our noisy, good-hearted, honest Charles; nor even yet of our little Benjamin.

---

* Dr. Pomeroy's daughter, well deserving of her aunt's praise, and who was, in after years, one of the victims of the terrible railroad catastrophe at Norwalk, Conn., where she employed her last strength to save the child who was in her charge, and died with the disinterestedness that had been characteristic of her life.

But they all shame my manufactures, and are as the Magnus Apollo to the waxen image of a country show."

Miss Sedgwick to Mrs. Channing.

"New York, March 14, 1830.

* * * * "I have a book in the press, and, as there is still a great deal to do to it, I am constantly employed. I am now hardened enough to talk of my *works* (oh! how the word and all its relations have made my blood tingle!) with perfect nonchalance. This treats of the present times, topics that concern every body, and the follies of the day. The scene is chiefly in New York, hazardous ground I am aware, but, at the same time, it seems to me of more popular interest than a tale of the olden time, which has more romantic facilities." * * * *

To the same.

"New York, June 23, 1830.

* * * * "I am delighted with your suffrage for my book. I shall never get the calm nerves of a regular-bred author, and I quake and tremble on every fresh appearance." * * *

Miss Sedgwick to Mr. Charles Sedgwick.

"Newport, Monday evening, Sept. 5, 1830.

* * * * "We came on very pleasantly, save a slight alarm from a sloop running foul of us—neither harming nor being harmed, but causing that general agitation, that running up and down, and to and fro, which indicates what a scene we might have in case of a real panic. We had one philosopher in the shape of an old woman, who made the most of the good and the least of the evil of life—who was quite willing to be laughed at by people who, she said, would never see her again, and in her turn to laugh at the follies' of the laughers—a species of simple wisdom that, if generally adopted, would save many a heartache, for, as my old woman observed, your people who are always jealous and suspecting **slights are the** ' *tiresomest* ***company*** ' you can have. L—— received me most kindly, and was excessively disappointed that you were not with me. **Your bed was made, and the** disappointment was general. For myself, **I felt** pretty flat when I was depressed with the full sense of the fact that I was here without you. Dear Charles, when some **of those** hours of depression which, in spite of the old general's example, will come over you again, arrive, think of what **a** blessing you have been, and are, and will be to me —of what power you have over me, and I am sure the consciousness of **such** angelic influence will exorcise any demon."

Miss Sedgwick to Mrs. **Channing.**

"Lenox, October 13, 1830.

"MY DEAR FRIEND,—I **can not let my** brothers **go to** Boston without a line to you, if it is merely a bait to **get a** letter in return. It is a long time since I have heard from **you,** and you know that I set *great store* by your letters. I **am afraid that some of our** friends may condemn our per- **mitting** Harry to go to Boston, but it is impossible for those **to judge** who can not understand the opposing evils and va- **riety** of embarrassments that attend a case like his. It is all-important to have his plans and wishes meet opposition, or an impassable barrier from abroad rather than from his friends, whose influence, while it is assuaging, may be sana- tive. I am particularly anxious that your brother Walter, who has been throughout so very and so effectively kind, **and** whose advice has been so useful to us, should not dis- **approve us.** I hope you will **see Harry.** He is very sus- **ceptible of** kindness from **his** old friends. Will this long **trial ever** cease? God grant us grace to endure it patiently. It has been attended with many circumstances to excite our gratitude and strengthen our affection for our friends. There *is* balm for every wound, and it is our own fault if we lose its healing influence. * * * *

"My summer has glided away peacefully and uniformly, with nothing very stirring of a private nature, so that my heart is free for public sympathy, and can exult in a French Revolution, and throb at the name of Lafayette. Your people of leisure are the true philanthropists." * * * *

Miss Sedgwick to Mrs. Watson.

"Lenox, October 24, 1830.

"MY DEAR SISTER,—I have thought of you since our parting as so bright and happy as scarcely to need any aid from us ; but I ought to have known better, for happiness is so much the element for which we are made—it so awakes the drowsy powers of our nature and stimulates our capacities, that we never, I think, more ardently extend our affections to our friends than when we are happy. It is the rich man and not the beggar who keeps his festival prepared and his doors open. But I do not see why I should go on to aggravate the sin I meant to excuse.

"How God has set his seal on love in all its modifications ! It is the life and health of the soul. It can not be violated without misery, and its restoration after loss or suspension is the return of the exile to his father's house. How strange that the benevolence of the Deity should ever be questioned, when we have its proofs in the operation of every faculty and every affection."

Miss Sedgwick to K. M. Sedgwick.

"New York, Dec. 14, 1830.

* * * * "My sweet Kate, I thank you for your letter. It is just such as I wish you to write. I have a notion that a

letter that is to be copied can never be quite so fresh from
the heart, never quite so deeply imbued with its tenderness
and sweetness as that which is marked down as the words
bubble out from the fountain. * * * * I should not have
seen your little beau ideal* if I had arrived earlier, as he did
not dine here. He has left town. Poor boy, he pays a
heavy penalty for his enchanting gifts. After being kept on
the stage till 12 o'clock, sustaining the most arduous parts,
his father takes him to Niblo's to a supper with *bons vivants.*
Oh, my sweet, bright-eyed Charles, how much more enviable
are you at that hour, in the arms of Nature's kindest nurse,
surrounded by the spirits of innocence and love ! * * * *

"If I had space I would give you a diverting account of
my visit to the Savings' Bank, whence I have fished out
M.'s money ; how, when the man asked me my occupation, I laughed, and confessed I had none, and felt inferior
to the meanest of the one hundred Irish about me." * * * *

Miss Sedgwick to K. M. Sedgwick.

"New York, December, 1830.

* * * * "We all, including Grace, went to see Charles
Kean in Hamlet, and Clara Fisher in Ophelia, Monday
night. Kean played extremely well for a young man under
twenty, and continually recalled to me his unequaled father.
Clara Fisher, in the first scenes, appeared like a little plain,
affected, spoiled drawing-room girl ; but when she came to
the mad scene, which is one of the very finest scenes in the
whole drama for effect, she seemed inspired. She was, indeed, the Ophelia of Shakspeare, 'a sweet bell jangled out
of tune ;' her little snatches of songs, the exquisite music,
and the delicacy, the pathos, the transient gleams of bright
light, and the deep shades that were shrouding forever her
sweet spirit, all was manifest, and all nature. I did not
think my old eyes would ever have wept again at any stage

* Master Burke.

sorrows, but it is the feeling that such sorrows are in life that makes us weep. Read that beautiful play aloud to your father, my dear Kate, *as* you read Shakspeare when he was gone. It is the most exquisite production in the English language." * * * *

Miss Sedgwick to K. M. Sedgwick.

"New York, January 14, 1831.

"I have been twice, dear Kate, to see your beau ideal, the miraculous boy! He is the only *prodigy* I ever saw. He is endowed with faculties that would make him pre-eminent at any age, that are prodigious at his. * * * * He plays tragedy with great propriety, but he is too young for the lover, and Romeo—a beautiful Cupid wooing an overgrown Juliet of a *certain* age—was rather ridiculous. He is a true son of the comic muse, and either in Looney M'Twolter, a wild Irish boy, or in Sir Abel Handy, a simple, kind-hearted, henpecked, wild projector of impracticable improvements, or in the Protean boy in the March of Intellect (a farce written for him), he is incomparable. But what would delight you are his musical attainments. He is said by competent judges—you know I am an ignoramus on the subject—to play a violin better than Segura. This would be a wonderful acquisition, if he had no other ; and the best of it is, that when he is commended for it, he says, with great modesty, that any body might play as well who would practice as much. To me it is very interesting to see the intense interest with which the orchestra listen to him, and to hear their leader cry, with all his heart, 'Bravo!' Indeed, the actors seem often to forget every thing but his presence and powers. It was amusing to see Mercutio fondly patting Romeo on the shoulder. My dear child, I would not turn your head with this dramatic genius, but I think we owe, and we can not help paying, a tribute of admiration to such beautiful gifts of Heaven, and it may stimulate your

own efforts **to know what acquisitions may be** made by intense assiduity. **His** brief life must have been a continued
study. He fences well, and dances beautifully. But there
is **a** sad reverse to this picture ; and when I **see him** come
forward in his own character, in his jacket and trowsers, and
square collar and frill, his fair shining hair brushed **smoothly** down, and feel that his youth and innocence **are in a**
tainted atmosphere, that he is exposed to moral death, **that**
his fine powers are almost sure to be blasted by such unnatural excitement and overdoing, that the rich bud must
perish,* I could weep—to tell the truth, I *have* wept over him,
and I have **breathed** a prayer of gratitude that those bright
and beloved children over whom my heart yearns are sheltered and nurtured in the retreats of purity, virtue, and love."
* * * *

Miss Sedgwick to K. M. Sedgwick.

"New York, January 25, 1831.

* * * * "There are few such persons as your father, **my**
dear child—few whose only question is whether others want
what **he** can give. His humanities are like the rain that
falleth on the just **and** the unjust, and, like the rain too, I
believe they sometimes bring forth fruit from very sterile
ground. If half the world were like him, I believe the other
half would cast their slough, and be so too. There is such
a principle of life and health in the atmosphere of the good
and lovely. Hark, the supper-bell ! If your father could see
with what eagerness I pick up all the little pearls dropped
in the corners and strung along the margins **of his** letters,
he would not doubt the **value** I set on the cross-readings.
Thank your dear mother for her very kind contribution to

---

* It is pleasant to say that this melancholy prophecy was never ful-
filled, and that "Master Burke," passing the fiery ordeal of precocity and
publicity safe in simple honesty of nature, is now living in New York,
sincerely esteemed by all who know him, both as a man and a musician.

my pleasure. Tell your Aunt Susan that I hear many of
her friends deploring her departure from the city. It is
colder to-night than ever, yet our parlor in every part has
been 74°! Dear Kate, remember the poor in this season
of their extremity, and forget not to be grateful, and to *express* your gratitude to that Being who has sheltered you in
your sweet home." * * * *

Miss Sedgwick to K. M. Sedgwick.

"Baltimore, February 2, 1831.

"MY DEAREST KATE,—We have arrived thus far without
any disaster. * * * * We left New York at 7 Saturday
morning; came as far as Amboy in the steam-boat; then we
mounted into wagon-boxes set on sledges, and were seated
on our baggage *dos à dos*, like an Irish jaunting-car, eleven in
our sleigh. Among the rest was an English woman, of their
fine sturdy breed, arrived from a ten-weeks' voyage the day
before, with a little baby born at sea! Some of our sleighs
had oversets, but we arrived safe in Philadelphia at 11 that
night. * * * * We traveled yesterday pretty much in Jo-
nah's fashion, shut up in a stage-sleigh, but had excellent drivers, horses, and inns, excepting one team, who, as a woman
told me, were 'pretty considerable wild and fractious, but
did not run away much.' They brought us safely to *Paradise*, though I am sure the way, to me, was through Purgatory. We arrived at Lancaster, one of the largest interior
towns in the United States, just after dark. * * * * We
crossed the Susquehanna at Lancaster. I thought, if you
could have looked in a magical mirror at that moment, and
seen us, you would have been amused. Fancy a lumbering stage-sleigh on a covered bridge, hail and rain beating
against it; the passengers with a lantern walking a mile and
a quarter (the length of the bridge). When we were mid-
way, a little bird fluttered over and was caught by one of

the passengers. **Poor little thing!** I thought she did not feel much more **out of place than I did.** We rode 25 miles to York, **and then put** into **harbor for the night.** York **was built by** Germans, and has **a** very **substantial,** comfortable aspect, as, indeed, every thing has in Pennsylvania. **The** house in which the old Congress sat when they **were** compelled by Sir William Howe's army to fly from Philadelphia is still standing in the middle of their principal street. Yesterday we rode 85 miles, to-day 48, without any discomfort. The horses 'run a little,' but the leaders soon cleared themselves from the sleigh, and we were safe. We came the longest, which is called the upper road. Every where we find civil landlords, good taverns (last night there were warm baths **in the** establishment), sober drivers, and every comfort. **To-morrow** we ride seven miles on the railroad. It is uncertain whether we proceed on wheels or runners ; either way will be bad enough, as the road is a sea of slush. **We** have been terribly incommoded **with turning out in the deep** snow for the transportation wagons. **We** passed more **than** 200 yesterday. They are '*awful* concerns' **in a** deep **snow.** This (Barnum's) is a most excellent house. We have **a** parlor, and bedrooms (each larger than your parlor) on each side. We have just supped on canvas-back ducks, and your uncle has sallied forth with Mr. B—— to **see** the city." * * * *

Miss Sedgwick to K. M. Sedgwick.

"Washington, February 2, 1831.

* * * * "We then went into the Supreme Court. Your father will tell you that it is the most dignified body in the United States. It is a small room, and looks like a handsome **cell in a** monastery. The ceiling is like a scallop-shell : **all is marble.** Chief Justice Marshall was presiding, and reading an opinion. His voice is feeble. His face has a

fine union of intellect and tranquillity, the seal of a well-spent life upon it. Judge M'Lean has a very fine face, an eye that moves like lightning. He looks as if he were a leader in the French Chamber of Deputies. Judge Story came down to speak to us, and told me that he had promised Judge Marshall to come with him to see me. If he does so, it will be a great gratification to me to see face to face one of the most venerable and honored men our country has produced. * * * * When we entered the House there was a debate going on relative to the reduction of the duty on salt. Some Southern members spoke with great vehemence, but nobody on the floor paid any attention to them. They spoke of their oppression, of throwing themselves on the sovereignty of their States, of being goaded to rebellion, of the time being near when ' vengeance should stalk about those halls.' It was melancholy to see such feelings aroused among our countrymen, and more painful to see them quite disregarded." * * * *

Miss Sedgwick to K. M. Sedgwick.

" Washington, February 5, 1831.

"*Monday P. M.* Dearest, 'most tired to death. Began with visitors the moment the breakfast was carried down. At 12, took a carriage and went to the House ; they were engaged in common business, and we hurried home before Cambreleng's reply to Burgess, to keep an engagement with Mr. Van Buren, who had offered to call to take me and introduce me to the President. He came in his beautiful coach, servants in livery, elegant horses, and two most beautiful dogs. We drove to the palace, entered a large, cold saloon, and then a drawing-room, in which is a fine full-length picture of General Washington. When the British came here in the last war, the President was obliged to fly. His wife, Mrs. Madison, cut the picture from the frame and took it with her—the only article she took! The President was not in the drawing-room when we entered. He came immediately, apologized for not having been there to receive us, as he had been that moment called out, was very courteous, and quite plain and pleasing. He has a wooden face, but honest and pretty good. * * * * It is still very cold here. Mr. Ridge, the Cherokee, and our connection, is coming to see us at ten this morning. We are waiting breakfast—what do you think for? Till Mrs. Webster has done with the tea-pot! Poor B—— is any thing but a landlord—an amateur in horses, a gentleman of elegant leisure, but he has some excellent subalterns in his establishment, who will probably own it in a year or two." * * * *

Miss Sedgwick to Mrs. Watson.

"New York, March 9, 1831.

"If I had a home (alas! how many sweet visions are comprised within that impossible *if*), I should wish F. to pass the next year with me. If I have any faculty (this is the common mode of speech of the self-confident), it is that of making young girls happy, and, in my opinion, half of all our amiability, not to say virtue, proceeds from our happiness—perhaps far more than half of that of the young. The stream that runs clear must be clear at the fountain. My dear sister, you quite over-estimated my writing you from Washington. What is there in a passing tribute from the world that weighs for one moment against that love which began with life, and which is as indestructible as the soul? If you were not my sister, my dear Frances, your friendship, the friendship of a heart so ardent and warm as yours, would amount to more than all the *world* has ever offered to me; this is simple undemonstrable truth. I deserve no praise for what is a part of the constitution of the mind—a part of that chain with which He, who is love, hath bound us together."

Miss Sedgwick to K. M. Sedgwick.

"Newport, August 13, 1831.

"MY DEAREST KATE,—I have not written to you since I arrived here! Marvelous, is it not? Well, you will not disbelieve me when I say that you are almost always present to my mind. At first when we arrived here, M. and I felt pretty doleful. We have an apartment that has no view but of potatoes and ragged seringas, and the walls, in consequence of the prevailing dampness here, smell like mouldy plaster—something of a contrast to our home privileges. Then every thing is in such a rude and homely style, compared with our other watering-places. But, on more experience, we find pleasures and comforts developing. There is no ceremony, no fussing about dress. The family are all friendly, the walks and the rides are beautiful beyond description, and the bathing! Oh, dear Kate, I am sure the breakers never swell over me that I do not think of you. How you would scream with delight as you rose from the passing wave! * * * * We are, I assure you, droll figures when we are rigged, and then the variety of groups that go in, in black, white, and gray! portly old ladies, and slim young girls, now and then a beautiful young creature whose head looks like a mermaid—M—— C——, for instance—when her head rises from the water, and her beautiful hair wreathes in its natural curls over her swan-like neck. Then the groups are varied with nurses and children, and strapping black women bathing their over-delicate young mistresses."
* * * *

Miss Sedgwick to Mrs. Watson.

"Stockbridge, November 25, 1831.

"MY DEAREST SISTER,—It is just one week to-day since you left us. Had any marked change occurred in the ob-

K

ject of all our present cares and watchings, I should have
apprized you of it.   Jane and I both think there is a gradual, though scarcely perceptible diminution in the operation
of the functions of nature.   For the last three days Harry
has articulated but once, and attempted it but twice.   How
long his mind will remain in its silent prison we can not tell.
That he is spared a consciousness of the intense and throbbing interest with which we watch him is a mercy.   I sometimes realize that this profound repose is given to his mind
the better to prepare it for the intense joy of release, for the
love, the rapture of heaven.   But you know, my dear sister,
how bitter thoughts of the past will cloud our brightest
hopes, and how our kindred flesh shrinks as we advance to
the last struggles of mortality.   But I hope that our trust in
God will enable us to sustain every trial with meekness and
thankfulness, and that we shall be able to say, as our suffering brother said, as our earthly happiness is all vanishing
away, 'I love God better than I did in health.'   'Though
he slay me, yet will I trust in him.' "

On December 22, 1831, Miss Sedgwick wrote in her diary:
"Days of sorrow, wintry days, have followed the serene, lux-
urious days of summer.   My life is now passed under a
deep, desolate shadow.   My brother—he whose web of life
from my cradle has been interwoven with mine, so that it
seems to me they can not be parted without shattering the
whole texture—my dear Harry is sinking away.   Day after
day Jane and I watch over him, but we can convey no feeling of ours to his mind ; we can get no intimation from that
silent prison-house.   We look on the features that have always been the medium of kindness and ardent affection—
they are the same ; intelligence, composure, and deep seriousness are expressed there—no inanity, no approach to vacancy nor weakness.   The mind must still exist, and He

who breathed into him that glowing, ever-active, ever-soaring spirit, will guard and keep it, though it has pleased Him to close up all the avenues by which we approached it."

The next day the merciful gates of release were opened. The sister's mourning was as if a portion of her life were rent away, but without a shadow of repining, and the next year she was able to write: "This is the anniversary of my dear brother's death. How vividly has memory presented to me that day of anguish! I have lived it over again, but softened by time, by a more grateful sense of the mercy that closed his life without more physical suffering, and, I think, with a more distinct anticipation of a reunion. I seem sometimes to catch the glimmering light of another morning. My dear Harry, my heart has been faithful to your memory."

When time had softened the anguish of this blow, and passionate grief had calmed into tender recollection, a series of happy and prosperous years opened to Miss Sedgwick. She drew fresh life from the charming groups of nephews and nieces growing up around her, to whom she was a radiant centre of entertainment and affection. She loved them with a triple love, made up of her strong natural interest in young people, her devotion to these as the children of brothers and sisters who were dearer to her than life, and the affection called forth by their individual characters; and they, in return, made her their confidante, their adviser, the sharer of all their hopes, pleasures, and anxieties —their mutual rallying-point of inspiration and excitement. No plan could be carried out without " Aunt Kitty's" counsel, no amusement complete without her participation. Her coming was the signal of happiness and festivity, and her departure never made her friends " twice glad." One of her oldest nieces writes her in 1832 :

" I never went into your room in one of my saddest

moods that I did not come out with a smile that you had
conjured up, and most mysteriously, for I am sure I could
never account for it; and when I have thought of the change
in my feelings in going to and returning from you, I have
been almost disposed to believe in fairy work. But, not to
derogate from you, I have accounted for it in the only rational way—the supremacy a superior mind must always
have over an inferior, so as to turn darkness into light, and
perplexity into peace, if not joy. All must be darkness and
perplexity now, for you are not here to turn them into light
and joy, and can you wonder that I miss you?"

This expresses the common feeling of her family, and, to
the day of her death, her presence was always felt by each
as an honor as well as a comfort.

Her love for children was peculiarly tender. "She and
every child who came near her," says her niece, "were always bound together by the strongest mutual attraction, and
her devotion to her particular pets was sometimes a source
of annoyance to older friends. Until I was quite a big girl,
she made it her practice always to lie down beside me when
I went to bed, and tell me a story—no matter what friends
were impatiently waiting for her to reappear—and she continued the custom with my children. Her stories were in-
vented at the moment, and often continued, like Schehera-
zade's, for a number of nights, and in that case she was occasionally reproved for mistakes in the names of the characters, or in regard to the various incidents. At seventy-
five I have seen her sit on the floor and play 'Hunt the
Slipper' with as much zest as any of the children. She encouraged the most affectionate familiarity of manner. A
lovely little girl, one of her nieces, once exclaimed, on
hearing some one say how much she *respected* Miss Sedgwick, 'Rethpect Aunt Kitty! why, I couldn't rethpect Aunt
Kitty!'"

Nothing could have delighted "Aunt Kitty" more than such evidence of that love which "casteth out fear."

Miss Sedgwick was now at the height of her literary popularity. The rapid sale of her books was proof positive of their acceptance with the public, while from friends and strangers came the most gratifying testimony not only to their artistic merit, but also to their moral power and real usefulness. It was at this time that she began to write especially for the young, and for those who needed instruction in some of the primary studies of the world's great school, and between 1834 and 1837, besides the "Linwoods," one of the most beautiful and elaborate of her novels, appeared "Home," "The Poor Rich Man," the "Love Token," and "Live and Let Live," names fragrant in memory for the exquisite dramatic truth and beauty which carried straight to the heart their lessons of human brotherhood, healthy living, plain practical sense, and deep religious feeling. The following extract from the letter of a country physician, a personal stranger to Miss Sedgwick, is given, although of a somewhat later date, as a specimen of the heartfelt tribute constantly paid to her from this time — a tribute making thankful both the giver and the receiver.

Dr. Cummings to Miss Sedgwick.

"August, 1851.

* * * * "Were I not in a most difficult position to leave (having wound myself into the affections of parents and children), I would devote the remainder of my life to the diffusion of your books among my fellow-mortals, which I think would be doing God service, and one of the best missions yet undertaken, and would do more to hasten forward the millennium, that all are so anxious to see, than all the sectarian preaching in the land. This may look a little like enthusiasm—perhaps it is—but to me it is Gospel truth, and

I have now put more than fifty volumes of the books in circulation in this region, and have got our Unitarian minister to say he will give a copy of 'Home' to every couple he marries."

Nor were letters of praise and gratitude the only ones that poured in upon her from unknown correspondents, but letters of inquiry, of suggestion, demands of sympathy, requests for advice on private or literary concerns, for assistance from purse or pen, crowded upon her, and all received kindly attention. Compliments of every kind were offered to her, some gratifying, some amusing. The Historical Society of Pennsylvania elected her an honorary member, and the Nu Pi Kappa Literary Society of Kenyon College, Ohio, did itself the honor to inscribe her name upon its list.

Meanwhile she kept up a constant and active correspondence not only with her brothers and sisters, but with nieces and nephews, cousins and friends innumerable, both in this country and in Europe. She exchanged letters with Sismondi for more than twenty years, and with Miss Martineau for several years after her visit to Stockbridge, of which an interesting sketch will be given later in this volume. Her interest in the concerns of her friends went into the most minute particulars, and she was, in the words of her niece, "The confidante and adviser of every body who came near her. I have often," she says, "known her make some new acquaintances at a watering-place, who, after two or three days' intercourse with her, would pour out to her the whole secret history of their hearts."

Her long and affectionate friendship with Mrs. Jameson dates from this period, and it was now also that she first saw Mrs. Fanny Kemble, and that her enthusiastic admiration for the inimitable actress warmed and deepened into a love for the noble woman which proved a bond of life-long strength and beauty.

About this time, also, her warmest sympathies were aroused
by the arrival in New York of the noble band of Italian pa-
triots released by the Austrian government from the dun-
geons of Spielberg on condition of eternal exile from their
native land. She and her brothers were among the first to
welcome Confalonieri, Maroncelli, Foresti, and their fellow-
sufferers, and to give them, in fervent sympathy and admiration, cordial hospitality and generous assistance, all that a
foreign country could offer in compensation for their misfortunes. They came as strangers, but strangers they were not
long, for the noble personal qualities of most of these martyrs for freedom soon changed mere respect and compassion into devoted friendship, and the Sedgwick family in
especial entered upon intimate relations with nearly all
of them.* No one can remember without strong interest
either the personal appearance of these gentlemen—their
stately forms, bent and sometimes crippled from long im-
prisonment; their faces, where the well-known beauty of
their race was marred by the deep lines cut by grief, anxiety, and privation ; their great earnestness of manner, which
seemed to spring from latent passion held in strong check,

* Miss Sedgwick herself says, speaking of the Italian exiles, "Several
of them became intimate in our family, and closely bound to it by reverence and affection on our side ; they were men of superior intelligence
and education—honorable gentlemen, true-hearted, loving men, ingots
of gold that had contracted no alloy in the subjection of their country. Confalonieri, Foresti, Albinola, and our Castillia became our dear
friends. Castillia came to pass a few months at my sister Jane's; those
months extended to years. He was as a brother to her—an elected
brother to us all—and most tenderly beloved by her children. He possessed all the virtues that one can name, and in their most attractive
forms. He was a Catholic—such a Catholic as Fénelon was, as St.
Paul was, 'clothed in the whole armor of God.' But Castillia had
more of St. John than St. Paul, and as appropriately might that apostle,
who is to us the impersonation of all Gospel love and gentleness, have
been *chained* in a dungeon as Castillia."

or the honorable resolution with which they supported themselves by teaching their own language, and the accomplishments which had been the ornaments of their youth. Miss
Sedgwick was indefatigable in obtaining pupils for them.
Her love of liberty and hatred of oppression ; her reverence
for those who had risked and lost all for freedom's sake,
and her regard for them as her friends, all kindled her zeal,
and for some time she was so engrossed by these interests
that her older acquaintances protested that all attempts to
gain her attention were bootless unless the subject were
stamped with the magic seal of Italy and patriotism. She
was now in the midst of a large and brilliant circle, constantly courted and flattered by the world, her presence every where sought, and her notice eagerly coveted, and she
used all her power and influence to benefit the exiles. She
had the full sympathy and co-operation of her family. The
younger members were all seized with an enthusiastic desire to study the Italian language and literature. They
spent much time on it even in the busy winters of New
York, and in summer, when the clan was usually gathered
in Berkshire, where Stockbridge and Lenox were becoming
more and more attractive each year to visitors in the warm
season, large classes were easily formed to provide employment for the fascinating teachers, and delightful months
were passed by instructors and pupils among those beautiful hills and valleys—months of refreshing out-of-door freedom and enjoyment, enhanced by intercourse with refined
and cultivated people. Miss Sedgwick heartily enjoyed this
country life, and, though a busy woman, always found leisure
to encourage and share its wholesome and inspiring pleasures. Her summer home was now at Lenox, in her brother
Charles's house, to which, for her especial accommodation,
had been added a wing, gradually enlarged till it contained
four or five rooms, and gave her space and opportunity for

independent hospitality, in which she took great pleasure. Her little guest-chamber was seldom empty during the summer, and endless were the entertainments, pic-nics, tea-drinkings, evening gatherings over which she presided, receiving the distinguished and the insignificant with equal grace and welcome. Yet hers was not a loose and undiscriminating kindness. No one had a keener eye for pretension and folly; she was too quick-witted not to be very sensitive to the attacks of that ravager of society, the bore; and she was so alive to the ludicrous side of all things, that if the natural sweetness of her disposition had not been re-enforced by an intelligent and highly-cultivated humanity, it might not have restrained her wit from scorching where it touched, instead of brightening her social circle as it did

> " With summer lightnings of a soul
>   So full of summer warmth, so glad,
> So healthy, sound, and clear, and whole,
>   Her memory scarce makes us sad."

*Miss Sedgwick to Dr. Pomeroy.**

"New York, April 29, 1832.

" MY DEAR DOCTOR,—I am seldom bold enough to doubt the wisdom of your decisions, but it seems to me that your better judgment has been led captive by your humanity toward a portion of the community who, from having been the objects of desertion and despair, have suddenly become the chief subjects of effort, hope, and Christian love. I am not surprised at Louis's zeal, but that you and other judicious, and thinking, and patriotic members of our village society should have banded together to introduce into our still pastures and by our sweet water-courses, amid our flocks of defenseless sheep and lambs, these state-prison wolves, is, I

---

* Dr. Pomeroy was interested in the establishment of a Home for Discharged Convicts, which it was at this time proposed to place in the neighborhood of Stockbridge.

confess, a mystery to me. I entreat you to reconsider the matter—to think how great a portion of our peace and happiness results from the safe character of our people, from the security with which we can go out and come in, and lay our heads on our pillows at night. If the effort must be made, there are places thinly inhabited, remote from villages, that would be more suitable. Has a colony ever been thought of in some part of our fine unoccupied territory? In the name of Heaven, let some other portion of this habitable globe be selected than our village. It seems to me that the well-being of the virtuous and moral part of the community, those who have done nothing to forfeit their rights, ought to be considered. Think of the amount of fear that will be inspired by these people ; and that, as soon as experience (should experience teach us they are as harmless as Louis* thinks them) has reconciled us to the presence of a certain portion, another untried, unproved, arrives. Think of the defenselessness of our community, composed as it is chiefly of women. Think, my dear brother, of what will touch you as nearly as any thing—that it will probably drive Jane to a removal from Stockbridge, and keep all who have a choice of residence from going there. Brother Theodore was quite displeased with the view we all took of the matter—by *all* I mean Robert, Elizabeth, George, and myself; but he has received a remonstrating letter from Susan, and has written to Louis to suspend his subscription. What does your son Theodore think of the matter? and what may be the amount of the probability that the project will be carried into execution? We are all rejoiced that you are coming to town. My best love to all, and, with the most earnest prayers that you will not aid or abet the building up of this charity, I am, as ever, yours truly,   C. M. SEDGWICK."

---

* Louis Dwight, a cousin of Miss Sedgwick, long connected with the Prison Discipline Society in Massachusetts.

Miss Sedgwick to Mr. Robert Sedgwick.

"Stockbridge, September 11, 1832.

" MY DEAREST ROBERT,—I received your letter last night by T. S. P., who arrived here at 8 o'clock, only thirteen hours from New York. This is an annihilation of space of which our forefathers never dreamed. And what would the Indian of three centuries ago say, who probably considered it the work of a lifetime to find his way through the various tribes that intervened between him and the great waters? * * * * L. did not go till this morning. However, I do not think she lost yesterday, as it was one of the most golden days ever breathed upon this earth, and I devoted almost the whole of it to rambling over the hills and by the river-side with her and F.—myself almost as much a child as either of them. L. has what I consider one of the most fortunate gifts—an exquisite susceptibility to the beauties of nature. She is the most delightful creature for a scramble."

Miss Sedgwick to Miss K. M. Sedgwick.

"New York, December 9, 1832.

* * * * "Oh, my beloved child, how lonesome it is here without you! If you could have seen how I felt in filling the drawers, and the various nooks and crannies that you had occupied, you would have pitied me. * * * * You have grown from being my pet to be my companion and friend, and from filling that little snug cabinet-corner in my heart you have diffused yourself over my whole existence, and what can I do without you? But I am not without you; you are present to my thoughts—always in my memory of the past, and hopes of the future. * * * * * It strikes 11. Good-night, my beloved Kate. Good-night to all the dear dwellers in Lenox. * * * *

" 7 *o'clock A.M.* What a glorious morning! It is strange,

but true, that I never missed the country—quasi-country (I tremble at my temerity in using a crumb of the learned tongues in such a presence)—as I do this year. I long to have my eye rest on those mountains. I had rather see the muddy roads, even, than the pavements; rather stumble down to Debby's in the dark than go by lamplight; and the brick walls make my eyes sore. I meant to have written a farewell note to your dear mother to thank her for hers, and to tell her how sadly I was disappointed not to see her again. My tenderest love to her and to father; tell him I hated to untie the cords that were the sign to me of his last labor of love—last of what a host!" * * * *

Miss Sedgwick to Miss K. M. Sedgwick.

"New York, January 31, 1833.

"MY DEAREST KATE,—You will, I know, be disappointed at receiving no intelligence from me this week. Mr. ——! the very mention of his name gives the explanation of all delays. Our packets of various kinds, after awaiting him for weeks, were put into his hands last Saturday—bundles, letters, notes, and all; and when nothing else could detain him, his evil genius appeared in the shape of gout. When he will go time only can decide. I dare not venture to re-claim the things to go by the colonel, for I am sure he can not take them; and when Mr. —— does go, they will go safely, and no man on earth is so generous in this way as he. He is like the horse that had but one fault under heaven —he never would *go*. I have been all day sitting with Mars-ton, getting a smart handkerchief made for a party, and no old miser could have groaned more than I have over the cost of satin, blonde, etc., outwardly and inwardly. I have thought of at least the hundred and one good uses that I might have made of the money. Your Aunt Lizzy, whose energy worked me up to the extravagance, sits by and says,

'Nonsense ; you'd think nothing of it if it were for Kate.'
Ah ! that alters the case. 'For Kate !'—ah ! there I feel the
old-fashioned love that decked 'in silks and jewels sheen.'
Can not you see my room, the table, the old plaid cloth, the
writing-desk, the medley of portfolios, books, and manu-
scripts, here a little bit of satin, there a bit of tulle, and poor
Marston deep in the mysteries of piping and folds ? I was
sorry you were not here for the fancy-ball at Berteau's. * * *
L. was very prettily dressed, but not in fancy. Her mother
told her she sent her as an American lady, a character Mrs.
Trollope would think the most fanciful of all." * * * *

Miss Sedgwick to Miss K. M. Sedgwick.

"New York, February 8, 1833.

* * * * "I wish you would read Mercutio's description
of the fairy's car that causes dreams, and then could imagine the effect Kemble gave it by his recitation. It seemed,
as he delivered it, as if one brilliant conceit after another
flashed through his brain.

"We had a person to pass the evening a few nights since
who is a kindred spirit of Mr. Tuckerman.* He is a mechanic, a jeweler—Mr. Joseph Curtis. He has about thirty
boys, who all live with him. His object is to have them
well taught their trade, and well educated in other respects,
and to have vigilant moral education going on. They have
a republican self-government. They select juries from their
own body, and always submit to the verdict rendered. During the cholera he determined it was best to keep up the establishment. One of the boys had a dramatic turn, wrote
dialogues, then a little play. Some of them were fond of
music, and others had a taste for drawing, and made some
scenery. Among them they got up private theatricals, and

* Joseph Tuckerman, the well-known philanthropist and missionary
at large in Boston.

when all the rest of the city were flying, or in consternation,
they were well and gay, did their day's work, and had their
regular evening-school, and their occasional theatre. Tell
your Uncle Major this. Some of the boys learn French and
Spanish. He has journeymen whom he credits $50 a week.
He is one of the most interesting philanthropists I ever met
with. Simple, apparently *quite* free from vanity, benignant,
and acute, but uneducated, which he deeply regrets. I have
enough to fill a folio about him. He is at present engaged
in a plan for instituting an efficient moral police for the
whole city." * * * *

Miss Sedgwick to Mrs. *Frank Channing.*

" New York, February 12, 1833.

* * * * "We have had a droll time getting up a society
in our Church. I do not think it is within a woman's prescribed destiny to do any public duty. We are, some of us,
very ridiculous persons in full light. After claiming rights
and surrendering them, caballing and diplomatizing—no, I
will not ; I am betraying the secrets of our order, and we
ought, for our own dignity, to be as secret as the Freema-
sons.

"We are just now in the full flush of excitement about
Fanny Kemble. She is a most captivating creature, steeped
to the very lips in genius. You will not see her till the middle of April. Do not, if you can bear unmixed tragedy, do
not fail to see her Belvidera. I have never seen any woman
on the stage to be compared with her, nor ever an actor that
delighted me so much. She is most effective in a true
woman's character, fearful, tender, and true. On the stage
she is beautiful, far more than beautiful ; her face is the
mirror of her soul. I have been to see her : she is a quiet
gentlewoman in her deportment." * * * *

Miss Sedgwick to Mrs. Watson.

"New York, Feb. 20, 1833.

"We have been very gay of late, and excited by the enchantress Fanny Kemble. I owe her some delightful hours, when I have felt something approaching to the enraptured feeling of youth. There is no sensation more delicious than that you experience from the mastery of genius, that restores for a moment the flexibility of youth, and fires and melts you at will. She is a most gifted and accomplished creature, and very graceful and attractive in her manners. Her father is a gentlemanly man and fine actor, but he has not her moments of inspiration. She resembles E., and at first you would not think her handsome, but her face has the whole range of human expression."

Miss Sedgwick to Rev. Dr. Channing.

"New York, May 20, 1833.

* * * * "I have been particularly desirous to ask your advice in relation to the publication of a MS. article sent to me by Sismondi to translate. He is very anxious that it should be disseminated and *read* here. It is a very interesting communication on the emancipation of slaves. We have been at a loss whether it were best to make a pamphlet of it, or to attempt to get it into the North American. I have hoped that you might, if your health permitted, write a review of it, as it is a subject that transcends almost every other in its importance to the interests of humanity—that great *best* cause to which it is your happiness to be devoted."

In the summer of 1833 Miss Sedgwick made a journey to the Virginia Springs in company with Mr. and Mrs. Robert Sedgwick and a charming young friend.

Miss Sedgwick to Miss K. M. Sedgwick.

"Richmond, Va., June 18, 1833.

"My dearest Kate,—I have just finished a letter to
your father, and am beginning a journal to you, to be written more leisurely. The boat we were in yesterday from
Norfolk was delightful. Imagine how different from the
North River boats—not more than fifty passengers, almost
every one of the respectable order ; a little cabin on deck
for the ladies, a sort of lounge or boudoir, furnished with
three delightful sofas, low chairs, a Boston rocking-chair,
and mirrors enough for a party of Circassian beauties, which
certainly we were not, bating F. C.

"Richmond is a pleasing-looking place as you approach,
and, from a distance, does not look unlike Albany. The
Capitol, an imposing edifice, is on the summit of the highest
of the three hills on which the city is built. There are some
very handsome houses, but, for the most part, the town has
a dilapidated aspect. Yesterday morning a nephew of our
friend Mr. Randolph—'Randolph of Wilton' (this is their
feudal manner of designating the proprietors of their great
domains)—called to see us, and invited us to take a drive
six miles to his estate of Wilton. His parents are dead,
and this young man—a fine specimen of Virginian character, his face expressive of frankness and generosity, and his
person of the fearless, bold habits of a country gentleman
and sportsman—has succeeded to the estate. We went in
a carriage, and he on a fine blood-horse, and his cousin
Harrison, on the best horse he could get, attended us. The
estate comprises 2196 acres of land on the James River,
and about one hundred and fifty slaves. The house is of
wood, and more than a hundred years old. The spacious
wainscoted rooms, the high ceilings, the broad staircase and
fine hall, give you a very magnificent idea of the grandeur

of its former proprietors, who so long ago **had an establish-ment that wants** nothing but a *fitting up* to vie with **modern elegance.** But such ruin !—broken-down fences, **a falling piazza,** defaced paint, banisters tied up with ropes, **etc.** At the gate we were met by two little slave urchins whose limbs were scarcely covered with **rags.** The walls of one of the apartments was covered with ancestral paintings. The Wilton Randolphs being the eldest branch, they have all the pictures. The slaves fancy this room is haunted, and it is a common punishment for the young offenders to shut them up in this spectral apartment. There are some fine old trees on the place, two superb catalpas, and I should think many beautiful walks, but a pouring rain prevented our see-ing any thing except from the house. The family **burial-**ground is on the estate. There are a few pieces of modern furniture, but the general aspect of the house is that **of a** forlorn ruin. The gallant young proprietor has, however, an ample fortune, and is going **to** put it in complete order, and, as it is, he gives *déjeûners* and balls. He pressed us to stay and take a ' snack' (a lunch), but we returned after wander-ing up and down the long arcades, and taking the Virginia beverage, a *bona fide* ' mint julep.' * * * *

"There would be much, my dear Kate, to interest you here. There is nothing, of course, offensive in slavery as **we** see it in this hotel. The servants are well dressed, civil, and accomplished in their way. I have, as yet, seen noth-ing on the table different from ours except their varieties of corn-bread and cakes. They have chickens, but they are not bigger than pigeons. Their raspberries are nearly gone, and apricots are ripe. The streets are not paved nor light-ed. No slaves are permitted to be out after nine. The houses are not numbered, nor the streets known by their names ; their only directions are this side or that side the Bell or the Eagle. The slaves that **I see** about the streets and in the country **look to me downcast or** surly, but this may be fancy." * * * *

Miss Sedgwick to Miss K. M. Sedgwick.

"Warm Springs, Bath County, Va., June 26, 1833.

"MY DEAREST KATE,—Here we arrived this morning **a little** past nine. It is the first in the line of springs in this mountainous country—a basin scooped out of the mountains, and guarded and fenced by them on every side. In coming from Cloverdale this morning—but stop! just fancy us at Cloverdale, **after a** most fatiguing ride of sixty miles, fully equal **to a hundred in** our country, over sands that, for the most part, we should consider impracticable there—called before three on a **rainy, dark** morning, to resume our traveling over roads that **we** were told were worse than any thing we **had seen!** **Twelve** passengers were our complement, and we broke our thorough brace three miles on our way, just **as a** fresh shower set in! Half a dozen negroes **were** summoned; we all alighted except Aunt Lizzy, who never leaves **her seat;** the coach was pryed up, a chain, made for **the** wheel-shoe, substituted, and we came on safely. The **coachmen** and horses **are** most excellent throughout the **country.** After jolting our lives out, we struck a very fine turnpike which crosses the Warm Spring Mountain, a branch **of the** Alleghany. We ascended for four miles, winding up **a** road resembling the ascent of the Catskill, but affording glimpses of far more beautiful mountain scenery. When **we** reached **the** summit, or, as they call it here, the 'Notch,' the grandest **scene** my eyes ever lit on, save Niagara, was under my eye. An amphitheatre of **deep,** *deep* glens below, mountain rising over mountain, one stretching beyond another, some in conical peaks, others in soft, wavy lines, and others broken into fantastic shapes, the sunbeams here and **there piercing the dark,** flying clouds, and giving **to the** whole scene the effect of a painter's light; and the most beautiful point of all, a shower streaming from the clouds over one of the peaks, like Niagara etherealized. If we were heathens we should have imagined it the descent of a god, but, being Christians, dear Kate, it appeared to us one of those ineffable forms of beauty to which the Divinity had said, 'Let it be,' and it was. We forgot all our fatigues, anxieties, joltings, and hair-breadth 'scapes, but it was such a brief pleasure that I am going up the mountain again this P.M. to enjoy one more view of it. * * * *

"We found a delightful breakfast awaiting us, and fine venison steaks. Venison is the staple meat of this part of the country, and is not like the dry, half-fattened, uncooked meat that our Epicureans feast upon. The country taverns of Virginia are the beau ideal of inns, shaded, quiet, and clean, with the greatest abundance of the prime luxuries of life, and, above all, attendants good and plentiful. This is one good of this horrid blight of slavery, which seems to me far worse since I have seen it. The Virginians resemble strikingly our plain, country, New England people. They are better-mannered, more frank and cheerful. Our land-lady here—Mrs. Fry—looks like a respectable farmer's wife of Lee; her cap and gown must have been cut somewhere about the paper factory. Their house—the only one here —is as unpretending as Deacon ——'s, but abounding in comforts. They have a fashion here which is peculiar to the Virginia Springs. We are lodged in cabins about forty yards from the main building. F—— C—— and I occupy one of two apartments. I am now sitting by a door that opens upon a green field bordered by the mountain. This may be inconvenient in bad weather, but the quiet retirement is delicious, and so is the separation from all the bustle and slam-banging of a hotel like Lebanon. Below the main building is the great bath. It is inclosed by a sort of rotun-

da as much as **thirty feet** in diameter, and this filled from
four **to six feet deep with the warm water,** at a natural tem-
perature **of 96 degrees.** No warm **bath can be more** delicious ; **the water** is bubbling about you, and, instead of the
beautiful Princess Zorahayda, you may imagine a thousand
water-spirits dancing and sporting about you." * * * *

Miss Sedgwick to Dr. Pomeroy.

"White Sulphur Springs, July 3, 1833.

"Tell **the** girls that F. and I are in great hopes that one
of us has captivated an Orleans planter who has some dozen
sugar and cotton plantations. The favorable symptom on
my side is that he confides to me all his lamentations over
his ' dear first wife' (her miniature is actually under my pillow at this moment) ; but then he is at a very *suitable* age for
me, which a widower is apt to think the most unsuitable in
the world, so I fear F. will get the plantations. This region
is an inestimable gift to the Southern people—such a cool,
delicious, invigorating atmosphere. It makes these liver-
colored men at least think of youth and roses. Robert has
just been up to my cabin to say that we proceed up to the
Salt Springs to-morrow morning. He has ascertained that
'**the Lexington road** can be traveled " with faith"—bad as
the Purgatory hills are—but that the devil can't get through
the Valley of the Shenandoah ;' so we shall probably go
from Staunton to Fredericksburg, City of Washington, and
home ! Blessings on the word. Love to all. Yours as
ever,   **C. M.** SEDGWICK."

Miss Sedgwick to Mr. Robert Sedgwick.

"Lenox, September 15, 1833.

* * * * "How happy must you be to hear nothing but
good of your children ! L. is a charming creature. I have
hardly ever seen a child of such promise. This is not flat-

tery or exaggeration. Should she live, I trust she will be a creature of rare intellectual and moral superiority. Her affections are strong and tender. Truth (which seems to be the foundation of moral power and dignity) is not only with her a principle, but it is an original constituent of her character ; and with this, which is rare, she is imaginative. She has that spirit of poetry that gives a soul to nature and a charm to feeling. Her aunt thinks she has remarkable capacities for acquisition. She studies her Latin 'con amore.' It would delight you to see how she is beloved here, and the intercourse she has with her uncle, who mingles with the natural affection of his relation to her a sort of playful, lover-like fondness, inspired by her individual character. E. is an excellent boy, and, I think, deriving great advantages from his residence here. Whatever the country may be to girls, it certainly develops the character of boys much faster than town can. Other things equal, the boy who is partly educated in the country must be superior to the town boy. This driving, riding, harnessing (E. can partly harness the horse), taking care of the cow, feeding the pigs and the chickens, are some of the best lessons in education. It seems to me a great blessing in yours and Charles's condition that this arrangement in relation to your children can be made with such mutual advantage. It is delightful to me, who stand in an equal relation to the children, to see them growing up more like brothers and sisters than cousins. God grant that that affection, which was our most precious inheritance—which has been the sweetest blessing of our lives, may continue long after we have ceased to watch over it. Elizabeth is an admirable woman, and every day improving in her qualifications for the task which she so heroically performs. My dear Kate is this day thirteen years old. I feel deeply thankful for the blessing she is and has been to me. Few ever arrive at the threshold of woman-

hood with brighter prospects. * * * * We have had the religious *agitators* among us lately. They have produced some
effect on the factory girls, and such light and combustible
materials. One of the fanatics, being met by Blum, asked
to take a seat in his wagon. He began an exhortation by
asking him if he were a Christian. B., who had no other
idea of a Christian than as contradistinguished from a Jew,
took fire. He said it was very 'extrordinaire question—
certainement, he was a Christian.' 'Do you read the Bible
every day?' 'I read it as often as is profitable.' And, repeating the conversation to Ashburner, he said a man might
travel from one end of France to the other without such an
impertinence as being asked if he were a Christian. We
had an interesting religious address from Mark H. (who has
taken orders) a few evenings since. It was almost free from
sectarianism, and dwelt on topics that were familiar and affecting to the dwellers within the circle of our mountains.
How much our preachers might gain by touching those
strings within us which are attuned by an Almighty hand!"

*Rev. Henry Ware to Miss Sedgwick.**

"Cambridge, January 31, 1834.

"My DEAR MISS SEDGWICK,—It was some time last year,
or last month, that I said I would write you a letter; that I
do it now, and not a month hence, is to be considered by
you as more wonderful than that I did not do it three weeks
ago. My performance always marches in the rear of my
purpose.

"My first wish was to secure the use of your pen in the
composition of a volume for the Sunday Library, with a view
to which I wrote you a year since (nearly), but was prevented from sending the letter by a new scheme which came

---

* This letter induced Miss Sedgwick to write "Home," the first in
the series of her minor works.

into my head, and in which I should wish to have your aid. That scheme I had at length given over, but have now, within a few days, returned to it again ; and when I have laid it before you, I beg you will give me your advice about it, and say whether you will give your aid to the first or the last. It is a scheme for offering to the public an exhibition of the practical character and influences of Christianity, illustrating its principles, its modes of operation on the heart and character, and the manner in which men may avail themselves of its power and peace. This may be done, it seems to me, in a series of narratives, between a formal tale and a common tract, so as to present to view an image, a portrait of the Christian religion according to our understanding of it, and at once enlighten readers by a familiar exposition of principles, and improve them by a display of their modes of operation. In a word, I fancy that a succession of *Illustrations of Christianity* might be made to do as much for religion as *Illustrations of Political Economy* for that science ; or more, I fancy that the nature and efficacy of *faith*, the doctrine and duty of *regeneration*, the whole theory of the *religious life* in education, in the *relations of life*, in temptation, etc., etc., might be thus developed to great advantage, and more efficiently than in many sermons. What should you think of such an undertaking? Will you take part in it? Will you tell me your mind respecting its feasibility, etc., etc. ? My idea is that several persons might be found who would each write one or more numbers, and that they should be published monthly. Another idea has been that you should be persuaded to undertake the whole—which I hardly dared to propose, and therefore mention last, that it may not come to you abruptly, and that it may hold the place at the top of the climax, which always belongs to the best suggestion. You could hardly be engaged, I think, in a more useful service, or one of deeper interest. Will you think of it seriously, and relieve my impatience to learn the result as soon as may be? For, though dilatory myself while a subject is in my own keeping, I am apt to be in a hurry when it is out of my hands. Very respectfully and sincerely, your friend and servant,   H. WARE, JR."

Journal.

"*April* 29, 1835. I have read Fanny Butler's book, most of it with intense pleasure. It is like herself, and she is a complex being, made up of glorious faculties, delightful accomplishments, immeasurable sensibility, and half a hundred little faults. Let those find them and mark them who have an appetite so to do. I have not. * * * *

"*Saratoga Springs, July* 1, 1835. Here am I again at this most vapid of all watering-places, but I have come, not for pleasure so called, but for that in which to me is included all pleasure, and happiness, and comfort, and joy, and whatever has a *pleasurable* name—my dear Charles's health. * * * * A more leaden *batch* of women I never saw; nothing of the brilliancy of fashion, and nothing of the charm of nature and individuality. They have gone just far enough in civilization to obscure nature, and not far enough to polish it. The varnish is on, the last touches not given. Well, I care not for myself, though I would fain leave the drawing-room and gossip with the laundresses under our windows. * * * * Mrs. R. told a good story to-night of a down-Easter, who, being charmed with her waltzing, begged her to repeat it, and said he "would make it up to her," taking her for a stage *artist.* The man was honest. * * * *

"*Stockbridge, August* 9, 1835. Miss Martineau and her attendant have paid their last visit to our valley. I intended to have been diligent in taking notes of our extraordinary guest, but the time was so filled with quickly-succeeding pleasures that it passed without any written record. She

was here eight days. She has just returned from her Southern and Western tour. She had been honored, praised, and
homaged, not to say worshiped, by the great as well as the
small. No woman has ever, perhaps, received so rich a
recompense of reward, and why? I think, because her spirit and influence have been in harmony with the spirit of the
age—because she has gone with the current. She has devoted God's good gifts to the use of his creatures. Other
women have shown as powerful a genius as hers, Mrs. Barbauld, I think, superior; Miss Edgeworth, more various tal·
ents, and a fuller demonstration; Mrs. Somerville, higher
attainments in science; Mrs. Hemans, a more exquisite gift
in the loftiest department of imagination; and Mrs. Jameson, a more general cultivation, a richer imagination, and
the power of embodying her own rich thoughts in a more
poetic, more drawing-room, if not as vigorous a style. But
Miss Martineau, with a single eye to general good, has, with
the light of philosophy and religion on her path, devoted
herself, not to the intellectual amusement or advancement
of the gifted and educated, but to make bread more plentiful
in the husbandman's dwelling, and to still the cry of hunger
forever in the poor man's cottage, and with the bread that
perisheth to give him that which cometh down from heaven.
It is this that makes us all cry to her, Hail, thou favored
among women! * * * * Her dress is simple, unexpensive,
and appropriate. Her voice is too low-toned, but agreeable,
the suitable organ of a refined spirit. Her manners, without any elegance, are pleasing, natural, and kind. She seldom speaks unless addressed, but in reply to a single touch
she pours out a rich stream. She is never brilliant, never
says a thing that is engraven on, or *cut in*, to your memory,
but she talks on a greater variety of topics than any one I
ever heard—agreeably, most agreeably, and with sense and
information. She is *womanly*, strictly, with sympathies fresh

L

from the heart, enthusiasms not always manifestly supported by reason, now and then *bordering* on the dogmatical, but too thorough a lover of human rights ever, I think, to overstep the boundary, and she is, I think, not conceited— no, not in the least, but quite aware of her own superiority, and perhaps a little too frank on this point. But this may be from a deficiency instead of excess of vanity. She is a genuine lover of nature, a person quite superior to the miserable little traveling vanities of her forerunners. She never remarks on our conventional manners, and usually adopts them ; for instance, she eats her egg out of a glass, holds her fork in her left hand, and eats a hearty dinner without grumbling, at one o'clock. We had some delightful drives together, when Nature, too, seemed paying her its beautiful tribute. She expressed herself as nauseated with slavery; as having seen, or rather been let into, its demoralizing tendencies by the communications of the Southern ladies, who, she says, are bewildered with the perplexities of their condition. She likes the Western people. But I perceive that, like all travelers, she is liable to false judgments from one-sided views. * * * * The most interesting part of her character is the sincerity and earnestness of her religion, her lively, effective faith, her knowledge of the Scriptures, and her delight in them as the records of her best friend. How few of us read them even with the interest with which we read a letter on *common topics* from one we love. I was to have joined Miss M. at Boston, and accompanied her to the White Hills, but Mrs. B.'s visit intervenes, the season is getting late, she can not put off, and I can not hasten, and so I lose this delightful opportunity of going up to the high places to worship with her.*

"*Lenox, September* 5, 1835. A little circumstance occurred

---

* Miss Sedgwick's views of Miss Martineau's character were in some respects painfully altered by subsequent developments.

to-day, so characteristic of Charles, and so illustrative of the happiness of the disinterested course, that 'meet it is I set it down.' As we were sitting at dinner expatiating on the *intense* beauty of the day, Mr. Parker proposed a ride to Stockbridge. Charles eagerly accepted the proposition, and was evidently anticipating as much pleasure as a ride in *perfect* weather with an agreeable companion could give him. Presently came a little urchin with a request from Mrs. W. for the horse and wagon. Charles made some inquiries as to the when and where she wished to go, but could obtain no satisfaction. I remonstrated against his lending the horse, and said, petulantly, that if he would only be just to himself, I did not care how generous he was to other people. He went off to see, as he said, how the matter stood, and end, as I was sure he would, in giving up the horse. In returning from our twilight walk we called at Mrs. W.'s, and such pleasure as she and the children had had, such gratitude as she expressed! She had asked one of the little children going down whom she loved. She replied (more heedful of the source of her pleasure than most persons), 'Mr. Sedgwick.' Charles had his reward. He had made five, great and small, rationally happy, and the best of it was, he was the happiest of all. * * * *

"*Monday evening, September* 14, 1835. We have attended the trial of poor young Benjamin Collins, a youth who, in a moment of passion and intoxication, killed James Bevin, or, as he was familiarly called, 'Uncle Cobe Beaver,' who seems to have been a sort of tame outlaw, one of those domestic wild beasts that hover on the skirts of civilization. The witnesses are the very lowest of our population, their language a dialect peculiar to themselves: for instance, I had the *temptation* to go, for *intention; I exposed*, for *supposed;* made a *hilt*, for *halt; sluiced* and *slung*, for *tipsy.* * * * *

" Collins's case was terminated yesterday, and the verdict

of manslaughter rendered. Poor fellow! and yet it was the
best we could hope for him, as the 'law and the testimony'
were against him—the *inflexible law*. This innocent youth,
who, as his brothers say, never had murder in his heart, excited much interest—the victim, as we feared he would be,
of an accidental meeting with a gang of outlaws. His two
brothers, men of good reputation and habits, sat near him,
and must have been a most merciful support to him. Cobe
Beaver, as it was testified, was a most ferocious, tiger-like
wretch in his aspect; 'an untamed, two-handed man,' said
one of the witnesses; 'a hairy, swarthy savage,' said another, 'that I should have thought myself justifiable in taking an axe to defend myself against.' What a lesson! this
man, in the midst of his drunken comrades, was knocked in
the head like a bullock by an inoffensive, peaceable strip-
ling of nineteen! Collins's brothers came to see me this
morning. I like them—good-hearted young men. A curious instance of the remains of a spark of heavenly fire amid
the ruins of human nature came out in the course of the
examination. It appeared that when Beaver fell, Tone (Anthony), his son, stood near Case Brazee. Tone was so
drunk that, though he was not more than two rods from his
father, he fell in getting to him. When he got to the body,
he fell on his knees beside it, screaming, 'Jesus Christ! my
father is dead!' and then, pulling over the body, kissed the
face!

"The attorney general mentioned an interesting case here,
recently tried. A man, whose moodiness and sulkiness (and
nothing else) had for some time indicated insanity, shot his
wife. The only witness on the trial was a most interesting
little girl, a child of twelve. She told her story on the stand
with considerable composure after being most kindly questioned. When she came to that part where she said, 'I was
sitting by my mother; my father came in with a pistol in his

hand, pointed it at my mother, and fired it,' she stopped. 'And what then?' asked the examiner. She hesitated, and, clasping her hands, burst into tears, and replied, '*My mother died.*'"

Miss Sedgwick to Mr. Charles Sedgwick.

"Boston, October 21, 1835.

" I believe, dear Charles, I was waked by the inspiration of Boston, for I was wide awake with the first ray of light, and up and dressed betimes, and, in the interval before breakfast, have time to relate to you our divers adventures, beginning, however, by telling you that we arrived most comfortably at 6 o'clock last evening at the railroad dépôt in Boston. Blessings, say I, on the inventors of railroads, which shorten distances, lengthen life, and save wear and tear of body and mind. The cars here are as large as a good-sized parlor, and nice stuffed chairs, each holding two persons, give them a most comfortable aspect. Every fresh experience confirms my belief that K. and G.'s stage arrangements are the worst in the country. With no extraordinary reason for delay, the coach did not arrive at Stockbridge till after 11. We then proceeded toward Becket, stopping and lingering at every inn on the way, doing errands, etc., and finally drove up to Chaffee's after 2. In turning up that sidling approach to his step with a heavy loaded coach, the driver gave one of the professional whirls round, and we had just a flash-of-lightning gleam of our fate when we were *whacked over.* Thank Heaven, no one was materially injured. Mrs. Minot got a severe bruise on her forehead, and one eye is now nearly closed, and the blood so settled around it as dreadfully to disfigure her, but there is, I believe, no injury to the eye. Mr. Davis and I, and I believe the rest of the company, escaped without even a bruise, and so the matter will pass, as the woman assured me at the inn it was no uncommon thing, and no fault of the driver's, which the driver loudly reiterated. Whose fault, then, is it? Mrs. Minot suffered a good deal of pain during the day, and excessive anxiety, in consequence of the jarring of her nerves. We left B. just at sundown with twelve passengers, a fair lot of customary baggage, a box of carpenter's tools, and a box containing black walnut extending the whole length of the coach; the consequence was, that at the first ascent the horses refused to draw. We were unloaded, and it was some time before they started; and, to finish the whole, when near Springfield, the coach-wheel was run off a bank, and, in consequence of its being top-heavy, we should have inevitably been again overturned (as the driver said) if he had not stopped at the precise instant, turned us all out again, and righted his coach. All this, and plenty of time during our evening's drive, gave me leisure to reflect on our highwaymen, who, with sleeping consciences, rob you of rest and peace of mind (who would not rather be robbed of his purse?), often break your bones, and not unfrequently take your life; and, in addition to these crimes, inflict hardship on the poor defenseless horses, that, as there is no human tribunal to take cognizance of them, will, *I guess*, make a pretty heavy part of future settlement. But now to the agreeable. I was pretty tired at Springfield, but, going supperless to bed, I felt very well in the morning, and the coach not starting till 6, and Mrs. Minot feeling *travelable*, we did not hesitate to come on, and reached Worcester five minutes before the cars started, making no pause for dinner, which was greatly in my favor, as I seem to want nothing but to be compelled to live without eating."

The last sentence refers to a severe attack of dyspepsia with which Miss Sedgwick had just been afflicted. "She had always," says her niece, "a vigorous constitution and

very hardy habits ; but, owing probably to her early ignorance and disregard of the laws of health as we now understand them, she suffered all her life (till past fifty at least)
from very severe sick headaches. In her youth she was
treated for them in the 'heroic' style then in vogue. Bleeding, blistering, and calomel were freely used, to her great
detriment, as she was afterward convinced."

Her hygienic knowledge, though late learned, was so well
seconded by these "hardy habits"—the result of her early
country training—and by her remarkable elasticity of body
as well as spirit, that her health, in the latter half of her life,
was generally good, and she gave the impression of uncommon bodily ease and activity.

Journal.

"*Boston, October* **28**, 1835. The funeral was at **12**, attended only by the relatives and nearest friends of the family.
This is as it should be. Dr. Channing made the prayer.
His filial sentiment to the Deity always impresses me ; it is
not merely the confidence of a child to the father, but the tenderness that is most commonly felt to the mother ; he is like
the child who throws himself on the mother's bosom, sure
there is repose there, and love enough for all his wants.
His voice is the most tranquillizing sound I ever heard. I
think, if my passions were in ever such a storm, it would
calm me as if it were the very organ of the Spirit of Jesus.
* * * *

"*November* **2**, 1835. Went to hear Mr. Taylor at the Sea-
men's Bethel, and there was something like what the ministrations of the Christian religion should be—the poor, the ignorant, the neglected taught wisely and with a glowing zeal.
Such men should be the messengers of Christ ; they are
sent. His heart is full, and his lips touched ; he does not
scourge his brains by midnight lamps, but comes panting

with good news from his Father's house to the wandering and wayfaring children. * * * *

"*November* 11, 1835. Miss P—— gratified me very much with the testimony of an intelligent, **orthodox** factory girl about 'Home.' She said, if **they would spend their** Sundays in Lowell, as recommended in this book, much **good** might be done. This is **better** than the opinion of half the **ministers** in New England. She said a gentleman had said **to her, 'I must go home and read the** Linwoods. It takes me half an hour to read a page. I should as soon think of galloping **through Paradise.' I like to save** up these bonbons when **they are so very sweet.**

"*November* 13, 1835. Expect my blessed brother to-day, who, I fear, will scarcely give me a blessing for bringing him in these November winds. **How the heart** clings to its dearest **loves! how common** *surface* **pleasures** fade before such **a happiness as seeing** Charles! **Do not blow, ye** winds! **Shine out, fair sun, on this** best **being that walks** beneath **thy beams!** * * * *

"Called at Commodore Downes's, a man with a face sealed by Heaven, and a life that bears out the seal. 'A good father, son, husband,' said the severe-looking Captain Percival to me. This Captain Percival spoke of the *bewitching* interest of a sea life, which he has pursued for forty-three years. 'A man feels independent aboard his good ship, when he's only to snap his fingers, and three hundred men stand before him, ready to do his will.' My sympathy was with the three hundred men that had to obey, not the *one* that could command. * * * *

"Had some *very* agreeable conversation with Judge Story, in which he repeated to me an old message from Chief Justice Marshall. 'Tell her I have read with great pleasure every thing she has written, and wish she would write more!' Had some talk with Judge Story about death. He did not agree with me that Calvinists died with more animation than Unitarians. He said his father (a physician) said young people died most happily, middle-aged with most clinging to life, and old people with most regret.

"*November* 20, 1835. Went to see Mr. Wells's school at South Boston. The house is on a point of land that runs out into the bay, and gives an extensive view of it and the islands that stud it. Wells looks like a fine old Italian picture, and has a voice that is a fit musical organ for an harmonious soul. From his childhood he has loved boys, and for many years devoted himself to their moral advancement. He has now the care of ninety-eight! and keeps them orderly and happy. If they do not learn quite so much Latin, Greek, etc., of him as at some noted schools, they learn infinitely more of what is of more important and universal application. He said he had read all my books to them, 'all except the last, and in that were some bad words, some profanity!' This is a criticism worth remembering, and in the next edition I will correct, wherever I can, without sacrificing what is essentially characteristic, this fault. * * * *

"*New York, December* 17, 1835. More than a fortnight has elapsed since I came to this city—a fortnight of my short remainder of life passed away without exertion and without fruit. I have been met by every one with congratulations about my book, which has, I think, proved more generally acceptable than any thing I have before written. My *author* existence has always seemed something accidental, extraneous, and independent of my inner self. My books have been a pleasant occupation and excitement in my life. The notice, and friends, or acquaintance they have procured me, have relieved me from the danger of ennui and blue devils, that are most apt to infest a single person. But they constitute no portion of my happiness—that is, of such as I derive from the dearest relations of life. When I feel that my

writings have made any one happier or better, I feel an
emotion of gratitude to Him who has made me the medium
of any blessing to my fellow-creatures. And I do feel that
I am but the instrument.

"This is the 17*th December*, 1835, a day that will long be
memorable to our citizens, a day of the most sudden and
overwhelming calamity. Last night, a little before 10, brother Theodore came in, and said there was a great fire near
Robert's office, but, as the wind set the flames away from it,
neither apprehended any danger. When we went to bed at
half past 11, the fire appeared to us going down, but it still
raged ; the extreme cold—mercury at zero—accelerated the
flames. The hose froze, the firemen were impotent, the
flames spread through the packed warehouses of the wealth-
iest portion of the city. It was a scene of helplessness, be-
wilderment, and dismay. The flames were only arrested by
blowing up houses—they are not yet extinguished. It is a
scene of desolation, from the ruins of the noble exchange to
the water's edge. There is no calculating the extent of
loss—the direct loss—the loss from suspension of business,
and payments, and interruption of industry, and the failure of moneyed institutions. All the fire-insurance companies being bankrupt, the city is at this moment uninsured.
The town presents a curious spectacle ; churches and private houses turned into receptacles for merchandise ; carts,
coaches, going in every direction filled with boxes, cans, and
every species of commodity ; the sidewalks filled, guardians
stationed over them, companies of firemen, and companies
of militia and beggars, their shoulders covered with piles of
half-burned blankets, bits of shawls, and pieces of calico.
Some fine morals may rise the phœnixes of this fire. The
poor may learn that, though the individual rich man has no
humanities, his wealth—Heaven-directed—must wander to
the poor ; and this striking manifestation of the instability

of human possessions must, in all our eyes, amazingly de-
preciate their value. The *millions* of yesterday, the *ashes* of
to-day.

> "'Take physic, Pomp :
> Expose thyself to feel what wretches feel,
> That thou may'st shake the superflux to them,
> And show the heavens more just.'

"'This,' said a man, looking on the falling warehouses,
'is a leveling system with a vengeance!' * * * * Two miserable nights since the fire ; my room is a watch-tower
whence I watch the brightening glare of the flames from the
ruins as they rise and fade away on the cold sky. The city
is virtually uninsured, the firemen disabled, the hose so
spoiled that very little of it is in a usable state, and the lights
now threatened with extinction from the injury to the gas-
pipes. No wonder that hearts beat when we are repeatedly
wakened by alarm-bells, and cries of fire from tremulous
voices.

"*Sunday, 20th.* Last night the Philadelphia firemen, who
had generously come to our assistance, kept watch, and I,
relieved from duty, slept quietly till daylight. Mr. Ware has
preached an excellent sermon to-day from that most appo-
site text, 'Who hath done this unto this great city?' * * * *
It is beyond any desolation I ever witnessed, and in the
hazy, murky atmosphere of this day, where you do not see
the bounds, but only fragments of walls dimly defined in the
mist, it appears a world in ruins. Here and there are still
dense masses of smoke and flames issuing from cellars where
there must be at this moment piles of merchandise consum-
ing. And is this mass of ruins all that remains of the exul-
tation, projects, and hopes of the past week, the vulgar pride
of the mere merchant, the natural complacency from the
rich results of years of skill and toil, the plans of the young
husband and father, the hopes of the lover?" * * * *

Miss Sedgwick to Mr. Charles Sedgwick.

"New York, February 4, 1836.

"With characteristic confidence in another's ability and success, you put me up to making money out of my poor brains. Depend upon it, this is a dream. I may go on as I have, if my life and health continue, earning a few hundred dollars a year, and precious few too; but, while such a novel as Rienzi can be sold here for fifty cents, as both editions are, I can not hope, even if I could call to my aid the 'cutest stock-jobbers of Wall Street, to continue, by any play upon the gullible species, to make much out of my handicraft. However, I am as eager to make money as you are —to make it for me. Harper promised, as soon as the French question was settled, to make me an offer; but, I suppose, our President-king's offer to his brother sovereign must first be known to have been accepted. I trust Harper will choose to repurchase the copyrights that have been sold, and then, for better or worse, we shall have it in our own hands. I shall have a successor for Home out in the spring. It will not be nearly as good as that, and it is far from being as strong an illustration of my subject (poverty and riches) as I hoped to have made it, but then I think there are good notions, suited to the American market, in it. To-day I have begun my souveniring campaign. I hope to get something from the English edition of the Linwoods. That book has, I believe (but am not certain), been translated into French.

"*Friday morning.* The weather continues as cold as ever —beautiful, bright winter days. But for the thought of the suffering around us, of which we are ignorant, I should enjoy them, for there is such stimulus in the air, and such a consciousness of the warmth from the good fire that seems to fold you around like a blanket. I asked my little Sunday-scholars the other day to tell me what the rich had that they had not and yet desired. One of them replied, 'A good warm fire *all* day!' Their luxuries are our necessaries."

To the same.

"July 4, 1836.

"MY DEAREST CHARLES,—I can not return my child to her parents without sending my blessing for the delight and comfort she has been to me. I am glad she is to be released from the unhappy condition of human existence in midsummer—life in town; and pray take notice, all concerned, that I have not detained her for a moment. She has made all her own arrangements without the slightest interference on my part, and this, considering she is somewhat like the breath of my nostrils, I wish to have credit for. I do not feel so badly at being left as I thought I should. I am very well, and have plenty to do, as I am going to begin to-morrow on my second Home : Harper prints it. I suppose I shall just about get through with it when the time for my departure comes. If all goes well, I do not see why I may not be with you by the first week in August. A month is not very long. This is a most odious day here. All our liberty seems made into gunpowder, and noise to be the only expression of rational beings."

To the same.

"New York, July 22, 1836.

"DEAREST CHARLES,—I thought I mentioned in my last that I should leave here the first of August, which will be a week from Monday next. Now, much as I delight in having you with me, I would not, on any account, have you come down just to give me that indulgence. If you have any *pretext* of business ; if you want to do Robert good, and see him look as Christian did after he threw off his burden, and see L. tranquil and prospering in all respects ; and if you want to get some family stores, or if you have any reason besides making a spoiled child of me, then pray do come. * * * *

"I am daily sitting at Ingham's, and want you very much to see the picture ; and I want you, too, to come to some conclusion with Harper. I want you to speak or write to them before the publication of 'The Poor Rich Man,' to urge upon them the policy of letting it be known to their correspondents in the New England country towns what sort of a thing it is, intended for popular consumption, that it may at once be for sale in the country towns. If I should continue the series, this may be important. Ask Webster if he will take fifty, or less, as you think proper, to sell on commission."

Journal.

"*May* 19, 1836. Sir James Mackintosh has an admirable argument for fictitious writing which all who have dabbled in it should cherish : ' Fictitious narrative, in all its forms, epic, poem, tale, tragedy, romance, novel, is one of the great instruments employed in the moral education of mankind, because it is only delightful when it interests, and to interest is to excite sympathy for the heroes of fiction—that is, in other words, to teach men the habit of feeling for each other.' * * * * Sir James says, after reading Coleridge's '*Friend*,' ' It is not without ideas of great value, but it is impossible to give a stronger example of a man whose talents are beneath his understanding, and who trusts to his ingenuity to atone for his ignorance. Talents are, in my sense, habitual powers of execution.' * * * *

"*May* 27, 1836. What a portion, and valuable portion of my life has passed without scarcely a record ! What Sir

James MacIntosh calls the incorruptible honesty of dates is a witness against me.

"*June* 6. The Farm near Philadelphia.—Here am I again, just where I began this book. I have since reeled off fourteen knots of my unproductive life—alas! alas! Charles, Kate, and myself, after having waited two days upon this northeaster (which has now blown, with rain, *every* day fifteen days), came on Saturday, and found the weather, like all other bulls taken by the horns, not very mischievous.

"I have just begun the printing of the 'Poor Rich Man,' etc. May it go forth on its mission with God's blessing! My next task is to write the memoir of Lucretia Davidson, which will be little more than reforming her mother's most affecting record. This has brought me acquainted with her mother, and her sister, a flower from Paradise, and soon to bloom there.

"*Newport, Sept.* 12, 1836. After a railroad ride, and a slight accident, which scared the life out of a poor woman who had selected the *safest* car because the preceding night she had been jostled off the track, and her unlucky husband's nose broken, we arrived at Troy, where, after telling her woes, she said, 'I was in the spirit of prayer all the way. I am pious, and my husband, and my daughter (a little sprout), and my niece, this young woman, but my son is not, and for him I was in prayer.' The son was an unlicked cub, who looked as if he had still less notion of piety than his pious mamma. Piety, in her acceptation, is a certain password which is a sure passport to heaven. She by no means meant she was devout and beneficent. * * * *

"*Stockbridge, Oct.* 12, 1836. I heard a touching anecdote last evening of J. F. She is just three; her mother has been dead nine months, her infant sister died one month after. She was ill (J.), and awoke sobbing, and saying to Miss W., 'I want to see my mother and Isabella.' 'They are in

heaven, J.' 'What are they doing there, Miss Abby?'
'Singing praises, I believe.' 'Can't we sing too?' 'Yes, J.;
what shall we sing?' '"How glorious is our heavenly
King!"' and thereupon the little creature, in the darkness
and silence of the night, raised her voice, and fell asleep
singing! Did not her accents mingle with her mother's?
Was not her mother's spirit hovering over her pillow? Surely where there is a tender and loving child there is heaven.
* * * *

"*October* 17, 1836. Came to Lenox to enact housewife in
my sister's absence, and I find I can do little else. * * * *
Yesterday I illustrated the day by making a batch of pies
among other domestic offices, and then, in spite of the Puri-
tanical clouds that hung over us, I had a delightful ride on
my Lady Blanche. To-day I have 'pottered an immensity,'
read some of Ford's plays, and the review of Henningen's
War in Spain. Sad, sad is it that in a Christian country, so
called, at this era, there should be something worse than
savage barbarities, the cruelty of the wild man, with the coolness and premeditation of the civilized man. * * * *

"*Friday, March* 31, 1837, 11 *o'clock*. Just put the last word
to my first draught of 'Live and Let Live.' I hope it will do
some good. I do not expect for it the popularity of the
'Poor Rich Man.' It will offend some and shock many, but
I am satisfied that it is in the main right, and in the consciousness of having written in the hope of doing some little
good to the high and the humble, I commend it to God's
blessing.

"*May* 23, 1837. This has been an eventful and exciting
spring. When I came to New York in February, I found here
Foresti and Argenti, two of the Italian prisoners of state, who
had been in Spielberg—Foresti eighteen years, Argenti six,
Tinelli at Milan and Gradisca six. Foresti is now forty-five.
He is a native of Ferrara, and before he was twenty-one he

was prætor of his province. He is a man of a perfectly original character, an independent thinker. A strong love of justice and an inflexibility of opinion seem to me to distinguish
him. He is not obstinate nor opinionated, but, having once
thought out for himself, examined, and weighed, he seems as
certain of the result as if he had come to it by mathematic-
al rules. He is modest, and the tone of his voice indicates
a certain melancholy and gentleness that reminds you at
once of suffering and wounded affection. His face, too,
speaks of Spielberg. His spirit was never subdued by suffering, never calmed by the Christian faith which always has
a calm for the submissive sufferer. Of all the prisoners at
Spielberg, he was one of the three who did not there become
Christians. He has a strong religious sentiment, and a love
of his country that is almost religion. It is like the inextinguishable fond feeling of a child for its mother. This
man interests me deeply. In some points he strongly resembles my brother Harry, that dear brother who loved me
so much better than I deserved. There are moments when
the impression of this resemblance is so strong that I could
close my eyes and fancy my brother's spirit was with me.
Foresti, too, had a sister *Caterina*, whose name he never
pronounces without emotion. He is so true, so unfaltering.
Argenti is good-hearted, but a common material, and *very*
tiresome, poor fellow! Tinelli is a gifted man, with a brilliant intellect, a quick perception, and the figure and face of
a handsome brigand. He is irritable and impetuous, resisting a destiny that no resistance can even modify. His present intention is to go to Texas. He married the daughter
of General Battaglia, a man who commanded the Italian
troops under Napoleon. She is now ill, and living with her
old and rich father. Every obstacle will, as Tinelli expects,
be thrown by the government in the way of the expatriation
of his two sons. Castillia is my interesting correspondent,

and, as I believe, the St. John among these apostles of liberty. Confalonieri is the *distinguished* man among them, the man who sacrificed most to the cause, who endured with most dignity and gentleness, and who now shows himself a man that no circumstances can subdue, but whose spirit, like angelic spirits, makes all circumstances subservient to his progress. I have never seen any man who has so realized to me my beau ideal, the dreams of my youth, and the *sane* portraits of my maturity. I have always been fond of a sort of character-drawing reverie. When others build castles in the air, I fill them with tenants. I have imagined, but never before seen a man who seemed to me to have the tone of high breeding which, in spite of our democratic theories and principles, we associate with the old aristocracy, blended with that humility, respect, and tenderness for his kind which marks the Christian philosopher of the present day. He is enlightened, cultivated, but never theoretical or pedantic. Under the external of courtesy and deference in which most foreign travelers invest themselves, a certain consciousness of superiority, a certain contempt of us as parvenus, is betrayed, but not so with the count. He seems perfectly earnest and sincere, and inspires as unwavering a faith as if his soul dwelt in the transparent body Dr. F. recommends. * * *

"*May* 23, 1837. I have just seen, in an album of Miss Emily Ward's, two lines from Racine, written by Prince Louis Napoleon Bonaparte, the young man whom I have recently seen, and who is unpretending, sensible, and indescribably *ugly*. The words are happily selected by one of the Bonaparte race, whose chief has so strikingly illustrated them :

> "'Le premier qui fut roi fut un soldat heureux ;
> Qui sert bien son pays n'a pas besoin d'aieux.'"

Dr. Tuckerman to Miss Sedgwick.

"Boston, October, 1836.

" I will not attempt to conceal from you, my dear Miss Sedgwick, the very great pleasure with which I read the 'Inscription' in your little volume, 'The Rich Poor Man and the Poor Rich Man.' This morning Dr. Channing came into my chamber, where I have been since the close of August as an invalid. I put the volume into his hand, directing his attention to my name. 'Well,' said he, '*it is* an honor to have a book inscribed to one by such a woman.' And an honor I feel it to be, far higher than would be any mere gratification of ambition or of vanity. I have read this little book with increasing interest to its close. God has given you, my dear friend, a great power over the human heart, and most gratefully do I rejoice that this power is consecrated by you to the highest and noblest ends. You have entered upon a rich and boundless field—as boundless as the wants of our spiritual nature, and as rich as our capacities of never-ending moral improvement; and the 'sheaf' you have gathered and sent to me is of the purest wheat, which, I trust, will be for life-giving aliment to many a soul."

Miss Sedgwick to Rev. Dr. Dewey.

"Lenox, January 9, 1837.

" Nothing can be more simple than my days, which are about as much alike one to the other, and reeled off about as fast as the threads of a skein of yarn. I rise at dawn, by a fire—a roaring one, not imprisoned in a stove, but looking kindly on me, like an honest old friend. I take a fair two-mile walk every day, not by ' Shrewsbury clock,' but by an incorruptible mile-stone, with my Hebe at my side. Do you know what it is to face a winter's storm—to beat against

the gusts that sweep over these hills—to plow through the
unpathed snows? If you remember aught of all this, you
will give me credit for my resolution—more than I deserve,
perhaps, for I have my reward in unexpected renovation of
health, and in an enjoyment that I had forgotten or never
have known of the sublimity of these hills in their winter
desolateness, and in the poetry of the skies that have each
day as new an aspect as if they were a new creation."

Miss Sedgwick to Miss K. M. Sedgwick.

"New York, February 26, 1837.

＊ ＊ ＊ ＊ "Your uncle went yesterday to call on Frederigo
Count Confalonieri. He was very much interested by him,
and says he was completely overcome with seeing him. He
has had a horrible passage of three months. The *Houstri*-
ans sent an Austrian captain along who did all he could to
embarrass and confound them, and, but for the American
captain, Confalonieri says they never should have reached
this shore. Castillia was with him, having come on at the
first news of his arrival. We are to have a supper-party for
the exiles this week."

Miss Sedgwick to Miss K. M. Sedgwick.

"New York, March 8, 1837.

＊ ＊ ＊ ＊ "Mr. Joseph Curtis came to see me last evening, and told me that, in all his experience, he had never
witnessed so much good fruit from the publication of any
book as from that of the 'Poor Rich Man.' This *pleased
me.* I knew he would not flatter, and that, though he might
overestimate its merit, he did not grossly misjudge. I trust
my vanity is not fed by the praise of this little thing. I
think I understand the secret of its success. It is, like breadstuff, or like the satinets and negro-cloths, to be a little more
modest in my comparison, suited to the market, the thing

wanted. I have finished and sent off an article for the Token. I hope to have the religious article done to-morrow; after that comes the Magnolia. I gave up that speculating affair; it was too water-gruelly even for a souvenir, which requires as thin potations as a *hôpital des malades.* I received the other day a letter from England with a 'Forget-me-not' of last year, and a request to write for the next number."

Miss Sedgwick to Miss K. M. Sedgwick.

"New York, March 9, 1837.

* * * * "If I had fulfilled all my engagements this week, I might have given a picture of the variety of New York society. Monday evening, at Mrs. C——'s; Tuesday, Mrs. J—— B——'s; Wednesday, Thatcher Payne's; Thursday, Mrs. L——'s; this evening, Ferrero's;* to-morrow evening, Mrs. Follen's, to meet the Grimkés and an abolition party! I did not go to Mrs. C——'s to see the last specimen of an age gone by—wit and sagacity without education—and all the pride of rank, now obsolete and forgotten here, neither did I go to Mrs. L——'s, where there still survives a certain elegance, and all the stiffness of a *société choisie.* I am not strong enough to go out every evening, and, except when I have some such motive as pleasing the children, my inclination is as weak as my strength.

"*Sunday evening.* Immediately after church I walked up to *Smith Court* to see poor Francis Brown. Do you remember the black-eyed boy I used to call Daniel Webster? The poor fellow had his arm mangled in a paper factory in consequence of the drunkenness of the engineer. It was amputated immediately. He says he neither felt the crush nor the amputation. His poor mother said 'he got applause for his bravery, but it was more than I could look on. They

---

* Ferrero was an Italian dancing-master giving a ball for his pupils.

wanted to take him to the hospital, but I said *no;* a mother
has many a *soothe* that no one else has.'   I just got home
in time for dinner.   Foresti dined with us, and staid till *five*,
talking to Aunt Lizzy, and telling tales of the Spielbérg heroes that made me 'cry like a wretch.'"

"New York, March 17, 1837.

* * * * "Well, dear, we have seen Confalonieri.   Your
Aunt Lizzy let Argenti know that we had penetrated his in-
cognito, and the poor man thought that courtesy required
his coming immediately to express his profound sentiments
to the 'famiglia Sedgwick,' or, as Argenti says, it was his
duty, and 'duty is a besoin du cœur.'   Well, he came; your
aunt was alone; had just returned from her drive, completely *en dishabille,* the room all upside down with preparations
for the party, when this elegant count, six feet high, rang.
Katy being out, Diana (the cook) came pattering up.   'We
are all out,' cried Aunt Lizzy; 'for your life don't let any
one in.'   She heard an altercation at the door; thought it
was Foresti, who is her *cavaliere servente,* and did not care.
But presently Diana floated back, crying, 'I can't get him
out, I can't get him out!'   Well, he staid half an hour, talking French and bowing with his hand on his heart, she
speaking English, and when I came home I never saw her
so completely flustered.   She says her house is no longer
her own; that she never expects to command a moment
when an Italian may not rush upon her; that her dreams
are haunted by Forestis, Ferreros, counts, etc.   But she is
devoted to them, and more enthusiastic than even the ma-
niacs of the valley.   The next evening the count sent his
servant to know if he might be permitted to pay his respects
to the ladies.   I was going out, and your aunt said no; but
yesterday morning he came, and a very pleasing, high-bred

nobleman he is. He talks as if he had been in his grave
for the last eighteen years, and said that I could not conceive the feeling with which the events of that period strike
on a man, when the knowledge of them comes all at once
after his disinterment. His contemporaries are gone ; he
asks for one, and another, and another—'mort! mort! mort!'
He is fifty-three—looks sixty. 'He has very superior heart,'
says Albinola ; 'he has fortune, and he offers it *importunate-*
ly to the companions of his misfortunes.'"

' *Miss Sedgwick to Miss K. M. Sedgwick.*

"New York, March 25, 1837.

* * * * "I received two singular epistles the last week :
the one from old Mrs. S—— I will inclose to you by Mr.
Sergeant, who leaves here Tuesday evening, and I think you
will have some merry shouts over it. 'Various is the mind
of desultory man.' Another from one of Fanny Wright's
men : if I conclude not to take any notice of it, I will send
that too. He concludes a eulogium on infidelity by begging me to put 'more morals and less religion' into my
books. This morning I had a letter from Cincinnati, begging two autographs—one for a namesake, another containing an application similar to Miss Stansbury's ; a letter from
Sparks, announcing the publication of Lucretia ; and after
—best, though certainly *least* of all—the most precious little
note from Confalonieri. * * * * Our company to-morrow is
the count, Albinola, Foresti—bless him!—Panon, Anderson,
Bryant, Mr. Johnson, Dr. Follen, Theodore, and perhaps
Tinelli and Haggerty. Mr. Gallatin and Irving declined,
Irving going to the country."

Miss Sedgwick to Miss K. M. Sedgwick.

"New York, April 16, 1837.

* * * * "Have I told you how I liked Ellen Tree? I

have seen her only once, and then in Ion. She is a very charming actress, very perfect in all the delicate details and by-play. Her readings are beautiful ; she is free from affectation of every sort ; in short, she is, *after* Fanny, incomparably the first actress we have had, but so far after her that you can not measure the distance. Ion is poor in dramatic effect, but I can easily believe that in her range of playing she is even better than Fanny in the quiet and passive parts. We called on her, and were at home when she returned the visit. She is very charming, perfectly frank and natural, and courteous to every one, and has a face beaming with expression. If it were not for her immense handle of a nose, she would be very handsome. We had tickets to the College celebration, and went ; and such a jam I have seldom witnessed. You may fancy what a collection an Alma Mater would assemble who called together the progeny of fifty years, and all the collaterals of that progeny. 'Oh,' whispered Mrs. C—— to me, 'the worst of the American parties is that we must have the people !' Foresti told me last evening that he did not like liberal institutions, as he saw their effect here, for never, in any of the absolute or royal kingdoms of Europe, had he seen such aristocrats ! that a lady had said to him yesterday morning, she would that she were an empress, that she might say ' I will,' and be obeyed. Now isn't it a pity that silly women should give a stranger impressions ?"

Miss Sedgwick to Miss K. M. Sedgwick.

"New York, April 24, 1837.

" DEAREST KATE,—All my spare time yesterday was spent in concocting a report for a remodeling of our society, and I found it more difficult than writing a ' novel booky.' It is easier to get a heroine into a dungeon, and not much more difficult to get her out, than to decide how to impersonate persons and personify abstractions. We have come to the sensible resolve to have a school to teach little girls to sew, darn their stockings, etc., instead of a parcel of gossiping women meeting together to corrupt the 'less favored orders' by supplying them with ready-made garments. * * * * You can have little idea, who are surrounded by those who have been accustomed to live upon the fruits of their labor, of the confusion and dismay produced here by the general bursting of bubbles, and the consequent failure of the means of actual support.* The people are, as E. says, not *blue*, but *purple*. The panic pervades the community. The dry-goods' shops are almost deserted, save Stewart's, and you will see the line of counters, with clerks on one side walking up and down like so many ghosts, and no buyers on the other. Even Broadway, to use the slang phrase, *feels it*. This is the season, you know, of spring butterflies—the gay season of Broadway—but now it is almost as dingy as it was in the cholera season. Nothing is talked of but 'who has failed to-day?' and the buried carcasses of to-day are covered by the fresh ones of to-morrow."

Miss Sedgwick to Miss K. M. Sedgwick.

"New York, May 8, 1837.

"DEAREST KATE,—So late, and my weakly weekly not begun! A dress-maker converting the bag-sleeves of last year into the puffs of this; my hat on to sally out to Stewart's to make bargains and save a little rag-money by getting more necessaries than I *want*—a common illusion of economy; your mother, Rie, and Molly gone to the Narrows with Captain Delano; and the pleasant expectation of seeing Ellen Tree to-night in Beatrice—*voilà nos affaires!*

"*9th.* Ellen Tree is a charming Beatrice, but not the rich, keen Beatrice of Shakspeare—not the Beatrice of Fanny

---

* This was the winter of the great financial crash.

M

Kemble. I never **observed** till **last** night how truly, how nicely Shakspeare **has** marked the distinction between man and **woman in the** different emotions experienced by Benedict and Beatrice on the first mutual discovery of their love. **He is a** little shamefaced—conquered, but ashamed **to** yield —and yet has the manly feeling of generosity to the *weaker* **party.** She at once is touched with love, and you **see** through the sparkling the tender beam of a woman's **eye.** This was well marked by Miss Tree."

Miss Sedgwick to Miss K. M. Sedgwick.

"New York, May 19, 1837.

* * * * "I have been reading Mrs. Hemans's Life, and **am** disappointed in her. **She seems to me** to have belonged to another age of the **world**—to have been a Sappho or a Corinne—a creature of those times when the elect few had no sympathy with their race, when they were born for music and song, for *pas seuls* and *pas de deux*, and *not* to **be** linked in with their kind, to lean on the strong and sustain the **feeble.** **She** shows **how** inadequate sentiment is, how feeble **the theory** of beauty **compared** with that sense of duty, that **perception** and love of the image of God, which gives an interest to the meanest of our fellow-creatures, and a dignity to the commonest office of social life. In our practical, working-day world we can scarcely conceive such **an existence** as Mrs. H.'s. * * * * What I like least of all is a littleness of vanity that is betrayed in blowing off with a *gale* of contempt the incense offered to her. **She does not,** like an intoxicated mortal, snuff up the cloud of incense, nor, like a propitious or good-natured divinity, permit it quietly to ascend, **but** she betrays her wish for something more and better by her continual consciousness **and** contempt. Her **American** admirers come off with most mortifying proofs **of** *ennuyant* their idol. She evidently regarded them as **I** should

so many Chatham Street admirers. A good lesson to our travelers not to go lion-hunting. Toward the last her character became more earnest and natural. * * * * I am going off with L. and E. to visit our sewing-school children. My office is no sinecure, I assure you, but I like this ministry at large."

Miss Sedgwick to Mr. Charles Sedgwick.

"New York, May 24, 1837.

* * * * "Our agitations here seem to be pretty much over ; at least there is less of it on the surface.* Men have become accustomed to the new state of things, and, though you see many an anxious and many a despondent countenance, yet they no longer look amazed and on the brink of madness. How we are to get out of this hobble I know not ; but if we are true to ourselves, I am sure it will be, as the old women say, a *sanctified* Providence. The exclusive love of riches must abate when their uncertainty is so proven. Men must learn the worth of those acquisitions, those fountains of respectability and happiness that are independent of the fluctuations of the money-market—that a man need not look at the price of stocks to graduate his enjoyment of the caresses of his children, the pleasure of a good new book, or the enjoyment of nature on one of these exquisite spring days—that he need not speculate to relish a simple dinner—that Champagne and *pâté de foie gras* are not essential to his happiness, nor blonde nor Mechlin to his wife, nor Italian and music to his daughters. I wrote a little article for John O'Sullivan† called 'Who and What has not Failed,' which it seemed to me showed a great balance in favor even of the real bankrupts."

* Alluding to the financial crisis of 1837.
† Editor of the Democratic Review.

Miss Sedgwick to Miss K. M. Sedgwick.

"New York, May 30, 1837.

* * * * "Oh, Kate, I witnessed such a scene to-day! I heard Mme. Gérard* was ill, and went there. As **I went** up **the** steps, two gentlemen opened **a** window up stairs, and beckoned to a hackman turning the corner. Angélique came to the door, and said her mother was better; she had her bonnet on, and looked bright as usual. **I** asked her to go **up and ask** her mother if I could do any thing for her. She **came back** and beckoned me up. When I entered, Mme. G. raised herself from the pillow in a paroxysm of **grief,** and, stretching out her hand to me, said, 'Oh, made-moiselle, j'ai tant souffert! j'ai tant souffert! bon Dieu! bon Dieu! bon Dieu!' I looked round for an explanation, and poor Gérard was screwing up a little coffin, while the girls, evidently excited with the novelty of the scene, and the pros-pect **of** a drive, though to a *funeral,* were hovering round him. Not death could suspend madame's observance **of** politeness, **so** monsieur's office was interrupted for an intro-**duction to** me. It seemed madame had given birth yester-**day to** a still-born infant. She said that, through months of anxiety and pain, the expectation of having a child had sus-tained her, and it was a boy—a boy, so long desired by her husband, and Angélique, and Loo. A friend who sat by said, 'But you will live to see it is all best.' 'Ah! **mais je** suis mère, et je l'ai attendu avec une telle joie!' 'Oui, madame, mais l'homme propose et Dieu dispose.' These obvious truths fell as impotent as such consolations usually do. I could not help crying with her, there was something so sim-ple and true in her **grief,** though it seemed to me an inesti-**mable** blessing that the child was taken. Angélique is her **nurse. They** are obliged to move to-morrow, and Angélique

---

* An accomplished Polish lady whose husband was a political exile.

has packed every thing. 'Ah! my dear Miss S.,' said Mme. G., 'there is nothing like necessity.' Truly there is not. Angélique is ten or eleven years old! There was a German woman who looked like one of Scott's old women, and was all the time haranguing madame on (as I supposed) the inutility of weeping, and finally came up to the bedside, the little coffin tucked under one arm, and gesturing with the other!"

Mrs. Jane Sedgwick to Miss Sedgwick.

"Stockbridge, June, 1837.

"MY DEAREST KATE,—Never did so precious a morsel fall from your pen as your letter! I would not give it for all Redwood, Clarence, Hope Leslie, and the rest of those very precious books. It was just what I needed—what I longed for. Of all the abundant good gifts you have received with such liberality from God, there is not one for which you ought to be so grateful as the power of your sympathy. What would your genius do without it for those poor exiles, what for that host of children who are fed with your smiles, for all that crowd of poor in spirit who are the chief paupers in our community! What has it not done for me, my sister! I look to you with a certainty that every thrill of pain or pleasure will find its echo in your heart, and this sentiment often stands in place of society to me."

Mrs. Jane Sedgwick to Miss Sedgwick.

"Stockbridge, March 4, 1837.

* * * * "You, I know, will not be wearied with any details of our hero.* As soon as he heard of the arrival of Confalonieri, he came in, looking like a real seraph, or Gabriel, or any other nature that existed before the fall. 'Madam,' said he, 'my friend has arrived safe, and I come to re-

* One of the Italian exiles who was passing the winter in Stockbridge.

lieve my heart to you.' You may be sure it was all I could
do to keep from crying, there was something so touching in
the idea that this poor fellow could find nobody nearer than
myself to be interested in an event which filled his whole
soul with the deepest emotion."

Rev. Dr. Channing to C. M. Sedgwick.

"August 19, 1837.

" MY DEAR MISS SEDGWICK,—I can not, without violence
to my feelings, refrain from expressing to you the great gratification with which I have read your 'Live and Let Live.'
Thousands will be the better and happier for it ; thousands,
as they read it, will feel their deficiencies, and resolve to do
better. No relation is so little understood among us as
that of head of family and domestic. The false notions of
it which prevail in England, even more false, I suspect, than
are to be found on the Continent, exist here, in defiance of
the spirit of our institutions and of Christianity. Thousands,
brought up under this pernicious system, are wholly unconscious of the inhumanity (I use this word in a large sense)
with which those living under their own roofs are treated,
and, as a general consequence, the domestics carry into their
service no generosity or affection. Instead of feeling the
dignity of their vocation, that they are contributing essentially to the happiness of the family, and may render services for which wages are a poor equivalent, they connect
ideas of degradation with their work, and try to maintain
their dignity by jealousy of rights, resistance of imagined
encroachments, bad manners, and sometimes positive rude-
ness. No relation needs reform so much. Domestic happiness is too often sacrificed to the unfaithfulness of both
parties in it. Your three last books, I trust, form an era in
our literature. May you be strengthened to go on, and expose the errors in our social system."

Miss Sedgwick to Rev. Dr. Channing.

"Stockbridge, August 24, 1837.

"MY DEAR FRIEND,—I can not tell you how much your very kind letter has gratified and encouraged me. I thank Heaven that I am not now working for the poor and perishing rewards of literary ambition. Unattainable they might be to me, but, whether so or not, they are not my object ; and I think the time has gone by, or, perhaps, has not come to our country, when they are legitimate objects. With the great physical world to be subdued here to the wants of the human family, there is an immense moral field opening, demanding laborers of every class, and of every kind and degree of talent. Neither pride nor humility should withhold us from the work to which we are clearly 'sent.' No one can feel as I do the imperfection of the labor I achieve ; but I do gratefully feel that it is something done in the good cause, and such a Godspeed as yours, my dear friend, gives me heart and courage to proceed. There is much sin from mere ignorance, and I have been told by persons, in whom I could not previously have believed such ignorance to exist, that my view of the relation of employer and employed was entirely new to them. A gentleman asked an introduction to me, a very clever man, who has been the commander of a privateer on the South American coast, and who has rather better morals than could be expected from such a position. He thanked me for the light I had given him, and said he had always supposed the Irish were to be treated as you would treat slaves ! That slaves are the subjects of Heaven's equal laws he has probably yet to learn."

Mrs. Jameson to Miss Sedgwick.

"December 22, 1837.
"I can not allow your niece to go to New York without

a few lines from me, though the lines must be few, and not
worth much—not worth postage at least, yet they will tell
you that I love you and think of you, and never do think of
you without feeling glad and grateful to have known you, to
have you to think of and talk of. * * * * Farewell, and God
bless you, and keep me a little wee corner in that good
heart.   How full it must be !   How crammed and crowded,
unless it has an India-rubber capacity of extension—has it ?
Put me somewhere, stick me behind the door, any where, but
let me in."

In the spring of 1838 a sad reverse clouded this bright
season.   Mr. Robert Sedgwick was stricken with paralysis,
and the following year was passed in anxious and devoted
nursing, and in watching his gradual recovery.   In June he
was well enough to pass a short time at Rockaway, Long
Island, where the following letter is dated.

Miss Sedgwick to Miss K. M. Sedgwick.

"June 23, 1838.

"MY DARLING KATE,—Your aunt writes to your uncle
that you are to be in Warren Street to-morrow, provided the
weather is good, which proviso indicates that you are coming with Mr. B.   I hope so, and that when he has done the
good deed of getting you to Warren Street, he will fill up the
measure of his virtue by coming forthwith and bringing you
to Rockaway.   If he can't come, drum up some excellent
person who will—excellent, I mean, from the odor of sanctity which bringing you to me will steep them in.   As to their
other qualities, I will not stand upon them.   Your uncle will
probably, at any rate, remain here for a day or two next week.
* * * * My beloved child, I have set my heart on enjoying
with you your first sight of the sea-shore, the most sublime
of all the spectacles of this earth.   I do not enjoy the cli-

mate here ; it is too cold, and I miss the beautiful witnesses of God's bounty and love that are on our sunny hill-sides and in our fruitful valleys. But there is something here that brings you more into his actual presence, and when you turn from it you feel as if you were going down from the mount. Your uncle has had a delicious day. I do not think he has ever enjoyed his existence so much. His mind is in such a tranquil, grateful, and loving state—it seems to me so precisely the condition of a saint at his departure, that I really am at times awed as if I saw him standing on the threshold of another world." * * * *

Mrs. Jameson to Miss Sedgwick.

"Windsor, August 20, 1838.

"On the very day I left London to take up my residence here, Mr. Putnam brought me your letter. You are the dearest, kindest creature in the world, *that* is certain, thus to find time to write to me in the midst of your anxieties, distresses, and avocations ; but believe that I am grateful. And then your letters, no matter how short, how long, are sure to contain some word or words which lie on my heart like balm for hours and days afterward. You have this instinct of benevolence and affection in a degree that no other possesses—no other that I have ever known : how can I but love you dearly? * * * * Have you yet begun the tale you mentioned to me ? Which is to be next in your series? Can I make any arrangement with my publisher for you, by which you might have some share of the profits of the English editions of your books? You are *very* popular here. I sent you, or rather Kate, the third edition of one of them, for I thought it would please her."

Miss Sedgwick *to Mrs. Frank Channing.*

"Lenox, October 24, 1838.

"My dear Friend,—Your letter gave the truest pleasure to one and all of us ; the storms and toils seemed passed, and your minute account of your pleasant haven was delightful.* Some of us even began to feel an incipient emigrating fever—to feel the pressure of the burdens of our present social existence very heavy upon us ; however, I rather think we shall go on fretting in the old harness, and content ourselves with rejoicing in your joy, or, if that is a stronger term than the case will warrant, in the cheerful resignation with which you have given up, and the energy and hope with which you are striking your roots into a new soil. How true it is, and how constantly illustrated in all the various experience of life, that, as Fénelon says, when ' we cease to resist we cease to suffer.'

"*3d November.* My dear friend, I was but well started in my letter to you when I was interrupted, and it has had the fate of interrupted letters. For the last ten days we have been quite absorbed in preparing to part and parting with our dear and good friend Castillia. He and others of his companions have returned on the faith of the amnesty granted to political offenders, but already they have been annoyed by the vexatious tyrannies that clog even the mercies of the Austrian government. Castillia's affections had struck such root among us that his recall seemed like a second banishment—a most hard case—and I am sure he has left behind a family that might be mistaken for weeping parents, brothers, and sisters. Such is the effect of pure goodness. It finds every where *missionary ground.*" * * * *

* Mrs. Channing had removed with a married daughter to one of the Western States.

Mr. Robert Sedgwick was so much better by the following spring that Miss Sedgwick, with his wife and eldest daughter, and accompanied by two other nieces, went with him to Europe, in the hope that rest and change of scene would prolong his life. They were gone nearly two years, and he was so far restored as to enjoy the journey himself, and to contribute to the enjoyment of the others with much of his former wit and geniality.

Another severe blow fell, however, during their absence, upon the whole family in the loss of Mr. Theodore Sedgwick, a man of great nobleness of character, who died, not exactly in the melo-dramatic manner described by Miss Mitford, but from an attack of apoplexy, with which he had been for some time threatened. In several members of this rarely-gifted family the physical brain seems to have lacked the toughness necessary in the agent of such brilliant, energetic, and untiring spirits.

Miss Sedgwick to Rev. Dr. Channing.

"New York, April 17, 1839.

"Many, many thanks to you, my dear friend, for your kind letter, which is truly a parting blessing to me; and pray accept all our thanks for your letters of introduction. Is it not a privilege to have made a name which opens the doors of strangers to your friends as well as to yourself? It is not true that love always casts out fear—probably because some imperfection attaches to it. We erect barriers about ourselves, and then are all our lives complaining that we can not overleap them. In my early intercourse with you I participated the vulgar feeling in relation to your superiority, and was awed by it, not knowing that that was the very circumstance that should have drawn me nearer to you, and to a more frank intercourse. I hold your friendship as one of God's best gifts, and imperishable."

Miss Sedgwick to Rev. Dr. Dewey.

"Kronthal, September, 1839.

* * * * "What a lifetime I have lived since the night
dear M. gave me a shelter—since that ominous shake of
your hand at the Astor House ! What have I not seen ? It
would be more to the purpose to tell you what I have seen.
The great literary people in London—thanks chiefly to F. B.
—Hallam, Sydney Smith, Lockhart, Milman, and many others. I had a glimpse of the fashionable world too ; was
twice at the Marquis of Lansdowne's, and at a grand soirée
at the rich Miss Coutts's ; saw a great deal of Rogers, who,
by-the-by, is one of the most agreeable men I have seen,
living without fear of boring or being bored, the prevailing
terrors of London society. Oh, it is a horrible arena, where,
like trained gladiators, each awaits his turn to spring into
the place of action and display his strength, while others
are breathlessly waiting to succeed him. It is a state of society that belongs to a high degree of civilization—but the
civilization of savages. I would rather die at once than to
struggle as they do there to maintain an existence in *society*.
But these are only reflections afterward ; for the time, it
was all delight, animation, and *fatigue*. My six weeks in
England were six weeks of prolonged surprise and amazement. What a magnificent country it is ! What perfection
of physical cultivation, and beauty, and comfort ! How essentially the people are like us ! I never had a feeling there
that I was out of my land except when I was reminded by
some question indicating that we were about as dim and
distant to them as heaven—or that other place, which I hope
few among them will ever make acquaintance with. I saw
a good deal of Joanna Baillie, and had very nice talks with
her about you and Dr. Channing. She is a most sweet lady,
with an intellectual freshness that is striking at her age, and

a mental strength that would be striking at any age. Our friend Mrs. Jameson I found much quieter and happier than when she was in America—as she should be, when, instead of fighting against the demons of ennui, she is quietly doing womanly domestic duties. What a safety-valve they are!"

On her return home, Miss Sedgwick published "Letters from Abroad to Kinsfolk at Home," and tells the story of her travels with so much grace and such graphic description, that not much is left to say about them except what her modesty prevented her from intimating—the warmth of respect with which she was received both by old friends, known personally or by letter, and by those to whom she carried introductions, many of them the people best worth knowing in England and on the Continent. Thus the party found active social interest in almost every place they visited. The Sismondis were affectionately devoted to them at Geneva ; and foremost in Italy to welcome them with open arms were the friends of the exiles to whom they had shown such generous hospitality. "Wherever we went," says Mrs. Minot, "Aunt Kitty, then fifty years old, was the most eager, the most enthusiastic, the most untiring of the party, and put us young girls to shame by the zeal with which she would rush out before breakfast, at any place where we passed a single night, to see the most of it before leaving it."

It is touching to see, in Miss Sedgwick's record of the journey, how the sweet humanity of her character found exercise every where, from the little girl on the Alpine pasture "who had got her arm about my neck," and Baptiste, the honest Switzer boy who intrusted her with a letter for his brother in Buenos Ayres, to her feeling on the play-ground at Eton, and in the ship's cabin where Nelson died, and her genuine sympathy with the newly-crowned Queen of En-

gland ; and then, again, in her wise tenderness for Clotilde
Poggione, the young Italian girl of whom she gives so lovely
a sketch at Magione, and her compassion for the poor peas-
ant of Foligno lamenting over his dead ox with grief both
deep and loud.

On their return, it was found that the relief to Mr. Sedgwick's health had been only temporary, and within a few
months he died, leaving a chasm in his sister's life to be
bridged only by religious faith now, and the hope of reunion
hereafter.

Miss Sedgwick to Rev. Dr. Dewey.

"Lenox, September 7, 1841.

" MY DEAR FRIEND,—Your letter was a comfort to me—
the greatest comfort, I think, that words from a friend could
give me. You understand the heart. You know I do not
want to be told how many reasons I have not to grieve.
This is cold—selfish. I always feel it so ; but you make me
feel that I am *not* alone—that I am not unreasonable in feeling my sorrow to be as much as I can bear. You speak to
me of my lost treasures as knowing their worth—their worth
to me. God only knows how I have loved my brothers—
the union of feeling, of taste, of principle, of affection I have
had with them. No closer tie has ever weakened that which
began with my being. I have no recollection beyond the
time when they made my happiness ; our lives have flowed
in one stream ; and with Robert so long, that now I feel as
if half my life were buried in his grave. To others I know
he seemed a broken man, but not so to me. I saw through
the clouds that had gathered over his mind—the mind was
there, and that which was the best part of him, as it is of
all God's creatures, his affections, were more constant and
tender in their manifestations, and to me he often turned
with the enthusiasm of our younger and happier days ; he

fell back upon the worn, accustomed channels that had been somewhat clogged by newer ties and business cares. We had a thousand points of pleasant memory and sympathy— we have been each the chosen friend of the other. From the time of my father's death he added to every thing else a father's care of me ; and, till his sickness, I never gave a thought to my affairs, any more than if I still lived in my father's house. But he is gone—gone when I did not expect to lose him ; prepared I never should have been, for I should have clung to him while there was one gleam of intellectual life.

"The time will come, and soon, I trust, when I shall think with a cheerful gratitude of his firm faith in immortality, of his calm waiting for death, of his preference to it over diminished life, of the comfort of his last days, of his pure unspotted life in the midst of the overburdening world, of his unswerving fidelity, of his exquisite tenderness, of our near reunion ; but now I can only feel as a child that is torn from the arms of its mother—my tears must flow till my sick soul is relieved. I look upon my *only* brother with a fear that he will vanish from me while I look at him. My dear friend, I am pouring out my heart to you. Do not— no, you will not think any thing unkind of me. I dread now your going away. Weakened as I am, the lights seem all going out. I shall certainly come to see you—at least I think I shall, for I trust in one fortnight I shall rise from this blow, and be able to see you without distress. I have lived to feel a vivid memory, such as you express of Harry, most precious to me. You do not know, I trust, what it is to have those whose memory to you is as fresh as if they had left you yesterday almost forgotten by the world. Your friendship will last me while I live, will it not? I have had praise and flattery, and I have not been insensible to them ; but God knows they never weighed for one moment against affection, and I would give all the world could offer to me of them for one tone of Robert's voice.

"God bless you. Ever yours, truly and affectionately,

"C. M. SEDGWICK."

Miss Sedgwick to Rev. Dr. Dewey.

"New York, Feb. 26, 1842.

* * * * "You see our papers, no doubt, and will—won't you?—rather partake than laugh at our 'entusymusy' about Dickens. No doubt there is some admixture of egotism, and those poor vanities that always explode in noise and nothingness ; but, for the most part, it is a genuine senti- ment, an involuntary effusion of gratitude, an instinctive hero-worship. It marks the age and our country, for it per- vades all classes. After making a journey from Boston here like a royal progress, being welcomed with shouts, visited by thousands, sculptured and painted, serenaded, dined in pub- lic and private, and fêted in every mode, he has the discre- tion and good sense to decline any farther public demon- strations. It is a proof of his power that he has stood as steadily in this focus of sunbeams as if he were in the cool shade of private life. He has a *beautiful* face—his full dark eye (if your wife asks the color, tell her whether it be brown, hazel, blue, or gray, is yet a mooted question) is, in truth, the spirit's throne of light. Some of our exquisites say he is not high-bred—has not the manners of the *haut ton ;* and, to tell you the truth, if I had met him coming out of the Carlton, I might, at a hurried glance, have taken him for one of the officials of the establishment, but I should certainly have stopped to look at him, and should have thought, 'My friend, what gifts are lost on you !' But he does not want good-breeding ; he is cordial, natural, and, thank Heaven, unconventional. It was beautiful to see, at his dinner here —of which I, with about fifty other of womankind, had the

good fortune to be a spectator—the heartiness with which he took the laurels from his own loaded brow and covered Irving's, so that for the moment we all forgot, as he meant we should, that it was somewhat faded and shorn of its early glory. But I have no more space for him."

Miss Sedgwick to Rev. Dr. Dewey, then in Europe.

"Lenox, June 12, 1842.

* * * * "You are near the Sismondis—friends that I love and honor with my whole heart and mind. I fear, from their own accounts, that the shadows of age are gathering about them, but surely the sun of love and benevolence, that made their home the pleasantest resting-place in all our pilgrimage, must still give it a touching charm. Do, if you see them, as you certainly will, tell me just how they are. They seem to me like my own blood relations. I have lately got a notion that those persons toward whom we feel a sudden and lasting sympathy have been dear to us in some previous state of existence—that they are to be in a future one (if we are accounted worthy of the resurrection!) I do not doubt ; but that they have been can only satisfactorily explain to me the sudden, unreserved, unquestioning mingling of mind and heart, without the tedious process of 'getting acquainted.' Thus it was with the Sismondis, and with a few (very few) other pre-existing relationships. You will laugh at my philosophy, but can you give me a better?

* * * * "I believe I have never sent you a letter without some sad cloud over it, and now you will be sorry to hear that my dear sister*—long your true and earnest friend—is soon to be removed from us ; and yet, though I shrink—sore with wounds—from the stroke, I would not hold back her spirit from the joy that awaits it. She said to me a few evenings since, 'My heart is one echo to the infinite goodness of my Father!' and so it has been through a life of

* Mrs. Watson.

vexing trials that would have cooled any love, exhausted any enthusiasm but hers. Mr. Watson was turned out of office by the 'reform,' and lost his little pittance of a clerkship, and they came to Stockbridge to live on her slender means. There, at my sister Susan's, F. was married to L——y, and thus my sister's heaviest care relieved. She had been unwell, and very ill at intervals all winter, and since the marriage she has steadily declined. She is now confined to her bed, and suffers only the general distress which is involved in utter prostration. F. is tenderly devoted to her, and we are all by turns her nurses, so that she has those alleviations which her affectionate nature most needs."

Miss Sedgwick to Mrs. Frank Channing, after the death of Dr. Channing.

"Stockbridge, October 14, 1842.

" My DEAR FRIEND,—Your letter was a great comfort to us. We are anxious to learn all that can be learned of the closing scenes of a life so momentous, so cherished. You, dear Susan, have lost the friend that filled a relation to you that none else can. He has been always a bright point to us all ; to you an object of unceasing hope, joy, and happiness, and so is he now. Few persons seem, even to our imperfect vision, so completely to have fulfilled their mission. His spirit lives, to teach, to elevate, to comfort. It pervades his works, and they will go to thousands—millions of this and future generations. He was sent with a divine commission, of which he felt the power ; and now, though departed, he surely is not dead. This summer was a special mercy to us, and most grateful am I for it and for all its circumstances. What a prophetic close to his ministry was that most eloquent invocation !* I should never have known

---

* At the close of an address which Dr. Channing delivered at Lenox, on the 1st of August, 1842, the anniversary of Emancipation in the British West Indies, and which is included in his published works.

the affectionateness, the divine *simplicity*, the gentle playful-
ness of his character but for the intimate intercourse of this
summer. What a blessing that you were here, that you were
with him that last week, and that William, so dear to him,
should have received his last commission—a holy ordination
it seems to me."

Miss Sedgwick to Rev. Dr. Dewey.

"Stockbridge, November 20, 1842.

* * * * "You have heard of Channing's death, and perhaps that he passed the summer at Lenox, and in a free and
happy condition of mind and healthy state of body, such as
he often said he did not remember to have enjoyed from his
childhood, and such as his friends had never before observed. He seemed to have thrown off every shackle, to be
rid of his precision, and he was so affectionate and playful
with the young people that those who had not before known
him wondered any one should fear Dr. Channing! He liked
our anti-conventionalism—our free ways of going on—our
individual independence of thought and action; he enjoyed,
as if he had come home to his father's house, the forever-
changing beauty of our hills and valleys, and he went away
with more than half a promise to return to us next summer.
Before he reached Bennington he took the cold of which he
there died. Died! what a word, with its mortal associations,
to apply to the passage of such a spirit into the immortal
world!"

Besides the death of Mrs. Watson, other family afflictions
had saddened the last years. The loss of Mr. Charles Sedgwick's oldest son, a young man of uncommon promise, and
of a lovely daughter of Mrs. Jane Sedgwick, were deeply felt
by their aunt, and these were followed by an event which,
although happy and desirable, was at first to her, as it is to

tender mothers, almost as great a shock—the marriage of
her favorite niece, who in 1842 became the wife of William
Minot, Jr., of Boston, and from that time lived in Boston or at
Woodbourne, her beautiful country home in West Roxbury.

Miss Sedgwick to Mrs. K. S. Minot.

"New York, April 16, 1843.

"DEAREST KATE,—*I* feel it to be an age since I have
written to you. I have been waiting for a private conveyance. Postage with the three cents tacked on to the shil-
ling is quite too severe. I can put nothing inside the cask-
et to compensate for this heavy tariff upon it. Feeling the
cruelty of this heart-tax, I have been writing a little story illustrative of this evil of postage, when I would have been
writing to you, my darling. I think I feel more heavily every day my absence from you. I can not bear the rolling
away of month after month, the rising and setting of suns,
without one glimpse of that dear face that has so long been
my sunshine, my repose, my every thing. I do not complain. God knows that, stripped and solitary as I often feel,
I have still far more than I deserve ; but the companions of
my youth, the dearest friends of my happiest years, are gone
—from the *dearest* left I am separated—but it is useless,
even to you, to breathe the oppression of my soul. * * * * I
went last evening, through a fog that made our streets almost impenetrably dark, to hear Mr. Gallatin on the subject of the red-line map. To *hear* him was impossible, for,
though his mind is unscathed by the wear and tear of more
than eighty years, his voice is too feeble to fill a large chapel (the chapel of the University) crowded with people. I
suppose his exposition of the case will appear in print. I
passed an hour at his house a few evenings since, and heard
him talk with great clearness and interest on the subject.
There has been discovered, among the papers of Mr. Fay, a

very interesting document—a map used by the commissioners when they made the treaty, more favorable to us even than the late treaty, so that I trust one dark shadow, at least, will pass from our escutcheon. It is enough to have public officers defaulters, and our states and merchants bankrupts, without having our statesmen as tricky as tin-peddlers. Mr. G. reminded me of our dear Sismondi, and a fervent kiss he gave me at meeting seemed for an instant to blend his identity with our beloved friend." * * * *

Miss Sedgwick to Mrs. K. S. Minot.

"New York, June 6, 1843.

* * * * "Your mother went off yesterday P.M. in good heart and health, and in a cab packed as one packs a trunk. You could just see her face above a sea of things. I sent a basket of plants, taking it for granted that those already there that escaped seven months of steady freezing weather were sealed up under June ice.

"Anne A. and I went a few evenings since to take a sociable dish of tea with Mrs. Banyer, and Fenimore Cooper dropped in. I rather think the light by which we see the world emanates from ourselves. He moves in a belligerent spirit, waging war with classes and masses, boarding and broadsiding his fellow-creatures. He maintained that his own country was below France, Italy, and even England in civilization, intellectual development, *morals*, and manners ; that we were going in every thing backward ; that in common honesty we were below any other nation. Being in the presence of Mrs. Banyer and Miss Jay, who sanctify the very names of Christian and saint, he attacked the whole class with man-of-the-world slang, and wound up with promising me a pamphlet of his, just coming out, which is to grind M'Kenzie to powder. With all this, he was good-humored, and talked strongly and amusingly. He is a perfect John **Bull in** shape, dimensions, action, even to the growl." * * * *

"Lenox, October 22, 1843.

* * * * "We seem just to have got into a regular, profit-**able** mode of life as the breaking-up is coming. I get about **an** hour to write in the morning, and have finished two 'drafts' since you went away. Your mother is reading aloud Alison **in** the afternoons, and B. has been reading some of Smyth's best lectures to us in the evening. He **is** one of those great **spirits that** stand on so high an elevation that he has an almost unbounded horizon, and, seeing all around him, measures exactly the proportion of things. With what noble justice, philosophy, and truth he opens the field of history to his pupils! What an antipode is he to John-Bullism! We perhaps have not read enough of Alison to judge him. He is evidently yet in the low and obstructed region of Conservatism, and he reads, studies, and writes history to **confirm** the judgment he inherited. Religion and government are cast in a certain mould in his mind—a divine form that admits no change or variation. He has an animated relation of events, and when he is not misled by his biases, **he** is a very agreeable writer. A familiarity with Sismondi rather gives you a distaste to such a historian as Alison. My criticisms are made between runnings into the kitchen to look after a variety baking, so I do not choose to be responsible for any absurdities I may chance to write. The last mail brought me a delightful letter from Mad. Sismondi. Delightful! Alas! it is all a requiem." * * * *

"New York, Sunday, December 31, 1843.

* * * * "Last evening was a Berkshire at the O'Sullivans'. Alexander Everett is staying with them. They are living in one end of the University, the prettiest rooms in New York, with pointed Gothic windows and paneled doors, and the loveliest silver lamps lighted with gas. The pictures of five generations of the O'S.s over the mantel-piece in little, encircling a Madonna portrait of M. and A.—in short, every thing in keeping with these most picturesque of all the moderns. Dr. F., who was there, and who harangued to me all the evening, told me that he asked Ole Bull if Paganini had been his master. 'No,' he replied; 'poverty, wretchedness, and despair were my masters—greater than Paganini.' They truly are the great teachers and preachers, and yet he who is greatest among us has little affinity with any of them—Mr. Dewey. I heard him to-day preach a very solemn discourse suggested by the closing year. Its admonitory truths came home to my heart." * * * *

Miss Sedgwick to Mrs. K. S. Minot.

"Lenox, February, 1844.

* * * * "I have had several letters from Fanny K.* I am very much struck with the progress of her mind in the last four years. It seems to me that the intimate intercourse with the brilliant accomplishment, the wit, and the instruction of London has wrought her genius up to the highest polish of which genius is susceptible, while her bitter experience, falling on religious principle, has matured the best parts of her character. Her eloquence in conversation is marvelous; we sat up sometimes till one, and to the last the vigor of her expressions, and the flow of rich, fresh thoughts delighted me."

* Mrs. Fanny Kemble Butler, with whom Miss Sedgwick had been recently staying in Philadelphia.

Miss Sedgwick to Mrs. K. S. Minot.

"Lenox, August 14, 1844.

* * * * " I gave a picnic party on the lake last week to
the little children, and we mustered, with those who came to
look after them and look at them, seventy-nine. It was very
successful. Who ever failed when children and summer,
freedom and green fields, were the elements of the festival?" * * * *

Miss Sedgwick to Mrs. K. S. Minot.

"Stockbridge, October 18, 1844.

* * * * "My arrival at Lenox was rather of the dismal-
est. The afternoon was lowering and dripping, and when
Chaffee dumped me down at the gate—bag and baggage—
instead of the multitudinous sea of happy human faces that
I left there, all was solitary, silent, and cheerless. I opened
the door to rooms *un-souled*, un-carpeted, and stacked with
chairs and tables in apparent mutiny; no frolic, no Jessie.
"Tray, Blanche, and Sweetheart" all gone. At last, hovering over the kitchen stove (not the wide-mouthed kitchen
fireplace, once the concentrated symbol of home-charities),
I found a poor pilgrim from Erin, Anstey, and, at the sound
of our voices, in rushed Mary Brown, and finally came Jessie, doing all that faithful little dog could do to speak welcome and consolation. * * * I felt somewhat as the passengers on the Styx may—on a strait between two worlds, the
bright one I had left, and that gathered in the happy valley.
But with the morning came the angel of *our* life, and with
him G., sweet and welcoming. Your father had a most satisfactory cousining progress. He found ' Cousin Ben' wor-
thily filling the patriarchal place of our dear Uncle John.
Their reunion, after years of needless separation, was most
touching, and the good man's prayer, in his evening devo-

tion, with its thanksgiving and its supplication for the continued friendship of their descendants, was such as Burns's father would have uttered, or, rather, such as Burns, with his exquisite conception of the holiest feelings of domestic life, would have put into his mouth." * * * *

Miss Sedgwick to Mrs. K. S. Minot, after the birth of her first child.

"Lenox, November 11, 1844.

* * * * "Since that, you, as well as our darling, have entered a new world—a world of imperishable affection, of hopes, and fears, and projects. You have received the *best* gift that God gives to his creatures, the best treasure for earth, and a treasure to be laid up in heaven forever and ever. And this gift, I trust, my dear child, will find its due return of gratitude and devotion to the Giver—will find you guarding against that mere extension of self-love with which some parents love their children, but rather making this new spring of love an impulse of activity, of devotion to those to whom you have or can make the opportunity of doing good. Thus may our baby be the centre of concentric circles ; thus may the fountain she fills continually overflow and spread in many life-refreshing channels ; thus may she be the vestal that shall keep the fire ever burning in your holiest of holies. Take care that it be so, my darling. With the best, virtues do not spring up, or, rather, grow spontaneously ; they need continual tending, and, alas! sometimes watering with tears." * * * *

Miss Sedgwick to Mrs. K. S. Minot.

"Lenox, November, 1844.

* * * * "I am just now very much taken up with watching my poor little Jessie's* maternity. 'Ma chère mère'

* Jessie, a delicate little black-and-tan terrier.

N

I call her, **though I am sure from no** likeness to that most charming **of all odious** people, except in devoted love to her unworthy whelp, the ugliest little tyke **you** ever saw, and Jessie the prettiest mother imaginable—of the canine spe-**cies. It** is almost Beauty and the Beast ; and such tender **and** picturesque devotion ! What Infinite **Love it must** be that feeds all these multiform streams ! She has **a couch** nicely prepared under my sofa, where she stays excepting when her baby is so uproarious that I am obliged **to** carry her into the next **room."**

Miss Sedgwick to Rev. Dr. Dewey.

" Stockbridge, December 1, 1844.

"MY DEAR FRIEND,—That canon of the orthodox Church **which** proscribes letter-writing on the Sabbath seems to me **to have a** more than common infusion of their character of the mole which works underground and in darkness, and ut-terly without that divine light afforded to those who, though their wings are still invisible, hope, one **of these bright** com-ing days, to unfold them in the empyrean. **Is not letter-**writing (sometimes !) the exercise of that principle of love **by which we** are partakers of the divine nature? Is it not the utterance of our immortal spirits—of that portion of our being which alone will live through the eternal Sabbath ? Answering instinctively yes to these my own questions, I hold it fitting to devote this Sunday afternoon to writing to you, my dear friend, who are associated with my purest en-joyments **on earth, and** with the objects and substance of my faith **in** ' things hoped for.'

" I received your very kind note from West Stockbridge, and thank you earnestly for **writing it. It** was one of those impromptu expressions that, like the grasping of hands in **a passing** crowd, indicates, more than a predetermined **at-tention,** that the current sets right, that the heart of affection beats evenly and steadily. I wish you could have come to us, if it were only for an hour or two. Summer visits are somewhat like the notes of a favorite bird, so drowned in the general song of multitudinous life that they lose half their virtue; and what is there on earth like the presence of a friend? Nothing. It is a fitting type of heaven. I thought of you yesterday, and of your love and estimation of winter scenery, which I know corresponds with my own. After a pleasant Thanksgiving at Lenox, where we gathered the few fragments of our family together, and for the moment closed up the abyss between us and those departed by fond memories and living hopes, I came down with my sister to pass a few days at the old homestead—my only home—the only place on earth where forms, common and mute to others, have to me soul and speech; where voices linger in the walls of the rooms, and make their sweet and by-gone cheerfulness and tenderness ring in my ears in the dead of the night; where the stems of the old trees are still warm with the hands that once pressed them; where, in short, the dead are *not* dead.

"But it was not all this that I meant to write to you, but, alone here at this moment, I can not help feeling it, and what I feel when I am writing to you, that I must write. I was about to tell you of the beauty of yesterday morning, when Winter rose in her 'robes pontifical, ne'er seen but wondered at.' Summer is but a drawing-room scene compared to it. The sun of these days rises behind the highest point in our eastern horizon, and consequently his beams shoot down the sides of the mountains, and even into the laps of the hills, before he is himself visible. A newly-fallen snow covered the whole area between the hills from mountain top to mountain top, and every tree and shrub; not a breath of air had shaken the snow off the lightest twig. It was intensely cold, and the smoke from our village homes—

the breath of their nostrils—rose in a solid column white and bright as molten silver. Here a rose-colored light flushed the hills, and there the light dropped down into their hollows like cloth of gold. The whole vault of heaven was of the brightest blue ; not a cloud, not a paling hue over any portion of it ; and far up in the clear atmosphere, and relieved against this brilliant blue, stood the magnificent trees, with their winter foliage of snowy wreaths. Then up came the sun, and the trees that crested the summit all along his horizon glittered as if they were shining in another world.

"I should have feared boring most people with all these scenic particulars, but to you they will be open-sesames to the memory of Sheffield winter days.

"Shall I confess why I have not written to you for some weeks past? I will, to my own shame—because I had not read the sermon you sent me. It came while I was in Boston. C. lent it to some wicked borrower, and it was not returned."

Miss Sedgwick to Mrs. K. S. Minot.

"New York, March 2, 1845.

* * * * "There is a great stir here among the good people of various classes about an association in behalf of the tenants of our prisons. I wonder if a Humane Society could not be got up for the worst and most dangerous body of criminals in our country—our Congressmen. If Hope, Faith, and Charity can stretch to their case, they must be infinite in their capacity. This result of the Texas Question is most disheartening. I see nothing for us but letting the South fall off by its own dead weight. But to my own private cases of villains, etc. I went to a meeting of the Ladies' Prison-Discipline Society, where a committee from the men's society appeared to remind the women that they were

but a department ; that a report they had printed, and which was just ready for publication, would knock up all the magnificent plans of the House of Lords, etc., etc. The ladies' president meekly confessed a blunder. Some of her *collaborateurs* were disposed to stand upon their reserved rights, some modestly hinted they had privileges as well as responsibilities, and it finally ended in an agreement for a meeting to settle these somewhat important preliminaries, till after which I deferred my membership. * * * * The Texas Bill ! Who can tell what is to be the fate of the country. I do not despair, but I give up the Democratic party. They have covered themselves with everlasting and irredeemable disgrace." * * * *

Miss Sedgwick soon after joined the Prison Association, and was one of its most efficient members. A sketch of her connection with it, and with the " Isaac T. Hopper Home" for the reception and employment of women discharged from prison, will be found in the latter part of this volume, from the pen of her old and valued friend, Mrs. Abby Hopper Gibbons.

Miss Sedgwick to Mrs. K. S. Minot.

"New York, March 11, 1845.

" MY DEAREST KATE,—I received your letter after J. left us on Saturday, and did not answer it on Sunday because I used up my eyes writing to your father, and answering a beautiful letter from our learned cousin of Kent, Prof. Adam Sedgwick.* Then I put off writing till after our Monday evening, because I was sure J. would want to know how it came off. Yesterday morning was cloudy enough out doors and in, raining and snowing by turns. Your Aunt Lizzy,

* A delightful correspondence with Professor Sedgwick was kept up till Miss Sedgwick's death.

after a Sunday of fever and suffering, got up very feeble. S. was quite ill in bed, J. gone—J., whom all declared essential to the 'sweet security' of a party. 'If they are pleasant people,' said L., 'J. enjoys them ; if they are stupid, she entertains them.' I was for omitting the evening, it was so forlorn to have our gentle S. ill—she who is not like the sun, nor the serene moon, nor the beaming stars, for they are often clouded, but like the blessed beacon-lights that shine in all weathers. However, your aunt rose with good courage, S. put her veto on any intermission, and we concluded to light the lamps, the old ones to put on their t'other caps, and the young ones their pretty dresses. * * * * Catharine S., who looked, if possible, more lovely than ever, recited a piece of Landor's, which certainly deserves the praise that William Channing (who was here) gives to all Landor's poetry, of being done with the perfection of an antique gem. It is singular that this girl always selects poetry of the severe classic order, which seems so perfectly to accord with the style of her beauty and the order of her character. I have never seen any body like her. She has the serenity, the power without restlessness, not without consciousness, but content to bide its time, which is indicated in the concentration and tranquillity of the beautiful antiques. When she recited the Lady's part in Comus, she seemed perfectly to embody the idea of the poet. * * * * A great—*the* great circumstance of the evening to me was the reception of an answer to my letter to Cassius Clay—a noble 'letter, breathing the consecration of his high mission. * * * * I hope William will subscribe for the paper Mr. Clay is setting up to forward the anti-slavery cause in Kentucky. It is a sublime enterprise, and he should have the answering sympathy of all true men. Do talk with Mrs. D. and M. about it. There is always fire in their furnace, on their altar I might say, but that their fashion is to turn out work as well as to let the flame go upward." * * * *

Miss Sedgwick to Mrs. K. S. Minot.

"Linwood, near Rhinebeck, June 13, 1845.

* * * * "Do you remember my once receiving a letter from Miss G., with some verses, very pretty, from Maria T., a servant of hers, thanking me for having done service to the cause of domestics in 'Live and Let Live,' and do you remember that I gave her volume of poems to that good old Wesleyan missionary of the St. James? Well, being in the neighborhood of the G.s, I determined to go and see them, and a few evenings since, when we were taking our drive, the Dr. dropped me at their gate. I approached the house, a modest, old-fashioned structure, by a gravel-walk through an orchard covered with old trees, with their shadows sleeping on a bed of the richest clover. As I turned round the house I came to the piazza, and there an erect old lady, 'touched (sanctified), not spoiled' by age, was standing, explaining to a little girl, such as our Posy will be five years hence, a picture of Daniel and Belshazzar. It was a picture. Roses of all hues in their June bloom were trained about the piazza, a lawn with groups of noble old trees before it, and below it a magnificent stretch of the river studded with a little fleet of sloops. I introduced myself to the old lady. Her daughter soon made her appearance, a cheerful, intelligent, excellent person, living a truly godly life here, as far as a glorious scenery can make it so, in the vestibule of heaven. My friend Maria T. soon appeared, to my infinite embarrassment treating me with as much reverence as if her saints had appeared to her. She blends a nun-like sanctity and intellectual gleamings with the deferential manner of an English serving-woman—an odd mixture enough! I confess to *you*, dear Kate, that her expressions of gratitude and affection were very precious to me. She came afterward to see me, and when she took leave, 'God bless you, Miss S.,'

she said; 'may you never want a servant, friend, or what you
may please to call her.' I staid to tea at Mrs. G.'s. She is
one of the two last of the old race of L.s, a sister of the celebrated E. L., and of the chancellor. There were twelve of
them, who lived strong and joyous lives, all having lordly es-
tates in the Manor, with iron physical and rich intellectual
constitutions. They ate and drank after the old fashion—
turtle soups, mince pies, and Madeira wine for dinner, hot
suppers at night, laughed together over their breakfast-ta-
bles—*all* lived to slip far beyond the prescribed boundary
of man's life, and here is Mrs. G. absolutely unimpaired at
92. Oh, in what blessed ignorance they have lived and died
of dyspepsia and nerves! We had tea on the piazza; it
was prepared when I arrived, and one refreshing relic there
was of the olden time. . I heard Mrs. G. tell the maid 'to
change the tea-cups,' and the best china appeared. The
old lady presided with a sort of lofty grace, and drank green
tea, and ate strawberries and cream 'sans peur et sans re-
proche.' She became a Methodist, to the great scandal of
her aristocratic family, who were as aristocratic in their religion as in every thing else, and married, at 40, an honest,
good preacher after the old pattern of Methodism."

Madame Sismondi to Miss Sedgwick.

"January, 1846.

" I received your precious letter yesterday, my most dear
friend, and I prepare my letter while my heart is warm with
gratitude to you, as well as love, for I have received from it
great benefit as well as consolation. I find in it an almost
inspired perception of the invisible world, and such an out-
pouring of trust in God as, if it fails of permanently persuading me to the same beloved trust, for the moment excites a
sympathetic feeling that is inexpressibly comforting. It
gives me such a longing desire to see you, to talk with you,

to hear you, that visionary plans of meeting you again in
this world have been continually rising to my imagination,
in spite of knowing it can never be. I read and re-read
it, and it must supply my want of you, though it can not
hinder that oft-repeated regret, Oh, if I had her near me, I
would take all my documents and fearlessly lay them open
to her, because I know *he* would not have objected to her
seeing the inmost of his soul."

Miss Sedgwick to Mrs. K. S. Minot.

"Staten Island, Tuesday, July 28, 1846.

* * * * "Went off to the 'Home,' where I had a reception that did me a great deal of good. One of our inmates,
who has been *frail*, saw me from the third story window, and
made but one step from the top to the bottom of the stairs ;
and the outstretched hands and brightened eyes of these
poor creatures spoke to me an assurance that they have that
in them which will finally be worked out of the dismal swamp
of circumstances, and carry them back to Him who is love."
* * * *

Miss Sedgwick to Mrs. K. S. Minot.

"Lenox, August 23, 1846.

* * * * "A charming letter from our dear Madame Sismondi. The following are extracts she gives me from Sismondi's journal :

"' *Dimanche, 6me Octobre*, 1839. Miss Sedgwick est arrivée
avec sa nièce Kate. Nous sommes restés à causer ensemble jusqu'à midi. Plus nous passons de temps ensemble,
et plus je m'affectionne à eux tous. Un petit livre que
Madlle. à donné à ma femme m'attache encore davantage à
elle. Il est charmant, et de morale et d'art de conter—si
facile, si bref, si pittoresque. On l'aime et on l'admire pour
un si bel usage de ses talents.'

N 2

" '*Mardi*, 15me. **C'est le** dernier jour de nos Sedgwicks—
ils sont **arrivés** le 29me Septembre. Nos cœurs se sont
tout **à fait unis—ils** nous aiment tous, et nous **les** aimons
tous, et de tant de séparations **qui se renouvellent** pour
nous chaque jour, c'est la seule qui me laisse une vraie
melancholie.'

"Dear Kate, does not the rich **past flow** its strong **current
over** your soul as you read this? Do you not live over again
our long walks and pleasant drives **to** Chêne? **Does** not the
gate **of that** pretty hedged fence open again for us? and that
low house, which held such heavenly souls, again smile on
us? He **lives as** she lives to us—and the widest sea is between her and **us.**"

Miss *Sedgwick to Mrs. K. S. Minot.*

"Lenox, September 27, 1846.
* * * * "Our good friend Von Man* is drawing near his
departure with all that elevation of spirit that has characterized his life. I have never seen so heroic an endurance

---

* **Herr von** Mandelslohe, referred to in this letter by the affectionate
diminutive constantly used by his friends, was a German (from Hanover)
of noble birth, but an enthusiast for political liberty and social equality.
Bred to military life, he abandoned his profession and his country, and
came, without resources, to Canada, and thence, very destitute, to New
York, where he became known to Mr. Bryant, and was by him introduced to Theodore Sedgwick, who sent **him to** Stockbridge to earn a
support by teaching German. He was a very eccentric person. With
a warm, generous heart, and wide benevolence, he was proud and sensitive, and would receive no favors from those whom he did **not** love.
He taught with unwearied zeal and enthusiasm **those** who learned with
zeal, but **would rather starve than earn** money by teaching indifferent
pupils.

He lived two or three **summers** at Stockbridge and Lenox, receiving
the welcome which the **stranger, the** solitary, the poor, and the unfortunate always found there, **and was** tenderly nursed by Mr. Charles Sedgwick during his **last illness.**

of the miseries that heroism is rarely equal to resisting. Pain, the infliction of remedies in which he had no faith, the incompetence and annoyance of poor nurses and bad watchers, he has borne with unwavering fortitude and patience, concentrating his soul in unbounded gratitude, and keeping his whole spiritual nature sanctified with good affections."
* * * *

Miss Sedgwick to Mrs. K. S. Minot.

"Stockbridge, October 4, 1846.

* * * * "The last week has been a deeply shadowed one. We laid our good friend Von Man among our graves with a deep feeling of thankfulness that his spirit was unshackled, and that honoring hands, and those whom he best loved in this world, did the last offices for him. His feeling toward your father was worthy both. He once said to me, 'I love, Miss Sedgwick, to see you come in, and I love to see Mrs. Sedgwick ; but—you must excuse me—I love most of all to see your brother ; he is truly an angel to me.' And so he was, from first to last, from morning to night, providing every possible comfort for him." * * * *

Miss Sedgwick to Mrs. K. S. Minot.

"Lenox, November, 1846.

* * * * "Last evening I was apologizing to Mr. Field for playing cards in his presence, and said I hoped he was not of the opinion of a certain gentleman in New York, who had written to entreat I would change the game of marbles (mentioned in my little tract as, of course, one of the boys' plays) to kite, because marbles were immoral, as by betting they involved an appeal to God, as did cutting and dealing cards, it being all regulated by the interposition of Providence. 'So,' said Mr. Watts, 'is cutting wood, especially Billy Brogan's ; for, when he lifts up his axe, Heaven only knows where it will strike !'"

Miss Sedgwick to Mrs. K. S. Minot.

"Lenox, December 6, 1846.

* * * * "I have been very busy since I came from New York making additions to my *little-est* book,* and now they are nearly completed, and I think they will be, in rustic phrase, an *addition*, being, in fact, once and a half more than the original text, and more attractive than that, as illustrative of rules. I am much interested in the success of the thing, because I think it will do some little good to our district-school children. The school committee in New York have ordered ten or twelve hundred for distribution in the families of the children." * * * *

Miss Sedgwick to Mrs. K. S. Minot.

"Spring Bank,† Roslyn, May 30, 1847.

"MY DEAREST KATE,—Do you wonder where I am? In the guest-chamber of a generous, old-fashioned house, behind one of the mossy pillars that support a piazza which surrounds it, in front of 'Great Neck Bay,' a deep cut into Long Island from the Sound, of which, and its ever-passing home-fleets, there is a distant view, with a terraced garden descending to the water on one side, and a pond on the other, formed from the springs that descend from steep acclivities, with a little strip of land between it and a green ravine, like that which separates the Salisbury Lakes, along which there is a lovely shaded walk, and a rural bridge to the cottage (ornée) of the daughter of my host, well-grown trees hugging the old house, and lovely branches of light spring foliage floating round dark, solid pines. Little villages in the distance, with all pleasant signs of habitancy. But better than any outdoor life, nobler gifts of God than hill-sides and their rich borderings of trees, clear streams,

* The Morals of Manners.   † The residence of the poet Bryant.

and bays, we have within, and delightfully we have spent the day, though it has been cloudy and dripping." * * * *

"Lenox, September 19, 1847.

* * * * "I have heard our present Methodist ghostly 'father' to-day for the first time, and I regard it as a sign that the true millennium is advancing that this is the fourth pastor that we have had at this church who has so much sound sense and so much of the simplicity of the Gospel that a few doctrinal errors do not vitiate it. No one need be very zealous about the promulgation of Unitarianism when its salt is sprinkled throughout other creeds, and when, as it appears to me, there is some radical defect in it, or in its ministration, that prevents its general diffusion. As we approach another world its horizon enlarges, and the brightness of the light (perhaps the nature of it) beyond its portal makes that behind us dim, and distinctions and badges fade away, and we only see the general movement toward that great portal and the earnest aim to gain it.

"*October* 30*th*, 1847. Does William read to you the details of our Mexican affairs, Kendall's letters, etc.? Principled as we are by education, and all the habits of our minds against war, and disgusting as its savageness is, I feel it impossible not to have my pulses beat quicker at the valor, indomitable spirit, skill, and hardihood of our people. If there were virtue in those Mexicans, if there were any hope in their political existence, there might be sympathy for their wrongs. But as it is, it seems to me that it is the ordination of Heaven that this stagnant, putrefying race should give place to the fresh, strong current that is settling upon them. The achievement of our men in planting the 'stars and stripes' on the fortress of —— (I can't recall the name) will advance our reputation in Europe more than all our vast progress in the civil arts. But it won't do for me just now to condemn the vulgar judgment."

Miss Sedgwick to Rev. Dr. Dewey, after the death of Mrs. Minot's little child.

"Lenox, November 29, 1847.

" MY DEAR AND TRUE FRIEND,—Never were you wanting in sympathy with me in any moment of my trials, nor in the expression of it which, coming from those we love, *is* comforting, and that is saying a great deal when the whole being seems dissolved in tears. Neither to you or Mrs. Dewey will there seem to be any exaggeration in this. You know what space a child may fill—what gladness it casts over the path of life—what there is in the touch of its hand—in the beam of its eye—in that little form in which such joys, and hopes, and loves are centred. My darling little Posy ! She was the sweet flower whose sweetness I felt at every moment—a fresh fountain where so many springs had sunken away. I remember your Louise well. I remember the expression of her soft speaking eye. Such lives never—in one sense—never leave us.

" K. bears her grief so meekly, so unresistingly, so wisely as to be an unspeakable consolation to us. She has, with unqualified faith, resigned her precious gift to better teaching, better guidance than hers ; and while her eye is deprived of the loveliest object on earth to her, she has opened her spiritual eye upon an angel. The little child has been an interpreter of God's Word to W. too—revealed to him the mysteries of life, and death, and immortality—'opened,' as he says, 'with her little hands the ponderous gates of Death.' Ah ! my friend, death is the solution—death and its train of infinite hopes."

Miss Sedgwick to Mrs. K. S. Minot.

"Stockbridge, December 25, 1847.

"MY DEAREST KATE,—I can only think of you this Christmas morning, and my heart turns sick away from the joys of the little people about me—joys it never before refused to enter into. I have been to Anne's, but I could not bear it ; but one image was before me, and I have come to a solitary room where, by prayer and strong effort, I may see our darling in her spiritual life, where she has nothing of childhood but its innocence and its beauty. I can see her hovering over her parents, and calling upon you to look up—to look up from the dark, vacant space to that which can never be darkened, to behold in the brighter but transient joys of the little ones about you a faint type of that which knows no shadow. Her nature was too intense to have borne patiently the frettings of the harness of this life, and God spoke and burst the prison-gates. The Father took the child to his own presence. The more I compare her with other children, the more she seems to me like a fleet messenger, sent to return quickly ; and while I can keep my mind to this, I feel, my dear child, that you have enough to tranquillize you, and then the sight of a plaything brings the sense of intolerable loss."

Miss Sedgwick to Mrs. K. S. Minot.

"Lenox, January 2, 1848.

"Your letters, my darling, were never more welcome to me, and yet how changed from the uniform sunny aspect of so many years. I read them over and over again, and relieve my heart by many accumulated tears over them. As I foresaw, they are sadder and sadder as every day brings some fresh evidence and memorial of our loss ; for, with all the mercies and hopes that have attended it, heavy, heart-

sinking **loss it is.   I never wake in the** morning now without first thinking how sweeter than the sweetest bird's song
was the **sound of her morning tone to me ; and when** I wake
in the night, her name and yours are on my **lips.**   Associa-
tions with her here have revived that I did not **feel before.**
I see her sitting on the door-step, running over to Cook**'s**
shop, teasing and caressing Jessie, laughing on the foot-board
of my bedstead ; and I never now walk up the hill without
thinking of our parting there on the hill-side; and, indeed, the
old coach in which she once rode only speaks to me of her.
Dear, dear Posy !   She can never be absent from your mind ;
she is inwrought with all your consciousness.   She has taken
you to heaven with her, I sometimes think.   Dear Kate and
William, I can, without faltering, wish you a Happy New-
year, for I believe, as **you** have entered the portals of this
new year, it has been with eyes lifted to God, with an assurance of a happiness not dreamed of by most of those who
exchange the frivolous wishes **of** the new year—a happiness
more compact, more elevated as time flows away **and tem-**
poral things dissolve.   Do **we** not, in moments of great excitement, get gleams of truth that do not dawn upon us in
the common states of the mind ?   I do not know how much
we might win by faith from the spiritual world, but I do know
that there are moments when there seems to me to be but a
thin veil between me and the beloved who are there ; **when**
their eyes, with immortal life in them, are upon **me; their**
lips, with immortal love, speak to me ; and yet from **this I**
fall back to doubt and fear. * * * * Dear Kate, how **fresh-**
ly every thing of last year has been brought to my mind as
the days have gone on in sad procession ; the delight I took
in making ' Posy's Own Book,' more pure pleasure than in
all my other books ; how **you** came with her little letter !
Ah ! I should write of nothing else if I set down but the
thoughts of **a** single **hour** of her."

Miss Sedgwick to Mrs. K. S. Minot.

"New York, March 26, 1848.

* * * * "Oh, dear Kate, I fear I shall never carry out my journaling plan, there is such an infinity of things happening here. I breakfasted at Mrs. F.'s, then came home to Helen's lesson, which I do if I do nothing else ; then an audience with one of my 'Home' people ; then a very nice Protestant Irish woman, with a sad tale and a very handsome starving husband—she a godchild of Miss Edgeworth, with a sort of circular from her—both to be provided for ; action taken thereupon. L. announced, and a sad talk about the loss of two of his children. He told me the last words Von Man said to him (and said them with a 'joyful laugh'), 'I am sure I carry to heaven with me the memory of the good I have known here.' Subscription for a monument for Von M. had been made by his German friends, when two orphan girls, daughters of a good minister, arrived. Some friends of Von M. suggested that he would prefer devoting the subscription for his monument to their wants, and a portion was taken. Was not that a touching case of the spirit speaking from the ashes? The rest of the morning was occupied with visits."

Miss Sedgwick to Mrs. K. S. Minot.

"New York, April 7, 1848.

* * * * "After breakfast this morning your Aunt L. was 'running' your father about his present mania. She maintained that all his affections were merged in the French Revolution, and he declared that if he heard that you had a pain in your left hand, he should rush to Woodbourne and forget the French Revolution. This at least shows his estimate of his love for you, but don't put him to the test, my dear.

"Another king walked off! I propose a new society to institute a Home for Friendless Kings. Your father is quite brilliant this morning. You know Alison wrote a eulogy on Louis Philippe. Your father proposes for Punch that Louis P. in his pea-jacket and fugitive costume should peddle Alison's History about London, and the motto should be, 'History teaching Philosophy by example.' * * * *

"I have read this morning Lamartine's very fine speech to the Poles and to the Italians. I hope you see all these things. It is something to live while such history is enacting. I don't know how young men keep themselves steady. In their case I should sail by the first ship that would take me to the scene of action. Have you heard that 2000 constables extra to be sworn in at Liverpool balked at the clause 'loyalty to the queen?' This looks stormy."

Miss Sedgwick to Mrs. K. S. Minot.

"New York, May 21, 1848.

"I do not think, my dear Kate, that in your quiet, refined home you can have any idea of the 'incessant' life of New York, of the crowding and stuffing of every moment. It is now just ten, and I have come up from the City Hall, in whose dismal St. Giles precincts I have been to see a colored ragged school. My companion stared at me when I told her I should get into the cars and come home to write a letter in the intervening twenty minutes I should save before church. My Sundays are *not* days of rest. I wish you would recommend to those enlightened Bostonians who are on the ultra pinnacle, and wish to abrogate the restrictive institution of the Sabbath, to take a walk through Anthony and Orange Streets, etc., in New York, and see it virtually annulled, all the shops open, and apparently no recollection of this old abuse of man's precious liberty. * * * * The city is getting to be intolerable. I have yet a good deal of duty to do in our Prison Society, and for the last month, with the exception of a week at Lenox, it has occupied me for three days in the week. If I could feel sure that there is any service done in proportion to the trouble and time spent, I should be perfectly satisfied. I think the favored class of society owe an immense debt to Providence, which can only be discharged by attempting to rescue the vicious and ignorant from misery and degradation. But it seems to me they must be saved, and *can not* be *rescued*, and we remain as if there were a palsy on us. With the means of universal education and sustenance, we see creatures with the powers and faculties out of which heroes and martyrs have been made, covered with bruises and putrefying sores. My whole soul is sickened; and to-day, when I went into our church filled with people in their fine summer-clothes, and heard a magnificent sermon from Mr. Dewey, and thought of the streets and dens through which I had just walked, I could have cried out, 'Why are ye here?' Some good is achieved —I see that—but the work is struggling and inefficient. If the sea were to roll over the adults and leave the children, we could devise a future, perhaps attain it for them."

Miss Sedgwick to Mrs. K. S. Minot.

"May 27, 1848.

* * * * "I trust you have not, as we have, wasted your time on 'that little family in Hell,' living and dying at 'Wuthering Heights.' It is a most signal waste of talent. There is a certain resemblance to Jane Eyre, like a family look; the energy of thought and style, the Northern mind as well as air that breathes through it, the intimate and masterly acquaintance with a location and coterie, and exclusion from the world, the remarkable directness of style, are all qualities peculiar, and marvelously like Jane Eyre, so that I think the author must be her brother, the masculine of her masculine mind.

"I am exceedingly delighted with Dr. Channing's life. His youth was the fitting prelude and precursor of his maturity. There was more of the prophetic fire than I should have expected, more of the welding heat of enthusiasm, in which the souls of prophets and seers are fused and recast for their earthly mission. There is much precious leaven in the book—concentrated essence of spirituality—which I expect to do a vast deal of good in elevating and directing religious minds. His life was a monastic one; but in this 'incessant' age—this period of all-doing, amidst this ocean-life activity—we want calm, deliberate thought—a fixed star by which to direct the course."

Miss Sedgwick to Mrs. K. S. Minot.

"New York, June 11, 1848.

* * * * "I have been busy this week settling up concerns, and looking after some poor creatures who are poor enough to turn to me for help. I have now on my heart two lovely little boys, whom I hope to get provided with a pleasant summer home with the children on Randall's Island—the place to which our pauper children have been removed, and where they have it all to themselves; plenty of grass and woodland, and large, ventilated dormitories, and baths big enough to swim in, and good teachers, and plenty of healthful food. The tiny things have each a rocking-chair nicely constructed, so that they do not tottle out. This supplies pleasant means for their incessant natures without their running under their nurses' feet, and thereby provoking tempers not the best disciplined. A happier set of little creatures I never saw. The eldest of my little boys the girls think like our dear Posy. I do not see it; but perhaps it is this that draws me to him.

"Foresti sailed in the "United States" yesterday. He has left us, as he believes, forever. He hopes to assist with his counsels the Milanese government—to bring to its service his eleven years' experience of the working of a republican government. I trust the Italians will turn their enthusiasm into the channel of reverence for this man, who suffered seventeen years of living martyrdom ; but it is so much the way of the world to shove aside the old, and give to the young and aspiring all the prominent and active places, that I doubt if he is permitted to do all the good he hopes. Few foreigners have been so much respected here. His bold, upright, unflinching integrity has given a new impression of Italian character. There have been very discriminating and beautiful eulogies in the papers, which have pleased him. He left the kindest messages for you."

Miss Sedgwick to Mrs. K. S. Minot.

"New York, June 18, 1848.

* * * * "Dearest Kate, every hour here brings its pressing duty, and baths and sweet sleep keep the machine refitted. I left my letter Sunday for my second farewell lecture with my 'Home' people. These Sunday afternoons, in which I endeavor to mingle some social pleasure with the elements of moral teaching, really seem to be an enjoyment to these poor creatures. I went yesterday up to Sing Sing as one of a committee of the Prison Association, but, by the overturn there, and the putting in by the present Whig government of a new set of officers, our visit was perfectly useless."

Miss Sedgwick to Mrs. K. S. Minot.

"Lenox, July 16, 1848.

* * * * "This is rather an unpropitious scene for writing for one so unconcentrative as I am — S. sitting in B.'s lap, J. on the floor playing with the kitten, and M. D. and J. C. scattered about, and all talking ; but, if I live to my climacteric, I think I shall learn to write in town-meeting

or on a barricade.   This last news from Paris is appalling.
There seems **to be** nothing for France between the wildest
anarchy and a military despotism.   They have turned hope
into despair.   To keep back the wave of popular madness
by moderation and reason is as hopeless as poor Dame
Partington's exploit of sweeping out the sea.   The French
are not a reasonable people, brave and impulsive as they **are.**
Theatrical in every thing, instead of making the theatre **rep-**
resent life, they turn life into seeming, and deal with blood
and death as if they were dramatic pageants.   The cool
heads **of** the Puritans, and their repressed, 'governed' enthusiasm, compared with Parisian outbursts, are like the
forces of nature directed by Providence compared to the
explosions **of children.   Washington and** Franklin types of
the one race, Lamartine and Louis Blanc of the other!   F.
must feel intense interest in his French friends.   I see the
young men of the Polytechnic were fighting in one of the
battalions, so I suppose poor **Madame M. has had her cup**
of horrors.   We have had a man preaching here **to collect**
funds to send missionaries to France, and institute Sunday-
schools in the streets of Paris!   As sensible as sowing vio-
let seeds under the torrent of Niagara.   Kate says there
was 25 cents contributed.   There is more sense in Lenox
than I imagined."

Rev. Dr. Bellows to Miss Sedgwick.

"MY DEAR FRIEND,—I have this moment risen from the
reading at one sitting—a few pages last evening excepted—
of the 'Boy of Mount **Rhigi,' and it is with wet** eyes that I
hasten to thank you for this charming work, as full of wisdom as of genius, of love as truth, of piety as pure and solid
morality.   I feel it safer to have children—who may not al-
ways have even a father's care—when such books are ex-
tant, and waiting to throw their mantle of purity and pro-

tection over them. How precious is this talent you possess of bringing the highest and holiest truth within the comprehension of the humblest and feeblest minds, and that, too, without taking from it what is fitted to excite the admiration of the most cultivated and enlarged understanding, the most fastidious taste! I can not doubt that at this moment you are one of the most efficient missionaries of our Lord in his great vineyard below—a vineyard how choked, how calling for diligent and competent laborers! You will never know how much good you are doing, and are yet to do, until the great day, when the secrets of all hearts are revealed; but I know that you will not despise the testimony of any sincere heart to your eminent usefulness. I feel stronger, happier, more hopeful, wiser, this weary Monday morning for the reading and taking into my heart this delightful and heavenly story, and you will not be sorry for this."

Miss Sedgwick to Mrs. K. S. Minot.

"New York, January 27, 1849.

* * * * "We had the first high-school opened here yesterday—a very fine building, where the best scholars from the public schools are to receive a course of instruction in the highest branches of education. From this ceremony, which was fully attended in the large hall of the institution, and at which you may be sure there was 'nobody' present (in the fashionable acceptation of the term), I plunged into 'Vanity Fair,' and went to Mrs. ———'s reception. She requested one of her friends to show me through her apartments, which are prettier than any thing I have seen since we left Italy. The frescoes are done beautifully by an Italian artist. There is not much furniture, but all there is is of the order of Madam ———'s town house—one apartment in Louis Quatorze, another of another reign, and so on. There was to be a dinner-party, and a circular table

was set for 20 or 25. It was covered with the dessert, and a profusion of decoration, epergnes, plateaux, girandoles, and the most exquisite natural flowers springing up here and there, as if a genie had touched every vacant place with her wand. The *ware* was gold and silver plate ; the plates of the most exquisite painted china. The mistress of this Aladdin-palace, whom I knew a slattern at 17 (and a great heiress then), had a dress on so defaced that you could not tell whether it was silk, velvet, or tabby, and a gap behind showed that she had not drawn on the magic lamp for a dressing-maid."

Miss Sedgwick to Mrs. K. S. Minot.

"New York, February 5, 1849.

* * * * "Mrs. Farnham, the celebrated matron of the Sing Sing prison, is going to Boston this week on an enterprise which her circular will explain. She is, of all women ever created (within my knowledge of God's works), the fittest for the enterprise. She has nerves to explore alone the seven circles of Dante's Hell. She has physical strength and endurance, sound sense and philanthropy, earnestness, and a coolness that would say 'I know!' if an angel were sent to tell her the secrets of the upper world. Hers is an unprecedented crusade certainly, but in this stirring of the elements new combinations must be expected. She may not succeed in getting her company ; if she does, she will be a most able chieftainess ; and it seems to me nothing better can be done for the chaotic mass at San Francisco than to infuse into it the leaven of 130 intelligent and virtuous women. No better missionaries could be sent there. You will see Mrs. Farnham, and hear from herself her plan. I have promised her a letter to Mrs. Minot, who I know will be pleased to see so rare a specimen of womanhood, and who, if any body can in Boston, will aid her by suggestions as to the best mode of action in that vicinity, and any light as to her general plan Mrs. F. will gladly receive. At any rate, Mrs. M. will rightly appreciate this singular woman, and give her a patient and kind hearing."

Miss Sedgwick to Mrs. K. S. Minot on Mrs. Kemble's Shakspeare Readings.

"New York, March 8, 1849.

* * * * "The town—the town that I mingle with—talks of little else, and there seems to be a general voice of satisfaction and delight. I have never seen such assemblies in New York—the fashionable people, the old people, all the known clever people, the pious folk, the *mourners*, the Quakers. People study Shakspeare that never studied him before. In short, there seems to be a new soul in a lumpish world. * * * * We begin now to talk of our *rising star*, dear B. I feel a sort of warmth coming round my heart as when the sky kindles after a cold, dark night; not that my winter has been cold or dark, for that which is my chief happiness, my home, has been unusually pleasant—L. so bright, the girls all so loving to me, and your aunt so happy and so kind, and dear E. growing in grace every hour of his life."

Miss Sedgwick to Mrs. K. S. Minot.

"New York, March 18, 1849.

"My DEAREST KATE,—I expected to have had to announce to you B.'s safe arrival, but I can never regret a prolongation of pleasure to you, though it costs me privation, and *I truly never do*, which is what I think is called mother's love. * * * * There is a real, hearty, enlightened, enthusiastic admiration of her* here. One old lady, sans eyes, sans teeth, sans every thing but ears, rose after a morning,

* Mrs. Kemble.

O

and said she wished she would read oftener in the morning, for she could not come over from Jersey City at night! One lady is waked by a bird in the night, and finds it is ' Philomel' in the atmosphere. A little boy who did not wish to go ('he had heard Macready, and it was nothing to Uncle John's reading') heard her, and said that she 'did read *as well* as Uncle John.' A worthy friend of mine, a man of business, who never goes to the theatre, and has not yet heard her, has read Shakspeare in bed every night since she has been here. People who meant 'to go to " The Merchant of Venice" because *Desdemona* is such an interesting character,' have bought Shakspeare, and probably rectified their notions."

Miss Sedgwick to Mrs. K. S. Minot.

"New York, March 24, 1849.

* * * * "I shall be grieved if you permit any small matter to interfere with your going to M.'s wedding. We strike in one of the golden threads that make the history of human life when we are present at this great circumstance. I am not transcendental, as you know, but it seems to me that where there is a true, a spiritual friendship, there is a spiritual body formed by a delicate distillation from the events of mutual concernment, and that whatever we feel and act together adds to the vigor and beauty of that body."

Miss Sedgwick to Mrs. K. S. Minot.

"New York, April 8, 1849.

* * * * " Mrs. Ware* has gone from a ministry of generous love and unwavering fidelity to imperishable riches— riches that no scale can weigh. An angel has gone from among us—an angel who taught us how to live and how to die. It is seldom that my faith rises to what I desire to be-

* Mrs. Henry Ware.

lieve, but I do believe there was, in the last scenes of her life, a direct ministry to her spirit which enabled her, like the martyrs, to look serenely out from the fires that consumed her body."

Miss Sedgwick to Mrs. K. S. Minot.

"New York, May 12, 1849.

" MY DEAREST KATE,—I was about as much surprised to get the news of the great event as if I had never expected it. L. and I, on getting out of the omnibus on our return, were met by K. and M. W., and, before we reached our own door, were joined by half a dozen more of the 16th Streeters, and incidentally, before we reached home, 'Kate's boy' was mentioned. I jumped like a man shot (the most natural illustration just now*), and have ever since had a downy, soft feeling at my heart, and something very like a continual cloud of incense of joy and gratitude rising from it."

Miss Sedgwick to Mrs. K. S. Minot.

"Highland Gardens, October 13, 1849.

" MY DEAR KATE,—I meant to have journalized my visit here for you, but, as usual, I am behindhand. S. and I came up in the heavy rain on Monday, and found Mr. Downing awaiting us on the wharf, in defiance of the cats and dogs it was raining about him. When we arrived, Miss Bremer (who had already been to a morning wedding) was in her room. She has wisely stipulated that her mornings are to be sacred, and will probably thereby save herself from being sent to a mad-house by American hospitality. Lafayette's heroic humanity and French blood saved him ; but poor Miss Bremer, of the nature of the sensitive plant, or a lily of the valley, that would hide herself under a green leaf (and could, she is so small), how could she resist a twelve-hours' siege

* This was the day following the Astor Place Riot, in New York.

from the 'incessant' Yankee nation? She came down at the
dinner-hour, a little lady about G. A.'s height, slightly made,
with the most lovely little hands, a very florid complexion
(especially of the nose)—florid, but very pure and fair, and
far from giving any idea of coarseness. Her hair is somewhat grayed, parted with that ugly square bit on the top of
the head, and her cap is of that fashion universal some ten
years ago, of the shape of a pocket-handkerchief turned
back. She wears a gray gown and a black watered silk
mantilla. So she comes to breakfast, so to dinner, and so
she appears in the evening. . Her eye is a clear blue, I say ;
greenish, S. says. Her mouth is very like Longfellow's ; indeed, she looks about equally like him and like Maroncelli,
and might be the sister of either. But neither of them have
the modesty, the delicate recognition of every shade of feeling, and the most sweet gentleness that characterizes her.
She uses our language with accuracy and even elegance, but
her accent is so strong and her intonation so curious that it
is not easy to understand her. Her voice is one of the
sweetest I have ever heard—one of those soul instruments
that seem to be a true spiritual organ. She is simple and
sincere as a child in all her ways ; much, tell Mrs. Minot,
such a person as Miss Hannah Adams might have been if
she had been a writer of romances instead of Jewish geneal-
ogies, and the familiar friend of royal ladies—that is, very
slightly conventional, not at all rustic, but with all the heavenly qualities that, under the type of childhood, mark those
who are of the kingdom of Heaven. The first evening she
played us Swedish airs and taught us Swedish jigs. She is
much inclined to 'spiritualité' (I wish I could give the word
with her prolonged accent) in literature, and I believe that
the people she will most affect here will be the Transcen-
dentals. But she is not like them, foggy, but has, ' au fonds,'
a sound, rocky foundation, and clear atmosphere of good
sense.

" We had yesterday to dine with us Professor Bergfalk, a Swedish gentleman, ' a most *riche* man,' Miss Bremer says, in a higher sense of riches than any Yankee dreams of. He is employed by the King of Sweden to digest a code of laws, and has come here, I suppose, to observe the working of ours.

"*Tuesday*, *P.M.* Dear Kate, we went on to the mountain in four carriages, wagons, etc. Downing, Miss Bremer, and myself in one. I, as usual, walked up and walked down. It is a glorious view to see from the South Beacon ; but I have no time now for descriptions of out-of-door things. We had capon and Champagne, and all manner of merry things said and done. In the evening arrived W. R. and B. to attend S. home (I go in single majesty !). And this morning came charming C. E. and took me a long drive, during which we talked from earth to heaven. And then I sat to Miss Bremer, who makes capital water-colored sketches, and then we ate dinner, and had not all ' truths and *roots*,' but sound English . dishes, and such flowers and fruits as have rarely been seen out of Paradise. And since, I have given Miss Bremer another sitting, and here it is twilight. I like her more and more, and, as the soul comes out and overspreads the features with its beaming and beautiful light, I am ashamed to have called her ' plain.' She has tones of voice so full of humanity and of experienced suffering that they almost bring tears to your eyes.

" I think she has some expectations that will be disappointed. She expects a more distinct individuality, a development of originality unmoulded by precedents or imitations, or Old World conventionalities, that she will not find in a country saturated with canals and penetrated by railroads. There is a dignified, calm good sense about her, with a most lovely gentleness and spirituality. She occasionally tells us pleasant stories, as of a poor lady whose

husband often beat her. She one day took up a horse-shoe
lying on the floor, and straightened it with her hands. Her
husband was amazed. She said, 'This force is a gift in my
family.' 'And possessing it,' said the husband, 'you have
suffered me to beat you.' 'Yes, it was my duty not to resist.' He never beat her afterward."

Miss Sedgwick to Mrs. Channing.

"Lenox, October 21, 1849.

* * * * "Your anxiety about my health is just now quite
groundless. I was rather run down during the summer,
partly from the heat, and partly from a superannuated devotion to my little grand-niece. This I keep a profound secret, and let the world think it had a more dignified cause.
I sometimes get a little wearied in town, and often heart-
sick, but I believe that the little charity work I do is con-
servative in its tendency. It takes me out of doors, and is
solacing to the heart, after the heavy disappointments, and
amidst the wearing, small trials of life. Dear Susan, while
I fully realize the shortness of life, and do sometimes ardently desire to do two days' work in one, I feel its value
more than I ever did, and take far more pains to nourish it
than when I was younger and happier, and it seemed fairer.
The transition from 'beauty to duty,' if it takes from its
loveliness, gives it an infinite value. But again, my dear
Susan, thanks for your kind consideration, and believe me,
whenever I am inclined to any imprudence, I will think of
your counsel. It is Sunday, and nothing can be more profound than the stillness that reigns here. It is *our* Sabbath
too—vacation—and the one fly that is buzzing about me in
the warm atmosphere of my little room is a type of the
change that has taken place, and of my solitude. The summer visitors are all gone. * * * * The children are all gone
home, the family gone to church, and the stillness is startling."

Miss Sedgwick to Mrs. K. S. Minot.

"Stockbridge, November 25, 1849.

* * * * "We had a cheerful evening at H——'s, where we had a general family gathering. They have hung some very pretty cotton curtains in their little parlor, have bright piano and table covers, and every thing there, under H——'s regime, wears a cheerful aspect. H—— is one of the heroines of every-day life, bearing multiplied and exasperating evils without dejection or complaint, supporting mortifying circumstances without humiliation, and the general cares of labor and poverty with dignity and uniform cheerfulness. Such people pass along almost unnoticed, unpraised, but 'they have their reward'—as large a heaven here as their spirits can travel over, and a certain heaven hereafter. The great event of the past week has been the visit of the little female apostle of Abolitionism—Lucy Stone. Your mother, doubtless, will give you all the particulars of the Lenox protracted meeting, of the Burleigh of the true Balfour school who lectured to us there. The female impersonation of reform came here ; your Aunt Susan kindly invited her to her house, and we had great pleasure from her. She does not look older than you do—three or four-and-twenty !—she is thirty-one. She is a person of rare gifts, with a good New England education for a ground-work, and a collegiate course at the Oberlin Institution of four years, where the clever girls—good Grecians—found out that Paul—as such a generous, courteous spirit should be—was a 'woman's rights man !' where they ascertained that he only forbade them to *gabble*, not to talk in the churches, etc. She has one of the very sweetest voices I ever heard, a readiness of speech and grace that furnish the external qualifications of an orator (a lovely countenance, too), and the intensity, entire forgetfulness, and divine calmness that fit her to speak

in the great cause she has undertaken. She has some of
the slang words and slang phrases of her clique ; but if she
could have your Aunt Susan to travel with her, and be as docile to her wise hints as she was here, the ministry would be
quite perfect."

Miss Sedgwick to **Mrs. K. S.** *Minot.*

"New York, January 23, 1850.

* * * * "I have just come from ———; Cousin ———
opened the 'door for me with a smiling face that answered
all questions. Hope catches fire like a pine-knot, and burns
as briskly. The doctor says if nothing goes wrong she will
be out of danger in forty-eight hours. I called to see Miss
Robbins on my way home. She lamented her brother's
death with the eloquence of an old Hebrew. If your eyes
were shut, you might have fancied that it was a supplement-
al chapter of Job. It was a holy rhapsody on life and death.
I thought I should have remembered some of it, but I might
as well have caught a pitcher of water from the Falls of Niagara—its force carried it away.

"This is Tuesday, and, as it is a peerless day, I suppose
we shall have lots of visitors ; but, as my gown is ragged, I
shelter myself under the apology of a cold, and stay in my
room.

"$\frac{1}{4}$ *before* 4. You may laugh at my arrangements. At two
o'clock ——— sent for me to come down and see ———
———, who was looking very sweet and bright; then appeared Mrs. ——— and ———. ——— has turned her
back on the world since her engagement. Then Mrs.
———, like a bed of brick-colored poppies or red holly-
hocks; then ——— and ———, charming always; then Mrs.
———, and ———, and ———, all three in the *luxe* style,
as François used to call it—madame with the finest lace of
Paris, and the girls the finest velvet of Genoa. Then

———, all ermine, and Mrs. ——— ———, all nature and common sense, much more costly articles, if goods go by rareness. Then the Misses ———, one almost a beauty, and Mrs. ———, with sables half a yard deep. Excuse me, my darling, for these *sottises.* I know they are so, that is something; but what can one do with clothes? people but inventory their clothes. ——— ——— was here too, looking good, but rather rustical. I don't know what it is with our people—they are too conventional for nature, and not enough so for art."

Miss Sedgwick to Mrs. K. S. Minot.

"New York, February 18, 1850.

"MY DEAREST KATE,—I have just finished reading William Jay's noble article on Clay's resolutions, and my hands are as cold as ice. The blood has curdled in my heart. I thank God for the clear intelligence, the pure heart that comprehends clearly and states definitely the truth. I always distrusted Clay's *compromises.* That word compromise has a bad savor when truth and right are in question. Do get William to read the article to you. The print is too bad for your eyes. (I forgot mine while I was reading it.)"

Miss Sedgwick to Mrs. K. S. Minot.

"May 25, 1850.

"DEAREST KATE,—What blessings letters are! This wretched weather, the continuance of the east wind, that house in the mud,* and your father, have filled my atmosphere with blue devils, and I came up from breakfast begging Margaret to kindle a fire in my grate and disperse them, if possible. I had just settled myself at my table with notes to write to the Governor of the Almshouse, petitions to the public, notes of request and notes of thanks, when up

* See next page.

O 2

comes Nancy with a very nice note from 'a merchant,' with two $50 notes for the House of Industry and for 'the Home.' This was rather charming; and then dear Nancy again with a most cheerful letter from your father, with your delightful letter, and a note from William announcing a rush of population in the circle of our friends. I passed yesterday on Blackwell's Island, and had forgotten that there were any but low-browed, ophthalmic, blotchy people in the world.

"Mercy, how it pours! I wonder now that I ever before cared when it rained; but the vision of that wretched house!* If your father keeps up his spirits through this, I shall think they are water-proof, trial-proof, proof against all sublunary evils—of heavenly temper, as I have always thought them."

Miss Sedgwick to Mrs. K. S. Minot.

"New York, June 3, 1850.

"My DEAREST KATE,—I always feel as if it were a bad omen when Sunday passes over without my writing to you. But either I am getting shiftless, or I have each week more and more to do. I have just come from the House of Industry, from the infinite complicity of paying committees, purchasing committees, examining do., reference do., receiving do., cutting do., etc., etc. I received about two hundred registered names, etc., poor women eagerly seeking the boon of fifty cents' worth of work, upon which, by their account, a sick husband and any number of orphan children are to be supported. The best of it all is to see the ladies whose splendid equipages stand at the door in close contact with these exuberant daughters of Erin, earnestly devoting themselves to the relief of their wants. It will be a noble institution; at present it is, of course, crude and defective.

"I passed last week most delightfully, making a country

---

* Mr. Charles Sedgwick's house, which was just moving from its original situation to a spot nearly a quarter of a mile distant.

holiday of it from Monday till **Saturday**. **Mrs. L. came for** me on Tuesday. Wednesday we passed the **day driving to** the High Bridge, which, now that the Harlem **River is brim-** ming, the rubbish removed, the fresh woods and dark **pines** lighted up with dogwood, whose soft blossoms are like con- densed moonlight, is most beautiful. **I hope,** before I die, to show **you** how lovely this island **is—before I die,** and before all **Ireland has rained shanties upon it.** Much as you have been **in the city, I believe you are** unacquainted with its sur- roundings; the **suburban** neighborhood **is ruined, but** the **upper part of the island is not** yet spoiled of the beauty **its** Maker endowed it with when he set it amidst its waters **a young** sovereign. **The** worst of it is, that just **in proportion to the** increase of its power is the diminution **of its beauty.** Mrs. L. has a very pleasant society in her neighborhood; people who are not **philosophers or** literati, **but who have** immense wealth **and rural tastes; are naturally kind** and social; live, some of them, in patrimonial houses, and some of them in palaces of recent structure, with **all the means** and appliances **of** modern art. **I** will tell you all about **my** delightful visit when we meet, which, thank God, I hope will be soon, for to me, Kate, the 'world and the glory thereof' are naught to sweet Woodbourne and its inmates."

Miss Sedgwick to Mrs. K. S. Minot.

"Lenox, January 6, 1851.

* * * * "I took up Davy's Salmonia the day **of your** fa- ther's illness; **if** you and William have not read **it, do.** There may be **a little too** much description of the trout-fish- ing, as that is not William's particular hobby, but the acute and delicate perception of natural beauty and **life, charac-** teristic of a refined sportsman, and the occasional exquisite **touches of philosophy and** religion, **make it an** enchanting **book. Your father read us aloud last evening** some of Boccaccio's tales from a translation G. brought home. The translation is a paltry one, but when you consider that these tales marked the age in which they were written, it seems to me no species of manufacture has made greater progress than story-writing. Compare these tales of love, intrigue, cuckoldry, and death to the Scarlet Letter, composed of the same raw material, for these are the elements of the social compact !"

Miss Sedgwick to Mrs. K. S. Minot.

"Lenox, March 2, 1851.

" MY DEAREST KATE,—Many thanks for your letter. William goes to-morrow, and will take a basket for you, with a few eggs (which I hope will *remain* hermetically sealed), and a portion of the fresh marmalade I have just made from some splendid Seville oranges, and I hope that you and William will enjoy it. You had better take it out of the jar and put it in small containers, it keeps so much better. Your mother, I presume, has communicated the satisfactory result of Dr. Parker's examination. It is a great comfort to have the opinion of a man whose science, sagacity, and intelligence you feel confident of, especially when his opinion concurs with all your own observation. I have, for a considerable time, felt sure that your father's chief trouble was his stomach ; but a lay opinion is good for nothing, especially lay-feminine, till sanctioned by a medical one. You must, as your Aunt Jane says, pay five dollars for what you knew before, and then the knowledge becomes effective. Dyspepsia is bad enough, and you may think it no great matter of gratulation to have found out that this is the trouble. But your father has uncommon digestive powers, and a blessed tendency to a healthy reaction ; and, since he has given up the idea that mince pies and buckwheat cakes must now be harmless because they once were so, he has been gaining ;

and since he has confined himself—and he now does most resolutely and patiently, and apparently without a disobedient desire—to a strict regimen of meat and breadstuff, his complexion has changed, and every thing has gone comparatively well. He occasionally has a pink tinge, a healthy hue, and the yellow has nearly gone. To-morrow will be fifteen days since the last attack. He goes four or five times, for fifteen or twenty minutes at a time, on to my piazza, and he now walks there with a cheerful, quick step. Oh, dear Kate, you, who have not seen us through the long discouragements of this sad winter, can hardly imagine what a difference a little light has made. I should think it wrong, in almost any case, to cling with such tenacious desires to a life protracted to its 60th year ; but your father's life is such a blessing ! He is God's missionary to the poor and desolate, and to those *called* happy.

" *March* 8, 1851. The final decision is to send out a ship for Kossuth. I do not know how an act so disinterested, so suited to a model republic, has been carried by the same set of men who last year enacted a law for hunting down fugitives for freedom. Do not the angels laugh as well as cry over us? Certainly the inconsistencies of human action must make them either laugh or cry, and, as I believe healthy natures are most disposed to the agreeable emotions, I believe they laugh."

Miss Sedgwick to Mrs. K. S. Minot.

"Lenox, March 16, 1851.

* * * * "Last evening we were agreeably surprised by a visit from R.* St. Patrick's Day occurring to-morrow, the saint demands a general suspension of labor, and, like a boy coming to his home in a holiday, he has come to us. We certainly have had great happiness from exiles. R. is

* A Hungarian exile.

a most charming **fellow.** * * * * The education of a gentleman and a **soldier** implants its own vices, I have no doubt;
bnt it **is refreshing now and** then **to see** a man who has
grown **up** without the competitions, the selfishness, the base
money element of business life, in whom you see Nature's
material expanding without a thin and tarnishing plating.
R. has had, while his enthusiasm was fresh, full of **hope,**
and courage, and faith, an experience of a struggle in which
life was counted as nothing against national independence.
He has acted from and for thought; seen for it, read **for it,**
and, **having** acted, seen, and read much and variously while
he is in **the fervor of** youth, he is rather a contrast to Squire
T., who is **at this moment** sitting *vis-à-vis* to him.   He is a
good, generous, affectionate **fellow too, with eminent** good
sense, and just as much socialism **as** belongs to a well-de-
veloped Christian."

Miss Sedgwick to **Mrs. K. S. Minot.**

"Lenox, **March 23, 1851.**

* * * * "We had one of Betty's* Sunday visits yesterday, and, **as she** sat in the little parlor, amusing us with her
dramatic gossip, she fell upon an 'old nigger' (her own des-
ignation), one Frank Francis, who lives in the old halfway
house to S.   You may remember observing his illustration
of domestic economy; how, last winter, he enlarged his pig-
pen into a dwelling-house, and used the former habitation
as a wood-pile.   He lives alone apparently, but he **says 'in**
the best **of company — with his Lord.'**   I repeated this to
Betty.   'Ha!' she says, 'it's he with **the cloven foot,** I guess,
and why **the old Harry** don't take him **off nobody** can tell!'

---

* **The daughter** of Mumbet, the **admirable** and devoted negress mentioned in the "Recollections." Mumbet's only weakness was spoiling
her own children, and Betty grew up **a shiftless** creature, a mere pensioner upon the family **in** which her mother had been a trusted friend.

'Why, Betty!' 'Why, Miss Catharine, did you never hear
that he has killed three wives and burnt up one—Mary?
Mary came over here and borrowed a rope of Mr. ———,
and he said, "Mary, I charge you to return that," and she
said, "I will, sir, dead or alive." Well, the next news, folks
said Mary was burned to death, and buried in the Washington Woods. Mr. ——— was riding out one day, and he
saw a woman coming along with a rope over her arm, and he
up and says, "Why, that's Mary, as sure as life!" and so it
was; and she stopped him, and, says she, "I told you, dead
or alive, I would return your rope, and here it is." And
he took it and put it in his shay-box, and then she showed him all down one side where she was burned, and told
him if he did not make the case known and get justice done,
he too would be burned to death! and so he was. There,
you may see her grave now—open yet; he filled it, and filled, and filled, and as fast as he filled it opened; and Miss
Bradley will tell you that when he is working in her garden—
he is a nice hand there—she'll hear him say, "Let me alone!"
and he'll jump over the other side of the bed, and so he
keeps hopping.' Old ——— did die from a burn; he became a sot, and was probably in Tam O'Shanter's sight-
seeing condition when he met Mary with the rope. I have
told you this as a delightful proof that superstition has found
a retreat in our all-knowing land, though it be in the darkest recesses of these lees of humanity. The open grave
and the pinching spirit in the garden would not be bad for
a German story.

To the same.

"New York, March 30, 1851.

"You ask me what I have been doing all winter. Little,
my dear child, but watch your father's face, and do what I
could to minister to his comfort, and shift one heavy burden

for another.   I have written some small matters, and tried my hand at a heavy one ; but heaviness is the prevailing element."

Miss Sedgwick **to Mrs. K. S. Minot.**

"Lenox, May 4, 1851.

* * * * "Your mother, after reading Hawthorne's book,* has most kindly and patiently gone straight through it again in loud reading to your father and me.   Your father is not a model listener ; ten thousand thoughts of ten thousand things to be done call him off, and would wear out any temper but your mother's.   Have you read it?   There is marvelous beauty in the diction ; a richness and originality of thought that give the stamp of unquestionable genius ; a microscopic observation of the external world, and the keenest analysis of character ; an elegance and finish that is like the work of a master sculptor—perfect in its artistic details. And yet, to my mind, it is a failure.   It fails in the essentials of a work of art ; there is not essential dignity in the characters to make them worth the labor spent on them. A low-minded vulgar hypocrite, a weak-minded nervous old maid, and her half-cracked brother, with nothing but beauty, and a blind instinctive love of the beautiful, are the chief characters of the drama.   'Little Phœbe' is the redemption, as far as she goes, of the book—a sweet and perfect flower amidst corruption, barrenness, and decay.   The book is an affliction.   It affects me like a passage through the wards of an insane asylum, or a visit to specimens of morbid anatomy.   It has the unity and simple construction of a Greek tragedy, but without the relief of divine qualities or great events ; and the man takes such savage delight in repeating and repeating the raw head and bloody bones of his imagination.   There is nothing genial, excepting always little Phœbe, the ideal of a New England, sweet-tempered, 'ac-

* The House of the Seven Gables.

complishing' village girl. I might have liked it better when
I was younger, but as we go through the tragedy of life we
need elixirs, cordials, and all the kindliest resources of the
art of fiction. There is too much force for the subject. It
is as if a railroad should be built and a locomotive started
to transport skeletons, specimens, and one bird of Paradise !

In 1850, Mr. Charles Sedgwick's house was moved from
the somewhat cramped position it occupied in the village of
Lenox to a charming situation at a little distance, on the
brow of the hill, and commanding a vast and beautifully-va-
ried prospect. Here Miss Sedgwick's "wing" received still
farther additions, notably that of a broad and well-inclosed
piazza, looking to the south over twenty miles of valley,
meadow, lake, and hill, to the blue Taghkonic range, in
southernmost Berkshire. The terrace in front of it was
bright with flowers, which the assiduous care of their mistress kept in bloom both early and late, even upon that
height, still so bleak in early spring and late autumn. She
was an enthusiastic gardener, and thought no pains too great
to save a favorite rose or geranium, or to coax a bed of violets into early blossom. Nor did she confine her care to
flowers, but took a practical interest in the growing vegeta-
bles, and had her own strawberry-bed, from which it was her
delight, in the early morning, to gather the fruit with her own
hands. When she gave her frequent breakfast-parties, which
all who had the good fortune to be her guests must remember as among the most fascinating banquets in their memory, alike for the place, with its summer-morning beauty fresh
upon it, the delicacy of the viands, the piquant or interesting
talk that was sure to arise, and the radiant cordiality of the
hostess, she would be in her garden by six o'clock to gather
fruit and flowers for the table, and unconscious inspirations
of health and happiness for herself, of which she dispensed
the latter, at least, as liberally as the more tangible harvest

of her borders. ' Then, after arranging the table, and paying a visit to her tiny kitchen, where the more delicate dishes received the touch of her own skillful hand, she would make a rapid toilette, and appear, untired as the day, to greet her guests with that exquisite grace and sweetness, that genial warmth of welcome which made old and young, grave and gay, literary celebrities, distinguished foreigners, fashionable people from town, and plain country friends all feel a delightful ease in her presence. Her vivacity, shrewdness, and tact in conversation were never more charming than at these Arcadian repasts.

She piqued herself upon her cookery, and with reason. " Cooking is the only accomplishment of which I am vain," she said. A New England life, especially in the country, makes a strong draft upon all the executive faculties of man or woman, and Miss Sedgwick fully and cheerfully accepted all its obligations. She could make cake as well as books, and provide for all household exigencies as ingeniously as she could construct a story. Mme. Roland, speaking of her youth, mentions it as a rare and noteworthy variety of occupation, that the same girl who read works of philosophy, and could explain the circles of the celestial sphere, was often called into the kitchen to make an omelet, skim the pot, or dress a salad. To many Yankee women the apparent anomaly is a piece of every-day experience.

After her return from Europe Miss Sedgwick had very serious trouble with her eyes, and was for a year or more under the care of Dr. Elliott, the distinguished oculist. His treatment was of much service to her, but her eyes never fully recovered their strength.

Miss Sedgwick to Mrs. K. S. Minot.

"Lenox, May 4, 1851.

* * * * " Quiet indoors, but out, what a bustle ! What

uprooting and down-setting, digging holes and filling holes, moving fences, sowing, planting, building ! When the sound of the hammer shall cease, it will be a token of desolation indeed—of desolation or perfection. We have workmen here of every description, from Goodrich (who, you know, is employed as the ideal of amiability and honesty) down through the gradations of Oliver, Saddler, Matthew, to four 'jail-birds' who daily flutter their wings (and sing in heart, I hope) over our diggings. I had two of them in rather removed and close companionship on the rockery yesterday, and I could not help adjuring them not again to immure their strong arms. Some day when I am gone, dear Kate, you will take your children to this rockery, and tell them how, for love of you and them, I toiled on it, and if there should be visible tokens of my toil, you will tell them how many loving thoughts made an atmosphere of enchantment around me there. I every day feel more and more the happiness of our removal to this place—the escape and the benediction. Every day, every hour the earth has a fresh aspect of beauty. I do not know when (not since my childhood) I have been in the country at this season ; and if I could climb hills and fences as I did then, as far as my relations to nature go, I should be far more enjoying than then. Nature is now a more familiar, an older, and a richer friend ; and, besides what it is in itself, it is a medium of communication with the distant and the departed."

Miss Sedgwick to Mr. William Minot Jr.

"Lenox, May 15, 1851.

" MY DEAR WILLIAM,—It would, I know, please you if you could look into my heart, and see how much this last proof of your tender affection has increased my tranquillity and my sense of *riches* in that which alone constitutes inappreciable and permanent wealth. My besetting sin is a craving for love, and a miserly fear, and dread, and belief of its precariousness. This is partly nature, and partly the result of the fact that in the beginning of my life, and through so much of my existence that it gained the force of a constitutional habit, I was the most beloved of many hearts. Others came between me and these loves, and for the hardest trial of single life I was unprepared. What little fame I may have had, and general consideration, has not been the slightest compensation to me for the loss of that instinctive tenderness so like divine love, that which needs no suggestion or prop of duty, but acts spontaneously with all the qualities of fire but its destructiveness. If I have not moderated my desires, I have come to consider more rationally the inevitable in my condition, and, I trust, more gratefully what is left to me."

Miss Sedgwick to Mrs. K. S. Minot.

"Lenox, September 28, 1851.

* * * * "It is good, as the burdens of age accumulate, to shake them all off; to change old, tiresome ideas for new ones; to take a world of fresh impressions; to fill the storehouse of imagination with new and beautiful images; to gain assurance to uncertain opinions; to verify old fancies; to throw off some of your old social burdens while you extend the social chain; in short, to go to Italy and come home again! And I think it would be a good plan, Kate, to send out one of the family every year to bring home 'bread and fruit' for those that must stay at home. Plowshares and reaping-hooks are grand things, but one would like some of the delectations of life. It was a convenient way of watering the earth in the old times of Adam and Eve by dews, but the clouds and the rainbow are the fine arts of Nature."

Miss Sedgwick to Mrs. K. S. Minot.

"Lenox, November 2, 1851.

"MY DEAREST KATE,—What weaver's shuttle in Job's day went as the days, months, and years fly now! November, the last month but that which goes to 'manners' and does us no good, has come and is going, and the months that make up that solemn creature called the year seem to me to bear no record that will not pass with the leaves of the flowers that have dropped. But this is nonsense! If it is by continual dropping that the rock is worn, so it is by minute accretions that the gem is formed, and our meetings and partings, the minglings of our smiles and tears, the voices and caresses of our children, the cheerful 'good-mornings' and prayerful 'good-nights' that have made up the year's life, have nourished those affections that constitute our immortality, that inspire the hope of it, that assure the faith in it, that are *it*.

"The poor elephant is no more!* William's gay words were hardly a fit accompaniment for his sublimely dreary carcass. I saw him dying on Friday. He lay quiet, looking dreamily around, his proboscis curled up, without a struggle or movement, seeming to express the submission of the mightiest thing on earth to a stern, inexorable, omnipotent Fate. It is odd enough, but he reminded me of the 'dying gladiator.' Were his visions, in that wretched shed of Butler's, where his captors had brought him to die, with the leaden skies of our November over him, of his fellows tramping over the bright Indian fields, and drinking (two barrels

---

* This elephant, 'Columbus,' belonged to a traveling menagerie. In crossing a bridge in the northern part of the county, he broke through, and was so injured by the fall that he could go no farther than Lenox. He lived, however, for some days, and was, of course, an object of much curiosity and interest.

at a draught!) the waters of the Tigris? Like the 'gladiator,' too, his captivity has made him immortal—at least so long as the napkin-ring and our memory of William's wit lasts. Instead of dissecting him, as William anticipated, they are going to bury him to-morrow entire, and claim damages of the town of Adams, which town, your father thinks, is very like to sue the company for breaking down their bridge!'

Miss Sedgwick to Mrs. K. S. Minot.

"Stockbridge, December 21, 1851.

* * * * "I hope you see the papers, and all the curious, exciting, odd, and great things daily occurring. Did you see the Cincinnati address? Apart from the great interest of Hungary and her apostle, it is a delight to me to see the currents of small party politics, of business competitions, of money profits and losses, and all low materialities, overflowed by an inundation of generous sentiment—the nation for once, and (if it be so) for one moment, kindled with a disinterested sentiment, the higher part of our nature in general action."

Miss Sedgwick to Mrs. K. S. Minot.

"Stockbridge, December 27, 1851.

* * * * "This morning the mercury at 8 o'clock was, by your Aunt Susan's thermometer, 9° *below*, and that little instrument, like every thing in her domain, is made as comfortable as possible, snugged up in a little corner of her south porch. Others in the town fell to 15° below. I am thus particular for my own self-glorification, for I went to breakfast with Judge Byington and his little girls, walking the half mile on slow, slippery walking, and to-morrow, Kate, I am sixty-two years old! I never felt that I was old till the fact of sixty years stared me in the face, the years that

all hold old ; and even now, if there were any mode of evading time, any *charlatanerie* of self-delusion that could gainsay the fact, I should give in to my general sensation that I am yet in mid-life, a fit companion for you who are still in your zenith, a fit playmate for Alice and Will ! But that I am I will maintain, for there is childhood at each end of the road ; they have not taken up the threads, and I have pretty much let them go ! * * * * The whole town, at least the female portion of it, are up and doing.* Even the softly, calculating, most arithmetical wives of our farmers are co-operating with the Hungarian champions of the Plain. Kossuth's speeches have produced a deep conviction of the religious truth of his cause, and of the solemnity of the duty of a practical protest in its favor. An earnest soul creates souls, vivifies the principle of life that *sleeps* throughout their earthly pilgrimage in so many human beings."

Miss Sedgwick to Mrs. K. S. Minot.

"Lenox, January 11, 1852.

* * * * "——— and ——— seem to me to have the true idea of a home—a place guaranteed against all foreign intervention ; a sanctuary of domestic rights and freedom ; a temple with open doors, but never to be entered by the profane ; a missionary station, whence light is to go forth to the heathen around them ; a life-school ; an insurance office for the next generation ; a fortress of religion and morality ; a guarded passage to the holy land for them, tended by their two little angels. Such securities for the permanence of our institutions, carried wherever they go, will defend us against swarms of Irish, and Irish priests and German radicals. Would they not have preserved the French from the horror of being drilled for freedom through centuries of alternate revolution and despotism ? Is it not the utter moral un-

* Getting up a fair for the Hungarians.

soundness and homelessness of the French that makes the blood all tend to the centre and putrefy there? Homes where intelligence and affection have fair play scatter light and life throughout the land, and make the surest defenses against centralization. * * * * I suppose you have heard from your mother every particular of the fair.* B. and Mrs. N. worked like a whole army of beavers. * * * * We were all charmed by Colonel Perczel. He is about forty-five—a fine person, with a complexion not exactly fair nor delicate, but having a certain tone expressing purity, refinement, manliness, health, and giving to beautiful and harmonious features just the ground they want. An expression naturally cheerful, but saddened by circumstances, for you constantly see the light beyond the eclipse. His manners, too, have a high-bred quality, kindly and gentle, with a certain reserve of delicacy, and not hauteur. Poor man! poor people! what are they to do? Not Kossuth—he is exceptional— the prophet will die or be translated. He who can say, 'If I am disappointed, I shall go to prayer, to the Lord's Supper, to battle, and to death,' will be looked after reverently and with longing eyes by those who sit at ease, but far and far below-him. * * * * Whatever he does for the Magyars, he is doing good to people that want this bread from heaven as much as *they* want any thing he can give them."

Miss Sedgwick to Rev. Dr. Dewey, on the death of the Rev. William Ware.

"New York, March 22, 1852.

* * * * "But there are subjects of fixed interest, such as the death of our dear friend, toward whom I have something of the feeling his wife expresses, and which, I think, we always have for those who have made an essential part of our existence—very life of our life—as if he were not dead—as

* For the Hungarians.

if I should meet him again in those manifestations in which
I have met him—see his serene brow, his calm eye—hear
his voice—

> "'Oh for a touch of the vanished hand,
> And a sound of the voice that is still !'

How many times—for how many have I breathed this wish
in agony of soul ! But for the death of those we love, and
against the dread of death for ourselves, there are the omnipotent words, 'Whether we live or die, we are the Lord's,
for to this end Christ both died, and rose, and revived, that
he might be Lord both of the living and the dead.' Let
us be tranquil, my dear friend—the nearer the end, the more
tranquil.

"I am very glad that you are writing about our friend for
the Christian Examiner. You should put your testimony
on record. No one living better understood him. I have
not read Bellows's sermon, but I was exceedingly pleased
with it when he preached it. I thought he got at the secret
springs of William Ware's failures and success. I think
there was no one present who estimated William Ware more
highly than I do, or loved him so well, and yet most of his
old congregation thought Mr. B. did great injustice, or rather
that he was in great error in his account of the deficiencies
in his pulpit exercises. But it can not be denied that he
was a cold (not dull), and, to strangers, an uninteresting
speaker. No man felt this so painfully as himself. But, in
spite of this, I can testify that, as a pastor, and even preacher, he was so beloved that I believe not one consented willingly to his going. Robert again and again, when he had
resolved on the step he finally took, persuaded him from it,
and when he finally went, it was felt throughout that little
Chambers Street Church like the breaking up of a family.
He was all gold—gold too pure to be worked up into the
world's common currency."

Miss Sedgwick to Mrs. K. S. Minot.

"New York, April 11, 1852.

* * * * "My indisposition is gone and nearly forgotten, and ought to serve me merely to mark my great exemption from the commonest affliction of humanity.   And, besides, it brings an overbalance of pleasure in the unusual manifestations of love it draws out from those to whom we really are dear ; and, when one grows old, my dear Kate, one gets to be covetous of such manifestations, and to feel somewhat like an old miser I knew who carried his title-deeds about with him, and thought that if he could not see them his estate was gone to rack and ruin."

Miss Sedgwick to Mrs. K. S. Minot.

"New York, May 2, 1852.

* * * * "I feel, my dear child, incompetent to sustaining the part of a Protestant champion. I have been myself content with the great principle achieved and fixed by the Protestant battle—the right of private judgment. I never could—and now less than ever—feel the vital importance of one mode of faith over another. The Protestant, in all its modifications, seems to me to have an immense advantage in its political influence, and in its general development and advancement of the species. But that God should look with more favor on any individual because he is a Catholic or a Protestant seems to me incredible. That the infinite Father of all, looking over his universe, should respect the fences and pens set up by his short-sighted creatures ! Some of these, no doubt, are far better for us than others, but no one nearer to His love than another. The great thing is to choose that best adapted to our spiritual wants, or rather, I should think, to rise to an elevation above them all—nearer to God's universal charity, and farther from man's ignorant restrictions.

"I long to know if you heard Kossuth. I trust so. No such orator has been, or in all human probability will be heard again. And, for his cause, it is the rock of eternal justice. Among the tribes that have poured in upon us this last week came a Dr. Redfield, a professor of the art of reading physiognomy. He pretends that it is an exact science, and truly his readings here were wonderful. I have never seen any thing in phrenology that bore any comparison with his interpretations of the girls' characters.

Miss Sedgwick to Mrs. K. S. Minot.

"Lenox, May 23, 1852.

"MY DEAREST KATE,—At Lenox once more, in health and comfort ; a good color on your father's cheeks, cheerfulness abounding, and a lovely infusion of bursting blossoms of violets, eyebrights, and tender green over nature. In spite of the chill in the atmosphere, which we must have whenever the wind blows from the snows still unmelted in our Northern forests—in spite of this, there is a pre-eminent beauty in the spring ; the grace, freshness, and vigor of youth —a sentiment breathing through nature—and the renewed evidence that seeming death is not death. In this last there is to me a silent, potent, solemn assurance that the precious life hidden from us is not extinct—that those we have laid in the bosom of the earth in age and in childhood shall appear before us in the infinite beauty of their immortality.

* * * * "I saw Kossuth for the first time, and though he did not make one of his brilliant speeches, I was not in the least disappointed. It seems to me that our imaginations always fall short in conceiving the best things of their class. The masterpieces of poetry, of nature, of art, all surpass your expectations, and so does the exquisite blending of nature and art in this divinely-inspired man. He seems to me like melody perfected by the harmonies of art

—the whole man, intellectual, moral, and physical, all co-
operating in one result. I never had so profound an impression from the presence of any human being, and I think
this is from the conviction that he has been called to a sacred duty, and with his whole soul has obeyed the call."

Miss Sedgwick to Mrs. K. S. Minot.

"New York, June 13, 1852.

"I came to New York, as you know, with the intention of
staying a few days, and, having a few odd jobs to do up, I
was immediately involved in an address to Kossuth on the
subject of a lecture he had expressed a wish to give in order to raise funds for his family, but which he could not
thrust upon the public. This address, the obtaining signa-
tures, and the work to obtain an audience involves an infinity of labor. Kossuth has bitter experience of the incon-
stancy of popular favor. Five months ago this city was in
a fever about him ; the skies were rent with the general ac-
clamations. Now, the last Convention and the next Convention, Meagher, the sale of a house-lot, the dry weather,
M. F.'s wedding, any topic that comes up, has more interest
and takes precedence ! The ladies went on Friday morning to present our request. Mrs. Kingsland, the mayoress,
presented it. Kossuth, of course, received us with his
graceful graciousness. He looked sad ; but, as he said, he
is inured to adversity."

Miss Sedgwick to Mrs. Channing (1852).

* * * * "I did not answer your letter about Margaret
Fuller because I wanted time for that. I did not entirely
sympathize with you, and truly I distrust myself when I do
not. The book raised my estimation extremely of Miss Fuller, and the sadness of her life and the tragedy of her death
took from me all power to criticise her. From first to last

she was a woman of noble aims, and, with all her egotism, unselfish in action. The longer I live, the more presumptuous and futile it seems to me to attempt judgment of character, and Miss Fuller's was exceptional. Her self-esteem was so inordinate as to be almost insane, but it appears (and it is, I think, so stated) to have been a constitutional and inherited defect, and certainly without moral taint. Her truth was exemplary, and all her conduct after she left off theorizing and began the action of life in the accustomed channels was admirable, her Italian life beautiful. The close had the solemnity of a fulfilled prophecy, and, with all its apparent horrors, was it not merciful? Had she come safely to our shores, she must have encountered harassing struggles for the mere means of existence, anxiety, and all the petty cares that perplex and obstruct a noble nature, and, worse than all, disappointment! If she were permitted to enter at once with those dearest to her upon a higher state of existence, added to the ecstasy of a new life there was the joy of an escape from this. The arms stretched toward her will soon enfold her! * * * * I shake hands with you and your dear family on Kossuth. I rejoice in the conviction of his preeminent virtue, and I have been deeply moved by his divine genius. He seems to me to take rank with the noble army of martyrs, for is not his life a continued martyrdom? I saw him twice in New York. He paid us one beautiful visit, and once I went with a deputation of ladies to ask him to give the lecture for his mother. Would you believe that we had difficulty in getting names enough to publish to this call, and infinite trouble and anxiety in getting up the meeting? Dear William R. worked gallantly, and I worked hard, and after discouragement and almost despair we had complete success at last. It was one of the *blissful* moments of life when we got to the Tabernacle that memorable night and found it full—and what a lecture it was!"

*Miss Sedgwick to Mrs. K. S. Minot, in answer to an invitation
to come to Woodbourne.*

"June 18, 1852.

* * * * "It was a lovely vision, that **sweet place in all its
June** loveliness, and an escape from this dreadful heat. **But,
dear** Kate, I probably feel very differently about the **claims
of this** cause* from what you can. It seems to me a patri-
otic and womanly duty **to** give succor to these poor exiles,
and **very strange if** one can not feebly work for **a** few days
for him **who,** however mistaken his judgments may prove, has
toiled day and **night** for humanity for months and years, who
has been in prison **and in perils oft,** in sorrows always."

Miss Sedgwick to Mrs. K. S. Minot.

"**Lenox,** November 7, 1852.

* * * * "Was not the fable of the ass and the lion aptly
quoted in a New York journal **in relation to** Theodore **Parker's** funeral sermon? What sweet and bitter waters **has**
that great **man's** death caused to flow ! I do not envy him
who can 'draw the frailties' of a man **from** 'their dread
abode,' or who does not gratefully leave them 'to repose on
the bosom of his Father and his God,' when death has just
mournfully closed the scene. * * * * They have had a
charming little excitement at S., quite novel in its kind.
Your Aunt Jane with **a** surplus ! (wonders will never cease)
is at last building a wash-room and a drain, and in opening
the ground through **her garden** the skeleton of a 'delicately-
formed' female **has** been discovered. We have all our pet
solutions **of the mystery.** Schoolmaster Canning, learned
in skulls, pronounced it an Indian **girl's. Some** presume to
suggest it may have been a 'subject' **of a** doctor in the neighborhood. One intimates it may **be the** solution of the mys-

* **The cause of** Kossuth and the Hungarians.

tery of your Aunt Jane's mammoth squash, and threatens to institute an inquiry at the next Berkshire Horticultural meeting as to the nature of the manures she employs! Those of us most eager for romantic mysteries (the oldest inhabitant, too) remember a certain Dr. Tidmarsh, an Englishman, who lived in E. W.'s house, who was implicated in some dark concern, and left his abode to the traditionary horrors of a haunted house. But the poor skull tells no tales."

Miss Sedgwick to Rev. Dr. Dewey.

"Lenox, November 27, 1852.

＊ ＊ ＊ ＊ "While in New York I heard Thackeray's first lecture. It was an able one, written in classic English, and given with a manly dignity and simplicity. He is a nice discerner and skillful delineator—so skillful that, if there were a detective police for the follies and infirmities of human nature, he would be elected chief by acclamation. But I have no affinities for this sagacity, and no great admiration for his detective revelations. I prefer those nice analyses that find sustenance instead of detecting poison; the one work is for our Channings, the other for Thackeray and the wise in their generation. I apply all this, however, to the impression received from Thackeray's novels; his lectures, I believe, will be in a good degree free from this characteristic fault—much more humane and genial than his books, and a valuable model for our lecturers, who, I trust, will learn by him to strike their roots deeper, to cultivate a more healthy atmospheric growth, and to prune off the spindling, forced, transcendental shoots that betray a false, perverted, and ignorant culture.

"You will not perceive—but I do, and smile at it—how my present chief interests are betrayed in my modes of expression. How I shall best secure my precious roses outside, and how give a healthy growth to my geraniums inside,

employs all the energy I have left.   Mine is at least an innocent vocation, and I shall succeed in it better than Louis
Napoleon with his empire.   What strange tragedies are playing in our day, and we never seem coming to the last act!
You have read Victor Hugo's wonderful pamphlet*—can
the French nation fail to be kindled by such combustibles
thrown among them?   This does find its way there, as many
copies have been seized.   Is France to go on in the process
of rottenness to general decay and death, or is there vitality enough for resuscitation?   Who can solve these fearful
questions?   Easy enough to ask!"

Miss Sedgwick to Mrs. K. S. Minot.

"Lenox, November 28, 1852.

* * * * "The rain came most opportunely, softening the
earth so that we could stick down our hemlock boughs.   I
don't think you were ever better satisfied when you had put
Alice and Willie to sleep, and tucked them in their crib and
trundle-bed, than I am at looking out at the nice green hemlock curtains that are to defend my roses from the stern caprices of the coming winter—from that worst of all treatment, either in the moral or physical world, alternate cold
and heat.   I have been getting from Long Island a variety
of the most beautiful flowering trees, and have set them all
along the path to Alice's rockery, meaning them to be typical of my love for your children, and, if I live long enough,
that rockery shall be a beautiful spot."

Miss Sedgwick to Mrs. Channing.

"Woodbourne, January 4, 1853.

"MY DEAR FRIEND,—I have nearly given up the hope
of hearing that you are in Boston, and of meeting you there,
and therefore I must use this poor substitute (Heaven for-

* Napoléon le Petit.

give my ingratitude, for that which bridges the abysses of absence is not poor) for the seeing of the eye, and the hearing of the ear, and thus impart to you my earnest wishes for a 'happy new year' to you and yours. And how differently does this phrase sound to us as time bears us on ! These few words envelop our history, sparkle in our youth with presumptions and insatiable hope, and then grow dull and dim till they catch the ray from a better life ; and, brightened with this vitality, my dear friend of many years, I utter them to you. * * * * I am growing to like more and more this country residence. Besides the ever-fresh delights of an expanse of heaven, and trees, and fields, and the actual advantage of leisure, there is an escape from the infinite tediousness of city social life, an exemption from making and receiving 'calls,' which are the froth of a stagnant pool. I do not think much of it as teaching you your real value to the five hundred, for that secret a person of tolerable perception learns in various ways, but it is a wholesome rebuke to one's vanity to learn how very few will pay twenty cents and walk half a mile for the happiness of seeing you. You hear on all sides, no doubt, of Thackeray's lectures. I wish you could hear them. They are capital specimens of the best London talk, with the perfecting of careful revision, and given in a voice that indicates a perception of the sentiment of life, and a thorough baptism in its sorrows. Thackeray, with his great genius, has been no favorite of mine. He seems to me a libeler of humanity—the very antagonistic spirit to your brother William's. His last book is better ; the character of Esmond an '*amende*' to one half of the race. But his Countess, after all his elaborate laudation, is but an oversweet pretty woman, with the instincts and all the weaknesses of the weakest maternity ; and Beatrix is but his other phase of womankind, and neither have the merit of being natural." * * * *

Miss Sedgwick to Mrs. K. S. Minot.

"New York, March 20, 1853.

* * * * "I perceive that neither you nor William like 'Ruth' quite as well as I did. I agree with you entirely as to the enormity of visiting such an offense so vindictively, but it does not seem to me that the Pharisees of —— were much more oppressively righteous than our own people. * * * * The fault is in an undue estimate. The absolute necessity of chastity in a woman, as far as the certain transmission of property goes, has given a legal sanction to this blinding of the eyes and hardening of the heart. Women who violate every duty, who are pests in temper, who tear and rend their neighbors' characters, who are sensualists to the utter degradation of the soul, ride in the world's chariots (and no man or woman is so rich but they do them reverence), and in men the *permitted* grossness in thought, word, and deed, can't be spoken of, but a poor girl, ignorant of her own nature, with opportunity thrust upon her, and love blinding her, is the victim through life of a single offense. It is a perpetual punishment without hope of pardon, a rack from which the 'death penalty' is the only escape."

Miss Sedgwick to Mrs. K. S. Minot.

"New York, March 28, 1853.

"I passed last Saturday evening in C. F.'s ducal apartments, and met there Father Gavazzi, an Italian patriot priest, converted to Protestantism, or, as he says, to Paulism. He looks to me as if he had thrown off the priestly harness as joyously as Retzsch's Pegasus did the farmer's, but not from heavenly aspirations so much as carnal affections. He has nothing of the trained simulation of a priest, but looks strong and bold, as if he could lead or stay the multitude. His eloquence is said to have produced im-

mense effect in England. Perhaps its effect was partly owing to his striking the master-note in a full orchestra of
papist haters. I did not like his speech here, but he has a
rabble of orthodox 'mother of Babylon' haters crying ' hosanna !' after him. One has but to get up a stylish menagerie, and the lions are whistled into it like so many tame
pigeons ! I was looking through Mrs. F.'s vast arcades
when I saw *our* dear Mrs. F., looking lovely in black velvet
and lace, advancing with an Indian woman on her arm, arrayed in a theatrical costume composed of scarlet cloth, em-
broidered muslin, and tinsel, which she called an ' Indian
dress.' The moccasins were national, and the immense
Spanish fan might have been a gift from a Spanish king
of the sixteenth century to one of the majesties of the Mon-
tezumas."

Miss Sedgwick to Mrs. K. S. Minot.

"New York, April 17, 1853.

* * * * "We all went last Friday evening to hear Father
Gavazzi, and, if ever you have an opportunity in Boston, I
beg that you and William will go. It was in the brilliant
Metropolitan Hall, which holds 4000, and it was full to the
brim. He wears his priestly cassock, with the cross em-
broidered on the breast and sleeve, and an Italian cloak of
sufficient amplitude to give any effect of drapery he chooses.
He has the strongest of Italian faces, with that blackest of
hair that gives expression like the shadow of a picture. His
voice is powerful and flexible. He is melodramatic, and
has some *charlatanerie,* but is as great an actor as a man can
be who has these extravagances and purposes of effect ; and
you are less disgusted with this class of faults in an Italian
—their atmosphere is oxygenated. I have seen no such
actor since Kean's time. His lecture was on Italy. His
satire was keen, his contempt biting. He portrayed the

whole Popish church in Italy as an organization of police,
the pope being *chef;* and he described the throbbing of the
Italian heart under the pressure of foreign domination in a
way to make one's blood curdle. As I listened I could not
help running a parallel between him and Kossuth, whom we
heard this time last year. His angelic calmness, his Oriental grace, his flexibility, versatility, and the poetic quality
of his language, the white, heavenly light which invested
him, made him as one of ' God's messengers who hearken
to his word and do his pleasure.' Father Gavazzi was lighted with prismatic colors ; he dealt with thunderbolts and
flashes of lightning, and seemed sent forth by the Furies to
cry ' havoc, and let loose the dogs of war.' How many
spirits must there be in Italy seething under those priestly
robes !"   .

Miss Sedgwick to **Mrs. K. S. Minot.**

"New York, March 31, 1853.

"MY DEAREST KATE,—My heart turns to you as the only
one who can entirely feel, and will, in a good degree, share
my sorrow in the death of my—our dear friend Madame Sismondi. I have just received the news by a letter from
Mary Mackintosh. She says she died 'peaceful and happy;'
so she should, and so I am sure she would if she had her
senses. So, dear Kate, the dearest treasure of our journey
has passed away, and the sweet letters that came like the
holy dew of its twilight will be no more forever. To me it
will make no other difference. If I am worthy—I bitterly
feel that I am not—but, if God's mercy permits it, it can not
be long when, my weary journey, too, finished, I shall rejoin
her ; and even now she seems nearer to me than when she
lived. And you, dear Kate—I trust you will cherish her
memory, and the memory of that beautiful union which
showed us what a happy marriage was, and demonstrated

God's love in that institution which, I thank Him, you, my beloved child, have realized more intimately."

"April, 1853.

" Have you all read ' Villette ?' and do you not admire the book, and own it as one of the great books of the time? I confess that I have seldom been more impressed with the genius of a writer, and seldom less drawn to her personally. She has nerves of such delicate fineness of edge that the least touch turns them, or she has had an exasperating experience. Whether she calls herself Jane Eyre, or Lucy Snowe, it does not matter—it is Miss Brontë. She has the intensity of Byron—of our own Fanny Kemble. She unconsciously infuses herself into her heroine. It is an egotism whose fires are fed by the inferior vitality of others ; and how well she conceives others ! how she daguerreotypes them !

" You have read Jeffrey's life and letters ? What a privilege it is to read these best effusions of his spirit—strangers and aliens from him, to be permitted to read letters that have each been unsealed with expectation, reverence, and love by those whose right they were ! I have scarcely in my lifetime enjoyed any thing more, or felt a more glowing response (according to my poor measure) to the sentiments of any nature. How susceptible he was to the beauty of nature—to the clouds, the sky, the birds, the flowers ; how loving to children ; how warm and generous in his friendships ; how affectionate to women ; how every thing that a man should be ! I know you say amen to all I could say. Do you remember that beautiful letter about Burns ?"

"Lenox, June 6, 1853.

* * * * "Your kind proposal, dearest child, I can not

take up with.   I can not leave my garden for a month at
this season.   I am booked for the White Hills in July, and
am half engaged to make a little captivating journey with
Charles of Syracuse.   Besides, I have hired myself as dairy-
maid to Belle, and Lizzy is coming on Thursday, relying on
being my guest."

Miss Sedgwick to Mrs. K. S. Minot.   .

"Lenox, July **17**, 1853.

"My DEAREST KATE,—We arrived, having made a most
prosperous finish to our prosperous journey, at 3 o'clock yesterday.   I feel deeply grateful for the immense and unlook-
ed-for enjoyment I have had.   It is still in my mind a lovely picture, and the memory of my time (times) at Woodbourne as superior to the rest as Prometheus's state was
after he had brought fire from heaven to kindle it.   The
White Hills were full of melody, but the bird loves to fold
its wings in its own nest, and free as any thing mortal can
be from all that clouds and frets life seems the dear nest in
the covert of Woodbourne.   I found all very well here, and
the wheels rolling on smoothly.   C. is nicely.   Mr. W. and
Sixteenth Street breakfasted with me this morning ; Mr. H.
G. in addition, and W. B., who arrived last evening, and who
seems quite enchanted with Berkshire.   I found my flowers
looking like children whose mother has been spending the
day out—vines dangling, and long fresh spikes of rose-trees
running out in every direction, young plants disappeared,
etc., etc.   I fell to work in the rain (for it began to rain after we arrived) transplanting, etc., and to-morrow shall go
vigorously to work, and hope to get my wires up. * * * *
I believe I am losing, or have lost, my faculties, for I can
think of nothing else to say, a difficulty that never occurred
before in writing to you.   Thanks, dear child, and dear William, for your kindness to me ; kind you would have been

to any body, but I don't believe an own mother ever had truer happiness in visiting her child than I have in going to you."

"July 23, 1853.

" DEAREST KATE,—There are miseries in human life that Job, or Solomon, or Jeremiah have never described, because probably prophecy never revealed to them the folly of those fools who attempt to write after their eyes lie in a pair of spectacles. For the last *quart d'heure* (of infinite length) I have been looking for my spectacles with the desperate conviction that I have dropped them in my flower-beds, and shall *never* find them ! And I have looked up an old pair with one glass (typically) looking heavenward and the other earthward, and now I proceed to what I should have begun my letter with but for this accident—if that can be called accident which is as regular as my pulses.

" Don't grow too grand for your Berkshire annual migration while your *three* parents here survive. An old home is like an old violin : the music of the past is wrought into it."

"Lenox, October 2, 1853.

* * * * "What a blessing it is to look out daily on a scene that calls forth freshly and sincerely the song, 'O Lord, my Lord, how excellent are thy works !' My increased love and enjoyment of nature is far more than a compensation to me for the dulled relish of society, and the loss of anticipations and projects that age surely brings. But there are losses that but grow heavier as we go on. The sense of the loss of friends becomes even more acute as the interests of life diminish. Time hushes, but does not console. The manifestations are less and less, but the void is deeper and more aching.

"*Lenox, October* 27, 1853. I have just come from my ministrations to the poor jail-people. I do wonder if I do them any good. I have faith that seed may germinate at any distance of time—or eternity."

Miss Sedgwick to Mrs. K. S. Minot.

From a charming description of an agreeable evening at Miss Lynch's, 23d March, 1854.

"There was a Mr. M. too, a marked young man. After telling me in a very pleasant way—which, as I know, it requires an immense *savoir faire* to know how to do—how much his sister and himself had liked my books, he said his sister came in from walking one day, and said, 'I have seen such a compliment paid Miss Sedgwick! I saw a carman reading in the crowded street, and apparently absorbed. I crossed the street, determined to see what book he had, and it was "Live and Let Live!" Now, dear, don't involve my vanity by telling this to any one but W. It pleased me so much that I could not keep it to myself."

In the spring of 1854 Miss Sedgwick and her brother Charles were invited to join an excursion party of two or three hundred people to visit the Falls of St. Anthony, the cities of St. Paul and St. Louis, etc.

Miss Sedgwick to Mr. Wm. Minot Jr.

"Utica, May 30, 1854.

"MY DEAR WILLIAM,—You and Kate will be glad to know that we are this *one step* prosperously on our journey. I had many misgivings as to the propriety of my brother's undertaking it, and all opinions were against it except his wife's and Dr. Bailey's. But so far it has proved well. Owing to a change in the running of the cars, we did not leave Pittsfield till 3 P.M., and did not reach Utica till half past ten ; but he had nice naps, an excellent dinner at Pittsfield, a nice tea at the Delavan, and the news that the party was to be conveyed from Chicago to the Falls of St. Anthony and back free of all expense ! This, I think, set him up. A bargain is the delight of man's as well as woman's heart, and a man that does not care a straw for gold finds his mercury amazingly affected by saving it. He has been in fine spirits, and really seems quite well."

Miss Sedgwick to Mrs. K. S. Minot.

"Chicago, June 4, 1854.

* * * * "Your father has kept up wonderfully. He was tired last night, but would not confess it, and I have not yet heard the report this morning. He has certainly borne the journey miraculously ; he was the charm of the boat—young men hanging about him to hear his jokes.

"*PM.*—Your father came forth bright as the stars. Stars ! 'There is a glory of the sun,' and that is his. We have been dining out at the prettiest place in Chicago, and had a charming service at the Unitarian Church, and a communion, and your father staid, and it was truly a refreshing and rest. I wish I could give you any notion of the scene here. It is something new in the world—the meeting at the time of the gift of tongues was tame to it. There are people from all parts of the country. Many people of note, names long known and honored—by *some :* President Fillmore, Thurlow Weed, General Dix, Bancroft, Flagg, Judge Oakley, our dear beaming Chancellor M'Coun, painters, writers, sculptors, traveling Englishmen, Scotchmen, Italians, young ladies and old, old friends meeting in the doorways, loud and glad greetings, all with their 'steam up'— for the Mississippi. Young belles dressed for conquest, quiet interior matrons, young American lads, men of all ages, and all on the alert, plumed. To-morrow we start for

Rock Island at eight with a band of music. Five steamers, all chartered for the Falls. We are only to sail during waking hours, to stop at the mouths of all the great rivers, and if we *don't* blow up we shall have a grand time. I am now well fired up ; you would not know me for the be-drooft* woman that parted with you at Lenox. And your father—his mercury has got to the very top of the scale ! The people stared at him to-day at dinner, and laughed, and got more social vitality into them than they ever dreamed of before."

Miss Sedgwick to Mrs. K. S. Minot.

"Mississippi River, June 9, 1854.

" Going down this noblest of all rivers I have seen, dearest Kate, like a bird of swiftest passage. We are now one hundred and ninety miles above Rock Island, and expect to arrive there to-morrow at 7 A.M. ! The directors, our magnificent hosts, have extended their invitation to St. Louis.

" Your father has become quite fond of the people. Were there ever affections so abounding—so plastic ! His health improves, and he has more spirits than any one in the boat.

" I can not begin to tell you what we have enjoyed in this marvelous passage. I can not leave the deck long enough to describe one point of interest and beauty. One rainy day only gave variety to the scenery. Yesterday we drove over the prairie from St. Paul's to the Falls of St. Anthony, to Minnehaha—Laughing Water—a fall as beautiful as the Venus de Medicis—and to Fort Snelling. It was a day better than most lifetimes."

---

* A Dutch word Miss Sedgwick picked up in her early days in Albany, and was fond of using. The spelling is conjectural, but the word evidently corresponds to the German betrübt, and has the same meaning.

Miss Sedgwick to Mrs. K. S. Minot.

"On the Mississippi, June 11, 1854.

"We are running between **Missouri** and Wisconsin, and, when we stop 'to wood' or take in freight, we run on shore and hold a little talk with the Iowans, Wisconsians, and now the Missourians. There is proverbially 'no Sunday on the river.' At the bow-end of the cabin, on one side, is the clerk's office, on the other is the bar. On this boat, owning and serving the bar, is a personification of Dickens's 'fat boy.' He claimed acquaintance with me on my first appearance; showed me the daguerreotypes of his wife and two pretty children; said my writings lay on his table with these treasures, and how fond his 'ma' was of them. He begs me to go and see her at St. Louis; gives me 'Muscatine Journals' and 'Iowa Gazettes' to read, and as often as I pass his bar, begs me to stop and partake his ever-flowing hospitalities. The drinking of these people is inconceivable; still, your father and H. say they have not seen a drunken person.

"At St. Louis we shall have come nine hundred and seventy miles from the Falls of St. Anthony! These broad lands are the preserves of the Lord of earth's manor for his children, 'moulded by his forming hand' into an excess and perfection of beauty that is truly, Kate, inconceivable. It is in vain to say, 'Recall the most beautiful park-grounds we saw in England, the velvet lawns, the trees of centuries' growth, and then imagine them stretching to the utmost limit of sight; fancy precipitous hills, as steep as Monument Mountain, of all shapes, soft and wavy, and then running up into aiguilles, and all covered with this velvet carpet—trees planted in lines, in copses, in groups, in orchards, and here and there belted with a wall of sand or limestone, and surmounted with the most perfect mockeries of castle

foundations, and turrets, and towers—like the Rhine ; for
here is 'the cat,' and there 'the mouse ;' here Stotzenfels,
there Rheinfels and Rheinstein ; and yet how unlike any
thing in the Old World !   So fresh! so young! such abounding, vigorous vitality !   Not much historical embellishment ;
and yet here is 'Mad-axe ;' here, where Black Hawk leaped
on the bluff, showed his red flag to his people, and fled ; here,
the cross that La Salle, after traversing the country from
Quebec, planted ; and here, where Miss Bishop landed to
inquire, five years ago, for St. Paul's (four miles from it), and
was told there was no such place.   The New England missionary girl had faith in her instructions, hired two Indian
girls to paddle her in a canoe to the site of St. Paul's, found
two white families there, pitched her tent, opened her school,
had, to begin, eight white children, and now came on board
to tell us of her flourishing boarding-school, amid five thousand inhabitants !

"Here we are at Hannibal.   The 'Golden Era' coming
up ; the captain says we have 'half an hour ; will you go on
shore ?'   In half a minute we are patroling, like old citizens,
the streets of Hannibal, Missouri.   I had put my bon-bons
at the table into my pocket instead of my stomach (a salu-
tary substitution), and distributed them, Robin Hood fashion, among the black and white children, and bought 'gold-
en kisses' from bright young lips.   We went up the hill, took
a wide survey of the beautiful surroundings, were overtaken
by a violent gust of rain, and came scudding in.   I will not
afflict you by writing more.   I can not write better in this
jarring, trembling boat, and you can not read.

"*Niagara Falls, Sunday, June* 18, 1854. Here we are
again, my dear child, in health and safety, thanks to the
providence of God, and going out of this Western world by
the glorious gates through which we entered.   Yes, dear
Kate, how I wish you were with me for this day's ramble !

We have continued to enjoy, your father gaining strength, and by his infinite diffusiveness, and power of love almost divine, giving out more than any one else on this jaunt, binding people together, and spreading broad sunshine every where. As to noise, and dust, and all *discomforts*, we do not talk about them, or care much."

Miss Sedgwick to Mrs. K. S. Minot.

"Lenox, June 24, 1854.

"My dearest Kate,—My journey had its final crown and rejoicing when our precious little Alice sprang out of the dining-parlor door into my arms as I alighted from the last vehicle of our long travel. Twenty times that day it had occurred to me 'what a delight it would be to find Alice at Lenox!' but with no expectation of finding that vision, that seemed to me to rise like an *ignis fatuus* from my heart, realized. It was very, *very* kind of you and William to send her. Our journey was prosperous to its end. Not the slightest accident—not even a detention of more than fifteen minutes in a journey of 3740 miles! Providence must think better of rail-travel than William does. I would give a great deal to transfer to you the pictures in my mind of Western life, Western cities, illimitable prairies, and those beautiful, untrodden shores of the Upper Mississippi. No American can have an adequate notion of the future destiny of this land, of its unbounded resources, of the unlimited provisions awaiting the coming millions, without seeing—for seeing is believing—the great Valley of the Mississippi, and measuring by that 'the West' beyond. I would not certainly give up one of our hearthstones for it all, for my own life, but it is the soil for the young to take root and spread in ; and if they will but take with them the elements of moral as well as of physical growth, there need be no failure in this new world. The insane avarice of our people is worse than the

potato-rot, and how the real worth and work of money is to
be got into their heads and hearts is the problem to be
solved.   But there are people who are aware of their mission, and are 'about their Father's business.'   We saw Mr.
Eliot,* of St. Louis, who is said to have a wider religious and
moral influence than any man at the West of any sect ; and
one of the proofs is that he makes men of all sects tributary
to him, and co-operate with him.   The day we were there,
Colonel ———, their Crœsus (a man of a different faith
from Eliot), gave him property to the amount of $30,000 for
an industrial school.   He is a very attractive person, with
a spirituality and refinement that reminds you of Dr. Channing, but with the freedom, frankness, and facility that belongs to a more practical, out-of-doors man."

Miss Sedgwick to Mrs. K. S. Minot.

"Stockbridge, August 13, 1854.

* * * * " The event, to me, of the past week was a very
charming visit to Sheffield.   Mr. Dewey's domestic life is
beautiful ; it is to his fame what the rose-tints are to the
white rays of the sun.   His mother is eighty-two, with all
the highest attributes of age and none of its infirmities.
She listens to her son as to an oracle, and he treats her
with a filial tenderness and reverence that is as beautiful as
it is rare.   When we were there he was encompassed by
fifteen womankind, and he sat among us, hour after hour,
without being (seeming?) weary or dull ; talking wisely or
playfully, and always with an affectionateness that would be
called womanly in a less manly man.   The old house has
had various repairs and additions (he meditates more) ; the
old homestead is neatly kept, the old trees grow to vener-
ableness, and the simple *ménage* is ordered with the utmost
skill and ability.   I never saw a less ostentatious, or a more
cordial and effective hospitality."

* Rev. Dr. Eliot.

Miss Sedgwick to Rev. Dr. Dewey.

"October, 1854.

"I was reading Sydney Smith's life when I received your letter, and felt as if—in Mesmeric phrase—put into communication with you. He was not a speculative, perhaps not a spiritual man. There are some men in whom you can see wings germinating, but Sydney Smith seems to me like our own Franklin, perfectly fitted for his sphere, and perfectly performing his mission in that sphere, as eminent for his good practical sense as for the universally-accepted and unrivaled charm of his humor. What a blessed and blessing temper he carried into his restricted, humble life in Yorkshire! What a lesson to us country-folk is his enjoyment of 'Calamity,' 'Peter the Cruel,' and 'Bunch,' and the calico shades at Foston! The narrowness of his income (shame to the injustice and intolerance of the most civilized of civilized nations!) caused no wry look nor querulous word, and yet no man ever set a truer value on 'gold guineas,' or better loved the generosities and comforts they brought. And what a flood of sunshine he poured around him! how merrily he sent his shafts, so charmed by the holy oil of his sweet temper that the healing went with the wound, so that those oftenest pierced seemed to have felt only a pleasant sensation! Would not you have liked to have been one of those guests rescued from the 'Dumplin' soirée? Would you not have been Jeffrey on the jackass to have heard the doggerel salutation?—even to have been Jeffrey without it, heartily reveling with those rampaging children? Oh, it is a charming book! I thank God for his lovely character, and his daughter for her honest, earnest setting-forth of it. There is much wisdom, too, in his theoretical views of life, as well as in his uses of it. And at this moment, while I am shrinking from the future, I am rebuked by his admoni-

tions, and try to make the most of the happy present, much
as the light is diminished.   Charles is not well, and I look
on his pale face with a cowardly shrinking; yet, my dear
friend, I think I have gained something of tranquillity in
looking forward, and that I can say honestly and peacefully
those words that should never be vainly spoken, as they im-
ply the triumph of faith—'Thy will be done!'"

Miss Sedgwick to Mrs. K. S. Minot.

"Lenox, October 29, 1854.

* * * * "Your father read aloud after breakfast Henry
Beecher's sermon on the loss of the 'Arctic.' I seldom
have a pleasure that I do not wish to impart to you and
William, and if I can, I shall get this sermon for you. It is
adequate to the great tragedy that called it forth. Its solemn, exalted eloquence does not transcend your judgment.
It seems to me that language could scarcely express more
effectively the meanings of that fearful wreck, or more poet-
ically describe its concomitants. He is wrong, I think, in
making the commercial calamities of the last four years a
visitation upon the Compromise of 1850. We have no authority for such direct applications and interpretations of
God's judgments; but, with that exception, and leaving out
two or three phrases and words, it is unquestionably the production of a great head and great heart. It invests that
awful scene with a religious light, and sets in solemn order
the great truths to be learned from it. Beecher is a great
man for these times; 'bold, but not too bold;' outspoken,
and yet speaking advisedly, and with the power of genius
and scholarship; having those sympathies with the masses,
and intimate fellowship with them, which he imbibed with
his mother's milk, in the plays of his childhood, and the
competitions of his youth."

Miss Sedgwick to Mrs. K. S. Minot, after a long visit to Wood-bourne.

"Lenox, February 20, 1855.

* * * * "I came to bed as wretched as Lyttleton's night-howler; no softly-breathing child couched at my feet, no dear close neighborhood of beloved ones, no unfailing warmth, no loving green arms about the house with softly-whispering music, no nibbling mice! And in the morning —think of it, Kate!—why, I felt like one pitched out of a paradise home within four walls (a 'far sight' pleasanter than Adam and Eve's out-of-door paradise) into a snow-bank, with no stars, twilight, or dawn."

Miss Sedgwick to Mrs. K. S. Minot.

"Lenox, June 24, 1855.

* * * * "I heard of dear Judge Wilde's death, and with him has dropped the last link that bound me to my father's times, and passed away a friend, the very sight of whom made this life pleasanter, and strengthened the assurance of another by making me vividly feel there was no possible destruction of such qualities as made his life. Another sure and pleasant light has gone out, and those of us who are near the end must feel the dimness that it makes. But God surely has been merciful not longer to burden his weary old faithful servant."

To Mr. William Minot Jr., who was passing the summer at the sea-shore.

"Lenox, July 8, 1855.

* * * * "There is something to me solemn in the sea-shore without being sad; it hallows all days into Lord's days; it makes worship spontaneous, and utters a full an-them response to the sublimest tones of David's psalms. I

Q

have never been familiar enough with it to lose the awe it
first inspired.   I do not think I should like to live near it.
Its grand symphonies would overpower the sweet, soft, playful, bird-like tones of happy social life.   Prophets and seers
should dwell on the sea-shore, and apostles and martyrs
learn there to trample the earth under their feet.   But for
'common doings,' give me our smiling hill-sides and secure
little valleys."

Miss Sedgwick to Mrs. K. S. Minot.

"Lenox, July 1, 1855.

"DEAREST KATE,—Is it not a morning typifying the fur-
nace-heat of this hot summer-month *par excellence*, going like
a hot iron to the very marrow, fierce, destructive?   I am out
of humor; the plants are all belated, and they don't gallop
on as they should with this heat.   And I have a new and
most insidious enemy—a little green worm in the very heart
of each and every prairie rose-bud, eating its roseate life and
beauty out of it—a malignant little devil, corrupting the innocent life of all my little vestals."

Miss Sedgwick to Mrs. Channing.

"Lenox, July 27, 1855.

* * * * "I have felt very near you in reading the pleasant report of William's* intercourse with our transatlantic
brethren.   I think he is doing good there in many ways,
but most of all in breaking away from their old formulas,
and infusing a spirituality—a spiritual *life* into his ministrations which English preaching, so far as I know it, seems to
me very devoid of, or rather deficient in, for to be absolutely without it is to be dead.   It is a proof of William's power
that they take instruction meekly from him, for omniscience,
you know, is the ordinary gift of an Englishman." * * * *

* Rev. Wm. H. Channing, then preaching in Liverpool, England.

In 1855 there was much sickness and anxiety in the family circle, and in the autumn of that year Miss Sedgwick passed some weeks at a water-cure with an invalid niece. Returning to Lenox, she found her brother Charles still suffering from the effects of an attack of illness the preceding spring, and, as her anxious tenderness foreboded, he never recovered his health.

Miss Sedgwick to Mrs. K. S. Minot.

"Lenox, August 26, 1855.

"Monday morning, and the last minute's grace. Oh, Kate, what a morning I have had! company to breakfast; making pies and custards for Mr. M., your Aunt Jane, etc., for dinner, while K. J., here to spend the day, sat by to read me a MS. novel! Very beautiful!

"*Dr. Munde's Water-cure, near Northampton,* October 7, 1855. * * * * I have just come from reading Samson Agonistes to L. on the piazza, half frozen; any thing out of doors a regular water-patient can bear. They superadd to their human endurance that of birds and fishes. This establishment would please you if it were but a reminiscence of Germany. I can hardly believe myself in the heart of Yankeeland. The doctor is completely German, quiet and strong like their old Hartz giants. He looks like a victorious general. His wife, too, is a perfect German, uniting the lady and the housekeeper; the arrangements in detail, and all the operations, are German. It is an admirably ordered institution. The table is perfectly neat, bountifully supplied with the permitted edibles, but neither love nor money obtain favors. The provisions are uniformly excellent—bread, delicious butter, cracked wheat; farina, prepared better than ever I saw it; rice, and a sort of German toast—cold, of course, but very nice. There are but two women to wait on the table—about forty present—and I have

never heard a word spoken to them.   They seem both Argus
and Briareus.   There is a dumb-waiter that does all they do
not do.   We have a single sort of meat for dinner, always
good, prefaced by excellent soup, and followed by excellent
pudding, and accompanied by potatoes, tomatoes, and rice,
and stewed apples or prunes, and cabbage, which I believe
a German would eat on his death-bed.   'And Satan came
also among them,' I am ready to exclaim, when the maid
sets it down among its innocent compeers."

Miss Sedgwick to Mrs. K. S. Minot.

"Lenox, October 21, 1855.

* * * * "Your father will tell you how much he has
been relieved by the adjournment of the court till November.
* * * * We can not conceal from ourselves that he is in a
very delicate state ; and sometimes, dear Kate, when I look
at him, I feel as if he were on the verge of a translation ;
less of a change, when it comes, will it be to him than to almost any man who has passed through the earthly life, so
completely has he filled his with love and goodness.   What
will the world be to me without him?   Our separation can
not be long—for the rest God will provide."

Mr. Charles Sedgwick died on the third of August in the
following summer.   The lovely record of his character is
written indelibly on the hearts of all who knew him.   His
sister's love for him had been intensified by time and by the
loss of all her immediate family beside, but no one ever
thought her adoring affection unwarranted by its object.

Miss Sedgwick to Mrs. K. S. Minot.

"Lenox, August 2, 1856.

"MY BELOVED CHILD,—I got William's letter last evening.   God bless him for his most sweet words of comfort.

Your father had quite a comfortable day, comparatively, all through yesterday; talked a good deal, and slept without talking much in his sleep; spoke often of his delicious, splendid day. Three days ago, when he was very low, your mother said, 'It is hard Kate can't be with us;' he said, 'I think I shall see the little thing yet.' And yesterday both B. and I had a hope he might; but these are weak earthly desires; a higher love than ours awaits him, the brightness and happiness of which his whole life and character are a type. He shrinks from pain, he hates darkness, he recoils from sorrow—they are all earthly conditions—and oh! God grant us the faith and the love that goes beyond; grant us willingness to have this harassing struggle end, to suffer that he may rejoice. He has had a poor night and a restless morning, but is now sleeping quietly. He looks very sweetly, his face calm, and, for one so ill, not distressful. Bless William for his letter. Tell him it folds around my heart and staunches the bleeding. Dearest Kate, continue calm and cheerful. You have been a stay to your father all your life. For your own sake, for your husband's, for the little one, whom God bless to you, cherish all sweet and comforting thoughts. Don't make any unusual effort. Nature must have her dues. * * * * Each waits their turn to do all that he or she can do. E. is now at his side. F. is devoted. W. is sweet and most helpful. Dear little G. all she can be, and your mother never leaves him except for her meals and required sleep. She is a good deal let down, but I think she will be enabled to go through unfalteringly. The Stockbridge friends are here every day, and all friends thronging to offer aid and express kindness. The seed he has sown at broadcast springs up and yields the fitting harvest."

Miss Sedgwick to Mrs. K. S. Minot.

"Lenox, August 4, 1856.

"My dearest Child,—I want to put my arms around you, and see you look up in faith and love ; but I could not be more assured than I am that you thank God fervently that the last pang is over, and that your blessed father has gone from the heaven he made for us to the heaven that awaited him. Yes, the 'good and faithful servant has entered into the joy of his Lord.' His mind was perfectly clear up to the last hour. The last day was a day of continual oppression, excepting for an hour or two at twilight, when he slept. He took a part of a cup of tea from me at the usual time. His hardest night was Friday. H. watched, and even then his spirit rose above his mortal conflict, and he talked with him about Kansas, and urged exertion to be made to secure the Irish vote for Fremont. And now, relieved of the mortal pressure, how has his spirit expanded ! I am sure you and William will always rejoice in Alice being with us. She has been a consoling angel. Even on Saturday, when it was *labor* to your father to speak, he asked me 'where is Alice? She is a sweet little creature.' His last kiss was given to her ; take it from her lips, dear Kate, and feel that a breath of love was in it for you. I hesitated, after William's request to me, about taking her into the room, but after going up, and seeing how sweet he looked—how far more like himself than in the last scenes, and asking B. and all, I decided to take her up, and thought there could never be less of shock in the sight of death. She went, and, so far from recoiling, she stood by him of her own impulse, stroked his hair and beard, as she used whenever she approached him, kissed him, and continued to hold his hand in hers. How could it be otherwise? There lay that head in its natural posture, a little on one side—a head more expressive of dignity and sweetness never was. Last night, when she was undressing, she said, 'Is it not pleasant to think grandpapa's spirit may be in the room with us?'"

Just one week after Mr. Charles Sedgwick's death the expected "little one" appeared at Woodbourne, and the news brought the first throb of happiness to Miss Sedgwick's heart in that dark hour of bereavement and desolation. She felt from that time as if the child were sent as a special gift of consolation to her; her affection was even increased when he received the beloved name of Robert, and she cherished for him always a peculiar tenderness and devotion.

Miss Sedgwick to Mrs. K. S. Minot.

"Lenox, August 17, 1856.

* * * * "You know—you all know how my heart turns to you; how the light truly shines from the east upon my darkened spirit. But, my dear Kate, I can not leave here for the present; here only the vacant places answer to the cries of my spirit; here the form has not departed. I see my brother on the sofa—on the piazza. I spread his table for him. I start at the sound of his voice. I go down into the garden, and look at the 'corn,' and the 'Lima beans,' and the 'tomatoes,' and tell him how they are growing. He still sits at my chamber window; his light, as well as his shadow, is every where; and while the summer lasts, the season that bears his visible impress, I can not go away."

Miss Sedgwick to Rev. Dr. Dewey.

"Lenox, September, 1856.

* * * * "Here I cling, for here still lingers the twilight of my day. Here every object is associated with my brother—with sweet memories of pleasant or loving words, and

looks, and deeds. There is not one bitter thought—no failure. His life was one angel visit from beginning to end ; and, saying this without exaggeration, can I—dare I complain ? I know that gratitude for the past and faith for the future are my duty. I am not 'brave,' dear friend, but I try to be unreserved in my submission, and to give myself to all cheerful influences."

Miss Sedgwick to Mrs. Russell.

"Lenox, September 14, 1856.

* * * * "The loss of my brother has been the greatest that could happen to me—to me he comprehended all relations. There was, while he lived, a sweet breath of life and love through the great, aching, vacant space made by the departure of all my other nearest kindred ; and now, my dear friend, I have a sense of solitude that I find it very hard to bear. What he has been to me not even my aching, longing spirit can tell. His unfailing tender care ; his genial sympathy with every joy as well as sorrow ; the gladness he put into my life ; the sorrows he rooted out of it. Oh, I am not ungrateful for all that remains—for friends kinder and more loving than I have a right to ask or expect—but he is gone who made me feel my wants to be rights—who never disappointed an expectation. But, my dear friend, I do not often—I will not now—complain. I have an immeasurable joy in thinking of the completeness of his life ; of how many loved him, and remember him as having taught them, through his beautiful life, what humanity may be. All barriers fell before the power of his goodness ; bigoted Calvinists gave up their creeds, saying he had taught them they were nothing. 'The life was all ;' and his poor, ignorant Catholic friends, as they wailed over his sweet form, forgot their Purgatory, and said, 'He is in heaven.' But think, my dear friend, when the light is withdrawn that gave beauty to every thing here, what the home must be! But still there is a twilight upon it, and here I meet him and here I see him in his cheerful days, when the step was light and the voice strong."

The next letters refer to "Married or Single," the last literary work of its author, which, after Mr. Charles Sedgwick's death, it cost her a great effort to complete.

Miss Sedgwick to Rev. Dr. Dewey.

"New York, March, 1857.

"My DEAR FRIEND,—You are coming here to stay two or three weeks! And you may imagine how much I am expecting, for now we shall have no snow-storms, and no falling of the mercury that freezes every thing but the heart. I was glad you did not come to Woodbourne. Friendships that need 'proofs' are flimsy affairs; I can not imagine any thing that should weaken ours, and I look forward with a joyful faith to its infinite growth. What must be the joys that the heart can not conceive, when those that it can lift us out of all this muddle!

* * * * "I am getting a book ready, and working as hard as I dare, and therefore can not write letters. Is it not rather a folly (is it worse?) at my time of life to perpetrate a novel without any purpose or hope to slay giants, slavery, or the like, but only to supply mediocre readers with small moral hints on various subjects that come up in daily life?"

Miss Sedgwick to Mrs. K. S. Minot.

"New York, April 2, 1857.

* * * * "My book gets on very well—from eighteen to twenty-one pages a day. * * * * I have the miserable feeling of incompetence for my task; and sometimes, when my feeble interest in the future of my offspring is overcome, and

my old desire of success gets the better of me, I feel worried, and anxious, and utterly discouraged. A great deal of the whole needed copying, and much of it to be copied by myself; so you may imagine that I have worked and am working pretty hard—up to my last ounce of strength. But I am very well, and if there is no fatal mistake, omissions, or transpositions of pages or chapters from my weak memory, I shall be content. The book can't hurt any body, and it *may* be to some like a sprinkle in a dry time—lay the dust for a little while. But oh, dear Kate, there are moments when the full sense of my loneliness comes over me—when I think of all those whose hearts beat for me, and more than mine, at the publication of my early books, all gone, and he who shared and lightened every anxiety, and blessed all happiness—and then my strength all goes, and I *stop*. But better thoughts come—grateful thoughts for what remains to me."

Miss *Sedgwick* to Rev. Dr. Dewey.

"Lenox, July 19, 1857.

* * * * "I shall send you, in the course of the week, my new book. I hate to! I thought I cared very little about it, but I have overrated both my philosophy and my religion, and when I found a huge parcel of the things which I ordered to give to some of my peculiar friends, I could have burned them all if I could have burned the rest with them! We are told not to think of ourselves better than we ought to think, but there is one thing more important and more difficult—to be satisfied that those we most love should not think of us better than we deserve. All I now hope—my spirits are rather low—is that my friends may not be mortified either by the silence of the critics or their comments. The public, of course—and the public is right—takes no account of the sad and wandering states of mind in which you have written. But don't feel bad for me, my dear friend, and do not let your wife. * * * * My happiness is not at the mercy of success or failure."

Miss Sedgwick to Mrs. K. S. Minot.

"Stockbridge, July 20, 1857.

* * * * "I got home about 10 o'clock Saturday night, pretty well fagged out, so that I did not bear well the shock of seeing my book really out, and at every one's mercy. But that was lost in the vexation of that horrid English copy. That they should print it in that shabby style was mortifying enough. But that, I suppose, I could not object to ; they had a right to make the commodity most marketable. But do you know what else they have done ?—omitted the preface, which, being the greater part written by H., I was *sure* was worth printing ; changed the motto, all the captions to the chapters, inserted running-titles for the chapters, and varied the text—how much I do not know, but on two chance openings I found two most mortifying alterations : one, when Uncle Walter exclaims, ' " The devil take her !" (pardon him ; he was an old-fashioned man),' they have substituted ' Out upon her !' which, besides being an exclamation not fitting my character, makes the plea for him ridiculous. Then for suspect (in a letter of the heroine) they have put expect, in the vulgar use of the word. Heaven knows how many worse things I shall find. I shall write to Mr. Child, who I know will lovingly do me a service, to inquire of Ticknor & Fields the best mode of righting myself. Oh ! they have printed ' The Author's Edition,' which covers with my name the whole thing."

Miss Sedgwick to Mrs. K. S. Minot.

"Lenox, August 5, 1858.

"MY DEAREST KATE,—After having heard of the severe

attack* I had on Sunday evening, I know **you** will be glad to be **assured by** my own hand that, except a little weakness and **slight** dregs of cough, I am **as** well as when you left me. My rheumatism is much the same—less, I think, rather, **than** it was. The illness, though rather frightful, lasted **but a** short time, but long enough to make **me** feel keenly the **re**sponsibility of a spared life, and deeply grateful for the love **and** care manifested on all sides."

Miss Sedgwick to Mrs. Channing.

"Lenox, August 7, 1858.

* * * * "I received your last while I was in New York, and not very **pleasantly** occupied, and I had an impression that I answered it immediately ; but we are (I am) so apt **to** confuse intentions with performances, that I now do not doubt it was one **of those** easy letters which we write mentally and seal up in our hearts, and forget that we have not yet quite come to that spiritual state when **we may dispense** with the intervention of material signs. Your steady affection and incorporation with my family ties has been, and is, **one of the great blessings of** my life. **As** we near the end **we** feel more and more acutely the value of those treasures **that are laid** up in heaven, and have not a mortal destiny, **and** I think we feel, too, that nothing else is of much worth. The shadows are fast flying, the throngs of fellow-creatures that have obstructed us through life fade away, and the real people remain, and come out brighter and brighter, like the stars as the **day recedes."** * * * *

Miss Sedgwick to Mrs. K. S. Minot.

"Stockbridge, January 11, 1859.

"DEAR KATE,—I **came down** here yesterday after a very **good, or** rather startling **P.M.** sermon from Mr. Pynchon,

* Spasmodic croup.

which left me no reasonable expectation that I should not be 'cut down' this year, and considerable anxiety as to how I should lie in that case. Anxiety? No, I can not say that; whether it be the dullness of age, or (as I hope) a strengthening faith in the Fatherly goodness that has followed me all the days of my life, I am not easily frightened about the obscure future. It is true, as the child said of darkness in general, I do not know 'what is in it,' but I am sure there is nothing that Wisdom and Goodness does not appoint.

"It is a fearfully cold morning—seventeen degrees below zero at 8 o'clock; and I, though I had lain 'uneasy' as a monarch with a crown all night, being stiff with old age and growling rheumatism, went nearly to the bridge before breakfast, and saw the sun rising in a golden flood of light, the rocky bluffs of 'Monument,' as Solomon would say, 'as a bride at the coming of the bridegroom,' and the whole circuit of mountains that guard this sacred valley lighting up as the gates of heaven opened. The smokes from the village rose in solid white columns, and not a footstep outside the dwellings save G., and his lips were too stiff to answer to my salutation. I remembered William's repeated caution to me, and felt, in my toes and fingers, that discretion was much the better part of old age's valor."

Notwithstanding many sorrows, Miss Sedgwick's had been a very happy as well as useful life; but the point was now reached after which all change must almost necessarily be that of separation and loss. In her few remaining years, all her sisters-in-law were called to go before her, and she was left the sole survivor of four brothers and their wives, of two sisters and their husbands.

Mrs. Harry Sedgwick was the first to go, dying in 1859. With her Miss Sedgwick's ties had always been peculiarly close and tender, and only a short time previous she had written of her, 'I am never with this precious sister, who has been a cornucopia of blessing to us, without feeling, as old Herbert has it in his quaint phraseology, that "hearts within have propagation," and that "she has a whole heart for each one that she loves." And Mrs. Sedgwick's affection never varied in return, from the time shortly after her marriage, when she wrote, "If you ever need a sweet solace in a lonely hour, dearest Kate, think of what you have been to me, and feel secure of God's blessing for your reward." And again—

"The time I have just passed with you is without a parallel in the history of my pleasures. There never can be a spot which shall form a centre so dear to our family as Stockbridge, so deserving the name of home to us all. My right to call it so is only adopted ; I can not make the same blood as yours run in my veins, but I trust I can imbibe the same principles and feelings which have made that blood sacred to you."

Miss Sedgwick to Mrs. Russell, after the death of Mrs. Harry Sedgwick.

" Woodbourne, March 10, 1859.

"It was natural that I should turn to you, dear Lucy. You have known Jane as long as I have, and have loved her as long as you have known her. Our sympathies have run along parallel. There is now no one to revert with us to those glad days that were filled with social cheerfulness, with hopes some fulfilled, and some so long ago disappointed that they are now but as dreams. What days they were, dear Lucy, when the little church gathered in Broome Street, and your brother ministered at its sacred altar ; when Jane's sweet voice rose above all others in that small company ; when we used to meet at your house and at hers, in life so simple and yet so rich ! When Harry and Robert

were with us, and we had one heart, and dear Jane minis-
tering to all. How many years have passed since! What
a train of joys and sorrows to each and all of us! And yet,
let us thank God, the love and trust are unbroken. We are
one company yet. A part have gone before us, but when I
can rise above the feeling of vacancy and chill, I feel they
have not *left* us, and whither they have gone we too shall
soon go."

The latter part of the next letter refers to the funeral of
an infant daughter of Mrs. Charles E. Butler, a niece peculiarly dear to Miss Sedgwick.

Miss Sedgwick to Mrs. K. S. Minot.

"New York, June 5, 1859.

"MY DEAREST KATE,—I have just come from the morning service at our church, where I have been once more permitted to receive, through our dear pastor and friend's dis-
pensation, the communion. H. and N. were there. But the
crowd of images around me, the sad and the blessed memories, the real loneliness, and the clasped hands and living
eyes that I feel and see, are something strange even to me,
familiar as I should be with these strange contrarieties, that
follow upon my heart with the suddenness of chill and fever
to the body. There is a wonderful, an awful power in this
simple observance. To me it is like those moments when
persons are suddenly, in the strength of life, brought face to
face with death. The past life, its failures, its frivolities, its
sins, its supremest joys and keenest sorrows, are revived
with all the vitality of the actual and the present, and on
the tempest breaks the light of God's infinite mercy, the tenderness of Christ's sympathy. The bread *is* the body broken
for our sins; the wine *is* the blood shed for them.

"*Monday morning.* The service was performed by Mr.

Bellows as he does all these domestic services, as if his lips were touched with a coal from the altar of love, to which all hearts in sorrow come. It was most affecting to see the little creature lying in her bed of flowers, and baptized, as it were, into immortality, where she, so little while ago, received the solemn rite for her earthly pilgrimage."

Miss Sedgwick to Mrs. Rackemann.

"Woodbourne, December 31, 1859.

"The last time, dear Bessie, that I shall write this year. It is now 11, and beginning on the last solemn hour of the year—so solemn that I might be coward enough to slink to my bed and forget it; but I do not feel cowardly—thank God I do not. The cords that bind me to life are so firm that death can not part them, so elastic that space in no wise controls them. I feel such a sense, dear Bessie, of the mercies that have followed me to this *last station* of human life, that it would be the supremest folly, as well as ingratitude, not to trust for the future. Those that I began life with in my dear and most blessed home have *all* reached the other shore. There are times when I am crushed with this thought. *Now*, there is peace in it. I feel that the chain is not broken, and that I am the connecting link between them and their families on earth. And in these families what love, and beauty, and blossoming for heaven there is! This has been a year of the sorest trial, of loss to me, that you, as well as any other than myself, can measure. Your Aunt Jane was my dearest friend on earth, and yet how many cheerful hours the year has given me! I remember them; they have sustained me. And how many of them we had together at Lenox! You will think of them sometimes when I am gone, and when you feel low, my darling, remember you have been a joy as well as a sweet consolation to me. You have fulfilled your father's will, *realized* his wish, and continued the influence of his love in his home ; and so, truly, have all his children, and their mother. Am I writing a sad letter to you? I did not mean to. I let William and Kate go off to bed, and sat down to write cheerily. Never were children bound by prescribed duty, and impelled by filial instinct, kinder than they are to me."

Miss Sedgwick to Mrs. Channing.

"Woodbourne, March 10, 1860.

"MY DEAR FRIEND,—I have not written to you since the death of Eliza,* an event in which our hearts were blended. Her affection has been a precious boon to both our lives, her life full of rich memories, her character a light from heaven—an assurance of immortality, so much is there in it of that vitality which death *can not* touch. I have not experienced in her death any thing of that tremulousness, that clouded perception, that failure of faith, that recoiling from the extinguishing touch of death that I sometimes am haunted with ; partly, perhaps, because I did not witness the process of mortality. I heard of her illness only the day before I heard of her death, and I would not look at her after the light of her glowing eye was veiled, so that to my perception she passed over the gulf and into her inheritance. I did not see her after I came to Woodbourne. I was purposing to go over to Brookline, but put it off with that reckless delay which, in spite of experience, clings to us to the last, as if we had a secure grant of the future. She wrote to me an earnest invitation to go with her to *her* annual festival.† I declined it, assigning to her the true reason, that I shrunk from being with her on an occasion to her of the most elevating excitement which I did not partake. My feelings (perhaps I should say my judgment) would recoil when hers

---

* Mrs. Eliza Cabot Follen.

† The meeting of the Anti-slavery Society.

flowed on with the force of ocean waves to high-water mark. The last time she ever put pen to paper—the pen that has done so much blessed work—was with the intention of kindly convincing me I was wrong. Her frame was then shivering with premonitory ague, her hand was weak, and after writing one common note-paper page she could write no farther, and stopped at 'our festival'—words fitly her last, for her heart was in them. You will not misunderstand me, my dear Susan, nor imagine that I do not feel heartily in the great question of humanity that agitates our people. It seemed to me that so much had been intemperately said, so much rashly urged on the death of that noble martyr, John Brown, by the Abolitionists, that it was not right to appear among them as one of them. * * * * I wish I could know that you were as well and strong as I am, we so much need health in our old age. As the Irishman said of the sun, 'What is the use of it in the day?' So youth might spare a little of what is so essential to age. But if we can learn to resign contentedly, to live cheerfully in our narrowed quarters, and to await in tranquillity our Father's last dealings on earth with us, we may still hear those blessed words, 'She hath done what she could.' You have doubtless the two last great books, Hawthorne's and Florence Nightingale's — the last, one that will scatter blessings through the land. Like light and air, it is for universal good. It is rare for a person who has Miss Nightingale's wonderful powers of execution to write with such force, directness, and pithiness. I have but just begun the 'Marble Faun.' I am sure you will feel, as I do, that it pours a golden light into the dim chambers of memory, and revivifies the scenes that we, too, once enjoyed." * * * *

Recollections.

"*April* 7, 1860. I have been reading a portion of Kingsley's late edition of the 'Fool of Quality,' a book I remember as among my father's loves—one of the few novels in our old library at Stockbridge. How well do I remember the five duodecimo volumes, in their dark leather bindings. The favorite books of that time stand around the chambers of memory, each a shrine. In this there is much wit and pathos, nature and wisdom (nature *is* wisdom when it is evolved from the human heart and from life). The style seems to me admirable—something in the fashion of the quaint old coats of our grandfathers, fashioned for ease and use, and of the best broadcloth garnished with velvet. It seems to me an admirable book might be made out of it for children, and I have a great mind to try my hand at it. It might, perhaps, flatter a little too much the dynasties of the present day, the young usurpers of their fathers' thrones. * * *

"I learned, a few days since, by an obituary written by Bryant, the death of Mrs. Jameson. She was among the few friends of my happiest years left to me. She came to this country in 1837, with the purpose of a reunion to her husband, and at his invitation. She went to Toronto (in Canada), but his reception of her was such as to make it impossible for her to remain in his house with contentment and satisfaction, and after a few weeks she returned to New York and embarked for England, where her presence was essential to the happiness of her family, and her exertions to their support. Mrs. Jameson came to Stockbridge to see me before I had seen her. She repeatedly expressed to me a feeling of gratitude. She would say, 'You do not know how grateful I am to you, nor why.' I did not feel at liberty to ask her what she did not tell without asking. I had done *nothing* toward her, and I could only infer that some chance seed in my writings might have fallen on good soil in her heart. I say *chance*, but I believe, my dear Alice, that whatever utterance of mine has done good, was not

mine, but some good word that has passed through my mind
Heaven-directed. Now don't fancy that I fancy I have been
inspired! No; but to us all come thoughts, we know not
whence nor whither they go, nor how commissioned. She
left here in January or February, 1838. She and your Uncle
Robert were mutually interested, and when she went she
left him at the most prosperous period of his life—in the
very first class of New York lawyers, his profession pro-
ductive of respect, and honor, and profit, holding a high social position, and, as it seemed to me, essential to my happiness—to my life. On the 9th of the following March he
was struck down by apoplexy and consequent paralysis,
and from that time his life declined. This was the first
news from us that reached our friend. In May, 1839, we
(your Uncle and Aunt R., Cousin Maria, Lizzie, your mother,
and I) went to Europe. Mrs. Jameson received me with the
warmth of a true friend. She was then living at St. John's
Wood, near London, with her father (and all her unmarried
family), a paralytic, but still a jovial Irishman. He had
been an accomplished painter, and attached to the court of
George III. I remember well his cordial salutation, and
his saying (with a kind reference to my little book and to
his own consolations), ' Miss Sedgwick, *I* am the rich poor
man,' and, saying so, he looked with overflowing eyes upon
his devoted wife, whom I always found sitting beside him,
and on Mrs. Jameson, who was truly his joy, and pride, and
support. She had two unmarried sisters, and finally one
widowed one, and for the support of them all she labored,
as Mrs. Kemble says, valiantly to the last. I have never
seen her since our parting, when we left England for the
Continent, though from that time till within a year or two
we have maintained our correspondence, she always writing
more promptly than I, simply from my conviction that I
could give her no adequate return. She sent me her beau-

tiful books, and from to time love-tokens, which were taken impulsively from her room or table as she was parting from some friend coming here. The engraved name I use for my books she made for me. She drew the vignette, and engraved it while she was shut up with her father during his last sickness. She worked a worsted cushion for me, sent me a volume of poetry from Miss Baillie's library, and two letter-presses that had long been in her own use. I mention this to you, Alice, to show the steadiness of her feeling for me. I cherish this remembrance, for the impression she made was of an impulsive person whose affections would be rather showers than fountains. * * * * She had a pale, clear, intellectual blue eye, that could flash anger, or jealousy, or love; her hair was red, and her complexion very fair, and of the hue of an irate temper. Her arms, neck, and hands were beautiful, but her whole person wanted dignity; it was short, and of those dimensions that to ears polite are embonpoint—to the vulgar, fat. Her genius and accomplishments need no note of mine; they live in her books. I believe no woman has written more variously, and few, men or women, so well. She impressed me as the best talker I ever heard, and I have heard many gifted 'unknown,' and many known and celebrated. Mrs. Kemble, who has had far more extended opportunities than mine, as she has been familiar with men trained to talk in the London social arena, I have heard assign the first place to Mrs. Jameson. Her gifts and accomplishments are not now mere laurels on her grave, but have passed on, as I trust, to a higher sphere, and above them all the crown of her filial piety." * * * *

Journal.

"*Thursday, April* 26, 1860. My last day at Woodbourne! Sydney Smith well says that it is one of the pains of old

age that whatever we do carries with it the melancholy
thought of being 'for the last time.' Surely my experience
of the infinite bounty and goodness of God should fill my
heart with gratitude for the past and trust for the future.
I came here on the 23d of December. I have had since
uninterrupted health (save my habitual pains). I have had
the love and tender care of every member of this dear family, and troops of affectionate friends ; no serious illness or
overcasting sorrow among them. I have had the prime enjoyment of Mrs. Kemble's readings, and her society, and
many social pleasures." * * * *

Miss Sedgwick to Mrs. K. S. Minot.

"New York, May 12, 1860.

"MY DEAREST KATE,—It has struck 6 P.M. I have only
eaten a little fruit since breakfast, and feel rather like that
empty bag that can't stand up. But, as I have resolutely
shut up the 'Mill on the Floss,' not being able to meet the
storm that I hear rumbling in the distance, and that I am
sure is to pour down on poor Maggie's devoted head, I have
taken up my pen to begin to thank you and Alice for your
last letter. I have no greater pleasure than to hear from
you, and to know that you are all well. This 'Mill' has delighted me. It has turned out such an amount of good
grist, it is so filled with heart-probings and knowledge of
human life, so earnestly free from any attempt to dress up,
to express, or find a vent for the author's egotism ! It deals
sturdily with the real stuff that life is made of, and, like life,
constantly makes you wish that the characters were a little
different—that this and that would not turn out just so."

"Lenox, June 17, 1860.

"MY DEAREST KATE,—It is a divine day—a day when
hope and faith spring forth from the glorified earth in harmony with the soaring birds and the opening flowers. The

warm, gentle rain in June, such as fell yesterday (not quite enough of it, as Charlie, with his temperate gratitude, might say), falls on good ground, and, like spiritual grace, refreshes and multiplies God's good gifts. The air this morning is such as might come from Paradise when its guardian angel opens its gates to happy mortals. There is a worship of beauty, a sweet breath of praise from all this wide landscape before my door. Men, women, and children make the discords. Nature is the heavenly messenger whose voice is melody and harmony. Is it not strange that I, of all people in the world, should rejoice in the absence of humanity? Perhaps it is the novelty that makes it, for half an hour, agreeable to me. The family has dispersed to the various churches. Little Charles is not here, and therefore his flitting form does not pass in and out, and to and fro with this mobile resemblance (the only one) to the evil spirits.

"I have had far more than ordinary enjoyment in life, and in the affection and character of those nearest to me a foretaste of heaven ; and yet so painful are its uncertainties, so frightful its hazards, so certain its changes and disappointments, that I can not look upon its loss on its threshold as to be lamented. Why should it be if the life here is jumped, if the capacities and affections are saved from obstruction and blight, and pass to a higher school and infallible guardianship. Yet, dear Kate, the loss remains, the place vacant. Death has always been, and always must be, a tragedy."

Miss Sedgwick to Mrs. Russell.

"Lenox, July 17, 1860.

"My DEAR LUCY,—I sent to town by H. (and I am ashamed not to have sent it earlier) the Life of Perthes. He had an earnest intention to give it into W.'s hands, *but,* as he shares the infirmity of some of his family, he may forget it, and, to guard against that possibility, you had best ask W. to remind him.   I have often thought of you in your new and pleasant home, and rejoice that I can *locate* you in my imagination.   Not to be able to do that leaves the painful indefiniteness that we feel in regard to the disembodied spirits of our friends.   There are only rare moments when their present existence is realized to us.   Is this want of faith or defect of power?

"We have had a great occasion in our own dear valley— the laying of the corner-stone of a Catholic church in a beautiful spot just under the shadow of Laurel Hill.   It was a great day for J., and whatever makes her happier has my fullest sympathy.   She has been indefatigable in her exertions to effect this, and is half canonized by her Catholic friends and followers.   'Oh, see Miss J.'s good, beautiful face!' said one of them ; and, radiant with happiness as she was, it was hardly an extravagant expression.   Think, dear Lucy, of my living to see a close procession of Irish Catholics from one end of the village to the other, when I remember the time, forty years ago, when there was but one Irishman in Stockbridge—in the county probably—and he a Protestant.   Ah! the good old times, when Mrs. ——— declared the deacon's shop should not be turned into a cathedral, moved thereto by mass being held at the hatter's little shop for half a dozen poor Irish!"

Miss Sedgwick to Mrs. K. S. Minot.

"Lenox, 1860.

* * * * "Our life here is full, not of events, but of shifting scenes.   I called on Mrs. ——— and her daughter after our short service, which mainly consisted in a very pretty school-boy detail of the eminent example of friendship in the life of Damon and Pythias.   Do you know Mrs. ———?

She is a very pleasing woman, with more of the father in her than of the querulous worldly mother, who, through the mantle of renunciation and mourning, has always the bad flavor of low ambitions. Now, Kate, this is merely a philosophical observation of human character, and not a want of that lovely charity that thinketh no evil. I was making up for the clerical gruel I had taken by a little of Bishop Whately's strong meat, when I was surprised by a doze, which I should have stoutly denied but that I was roused in the heat of an altercation between the bishop and your mother as to the right mode of paving her garden-walk, and summoned to see Professor R., and J. Professor R. I am always glad to see. He is one of the 'peculiar people' associated with those now farthest from us, and yet always nearest. They both staid to tea, and after they went I was rushing off to make some calls that I had deferred two weeks, when entered the whole ———— race, whose voices are like—tromboids do you call them?—some instrument that is an imitation of a—fugue do you call it?—by a donkey and a peacock. * * * * Oh! tell my beloved Willie that I thank him for his letter, and that I have tried very hard to find a market for the pair of rabbits he offers. I have offered them to clergy and laity, to men and women, to boys and girls. The latter would be willing customers, but there is a restraining parental influence in the background. I see nothing for it but for me to buy them, and for him to kill and eat them! My love to dear Alice and to all. My darling Robbie, I am pining for him. Yours ever, C. M. SEDGWICK."

Miss Sedgwick to Mrs. K. S. Minot.

"Lenox, August 25, 1860.

"DEAREST KATE,—If any of the family have written you this week, and informed you of my illness, you will be glad to get a letter from me. I felt a cold coming on in the

night and increasing, and when I returned from depositing
my last letter to you in the post my voice was quite gone,
and in the course of a couple of hours I had a violent access
of croup. It was gradually relieved, so that before bedtime
the *distress* was over. I can not look back to any exposure
or imprudence. I ought only to be surprised that disease
comes so rarely to me, and to have renewed gratitude to
God for my continued health and sustained strength. The
end must come, my dear child, and before long—'the readiness is all.'"

Miss Sedgwick to Mrs. K. S. Minot.

"Lenox, October 7, 1860.

"MY DEAREST KATE,—I have just dismissed my little
Irishers, and come to my always pleasant Sunday office;
but I fear it will be brief and ill-performed to-day, as Grace
and I are going down to Uncle Stephen's funeral.* The
dear old man died peacefully on Friday, after having gathered in the last fruits of his faithful waiting on Mother Earth.
Since his strength has failed him to upheave the sods where
he has planted so much precious seed, he has tilled, to the
very last, his little garden-plot, opening the soil with his hoe,
the only instrument his weak hands could manage. Aunt
Visy sowed the seeds, his poor rheumatic fourscore body
refusing to bend beyond a certain angle. Visy says, 'Why,
he set up his tune every morning, and kept on humming it
till he had done his work; he enjoyed himself!' Talk of
gifts! What gift that ever God gave excelled in worth to
the receiver this cheery spirit, springing out of peace of conscience and good-will to man? 'He was not a professor,'
but I believe he has entered the kingdom of heaven without
the diploma of 'the Congregational Church in Stockbridge,
Mass.'

* Mr. Stephen Tucker, of Stockbridge, whose kindly nature made him
"*Uncle* Stephen" to half the village.

"Our sweet Louisa* will arrive soon after my letter. Tell her that Grace and I slept on guard last night as soundly as the soldiers did at St. Peter's prison, and the angels, like his, tended her children. Emilia, Annie says, waked often, but did not cry once, and Grace waked once, and instead of murmuring against Providence for taking away her parents, at the recognition of Annie's voice she merely said, ' I love oo in my 'art.' They are bright as new dollars this morning.

"I trust, my dear Kate, there will be no contretemps to mar your enjoyment this week, and that you will have a ' real good time.' I count days now as I once counted years, and feel far more eagerness to make the most of time —to use every ray of moral sunshine, and to escape the ' pestilent congregation of vapors' from moral diseases that overshadow and blight so much of life."

Miss Sedgwick to Mrs. K. S. Minot.

"New York, December 7, 1860.

"Never, in my lifetime, have we been at so interesting a point in our political history ; and if you and William did not talk on the volcanic topic before breakfast and after supper, I should think the blood of your fathers had lost all moral vitality in your veins. Oh, for the spirit of Wisdom and of Love ! But alas ! what hope of it, or what desert of it ! I suppose you will think it quite consonant to my cowardly character if I tell you that I feel most deeply interested in the poor mothers and maidens that are trembling in the midst of their servile enemies. As for that bullying State of South Carolina, one would not much care. As C. (cousin C.) says, ' Let the damned little thing go !' or as C. B. (two of the most humane men I know) says, ' Plow them under, plow them under ! It has been a little wasp from the beginning !' "

* Mrs. William Sedgwick.

"Woodbourne, January 5, 1861.

"MY DEAR LUCY,—Though I have received no answer to my last letter, yet it does not accord with my notions to stand on that very inconvenient footing—a point of ceremony—with you ; and my heart moves me to send my greeting to you at this season that sanctifies the greetings of old friends, and makes us feel how precious they are, and calls forth our gratitude for the preserved lives of those who are knit to us by the associations of a lifetime ; who have lived in the same social compact with us ; who have had the same friendships, the same joys and sorrows ; who have worshiped with the same heart at one altar ; who have the same treasures garnered in heaven, and who, in one hope, one faith, one baptism, are awaiting the summons, near at hand, to join the beloved who have gone before us to our Master. * * * *

"I came to Kate's just before Christmas. I have come to be considered by her children as a component part of the institution—a female manifestation of Santa Claus. You, dear Lucy, who knew me in my life of variety and excitement, will hardly credit the monotony and fair contentment of my present life. As I look at the great pines around us bending their branches to the ground, as they do now under a load of snow, and looking like large tents made of broad white plumes, with brilliant blue sky above and stainless snow below, I feel the living ministry there is in Nature, and should feel that

> "'The calm retreat, the silent shade,
>   With prayer and praise agree.'

* * * * "I wonder how, and how much, you are exercised on the subject of secession. I am hopeful as to the issue. I cling to the Union as an unweaned child does to

its mother's breast. But it seems to me we should stand in awe, and only pray that God's will may be done in this great matter. It may be that he will permit the Southern suicidal madness to rage and *prevail* to the great end of blotting slavery from the land it poisons. Massachusetts is condemned as the hot-bed of abolition fanaticism — I hear nothing but ultra concession and conservatism."

Miss Sedgwick to Mrs. Channing.

"Woodbourne, February 27, 1861.

* * * * "I have not yet come down to the level of the despairing of our country. On the contrary, I have strong hopes, perhaps confidence in the future. The Cotton States may remain out, but that may be no harm to us (God bless them!). The Border States may join them (I do not believe they will), and much trouble may ensue therefrom. But I have faith in the farther development, of the effect of our institutions. They are seed sown by the righteous— sown in love and justice to the *whole family.* We are making the first experiment of the greatest happiness to the greatest number, and Providence will not permit it to fail short of consummation. We have in our people the elements of life and health. We are in harmony with the great natural laws." * * * *

Miss Sedgwick to Mrs. K. S. Minot.

"Stockbridge, June 2, 1861.

* * * * "It is very uncomfortable to be all the time conscious of the working of your machine, and expecting that at any moment the chord will snap. We cling to life ; it is the law of our being ; and it is my continual prayer to trust ; to be delivered from fear and anxiety ; to be thankful for the continuance of my powers and faculties to this time ; to be fortified by the love of Christ, and unfaltering faith in him, and in God's mercy through him, to meet the summons that must come soon. I *am* cowardly.

" I am glad to have done with the subject. I quite agree with Emerson, who, in his chapter on Manners, says, ' If you have a cold, or have had a fever, or a sun-stroke, or a thunder-stroke, never speak of it.'

" Perhaps you know that our warriors of the Valley went on Friday to the Brook-farm camp. There were thirty-nine. Your Aunt Susan and half the village were at the station at 6 o'clock to take leave of them. Her blessing was the best munition of war they took with them."

Miss Sedgwick to Mrs. K. S. Minot.

" Stockbridge, June 23, 1861.

" I never before, my dear Kate (at least I think so ; but we go over our experiences again and again, and, when the scene shifts, forget them), felt such an insane desire to seize Time by the neck and hold him back to prolong this most lovely month of June. Every day seems a new revelation of the exquisite beauty of creation, an actual presence of God, a triumphal procession of the forces of nature. Life abounds, and grows stronger and richer from hour to hour, and there is no withered grass, no fading leaf, no faint song of the birds to foreshadow decay and death. It seems not a prophecy of heaven, but heaven itself. And we may listen to the great anthem without turning in upon discontents, and sorrow, and vain longings for what has been and can be no more, or looking out upon the raging of as disorderly and fiery passions as ever disturbed the peace of nature.

" One can not long keep up to the symphonies of nature in war-time ; and, with all my earnest feeling and love for this divine month, I was even to-day crying out of the window and breaking the Sunday stillness by an appeal for a newspaper H. had in his hand, we—your aunt and I—having missed that daily food yesterday, and being at the starvation point. He took off the edge of our hunger by saying a telegram had just been received announcing, from a 'reliable source,' that there would be no battle this campaign. Yesterday, you know, it was announced that a great battle was impending. And so from day to day we go on. It is a mere war of troops and rumors. A few days since, J. and M. were riding ; *en passant,* J.'s war fervor is up to the boiling point. M.'s horse stumbled, fell under J.'s, and upset him. Both were thrown—women, not horses—and when J. saw her horse's heels in the air, and coming down, as she thought, on her head, what one throb of anguish at parting life think you she had ? 'Oh, I shall never hear about the battle at Bethel !' It takes Berkshire to generate such enthusiasm as that."

Miss Sedgwick to Mrs. Russell.

"Stockbridge, November 16, 1861.

"My DEAR LUCY,—The year is fast waning, and our lives are speeding away, and few the lights still burning in our narrowed circle. Far as we are apart, and small as our visible intercourse is, I feel your rays upon my heart, and shall as long as we both live. I met W. when I was in town, and had a cordial grasp of his hand, and as much information as he could give me of you—not very satisfactory, as he told me you had been less strong than usual the past summer. We shrink from these intimations of change that must come, that is certainly near, and why do we, except from defect of faith ? If we believe that 'to depart and be with Christ is far better ;' if we believe that we shall be with Him who has brought us out of the darkness of the natural world into a revelation of immortality, who has made known to us the Father's love, the paternal character of God in all its bearings upon our destiny ; if we believe that death will deliver

us from temptation, from sin, from sorrows ; if we believe it
will reunite us to the beloved who have gone before us, who
were the life of our life—then, dear friend, should we welcome the twilight of our diminished day, and feel that 'to-
morrow will be fair.'   I must make an honest confession :
I have an intense desire to live to see the conclusion of our
present struggle ; how order is to be brought out of the present confusion ; how these adverse principles are ever to be
harmonized ; how peace and good neighborhood are ever to
follow upon this bitter hate.   I am willing to see South Carolina humbled in the dust—to see riches and honor taken
from her, and a full expiation of the crimes she has committed ; but beyond South Carolina I have no ill will.   The
people are cursed and borne down by their slavery, and
maddened by their ambitious leaders ; made to believe, not
a lie, but bushels of them, and they can only be cured of
their frenzy by being made to feel their impotence ; this they
seem now in a fair way to realize.   You and I, dear Lucy,
must find consolation for havoc and wide misery in the
many probable good results of this purgation.   It is delightful to see the gallantry of some of our men, who are repeating the heroic deeds that seemed fast receding to fabulous
times.   In a small way there is nothing pleases me better
than the zeal among our young women (young and old) in
working for the hospitals.   We hear no gossip, but the most
rational talk about hospital-gowns, comfortables, socks, and
mittens.   Our whole community, from Mrs. Kemble down
to some of our Irish servants, are knitting.   You may meet
E. any hour of the day going about to distribute yarn she
has purchased, to persuade some to knit for love, and to
hire blind women and old women to do the work.   Small
things become great with such motives and such actions.
Far better is this than the turmoil of city life !"

Miss Sedgwick to Mrs. K. S. Minot.

"Lenox, July 9, 1862.

"MY DEAREST KATE,—I have written to you (ideally) . twenty letters since the mail came yesterday, and brought to your mother the first dispatch from Will* since the *week of battles.* It was written late at night, after his first sleep after seventy-six hours of vigil with the exception of three quarters of an hour, after marches and fastings to men and horses too horrible to think of; and yet it is a connected and admirable account, and concludes with '*all right now;* the men restored to hope, except the few *vant-riens,* and I am ready to give the last drop of blood in my body to my country.' There is a pathetic description of the death of 'Sam,' General Sedgwick's favorite horse, who was pierced by three bullets when he was on him. But you will see the letter, and I will not garble it by any anticipatory fragments. You will be proud of your brother, dear Kate, and thankful, most thankful are we all that he and dear Cousin John† have passed through such dangers in safety. * * * * Your mother is calm, active as ever, and apparently cheerful, but I can see that there is an under swell of anxiety that I much fear will tell on her health. She is fit to be the mother of heroes, and she has certainly transmitted to her son her vigorous, hopeful spirit."

* William Dwight Sedgwick, son of Mr. Charles Sedgwick, one of the noble young heroes, and, alas! one of the victims of the War of the Rebellion. He felt his duty to his country paramount even to his love for his wife and children, and, entering the army, had attained the rank of major, when, after fighting gallantly in the early and disastrous battles in Virginia, he was struck down on the terrible field of Antietam, 17th September, 1862.

† General Sedgwick, who was a grandson of "Uncle John," Judge Sedgwick's elder brother.

Miss Sedgwick to Mrs. K. S. Minot.

"Stockbridge, August 1, 1862.

* * * * "It is strange how cheerily the world goes on, living as we do at this moment on a volcano. But, as I look out of the window on a lawn of the richest clover my eye ever fell on, and on one of the loveliest of sylvan scenes, with the mowers turning up the heavy, new-cut hay to the hot sun, it is difficult to realize that there is any worse evil afloat than the daily showers that discourage the husband-man, and yet a general dread pervades us all, not without terror, when the cheerful light of day is gone.

"*Lenox, September* 17*th*, 1862. * * * * I have plunged into the mêlée of 'Les Miserables.' I have just got to the story. It is a book that must be read, and will not be limited to the great congregation of novel readers. It deals with the greatest topics of humanity, and in such a mode as is possible only to a mind of the first order. The book is every where; the first time you lay your hand on it, read the chapter headed *L'Evêque en présence d'une lumière inconnue.* It is solemn, magnificent, and beautiful; full of thoughts that solve the mysteries of history. But you must read the whole book, and no better time than this, when we need to be *diverted* by other miseries than our own. The effect is sometimes impaired by the *extase*, the oxygenated atmosphere of the French temperament."

Miss Sedgwick to Mrs. Russell, after Mrs. Robert Sedgwick's Death.

"Lenox, September 12, 1862.

"MY DEAR FRIEND,—You will have heard, before my letter reaches you, that another dear member of my family has left us; your kindred too, and associated in your mind, as she is in mine, with the dearest affections and tenderest memories. I think she has been steadily declining, with a few intervals of slight rallying, for the last two years ; and since she returned to her home from New York in June, she has borne the impress of a fast-approaching change. I will not dwell on her sufferings ; there is no use to you and me, dear Lucy, in their contemplation. She had all the mitigations her state admitted, and immeasurable consolation in the presence and love of her children. Her character was a rare one—strong in the marked qualities of her family ; a more devoted and disinterested mother I have never known. And now she seemed to have earned her rest—to have laid down her cares, and, surrounded by prosperity, honored and beloved, to have a sunny afternoon before her. God willed it otherwise—transferred her, as we believe, to light and joy that fadeth never. To me she has ever been a most kind and faithful sister. She found herself adapted to country life. She took an interest in all its details, and she was much endeared to her country neighbors. She seemed to set out with the specific purpose of making my sister Jane's place good, and at first I thought she would be regarded much as step-mothers are ; but it was not so. Her sympathy with the sick, her unstinted and watchful generosity, her elegant hospitality, and her vein of humor, delighted our rustic people, and she is lamented with real and bitter sorrow. She was buried on one of our loveliest September days, just as the sun was setting and filling the valley with golden light. The cold tomb-stones seemed warm and soft in the flood of radiance. Her funeral room was filled with flowers sent in by friends and neighbors ; crosses of white lilies and roses at the head and foot of the coffin ; rings— types of immortality—hanging at the door, and baskets and bouquets elaborately and significantly arranged."

Miss Sedgwick to Mrs. Russell.

" Lenox.

"**You** perhaps have heard how manfully our dear Will be-haved—how, when he lay on the hard, plowed ground (and **he** was lying there seven and a half hours), fatally wounded, he managed to get his little diary from his bosom and write, with fond expressions and earnest prayer, the simple great truth, ' I have tried to do my duty'—the truth that takes the **sting from** death—the victory from the grave. So I am content that my beloved brother's son should die."

Miss Sedgwick to Alice Minot.

" Lenox, October 23, 1862.

* * * * " My love to *all*, and when I write this, I mean it from your grandfather *down*, to **each** and all, as is due from me, love and gratitude ; and mind you, kiss my darling for me. Which is that ? your father or mother ? Willie or Hal ? Charles or Rob ? It would puzzle me to tell.

"Yours, my very darling,

" CATHARINE M. SEDGWICK."

Miss Sedgwick to Mrs. K. S. Minot.

"New York, December 4, 1862.

" MY DEAREST KATE,—I received your long letter **and** Alice's addenda yesterday morning, and, though my stom-ach heaved a little **at my** darling—Cain !*—yet I felt like a man who, having been hungry, is well fed. Well, my dear Kate, you and William have a task, the most **difficult** in life, to work **up these grand** and diverse materials that God has **put into your** hands, to fashion them into the beauty of God's **likeness.** My hope is that you may be fellow-workers with

---

* One of Mrs. Minot's boys, who had thrown a stone at one of his cousins and cut his forehead.

Him, and then, if you are *faithful*, the result is certain. I
have unlimited confidence in William's wisdom and **power,**
but please give my compliments to him, and **tell** him that I
hold him responsible for the murderous propensities. The
Sedgwicks, if an imbecile, are a gentle race, and never till
now broke into the Decalogue. My darling boy! I am so
glad it happened before I came. I trust there were no lasting nor very severe consequences to dear little F.* I can
see the mother and sisters when the bleeding victim was
borne in! * * * * I had a disappointment yesterday. Mrs.
F. sent for me while we were at breakfast (we breakfast be-
fore eight!) to breakfast with her and go with a party to **see**
an iron-clad ship. I did not feel in the humor, and declined.
At four she came here flushed with pleasure, the rose color
of fourteen, and with more excited enthusiasm **than the**
whole present race of girls in their teens would have felt.
She had been over the ship; she had been shown all its
complicated resources by *Worden*, his face blind of one eye,
and ' blackened by powder that made it beautiful!' She
had passed an hour in company with Banks, etc., etc.; and
I had been to a dress-maker's, and going to and fro, up and
down, in search of a fine plaiter!—ignoble!"

Miss Sedgwick to Mrs. Charles E. Butler.

"Lenox, March 27, 1863.

* * * * "Oh Susy! it is so strange and lonesome here!
Louisa and her children are lovely and dear, but theirs are
new faces and new voices; and there are so many importunate memories, sad and solemn, and, thank God, some so
happy, that to me it is inexpressibly melancholy and dreary
—your aunt's condition most tragic of all. I go over the
house with some present purpose, but the past—the past is
always before **me.** My brother — my beloved brother is

* The wounded boy.

every where ; his children, the dead and the living, about
him. When I first came it was so affecting to me that it required all my fortitude, all my regard for others, not quite
to give up. Your aunt's *cheerful* voice, and Louisa's gentle,
sweet submission, reproved me—brought me to myself, and
now I hope to be able, in the few days left, to be of some
little comfort to Louisa."

This was Miss Sedgwick's last stay at Lenox. She had
passed the winter, as all her late winters, at Woodbourne,
and early in the spring went to visit her sister-in-law, already
attacked by the cruel disease which, after two years of most
courageous and sweet endurance, caused her death, and
Major Sedgwick's widow, who, with her little children, was
then living with his mother. She returned to Woodbourne
the first of April. The weather was snowy and inclement,
and made the journey more than usually fatiguing to her.
She suffered from severe headache all the next day, and toward evening was seized with an attack of epilepsy, which
kept her unconscious so long that it was not thought she
could survive twenty-four hours. But her strong constitution, aided by judicious medical treatment, prevailed, and,
though this was indeed 'the beginning of the end,' there
were long intervals of comparative ease and comfort before
her life closed. During these she saw her friends freely,
spent much time in writing to them and in reading, and
even made two more journeys to her beloved Stockbridge.
In less than a fortnight after this first attack she was able
to write to Mrs. Butler :

"Woodbourne, April 12, 1863.

"My dearest Sue,—I feel pretty much like one issuing
from a tangled wood, with paths leading in many directions
whither I would go, and one whither I *must* go, and that is
to you, my dear child, for during the last three weeks I have

been cut off from all intercourse with the absent except by those most subtle, imperceptible webs of thought that the heart spins out of itself by some process more incomprehensible than the spider's, and from secretions more mysterious, more admirable, for not liable to change or decay."

The rest of the letter, which is quite a long one, is chiefly occupied with tender inquiries and advice concerning the health of Mrs. Butler's husband. There are very few words about her own illness. A few weeks later she writes, " I am treated like a duchess by such friends as few duchesses have, and, as a proof of my amendment, I am writing before breakfast ;" and in the next letter to Mrs. Butler, dated in May, she says :

* * * * " The country, at this moment, is Paradise restored. Since my early youth I have rarely seen the country at this season, and each day is to me like opening a book of divine revelations. My walks seldom extend beyond the bounds of Woodbourne, but within them we have a great variety of deciduous trees and blossoming shrubs. The trees, in their infinite variety of shades of tender green, opening their leaves amidst the dark pines, seem like the freshness of childhood, and the flowers of every hue touch the chords of your heart like its laugh. Sickness and old age can not rob us of these pleasures, if God in mercy spares us our sense of them. But, dear Sue, I began merely to tell you that, though still weak, I find myself improving from week to week, and quite free from disease. I drive out daily, and walk moderately, eat with good appetite, and sleep well. Mercies to be mindful of. * * * *

" I went, on Saturday, to Readville (the Freedmen's camp), to call on A. S., and she and her husband drove over in the evening and took tea with us. To-day the regiment

is presented with a flag, and on Monday they move. Poor
young people! The Freedmen look remarkably well. I
saw colored *ladies* walking about the camp attended by some
fine, soldier-like looking men, and dressed very handsomely,
and, for the most part (there were some brilliant glimmer-
ings of color), in good taste."

Miss Sedgwick to Mrs. Charles E. Butler.

" Woodbourne, June, 1863.

* * * * "Since my illness I have in some respects be-
haved with the humility that one would think should always
attend us, holding the gifts of Providence by the tenure we
do. I don't lay out my future, nor count upon it. I receive gratefully my life from day to day, assigning its disposal to the good providence of God, and to those who are
my earthly providence. Whatever Kate tells me I may do,
I do, and none other. Is not that meekness? and certainly, so far, I have experienced the beatitude of meekness, for
I have enjoyed with contentment the sweetest comforts of
earth."

Miss Sedgwick to Rev. Dr. Dewey.

" Woodbourne, July 1, 1863.

" MY DEAR FRIEND,—Your letter was a great satisfaction
to me. I partook, in some sort, the parental joy and sisterly pride that must have risen in an anthem of joy and praise,
almost lifting the roof from the dear old ancestral home,
when you heard that your son* had, with so good a will—a
will so strong and victorious—paid his debt for his country,
and that he was *safe*—for the instinct of love can not be lost
in any secondary emotion.

* Dr. Dewey's only son had enlisted in the 59th Massachusetts Regiment, and was one of the volunteers in the forlorn hope at Fort Hudson, May 27, 1863.

* * * * " I expect to go to Berkshire to pass some months. * * * *

* * * * " I try to throw off all sad presages, and to live in strong, unfaltering faith in that sure Providence that has blessed all our days. My love and blessing to all yours, and in never-failing, never-ending affection believe me yours,

"C. M. SEDGWICK."

Miss Sedgwick to Robby Minot.

"Stockbridge, July 14, 1863.

"MY DARLING ROBBY,—It will be one week to-morrow since you and I walked round our flower-bed, and since then the kind showers have fallen, and I trust they are holding up their heads and smiling on you, and ready to send their love to me. How is our "lame tame" crow? and how is dear little Romeo? I want to hear all you can write me— of Will, and Charlie, and dear little Benjy, and you, my beloved boy. All the children here and at Lenox have been delighted with the walking doll. They all think it was so lucky that you drew the doll for so many of them to enjoy it. There was a party of little girls on Saturday, keeping F. W.'s birthday, and they all came over to see the doll, and they were delighted.

" It is very pleasant to let others enjoy our pleasures, and you, dear Robby, as you go along in life, will try to share with others your good things. We should be selfish, miserable creatures if we could do nothing for others. Twenty little girls enjoying your doll is just as good as having twenty dolls. God gives his good gifts to all—He sends the rain on the flowers at Woodbourne, at Lenox, at Stockbridge —every where. My dear child, continue in your resolve to 'grow up a good man,' and you will try to do, as far as you can, good to all.

"Give my love to mamma, and papa, and Willie, and

Charlie, and Hal, and all at Aunt H.'s, and to Aunt J. and
Cousin L., and the flowers that bloom, and the birds that
sing for you, and come to me as soon as you can—to me,
your loving   Aunt Kitty."

Miss Sedgwick to Mrs. K. S. Minot.

"Stockbridge, August 13, 1863.

"My dearest Kate,—I chanced the other day, in the
office of the President of the Senate and governor in futuro,
to see a box of quill pens. I was sorely tempted to steal
one—the grand official being occupied, I could not beg it.
Since, through J., I have obtained three, which, as Solicitor
Davis, or his grandson W. M. would have said, are as dear
to me as if plucked from the wing of the Archangel. Oh,
how it glides over the paper! how my heart's love fuses
and flows at its touch! Thank Heaven, I had almost finished my earthly career before I fell on the evil times of steel
pens, which turn my very heart's blood to hard steel. I
could as well write with the point of a javelin!"

Miss Sedgwick to Mrs. Charles E. Butler.

"Woodbourne, January 2, 1864.

"My dear Susy,—I can not let the second of January
pass without sending my blessing to you, my own dear
child, and to all my New York children, whether by the gift
of God or the authority of the law, which, certainly in some
cases, is to me 'vox Dei.' I have not been well, as you
probably know through your Aunt S., but I must have lost
all body, soul, and estate not to feel, at this season of memory and hope, the pressure of love and gratitude straining
across my heart for you *all.* * * * * It was a disappointment almost tragical to me to be removed* on the very day

* One of the attacks to which Miss Sedgwick was liable occurred as
she was on her way to church on Christmas Day.

of Christmas, and just as I was on my way to partake of its most solemn and dear consecration—the communion ; but I look back gratefully to the many returns I have been permitted to enjoy since we used to go in procession to the little tables in Warren Street. But from looking back, let us look forward, when all the shadows shall have passed away."

Miss Sedgwick to Mrs. Charles E. Butler.

"Woodbourne, January 27, 1864.

"DEAREST SUE,—I am deeply indebted to my New York children ; but, as I am under strict surveillance, I must limit myself to conveying to you a hint that may be of use in the regulation of your *fair. * * * * But, for mercy's sake, don't suggest that the oracular people of Boston claim superior sagacity. I merely suggest the result of experience, and a possible mode of avoiding the greatest bother here.

"I have a letter begun to B., asking her if F. can not set that grand heroic poetry of Bryant's to some patriotic German air—'Not yet.' I am so ignorant that I do not even know if it can be sung, but it struck me that the refrain '*No*,' if shouted by a multitude of voices at the opening of the fair, might be grand in effect. Do talk this over with B. and F. Thank dearest H. for a most delicious letter. Tell him the first Unitarian meeting was, I think, in Mrs. Russell's parlor. We met first as a society in a medical room, I think, at the corner of Reade Street and Broadway, and there, I think, we counted in all three female voices, and never shall I forget the thrilling sweetness of your Aunt Jane's.

"Oh, Sue, how has my heart been thrilled with the due

* Mrs. Butler was one of the managers of the New York Fair for the benefit of the Sanitary Commission, and had charge of the daily paper, "The Spirit of the Fair," issued during its continuance.

honor to be recorded to my brothers on the walls into which their very hearts were built !* Tell B. her letters have been nectar to me. I am much better. Love to dear C. and your children ; love and blessing. Don't exhaust yourself.

"Yours as ever,   C. M. SEDGWICK."

Miss Sedgwick to Rev. Dr. Dewey.

"Woodbourne, February 24, 1864.

"MY DEAR FRIEND,—Many thanks for your letter received yesterday. I must respond to its affectionate concern, if it be but by a 'bulletin ;' I hate to write by another's hand to those I love. * * * *

* * * * "I am better, though, from the nature of my illnesses, always in dread. But, thank God, I enjoy much—the sweet vicissitudes of day and night—my many and kind friends—W.'s *filial* care, and K.'s unfailing sweetness—the angel ministry of the children—this exquisite winter. I walk out daily, and every day, in spite of the cold and tempestuous wind of last week, I sat for hours on the lounge in the piazza, looking at the green trees, and thus healing my eyes, and basking in the sunshine.

* * * * "I too dread, but not fear, for I never so felt the goodness and love of God, and from the memory of his mercies springs trust. I hate to shut my eyes on the pleasant light ; but how came we, ignorant and helpless, into this world, and found every needful help, and a world of love !"

Miss Sedgwick to Mrs. Chas. E. Butler.

"Woodbourne, March 12, 1864.

"MY DEAREST SUE,—It is a *great while* since we have

---

* This refers to a proposition (never carried into effect) to place a tablet in Dr. Bellows's church commemorating Miss Sedgwick's brothers Harry and Robert as among the earliest and most zealous founders of the first Unitarian Church in New York.

had any communication except that mysterious one when spirit goes out to spirit. I have just come in from the piazza, where I have *disported* on my lounge, breathing in the elixir of life—the pure air, gazing at the pines and the clear, intervening blue sky. My beloved little boys are playing in the sunshine, and coming to me ever and anon with a shower of kisses, and bits of moss and green buds that are prematurely venturing forth on this wonderful spring weather. 5 *P.M.*—While I was writing, dear Sue, your letter, a missive on wings—angel wings—was on its way to me. It stood me well in place of all other company at my solitary dinner to-day—the sweetest of condiments. Glad am I to hear that you are getting well through your literary cares. And what a laurel wreath your letter from Gasparin is! I am not surprised by E.'s poetry. He has the divine elements of poetry in him. Make R. write for you. Send me your paper the moment it is out."

Miss Sedgwick to Mrs. Chas. E. Butler.

"June 1, 1864.

"MY DEAR SUE,—I wonder if Eve could write letters in Paradise! But, poor Eve, she had no one to write to—no one to whom to tell what Eden was, no beloved child to whom her love traveled through any or all space. Poor Eve!"

Miss Sedgwick to Rev. Dr. Dewey.

"Woodbourne, July 22, 1864.

"'You had better lay aside your writing materials, Miss Sedgwick, and take a nap.' So speaks my maid, Martha. No—no, indeed—not till I have told you that at last, my dearest friend, your book* is in my possession—not till I have thanked you for it. You know that I breakfast in bed,

* The Problem of Human Destiny.

and here write my letters.   My eyes will not permit me to read much at any time, and nothing, save a few verses in the Bible, before breakfast.   But I could not help opening your book, and opened, I read the preface, and the contents of the first chapter, and then felt an emotion akin in keenness (in nothing else) to that of a miser who, from an untold store, should have a guinea dropped into his lap!

"We are, indeed, all enriched if God has given you the key to these high mysteries; perhaps I should rather say, imitating your own modesty, permits you to throw a light on them; for has He not, in the mission and teaching of Christ, given the key to all who, in faith, obedience, and patience, use it?

"I am not now in condition to read such a book, but with caution, chapter by chapter, paragraph by paragraph, I may read it, and be instructed, encouraged, consoled—lifted out of myself by it; and I may hold it in my hand, and thank God that the writer is my friend.

* * * * "I have come to my greatest trial of self-denial from the contraction of my little income by the war.   I must give up the daily 'Evening Post,' which has been a great consolation to me ever since my exile from my New York friends.   It has been a sort of daily intercourse with the Bryants.   It is an old familiar friend, endeared by the recollections of my childhood.   From its first establishment— now sixty-three years—I have seen it.   Colman, the first editor, was my father's friend.   Since Bryant's editorship, I have looked upon it as my political text-book. * * * *

* * * * "Even my maid, witnessing my daily enjoyment of it, pleads with me to continue it; but alas! necessity, that knows no law, knows no indulgence, and this must go."

.

It can not be an infringement upon propriety to say that Mr. Bryant, on being made aware of the reason for Miss

Sedgwick's discontinuance of the paper, sent it to her, with equal delicacy and kindness, during the rest of her life.

Miss Sedgwick to Mrs. Charles E. Butler.

"Woodbourne, September 4, 1864.

"What a grand book is this ' Problem of Human Destiny !' At first I rather recoiled from the title, and feared to find it metaphysical, and dealing in subjects that neither he or we could understand. You will read it, dear Sue, and, reading, you will study it, and, studying it, you will distill from it instruction of infinite worth for your children. It is enriched by great thoughts—truths of immense magnitude, and beautiful illustrations, and is often even pathetic in the views it presents of the beneficence of the Deity, and is consoling to troubled, fermenting ignorance."

Miss Sedgwick to Rev. Dr. Dewey.

"Boston, December 10, 1864.

* * * * "I have been here for the last three weeks, and had much enjoyment from seeing old friends, and have had the honor and pleasure of a call from Whittier. He has a face and manner fitting his high gifts and mission. I have walked daily, and sat for two hours in the Public Garden. Am I not a brave old woman?

"Since I wrote to you, my heroic sister* has passed on— a blessed release in all senses—most blessed to her, if we can believe, as Jeremy Taylor says, that Death gives more than it takes away.

* * * * "A—— S—— bade me farewell Friday evening. She has returned to her hospital work at Beverly, New Jersey, where my Cousin E—— and S—— E—— are good soldiers in a holy warfare. What a different consecration from that of nuns ! How blessed are the single women of

* Mrs. Charles Sedgwick.

our country, who have found such new and blessed channels for those affections which crave and will have a channel! Surely more acceptable to God is the tending and solacing of sick soldiers than protracted prayers kneeling upon stone floors.

"Mr. M—— has had and enjoyed much a visit from his classmate, Governor Lincoln, aged eighty-two, and as vigorous and more nimble than most men of thirty! He says he has been a very temperate consumer of animal food, drank wine, tea, and coffee every day, and never lay down in the daytime during his life! Should not all the vigilant saints and nymphs guard his pillow? And we have had a visit from T——, a charming man, resembling in face and mind my brother Charles. I loved him 'peremptorily,' and should without other cause. Does not Choate deserve a crown for that saying, 'Thank heaven, there are not many that we hate peremptorily?'

"In advance, dear friends all, father, mother, and children, let me wish you a Happy New Year—fervently do I pray it may run a blessed course for you!"

The handwriting of this letter is very tremulous, and the few that followed it were for the greater part dictated. The invalid would, however, frequently send one or two lines only, written by her own hand, to a friend, as a greeting and remembrance from "a heart that yearned to give" to the last, and which no sickness could make forgetful. Her bodily powers were more affected than those of her mind. The disease made very gradual inroads upon the brain, and when these became manifest, her loss of judgment took the very characteristic form of increased and less discriminating admiration of every thing around her. And so, in the beautiful retirement she loved, surrounded by the tenderest ministrations, and without much acute suffering, her life wore gently away to its close.

Rev. Dr. Bellows to Miss Sedgwick.

"New York, October 7, 1866.

"MY DEAR FRIEND,—Thank you for thinking of me, and sending me one more written token of your continued affection! To-day has been our communion service, a day that has always brought me flocking thoughts of all those long-absent but once familiar guests at our love-feast. I miss you and your brothers and sisters there, but feel as if in spirit all of you were with us. I continually pray for all those whom sickness or age oppresses, and shall not forget how tenderly entitled to my best prayers you, who have been so much for all of us, are, in your seclusion and decline. You, who have 'loved much' all your life, are in the heart and in the prayers of hundreds of grateful, affectionate friends. I meet very often with fond, respectful inquiries about you, and I never hear your name coupled with any thing but reverence and love. Those retired from the world, who have served it well, seem to those still in it already above them, and in a sort of outer-court of heaven, and your words come to me almost as if the door of the celestial city were ajar, and I had overheard some of the angels talking."

Rev. Dr. Bellows to Miss Sedgwick.

"New York, May 16, 1867.

"MY DEAR FRIEND,—I write only to say good-by, for before another Sunday we shall be on the ocean. I have a delightful recollection of my short visit to you, and shall think of you very often, and pray for you as often as I think of you. God bless you, my dear friend. You have been trying all your precious life to make others happy and good, and the gracious Father, whose chosen name is *love*, knows your loving heart, and will say at the last, as he takes you into his everlasting acceptance, 'For she loved much!' Don't

S

let that pale slave we call Death—who is the mere porter at
the gate of Life—affright your heart.   He is the most *harmless* creature, spite of his grim looks.   Oh, if the brothers
and sisters who have gone before could only show you the
expression of their triumphant faces, how brave you would
feel to meet the change that will give you back health and
youth, and the past and the future, all in one !"

Miss Sedgwick to Rev. Dr. Dewey.

"Woodbourne, June 24, 1867.

"Since yesterday morning I have not expected to outlive
the longest days, but I must use this prolonged time to bless
my dear friend for the lifelong blessing of his friendship.

"I have suffered these last days from the cowardice of
my cowardly nature, from the imperfection of my faith and
love ; but I have enjoyed much from the tenderness of my
friends, from the transcendent beauty of nature, from its
revelations of love.*   I have longed to hear your voice in
prayer for me, sure it would have strengthened me ; but,
though I have not heard it, our gracious Father has.   I have
more mercies than I can remember. * * * *

"Yours *to the last,*   C. M. SEDGWICK."

Miss Sedgwick to Mrs. Charles E. Butler.

"Woodbourne, July 19, 1867.

"My DEAR SUSY,—I was in a wretched state when I re-

---

* And these she continued to enjoy till the last moment of consciousness.   She had the habit, in her days of health, of spending at least half
an hour every day before breakfast in out-of-door exercise, and, when
her increasing infirmities cut her off from this pleasure, she still welcomed the fresh morning air by throwing open all her windows.   Beside
one of them she daily knelt to offer her morning devotion ; then, going
to the chamber of her darling Robert, she knelt again by his deserted
bedside, to breathe prayers for him which may follow him with blessing
all the days of his life.

ceived your last letter. I was hypochondriacal ; but it disarmed hypochondria, and threw the blue devils on the other
side. I have been very poorly of late, and have driven out
to-day for the first time in several days, and feel much better for it. I had quite a long visit from Dr. Hedge, the
prince of divines. He tells me, to my great cheer, of dear
Dr. Bellows's success in his tour. * * * *

"I have a balcony out of Kate's window in the pine wood,
where I lie all day, and where the mercies and love of God
are continually pressing upon my senses. But 'tis hard
work, Susy, to be sick, and helpless, and useless !"

That mortal weariness was now to end. Before this letter reached its destination, the tired body was at rest and
the spirit freed. Mercifully unconscious of the final parting,
Miss Sedgwick crossed that 'narrow sea' which had formerly seemed so terrible to her timid, shrinking physical nature.
She had, indeed, attained that trust in God which is truly
willing to take all things from his hand, but she was too
much like Bunyan's tender-spirited Mercy not to have rather a trembling hope than confidence, and it is sweet to think
that she was spared all fear or suffering at the last.

She died, and left our world sadly the poorer for the lack
of that gracious presence. Many a one, even of those by
whom it was seldom seen, felt that

> "A light had pass'd from the revolving year,
> And man, and woman,"

now that it could be seen no more. In many a humble
room tears were shed for her who brought better than food,
or clothes, or even work—and she was liberal of these—in
the kindly sympathy, wise advice, and cheerful interest that
lightened the hearts of the poor ;* and many, in the midst of

---

* The day after her death, a young woman came hoping to see her and
carry from her some token of remembrance to the daughter of a woman

wealth, wept that they could never again receive the finer luxuries of wit, appreciation, and tenderness at her dear hands.   But in the large and loving circle gathered to meet her there must have been deep gladness as she came, and in the thought of her release from the body which had become a burden, and of the unchecked activity of her most loving nature, those who miss her most must find a true and tender consolation.

who, when a young orphan, had been taken into Miss Sedgwick's employment, and lived with her as a maid, though treated almost as a companion, and tenderly cared for, till she married.   *She* had long been dead, but the daughter had inherited her love and reverence for Miss Sedgwick, and the daughter's friend looked upon the lifeless form, and carried away as relics some leaves from the plants growing in the room, with almost the feeling of a devout Catholic to a canonized saint.

APPENDICES.

I. LETTER FROM MRS. FRANCES ANNE KEMBLE TO MRS. WILLIAM MINOT, JR.

II. SKETCH OF MISS SEDGWICK'S CONNECTION WITH THE WOMEN'S PRISON ASSOCIATION OF NEW YORK, BY MRS. JAMES S. GIBBONS.

III. LETTER FROM THE REV. DR. DEWEY TO MRS. WILLIAM MINOT, JR.

IV. REMINISCENCES OF MISS SEDGWICK, BY WILLIAM CULLEN BRYANT.

LETTER TO MRS. WILLIAM MINOT, JR.

FROM MRS. FRANCES ANNE KEMBLE.

Philadelphia, April 25, 1869.

You ask me, my dear K., for some sketch of my personal recollections of your aunt, and no one, beloved of her as you were, could ask me any thing that I would not endeavor to do ; but my recollections of your aunt stretch over a period of so many years, during which she was to me the tenderest of friends—years of such varied fortunes, of so much joy and so much sorrow, in all of which she participated with the whole sympathy of her most sympathizing nature, that her image calls up that of my whole life and all its vicissitudes, since first I came to your country in 1832, and fills me with emotions little favorable to any deliberate mental process. The days of enjoyment whose pleasures were enhanced by her companionship, the hours of misery whose burden was lightened by her compassion, the vivid intellectual pleasure of her conversation, the delightful fellowship of our walks and drives through the lovely hill country of Lenox, the life of intimate and almost daily communion with that bright spirit and tender heart, all come thronging back upon my memory, and I sit with my pen in my hand, *remembering,* indeed, but hardly able to write.

Your aunt did me the honor to call on me soon after my arrival in New York, and was among my first American acquaintances, and was my first American *friend.* She was then, I suppose, between thirty and forty years old, of a slight and graceful figure, the movements of which were remarkably light and elastic, and with a countenance in which bright intelligence, a keen sense of humor, and an almost pathetic tenderness of expression were charmingly combined. None of these winning attributes had departed from my dear friend's form and face up to the last time of my seeing her, and it is some consolation to me for my separation from her during the last years of her life that my latest vision of her was (considering the interval between them) but little different from the earliest ; the graceful figure had not grown heavy, nor the tender countenance harsh, nor had the liberal mind become narrowed, nor the warm heart chilled under the touch of Time.

Perhaps the quality which most peculiarly distinguished your aunt from other remarkable persons I have known was her great simplicity and transparency of character—a charm seldom combined with as much intellectual keenness as she possessed, and very seldom retained by persons living as much as she did in the world, and receiving from society a tribute of general admiration. She was all through her life singularly childlike, and loved with a perfect sympathy of spirit those of whom it is said, "of such is the kingdom of heaven." Nothing could be more affecting and striking than the close affinity between her pure and tender nature and that of the "little children" who were irresistibly drawn to her ; alike those who lived within the circle of her love, and those on whom only the kindly influence of her transient notice fell. I think, in her intercourse with the more "sophisticate" elder members of society, Miss Sedgwick's acute sense of the ludicrous, in all its aggressive forms of assumption, presumption, pretension, and affectation, was so keen that in a less amiable person it might have degenerated into a tendency to sarcasm, and made a satirist of one who was pre-eminently a sympathizer with her fellow-creatures. As a writer, I feel less inclined to speak of her very considerable merit, because the verdict of the public approval was deservedly awarded to her books as they appeared, and because, when thinking of *her*, I seldom think of *them*, feeling like the daughter of the admirable Pasta, who said to a friend, "You think my mother's singing beyond praise, and so it is, and yet, to *us who know her*, it is the thing we prize least about her." The pre-eminent characteristic of her intellect, as well as of her whole character, was its perfect womanliness, and assuredly, if she claimed a place in the honorable sisterhood of "Blue Stockings," it was among those most honorable members of it to whom the arch critic Jeffrey said he had no objection, for their petticoats "hid the hose." Of the society which gathered summer after summer to the pleasant hill region, the seat of her family home, attracted thither even more by the delightful intercourse of its various gifted members than by the pure air and fine scenery of Berkshire, Miss Sedgwick was the centre and soul, dispensing the most graceful hospitality, and doing the honors of her beautiful hills and valleys to her visitors with an unwearied kindliness and courtesy that must forever have combined in their memories the most delightful social intercourse with the most charming natural scenery.

To the poor, who were rich in having her for a neighbor, she was the most devoted and faithful of friends, sympathizing with all their interests, soothing their sorrows, supplying their wants, solacing their sufferings with an exquisite tact, which her knowledge of and skill in the homeliest, as well as highest feminine accomplishments, rendered as efficient as it was tender and unwearied. To be poor, sick, or sorrowful seemed scarcely hardships within the sphere of her gentle ministry of comfort. There is not one of the lowly dwellings within miles round Lenox and Stockbridge that her feet ever entered where her name is not synonymous with goodness, and her memory hallowed with grateful blessings.

Of what she was in that circle of good, gifted human beings to which by family ties she belonged, I may not speak while so many still remain who rejoiced in her daily influence, and whose hearts would find all words worse than inadequate to express how sweet and noble that influence was.

Early in my acquaintance with Miss Sedgwick, my admiration for her became affection, and the love and respect with which I soon learned to regard her increased and deepened till the end of our intercourse. Her memory now remains to me as that of one of the most charming, most amiable, and most excellent persons I have ever known.

SKETCH OF MISS SEDGWICK'S CONNECTION WITH THE WOMEN'S PRISON ASSOCIATION OF NEW YORK.

BY MRS. JAMES S. GIBBONS.

It was in the early days of the Women's Prison Association of New York that Miss Catharine M. Sedgwick appeared at one of its stated meetings as a visitor, on which occasion her grace of manner and pleasant voice so attracted me, and I was so much impressed by her presence, that I was about to inquire who she was, when she took me cordially by the hand, saying, "I understand you are the daughter of Isaac T. Hopper, and I must know you."

This was the beginning of an intimate acquaintance, and at once I besought her to become a member of the society.

To this request she readily assented, and the next year she was chosen our president, which office she held, beloved and reverenced by all, until her death.

We were soon brought into close companionship by visits to the prisons and kindred institutions, especially the Tombs, Blackwell's, and Randall's Island. The hospital claimed much of her interest, perhaps because there her tenderest sympathies were enlisted. In her visitations she was called upon to kneel by the bedside of the sick and dying. The sweetness of her spirit, and the delicacy of her nature, felt by all who came within her atmosphere, seemed to move the unfortunate to ask this office from her, and it was never asked in vain. So tenderly shrinking was she that she sought opportunities for such ministrations when no ear heard, no eye beheld her, and many an erring sister was soothed and comforted as she passed through the dark valley by the heavenly voice of this angel of mercy.

At the Isaac T. Hopper Home she labored faithfully for this class of humanity, and for many successive years during her sojourn in this city, attended by her niece Helen, with her favorite dog, she devoted Sunday afternoons to a Bible-class, and sometimes to the reading of such books as met the needs of the inmates. Sometimes the hours were passed in conversation, one and another relating their sorrows and misfortunes, and receiving in their turn the balm which flowed from a heart touched with a sense of their infirmities, and accepting the lesson that "to cease to do evil and learn to do well" was the way to a new and better life.

Miss Sedgwick was a woman by herself—so genial and loving, so easily wrought upon, and so readily moved to compassion for the sad and untoward experiences of her unhappy sisters, that her very presence was peace.

Those with whom she was associated in prison-visiting can testify to her wonderful power of winning the confidence of a class whose need was kindness, and such counsel as furnished food for reflection; consequently, her visits were attended with the happiest results.

Many of the prisoners were mothers of children who were in the nurseries assigned to the city's poor, and there began a work of never-failing interest and humanity. Seated on long benches, erect as their frail, emaciated bodies permitted, were rows of motherless and deserted children, lonely, spirit-broken to the last degree, suffering, without a ray of sunlight. It was not strange that she witnessed the scene in tears, and in these darkest of all days, sought some means by which to light up the existence, and strew flowers in the pathway of these little wanderers.   And so she initiated the Fourth of July Festival.   Listen to her call:

"We invite all who, like the good vicar, 'love happy human faces,' to go to Randall's Island on the Fourth.   Go there to see that lovely island in its rich natural beauty. Go to see the wise and generous provisons the city has made for its young pensioners, by which they are to become a crown instead of a curse to us.   Go there to make the bond that binds the children to their benefactors recognized and felt.   Let all who contribute to the festival go there and see the good to be done by addressing the sense and love of beauty ; how surely it exalts the angelic portion of our nature, and depresses the sensual and brutish."

These fêtes were seasons of great rejoicing to the children, and most liberal were the supplies of flowers and good things.   But the extreme heat made it a hard day's duty, and Christmas Day was fixed upon for bestowing dolls, toys, and books, and the custom has continued to the present time.

Christmas is alike regarded by rich and poor, and to come together for mutual enjoyment on this happiest day of all the year has become an institution which those interested are not likely to abandon.

It was on one of these occasions that a gentleman of the party placed a doll on the arm of a dying child.   Recovering consciousness for a moment, she pressed it to her lips, while a smile lit up her death-like face.   "Good doll!" she exclaimed, and again kissed it.   "These are among the last words she will speak," observed the doctor, and the next day the child died.

Innumerable cases might be added showing the effect of this charity, which may be recorded as among the sweet memories of our beloved friend ; but this will suffice to keep alive and active the spirit which prompted her to alleviate the sufferings of lonely and destitute children.

To return to "The Home," to which her labors were chiefly directed, we find her practical in this work of reformation. She employed the inmates in her own home, and recommended them to friends, believing that favorable circumstances and kindness were the means best adapted to save them from an evil life.

When she withdrew from active co-operation with us, the loss was unspeakable, although it inspired others with the necessity of greater diligence and activity. We were soon after apprised of her increasing infirmities, and in a private letter, accompanied by her resignation, we find the following words :

" I felt humbled in reading, and a confession of my unworthiness burned in my heart and trembled on my lips ; but the little that I could honestly take fell like precious balsam on my spirit, consoling and invigorating. My tearful thanks to you, dear friend, and my love and manifold thanks to our dear associates who authorized you thus to write. May God's blessing rest on them, and God's mercies, through their instrumentality, fall on many forsaken and helpless creatures."

To the " Ladies of the Home" she sent the following :

To the Executive Committee of the Women's Prison Association of New York.

Woodbourne, October 9th, 1863.

MY DEAR FRIENDS,—I rejoice in an opportunity of congratulating you, and the society of whose charities we have been the medium, on the great and unexpected accession to our means, from the munificent bequest of Charles Burrall, Esq. Of the generous donor we can say nothing but that we are profoundly grateful to him. He has passed beyond our praise and thanks to His presence who uttered those words of encouragement and immeasurable blessing to the Benefactor of the Poor—"Inasmuch as ye have done it unto one of the least of these, ye have done it unto me."

It is, my friends, with a feeling blending pain and pleasure that I resign the position among you with which you have so long honored me—pain at the disruption of a tie that, so far as I know, has never been jarred by a discord or dissatisfaction, and pleasure that your present affluence renders my co-operation of no importance to you. And, moreover, much as I may desire to linger with you, the infirmities of age, and my absence from the city, take from me even the pretext for such self-indulgence.

Your increased means enlarge your field of action, your blessed opportunities of doing good, and your responsibilities. May God give you the holy zeal, the wisdom, and the energy you need! And may He grant you that essential to the success of all great and good enterprises—*the right* officers to do the right thing in the right time and the right place.

Believe me, my dear friends, respectfully, gratefully, and affectionately yours,   C. M. SEDGWICK.

To this letter the following reply was sent:

Miss C. M. Sedgwick:

DEAR FRIEND,—At a special meeting of the Women's Prison Association, held at the "Isaac T. Hopper Home," October 13th, 1863, thy letter of October 9th, resigning thy position as First Directress, was presented. The reading made a deep impression upon all present, and, after a time of silence, succeeded by many demonstrations of loving kindness toward thee, our dear friend and counselor, the privilege was given me to answer thy communication, and to assure thee that, while we patiently abide the temporary separation from one whom we have held to be our strength in adversity, with one voice we call thee to share in our prosperity. When our days were darkest, thy presence and the might of thy influence sustained us. We remember, with feelings of gratitude, thy tender sympathy and substantial aid ; and now let the remembrance of thy goodness, and of all thou hast been to us, animate us to renewed exertion in behalf of our dependent family, and guide us in every act of the society of which thou hast ever been the pride and ornament.

We reverently acknowledge thee as our head. Grant us thy loved and honored name, and believe us, now and in all time, faithfully and affectionately thy grateful friends.

In behalf of the committee, A. H. GIBBONS.
New York, October 30th, 1863.

The Annual Report of the Women's Prison Association and Isaac T. Hopper Home for the year 1867 concludes with this notice :

" We can not close this report without some notice of the loss we have sustained this year in the death of our First Directress, our dear friend and fellow-laborer, Miss Catharine M. Sedgwick. Although it is several years since absence from the city and increasing infirmities have prevented her from being bodily present with us, we feel it as a fresh bereavement to lose her dear and honored name from the list of our officers. For more than twenty years Miss Sedgwick was an active member of our society—since 1848 its First Directress—and when, in 1863, she tendered her resignation of this office to the society, finding active participation in its labor no longer possible for her, it was received with an earnest and unanimous entreaty that she would still suffer her name to head the list of our officers, which was granted. And now that death must sever this last visible link, we feel more sensibly how strong and tender are the bonds which no separation can loosen, and how the memory of her gentle presence, and loving counsel, and efficient help will ever remain with us an abiding treasure. The touching modesty which formed so striking a portion of her character made it always impossible for her to realize the value of her own work ; but we, who can remember the spirit of love and tenderness which surrounded her like an atmosphere, know that it fell like balsam on thousands of wounded and weary hearts, encouraging the hopeless and comforting the forsaken, so that her memory is a perpetual inspiration and encouragement to us in the labor which she shared with us during her life."

LETTER TO MRS. WILLIAM MINOT, JR.

FROM THE REV. DR. DEWEY.

MY DEAR MRS. MINOT,—You have asked me to give you my thoughts of Miss Sedgwick, and also such of her letters to me, or passages from them, as were proper for publication. I am sorry that I can find only extracts of this character; for I think the special interest of letters, as such, consists in the whole of them being given; and these letters, though very precious to me and of rare beauty, are so full of the personality and the personal relations of the writer, that their very charm forbids their appearing in print. I send you such extracts from them as I think proper for your purpose, and I wish I could give you the biographical sketch that you desire—that is, any thing satisfactory to myself. But I have always felt it difficult, I hardly know why, to portray the character of my best friends; it refuses to yield to analysis—like music, which one feels but can not describe. But I will do what I can.

And with this view I should like to insert, if you think it proper, what I said the Sunday after Miss Sedgwick's funeral, in a sermon which I delivered in Stockbridge.

My friends, I have been led thus to speak to you of what we are, and may hope to be, by the solemn event and sad obsequies of the past week. I have been drawn to do so, invited by the considerate courtesy of your pastor, because

I could not bear that this occasion should pass without some word spoken of that with which my mind and many minds here are burdened and overburdened. That precious and beautiful life which has lately come to its end ought not to pass from us without some grateful and admiring comment. I was once in the French Institute, at the funeral of a member, when his fellow-members rose, one after another, and uttered their thoughts of him. I thought it a fit and excellent custom ; and if those who shared in literary labors and honors with our friend had been here with us at her funeral, well might they have spoken of her, and more justly and fully than I can undertake now to do ; but they could not with more affection and admiration.

But comment there will be, not only through public channels, but in many private words spoken in tones of respect, affection, and tenderness. Long will be pronounced among us the name of our friend as few names are pronounced. To-day it is uttered with tears, but in days to come it will be uttered with reverence and thanksgiving.

And let us be thankful now. Let not the only homage we pay to departed worth be grief and mourning. Let us not mourn as having no hope. We have a hope that enters within the veil. Were it not so, this hour, this place, this assembly would be covered with impenetrable darkness and gloom. But if we look forward we believe that all is bright —that the light of immortality is shining upon her path. "The souls of the righteous," says an ancient writing, "are in the hand of God ; and there shall no torment touch them. In the sight of the unwise they seem to die, and their departure is taken for misery, and their going from us to be utter destruction ; but they are in peace." Peace ! after the toil and weakness of life are over—peace ! after life's fitful fever, after pain and trouble, after weary days and restless nights —it is God's peace, and we believe it is given to her.

And when we look backward and commemorate the past, as we should, hers has been a favored life—a good and happy life. We have no need nor desire to speak of her life or lot in terms of ordinary eulogy. Life is no light thing to any. It is a hard strain upon every soul that passes through it. It is hard to live wisely and well. Doubtless she knew it and felt it all, sensitive and delicate as her nature was, though singularly controlled and balanced. Doubtless she had her faults, though I confess I could never see them. But there are inward records where are written trial, temptation, weakness, erring, regret, repentance ; and the greatest burden and sorrow of all the highest and best minds, I suppose, is that they live so poorly.

But hers was a good and happy life. Trained from her childhood in yonder mansion, though she early lost a mother's watch and care, by a father of singular dignity of character, of equally strong sense and affection ; with elder sisters, most affectionate guides and companions ; with four brothers such as are rare to be found in any family, all devoted to her ; with a younger generation of relations growing up around her, all drawn to her as a common centre of attraction ; and a home with one of them in her declining days, made sweet and loving as any home could be ; with a larger circle of constant and enthusiastic admirers ; with a still wider circle composed of all reading persons among us, whose hearts she touched with the wisdom of her thoughts and the grace of her pen—hers has been a life to rejoice over, and for which to be thankful and glad.

Her character was moulded, I always thought, of all good elements, with as few discordant ones, if there were any, as I ever knew in any human being—sense and feeling, reason and imagination, seriousness and cheerfulness, yet you could not tell which of them predominated, so blended were they all in her character ; and piety, deep and reverent, was hers.

I touch upon the **theme with awe.** Who knows the thoughts, the aspirations, the prayers that are **breathed in such** souls? Who knows what doubts and sorrowings over themselves are passing in them? But this world was pleasant to her ; **and** how much she did to make it pleasant to others !—did **it in** ways of philanthropy and charity, but did it yet more, unconsciously. Ah! one is tempted to hope that he does, **possibly,** something in that way, so little purposed and positive good are we sensible of doing. But certainly she did. **Her** life was **a** benediction, and a charm, and a blessing wherever **she moved.** Who that has seen her here, in former days, in **her** home walks, does not remember her very **step,** so self-poised, elastic, and free ; her manner and bear**ing, so** kindly and **cheering,** so full of **fresh heart-warmth and** inspiration ; her word, ready for every one, so fit and apt for every occasion of greeting or sympathy ; the neighborly love in which she lived with her people? Hers was a large humanity, stirred by **every claim** of sorrow or wrong, and yet a penetrating insight and tenderness **that never mis**took or missed the individual claim or call. **She had as keen a glance** into the faults and foibles of society as any **one had, but** her judgment always leaned to forbearance and **charity.** I might proceed, but who shall tell all the charm **of her** intercourse with her kindred and friends?

And all this character was expressed in her writings. **She** was not one whose private life was one thing, and whose authorship another—whose pen drew pictures of virtue and goodness that were all imaginings and dreams, and not realities. Her sweet and graceful nature welled up and flowed out in clear streams, **that** told of the fountain from which they came. Her **style was** one **of** remarkable clearness, simplicity, and beauty. She never **wrote a** letter, even the **shortest, without some** felicitous **turns of** expression, which **seemed as natural to her as** to breathe. She has written works which hold an honored place in our literature ; and her smaller and simpler tales, which occupied her pen mostly in the latter part of her literary career, are to-day running their rounds, bearing gracious wisdom and loving counsels to the homes of our people.

Her closing years, though with some painful and some halting steps, were a fit and beautiful ending to such a life. It seemed as if her setting sun suffused her spirit and all things around her with a golden radiance. Never did she seem so touched with the sense of all things beautiful. Never did the books she read appear so excellent, never her friends so admirable, never the scenes of nature so lovely. She saw God in all things ; for nothing hath its true beauty without that vision. She leaned upon an almighty arm, humble, indeed, and trembling, but held up by the great Christian reliance upon the Infinite mercy. And when at last a deep slumber fell upon her, and so she passed away, that seems to me a friendly veil, cast by the All-loving care over the tremblings and sorrows of parting. And when, for hours after, her features took on the form of the loveliest repose, and resumed all the beauty of earlier days, that seems to me an emblem of the soul's deep repose.

In speaking of Catharine Sedgwick, I would not use one word that was conventional or customary, yet neither would I restrain the natural language of friendship. Homage to whom homage is due, for it is well and dearly earned ; and it is, indeed, a notable thing to me, when I hear so much about this bad world, to see, rising amidst the general darkness—rising every where, this halo of admiration to the gifted and good. They are stars in this earthly sky ; and when men say "all is shadow and night in this world," it is meet that these stars should be seen and signalized ; and not remarkable persons—not authors nor artists alone, are such, but many another—many, indeed, from whose lives authors and artists obtain their best ideals.

Catharine Sedgwick was an author of no mean fame, and yet she was an original fine enough to draw from ; but she never seemed to know that she was an author unless it was forced upon her attention.   The freedom, the ease, the simplicity, the *abandon* of her manners, never betrayed, in any form, the slightest consciousness of success.   *Abandon*, I say ; and yet there was never any thing that touched the dignity and delicacy of her deportment.   A certain *freedom of genius* there was in her mind and way—a strain of sentiment in her conversation, that was not amenable to ordinary conventionalism ; but her good sense always came out, clear and fair, upon every question.   Her opinions were her own, but not eccentric nor singular ; formed by herself, but not for herself—for the sake of justice and the reason of things rather.   Her judgment was her own, and not another's—not a reverberation of the common talk.   The mingled frankness and fearlessness of her bearing told you that.

Fearlessness, I repeat ; and yet—for qualifications must come in, like many-colored threads in a woven fabric—yet there was a constitutional timidity in her nature.   But for a certain force, and even passion, in her whole constitution, physical and mental, it would have been weakness.   As it was, a blending of opposite qualities made a singular beauty.   There was a turn of the eye, I often thought, like a wild animal's, if I may venture upon the phrase, expressive neither of timidity nor fearlessness, but something finer than either, and typical of what we call a natural grace.   There was something of a Southern flexibility in her temperament and manners, a free swaying in her motions, and the very expressions of her countenance to the mood within, not often seen in a New England woman.   Her gait in walking showed this.   No one could see her in the streets of her native village without being struck with it—an unconventional freedom, a bearing independent of all constraint, and yet so generous and kind-hearted to all around her, as made one happier after meeting with her.

I am tempted to put into this too meager record a few words that I have received from the hand of another:

"Dearly as I loved Miss Sedgwick, I never had such intimate personal relations with her as would enable me to make a complete analysis of her character, while I stood too near her in affection and reverence to make it easy to draw a mere sketch. What I most loved in her, I think, was the exquisite, unfailing, abounding sympathy which was always ready for the need of great and small, and which, like the fairy tent of Prince Ahmed, could include a nation, or shelter one poor trembling head. And it was not a sympathy only with suffering, but a true taking into her generous heart all the feelings of people far less gifted than herself—their little joys, their half-formed desires, their crude aspirations; every thing in them that was true and natural found a response in her, while her quick wit and delicate perceptions made her easily see through any thing like affectation or pretension. And I think I admired most her perfect womanliness, which, adorned with beautiful refinement of manner, infused into every thing she said and did a peculiar feminine charm, gave an exquisite grace to the activity of her intellect, and pervaded the rich cultivation of her mind with a subtle sense of fitness and beauty.

"Her writings seem to me, in a remarkable degree, a reflex of her nature. Her books are not like reservoirs, into which thought is laboriously and painfully pumped up, or brought by elaborately-constructed conduits from afar, but rather like mountain lakes, which gather their sweet waters from the natural slopes around them, and reflect, in their lovely mirrors, the sources from which they are drawn. Her excellent sense, her genial feeling, her high-bred ease and grace, delicate sarcasm, and pure and tender tone of sentiment, are felt in each, and felt as a personal charm. I remember particularly the letters scattered through her novels for their fine ease of expression, and careless, graceful wealth of allusion and fancy. Some of those in ' Redwood' and 'The Linwoods' are especially admirable."

I have spoken already of Miss Sedgwick's family and her position in it. It was her great happiness to find it, from youth to age, the home of all protecting and cherishing affections. She had two sisters, one of whom only I knew— Mrs. Watson—and knew only to admire the elevated tone of all her thoughts and aims, the fervor of her sensibility, both religious and social, and her fine enthusiasm, almost conflicting with her natural good sense.

The four brothers of Miss Sedgwick were educated for the law : they naturally followed the profession in which their father, Judge Sedgwick, had been eminent, yet no one of them followed him in the political career in which he had been equally distinguished. The eldest, Theodore, practiced law in Albany ; Harry and Robert, in New York ; Charles, the youngest, at home. But he forsook the practice, which did not suit the sweetness and delicacy of one of the loveliest natures it was ever my fortune to be acquainted with. His name is fragrant in the memory of all who knew him. When he died, the Irish laborers who lived in his neighborhood asked leave, and were permitted, to bear his remains to the grave. His three elder brothers were all men of marked ability and equal integrity. Harry died earliest. The intellectual stamp upon him was perhaps strongest among the brothers—a man with a singular mixture of enthusiasm and penetration. He occupied the place of counselor in the office in New York, while Robert took charge of the active business of the firm, and had the confidence of those around him for sound judgment and high-toned principle. Theodore died of apoplexy. For some years he had looked to this as the end, and spoke of it so cheerfully that a friend one day by his side expressed surprise at it. "Yes," he said; "why not? It is the touch Ithuriel." All the brothers married women of marked sense and culture. Two of them, Mrs. Theodore and Mrs. Charles, were known by excellent writings; but the stately grace and sweetness of the one, and the practical intelligence and the full heart-life of the other, were finer than any books. Mrs. Robert many must remember for her beauty, and a cast of character in correspondence with it; for both were singularly high and high-bred, and rather exacting—not of homage, but of sincerity and sense from those around her. And Mrs. Harry—who can ever forget her womanly dignity, her strong sense, her large heart, and the flashing eyes?

And when all were assembled in Stockbridge, as they often were in summer days—and often with distinguished visitors from home and abroad—it would be difficult to find a family circle in which there was more good sense and good culture, more ease and freedom, or more gayety and affection. Catharine was, perhaps, the central figure of the group, at least to strangers; but it was a circle in which every one had attractions, and it was emphatically a family of love. The only contention about her, or with her, was who of them should have the most of her society in their homes. Hers was a position which, with its many and tender claims upon her, and her many philanthropic offices, and her large correspondence at home and abroad, added to her great literary labors, involved her in a life of cares. She once wrote to us, "My normal condition is one of fatigue." She is at rest. The busy day's life is over; and these families have passed like shadows over the earth. Peace to her memory! blessings so long as her memory shall endure!

REMINISCENCES OF MISS SEDGWICK.

BY WILLIAM CULLEN BRYANT, ESQ.

AT the desire of the friends of the late Catharine Maria Sedgwick, I have put together some notices of her early literary life, as it came under my observation, regretting that I am not able to speak of it more at large.

I became acquainted with Miss Sedgwick some time after the year 1816, precisely in what year I can not state. I had attempted the practice of law in a neighborhood where there was little employment for one of my profession, and, after a twelvemonth's trial, I transferred my residence to Great Barrington, near the birthplace and summer residence of Miss Sedgwick, in the pleasant county of Berkshire. It was on the third of October, in the year I have mentioned, that I made the journey thither from Cummington. The woods were in all the glory of autumn, and I well remember, as I passed through Stockbridge, how much I was struck by the beauty of the smooth, green meadows, on the banks of that lovely river, which winds near the Sedgwick family mansion, the Housatonic, and whose gently-flowing waters seemed tinged with the gold and crimson of the trees that overhung them. I admired no less the contrast between this soft scene and the steep, craggy hills that overlooked it, clothed with their many-colored forests. I had never before seen the southern part of Berkshire, and congratulated myself on becoming an inhabitant of so picturesque a region.

At that time I had no acquaintance with the Sedgwick family ; but the youngest of them, Charles Sedgwick, a man of most genial and engaging manners and agreeable conversation, as well as of great benevolence and worth, was a member of the Berkshire bar, and by him, two or three years afterward, I was introduced to the others, who, from the first, seemed to take a pleasure in being kind to me. I remember very well the appearance of Miss Sedgwick at that period of her life. She was well formed, slightly inclining to plumpness, with regular features, eyes beaming with benevolence, a pleasing smile, a soft voice, and gentle and captivating manners. The portrait of her by Ingham, painted about that time, or a little later, although not regarded, I think, by the family as a perfect likeness, yet brings to my mind her image as I saw her then, with that mingled expression of thoughtfulness and benignity with which her features were informed.

It was shortly after I became acquainted with her that, at her request, I wrote several hymns for a collection which one of her friends in New York was making. Two of these are included in the collection of my poems, one beginning with the line

> "Deem not that they are blest alone,"

and the other with the line

> "When he who from the scourge of wrong."

They were kindly received, and I was encouraged by her in my hopes of literary success. This was in the year 1820. At that time Miss Sedgwick had not appeared as an author, but her habits were understood to be literary, and in 1822 her "New England Tale" was published by Bliss & White, of New York, with a Preface written in March of that year.

I have a copy of the first edition of that work, the pages much thumbed, worn, and soiled, and with loose leaves, ready to drop out when the book is opened, attesting the number of times it has been borrowed, and the great number of times it has been read. The New England Tale became popular immediately ; every body was eager to see it, and it passed into the hands of thousands who were by no means habitual readers of novels, and who found themselves none the worse for having read it. It was the first time that the beautiful valleys of our county had been made the scene of the well-devised adventures of imaginary personages, and we all felt that, by being invested with new associations, they had gained a new interest. In the Preface to the work Miss Sedgwick had thought it necessary to say that "no personal allusions, however remote, were intended to be made to any individual," with the exception of the real personage whom she had introduced under the name of Crazy Bet. The experience of Mrs. Kirkland, after the publication of her sprightly and amusing sketches of western life, entitled "A New Home : Who'll Follow?" has since shown that this precaution was a prudent one. Mrs. Kirkland of course made her personal observation the basis of her sketches of life in the new settlements of Michigan, and, from the moment the work appeared, her neighbors in that region began so zealously and with such universal consent to appropriate to themselves the characters described in it, and were so little pleased with them, although they were not drawn with an unkindly hand, that the author soon became very willing to exchange her Western residence for one in New York, her native city. With regard to Crazy Bet, the sketch from real life which Miss Sedgwick, in the New England Tale, had wrought up with a fine poetic effect, I remember an incident to which I was witness while I lived in Great Barrington, and which I have always, whether rightly or not, associated with Crazy Bet. The village, unlike what it now is, was then a quiet little place—two rows of scattered dwellings under the shadow of the great elms which almost met over the road. An abundant shower had fallen on a warm summer day ; the clouds suddenly dispersed ; the sun broke forth in a flood of amber light ; the birds resumed their song ; the air was cooled and the verdure brightened, when suddenly I heard a loud, clear, and not unmelodious female voice singing, and saw a middle-aged woman marching along the street, in which was no other passenger. The notes were joyous and exultant, and seemed like an hosanna called forth by that glorious return of sunshine.

In 1824 appeared Miss Sedgwick's second work, Redwood, which by some is regarded as her best. I ventured to make it the subject of a somewhat elaborate criticism in the North American Review of April, 1825. This was my most ambitious attempt in prose up to that time. I took it up the other day with some misgivings, not having looked at it for many years, and was a little amused to see that I had dispensed both praise and blame with as magisterial an air as if I had been the most experienced of critics. Redwood was warmly received by the public, and such was its fame that it was translated into several languages of the European continent. Its success was fully deserved, were it only for the character of Debby Lenox, the clear-headed, conscientious, resolute Yankee spinster, a combination of noble and homely qualities so peculiar, yet so probable, and made so interesting by the part she takes in the plot, that as we read we always welcome her reappearance, and she takes her place in our memory with the remarkable personages we have met with in real life.

In 1825, by the advice of Miss Sedgwick's brother, Henry D. Sedgwick, I came to live in New York—a fortunate transplantation for me, for which I owe the Sedgwick family many thanks. I was kindly received by them all, and my interests were promoted by them as far as was in their power. I now saw more of Miss Sedgwick than I had previously done. The houses of her two brothers—the one whom I have already mentioned, and Robert Sedgwick—both men of high standing at the bar, were the resort of the best company in New York, cultivated men and women, literati, artists, and, occasionally, foreigners of distinction. Here I often found Verplanck, who had shortly before published his work on the Evidences of the Christian Religion, and was then occupied in getting through the press his able Essay on the Doctrine of Contracts. Here I met the novelist, J. Fenimore Cooper, who, however, soon after had a difference with Robert Sedgwick, which put an end to his intimacy with the family. At these houses I met Robert C. Sands, the wit and poet, whose Yamoyden, written by him in conjunction with James Wallis Eastburn, had just before appeared; and Hillhouse, author of Percy's Masque, and the finer drama of Hadad, which he was then writing. Halleck, then in the height of his poetical reputation, was among the visitors, and Anthony Bleeker, who read every thing that came out, and sometimes wrote for the magazines, an amusing companion, always ready with his puns, of whom Miss Eliza Fenno, before her marriage to Verplanck in 1811, wrote that she had gone into the country to take refuge from Anthony Bleeker's puns. Here was frequently seen Morse, then an artist, unconscious of the renown which was yet to crown him as the author of the most wonderful invention of the age; and Cole, the landscape painter, then in the early promise of his genius. Here, too, the clear, magnetic voice of Mrs. Nicholas was sometimes heard reciting Halleck's Marco Bozzaris, or one of Lockhart's ballads from the Spanish, to a spell-bound and breathless audience.

Henry D. Sedgwick was a philanthropist and reformer, without the faults which too often make that class of persons disagreeable. He was foremost in all worthy enter-

T 2

prises, but did not fatigue people with them. He took a deep interest in the project of reducing our statutes to a regular and intelligible code, and wrote an able pamphlet in its favor. I remember vividly the personal interest he took in one of the authors of that code—Benjamin F. Butler, then of Albany, and afterward, under the administration of Jackson, Attorney General of the United States—how much he was impressed with the purity of his character and the singleness of his mind, and how much we all admired him, on a visit which he made to New York, then a young man, with finely-chiseled features, made a little pale by study, and animated by an expression both of the greatest intelligence and ingenuousness. Mr. Sedgwick was warmly in favor of that change which has since been made in our laws—giving the wife the absolute disposal of her own property—the advantages of which he was fond of illustrating by the marital law of Louisiana. He was a zealous friend of universal freedom, and allowed no escaped slave from the South to be sent back if he could prevent it. I remember going with him on board a vessel just arrived from a Southern port, lying at a wharf in New York, in which it was said that a colored man was detained in order to be sent back into slavery. We found no indications of the presence of any such person, but if we had, he would have been immediately liberated by a writ of habeas corpus.

Meantime Miss Sedgwick was engaged in a work of somewhat humbler aim than Redwood, and in 1825 was published The Travelers, a work professing to give the narrative of a journey made by two very young persons, a brother and sister, with their parents, to Niagara and the great chain of our northern lakes. On their way these travelers meet every where some incident or some sight, which is made the source of entertainment and instruction. This was the first of Miss Sedgwick's books intended for young persons; the public gave it a ready welcome, and its **success, I suppose,** encouraged her in after years to write **the** series of works intended for young readers which became so deservedly popular. **I** was at that time one of **the editors** of a short-lived monthly periodical—the New York Review—in **which I** noticed the work, and gave one of the charming little narratives with which it is interspersed.

In 1827 appeared Hope **Leslie,** in which Miss Sedgwick **gave a picture of domestic life among the** early settlers of **New England.** Very distinct traces of that life, and of the peculiar ideas and character of the original Puritan colonists, **were then** to be observed in many New England neighbor**hoods,** though they have since, in this age of rapid changes, **almost** disappeared. With the aid of these, and the early **literature of our colonies, Miss Sedgwick accomplished her** task, as a skillful limner, by the help of a mask taken from the face of the dead and hints given **by surviving friends,** produces what is admitted to be a characteristic likeness **of** one who is no more. The old Puritan spirit, tempered somewhat by the gentler medium through which it has passed, informs every page of the book. It was now commonly **remarked** that Miss Sedgwick's literary reputation was entirely of home-growth, and that her **works were admired, and** added to our household libraries **without** asking, as had **too often** been the case in regard to **other American authors, permission from** the critics of **Great Britain.** Hope Leslie passed through several editions, and **was, I think, more** widely read than any of Miss Sedgwick's previous works.

Three years afterward, her fourth novel, Clarence : **a** Tale of our own Times, was **published in** Philadelphia in two volumes, and soon after it **was brought out in** London in three. I think this has been the least read of any of her larger works.

A little later the Brothers Harper conceived the idea of publishing a collection of tales by several well-known authors, and applied to Miss Sedgwick to become one of the contributors. She complied, and two volumes were published in 1832, to which Robert C. Sands furnished an amusing introduction, and gave the collection the odd and not very well-sounding title of Tales of the Glauber Spa. The contribution of Miss Sedgwick was a tale of the times of Charlemagne, entitled Le Bossu, in which she skillfully availed herself of the elements of the picturesque to be found in the customs of that warlike age, and the semi-barbarous magnificence of the court of that mighty monarch. The other tales in the collection were written by Sands, James K. Paulding, William Leggett, and myself.

In 1834 I went abroad, and remained for about two years, during which I could only observe Miss Sedgwick's literary career from a distance. During my absence, in 1835, she published The Linwoods, or Sixty Years Since in America, a charming tale of home life, with the incidents of which are in part interwoven those of our revolutionary history. This is thought by many to be the best of her novels properly so called, as it was the last.* There was no lack of warmth in the welcome which the public gave it ; edition after edition was called for, and the author had every assurance that other works of the same kind from her hand would meet with equal favor, yet she adventured no farther in this work. Whether it was that she feared that it might not be in her power to excel what she had already written in this way, or, as is more probable, that she determined to devote her talents to purposes which more directly regarded the good of

* This is a mistake, but, as it has been put in type, I prefer to correct it in a note. In 1857, twenty-two years after the appearance of the Linwoods, Miss Sedgwick gave the reading world another novel, entitled Married or Single, which by some is preferred to any of her previous ones.—*Note by W C. Bryant.*

society, from that time she composed only works of a less
ambitious and elaborate character ; all of them designed to
illustrate some lesson in human life, to enforce some duty,
or warn from some error of conduct, and all most happily
adapted to this purpose.   I recollect a singular attestation
to the power of these writings over the feelings of the reader.   Mr. Wesley Harper, one of the brothers who established the great publishing house which bears their name, and
which published several of these minor works of Miss Sedgwick, was in the practice of revising the proof-sheets before
they were sent to the press.   In performing that office, he
once remarked to me that he was fairly carried away by his
emotions, and could not restrain himself from weeping profusely.   I can assure the reader that it is no easy feat to
draw tears from the eyes of a veteran proof-reader.

About the year 1840 Miss Sedgwick visited Europe.   A
pleasant series of letters relating to this visit, addressed to
her kinsfolk at home, appeared in 1841.   I remember an
anecdote related by her of her sojourn in England, which
does not appear in her book.   A lady asked her, " Have you
any large old trees in America ? "   And then, checking herself before she could be answered, she said, " Oh, I beg your
pardon ; your country has not been settled long enough for
that ! "   I have since heard this anecdote matched by another, which is anonymous, and I fear not so authentic, of a
lady in England who wrote to her friend in Massachusetts
that a fair was to be held in her neighborhood for some
charitable purpose, to which she would be glad to send
something curious from America, and that if, in some of his
drives or rambles, he could, without much trouble, get for
her a vial of water from the cataract of Niagara, and chop
off a small piece of the Natural Bridge, and bring home for
her some little matter from the Mammoth Cave, she would
be infinitely obliged.

After this time I saw comparatively little of Miss Sedgwick. Both the brothers who resided in New York were dead; her time was divided between her friends in the neighborhood of Boston and those in her native Berkshire, and I was obliged to content myself with reading her works as they came from the press. One of these, which gave me particular pleasure, was her Life of Joseph Curtis, of New York, who passed a long life in works of charity and mercy, in labors for the relief of the wretched and the instruction of the ignorant, and whose example she has admirably held up to imitation. I often thought of her record of this good man's most useful, unostentatious labors when the Old World and the New vied with each other in paying honors to George Peabody, the opulent banker, whose whole life was occupied in heaping up millions to be bestowed at last in showy charities, whose funeral procession was a fleet furnished by two mighty empires, crossing the wide ocean that separate the two great continents of Christendom, from a harbor darkened with the ensigns of mourning in Europe to another in America, while the departure of Joseph Curtis called forth no general manifestation of sorrow. But the memoir of Miss Sedgwick is his monument, and it is a noble and worthy memorial of his virtues and services.

I am sorry that my materials for that part of Miss Sedgwick's literary life of which I have undertaken to speak are so scanty, and that I can recollect no more of it. Admirable as it was, her home life was more so; and beautiful as were the examples set forth in her writings, her own example was, if possible, still more beautiful. Her unerring sense of rectitude, her love of truth, her ready sympathy, her active and cheerful beneficence, her winning and gracious manners, the perfection of high breeding, make up a character, the idea of which, as it rests on my mind, I would not exchange for any thing in her own interesting works of fiction.

Miss Sedgwick's Works.

Miss Sedgwick has marked individuality; she writes with a higher aim than merely to amuse. Indeed, the rare endowments of her mind depend in an unusual degree upon the moral qualities with which they are united for their value. Animated by a cheerful philosophy, and anxious to pour its sunshine into every place where there is lurking care or suffering, she selects for illustration the scenes of everyday experience, paints them with exact fidelity, and seeks to diffuse over the mind a delicious serenity, and in the heart kind feelings and sympathies, and wise ambition and steady hope. Her style is colloquial, picturesque, and marked by a facile grace which is evidently a gift of nature. Her characters are nicely drawn and delicately contrasted; her delineation of manners decidedly the best that has appeared.—*Prose Writers of America.*

LIFE AND LETTERS OF CATHARINE M. SEDGWICK. Edited by MARY E. DEWEY. Portrait on Steel and Frontispiece. 12mo, Cloth.

HOPE LESLIE. A Novel. 2 vols., 12mo, Cloth, $3 00.

LETTERS FROM ABROAD to Kindred at Home. 2 vols., 12mo, Cloth, $3 00.

THE LINWOODS. 2 vols., 12mo, Cloth, $3 00.

LIVE AND LET LIVE; or, Domestic Service Illustrated. 18mo, Cloth, 75 cents.

LOVE TOKEN FOR CHILDREN. Designed for Sunday-School Libraries. 18mo,
Cloth, 75 cents.

MARRIED OR SINGLE? A Novel. 2 vols.,
12mo, Cloth, $3 00.

MEANS AND ENDS; or, Self-Training.
18mo, Cloth, 75 cents.

MEMOIR OF JOSEPH CURTIS. A Model Man. 16mo, Cloth, 75 cents.

*THE POOR RICH MAN AND THE RICH
POOR MAN.* 18mo, Cloth, 75 cents.

STORIES FOR YOUNG PERSONS. 18mo,
Cloth, 75 cents.

TALES OF GLAUBER SPA. By Miss
CATHARINE M. SEDGWICK and Others. 12mo,
Cloth, $1 50.

WILTON HARVEY, and Other Tales. 18mo,
Cloth, 75 cents.

PUBLISHED BY

HARPER & BROTHERS, NEW YORK.

☞ *Sent by mail, postage prepaid, to any part of the United States,
on receipt of the price.*

VALUABLE STANDARD WORKS

FOR PUBLIC AND PRIVATE LIBRARIES,

PUBLISHED BY HARPER & BROTHERS, NEW YORK.

MOTLEY'S DUTCH REPUBLIC. The Rise of the Dutch Republic. By JOHN LOTHROP MOTLEY, LL.D., D.C.L. With a Portrait of William of Orange. 3 vols., 8vo, Cloth, $10 50.

MOTLEY'S UNITED NETHERLANDS. History of the United Netherlands: from the Death of William the Silent to the Twelve Years' Truce—1609. With a full View of the English-Dutch Struggle against Spain, and of the Origin and Destruction of the Spanish Armada. By JOHN LOTHROP MOTLEY, LL.D., D.C.L. Portraits. 4 vols., 8vo, Cloth, $14 00.

NAPOLEON'S LIFE OF CÆSAR. The History of Julius Cæsar. By His Imperial Majesty NAPOLEON III. Two Volumes ready. Library Edition, 8vo, Cloth, $3 50 per vol.
Maps to Vols. I. and II. sold separately. Price $1 50 each, NET.

HAYDN'S DICTIONARY OF DATES, relating to all Ages and Nations. For Universal Reference. Edited by BENJAMIN VINCENT, Assistant Secretary and Keeper of the Library of the Royal Institution of Great Britain; and Revised for the Use of American Readers. 8vo, Cloth, $5 00; Sheep, $6 00.

MACGREGOR'S ROB ROY ON THE JORDAN. The Rob Roy on the Jordan, Nile, Red Sea, and Gennesareth, &c. A Canoe Cruise in Palestine and Egypt, and the Waters of Damascus. By J. MACGREGOR, M.A. With Maps and Illustrations. Crown 8vo, Cloth, $2 50.

WALLACE'S MALAY ARCHIPELAGO. The Malay Archipelago: the Land of the Orang-Utan and the Bird of Paradise. A Narrative of Travel, 1854-1862. With Studies of Man and Nature. By ALFRED RUSSEL WALLACE. With Ten Maps and Fifty-one Elegant Illustrations. Crown 8vo, Cloth, $3 50.

WHYMPER'S ALASKA. Travel and Adventure in the Territory of Alaska, formerly Russian America—now Ceded to the United States—and in various other parts of the North Pacific. By FREDERICK WHYMPER. With Map and Illustrations. Crown 8vo, Cloth, $2 50.

ORTON'S ANDES AND THE AMAZON. The Andes and the Amazon; or, Across the Continent of South America. By JAMES ORTON, M.A., Professor of Natural History in Vassar College, Poughkeepsie, N. Y., and Corresponding Member of the Academy of Natural Sciences, Philadelphia. With a New Map of Equatorial America and numerous Illustrations. Crown 8vo, Cloth, $2 00.

LOSSING'S FIELD-BOOK OF THE REVOLUTION. Pictorial Field-Book of the Revolution; or, Illustrations, by Pen and Pencil, of the History, Biography, Scenery, Relics, and Traditions of the War for Independence. By BENSON J. LOSSING. 2 vols., 8vo, Cloth, $14 00; Sheep, $15 00; Half Calf, $18 00; Full Turkey Morocco, $22 00.

LOSSING'S FIELD-BOOK OF THE WAR OF 1812. **Pictorial** Field-Book of the War of 1812; or, Illustrations, by Pen and Pencil, of the History, Biography, Scenery, Relics, and Traditions of the Last War for American Independence. By BENSON J. LOSSING. With several hundred Engravings on Wood, by Lossing and Barritt, chiefly from Original Sketches by the Author. 1088 pages, 8vo, Cloth, $7 00; Sheep, $8 50; Half Calf, $10 00.

WINCHELL'S SKETCHES OF CREATION. Sketches of Creation : a Popular View of some of the Grand Conclusions of the Sciences in reference to the History of Matter and of Life. Together with a Statement of the Intimations of Science respecting the Primordial Condition and the Ultimate Destiny of the Earth and the Solar System. By ALEXANDER WINCHELL, LL.D., Professor of Geology, Zoology, and Botany in **the** University of Michigan, and Director of the State Geological Survey. With Illustrations. 12mo, Cloth, $2 00.

WHITE'S MASSACRE **OF** ST. BARTHOLOMEW. The Massacre of St. Bartholomew : Preceded by a History of the Religious Wars in the Reign of Charles IX. **By** HENRY WHITE, M.A. With Illustrations. 8vo, Cloth, $1 75.

ALFORD'S GREEK TESTAMENT. The Greek Testament : with a critically-revised Text; a Digest **of** Various Readings; Marginal References to Verbal and Idiomatic Usage; Prolegomena; and a Critical and Exegetical Commentary. For the Use of Theological Students and Ministers. By HENRY ALFORD, D.D., Dean of Canterbury. Vol. I., containing the Four Gospels. 944 pages, 8vo, Cloth, $6 00; Sheep, $6 50.

ABBOTT'S HISTORY OF THE FRENCH REVOLUTION. **The** French Revolution of 1789, as viewed in the Light of Republican Institutions. **By** JOHN S. C. ABBOTT. With **100** Engravings. 8vo, Cloth, $5 00.

ABBOTT'S NAPOLEON BONAPARTE. The History of Napoleon Bonaparte. **By** JOHN S. C. ABBOTT. With Maps, Woodcuts, and Portraits **on Steel. 2 vols., 8vo**, Cloth, $10 00.

ABBOTT'S NAPOLEON AT ST. HELENA ; or, Interesting Anecdotes and Remarkable Conversations of the Emperor during the Five and a Half Years of his Captivity. Collected from the Memorials of Las Casas, O'Meara, Montholon, Antommarchi, and others. By JOHN S. C. ABBOTT. With Illustrations. 8vo, Cloth, $5 00.

ADDISON'S COMPLETE WORKS. The Works of Joseph **Addison, em-**bracing the whole of the "Spectator." Complete in 3 vols., **8vo, Cloth,** $6 00.

ALCOCK'S JAPAN. The **Capital** of the Tycoon : a Narrative of a **Three** Years' Residence in Japan. By Sir RUTHERFORD ALCOCK, K.C.B., **Her** Majesty's Envoy Extraordinary and Minister Plenipotentiary in Japan. With Maps and Engravings. 2 vols., 12mo, Cloth, $3 50.

ALISON'S HISTORY OF EUROPE. FIRST SERIES : From the Commencement of the French Revolution, in 1789, to the Restoration of the Bourbons, in 1815. [In addition to the Notes on Chapter LXXVI., which correct the errors of the original work concerning the United States, a copious Analytical Index has been appended to this American edition.] SECOND SERIES : From the Fall of Napoleon, in 1815, to the Accession of Louis Napoleon, in 1852. 8 vols., 8vo, Cloth, $16 00.

BANCROFT'S MISCELLANIES. Literary **and Historical** Miscellanies. By GEORGE BANCROFT. 8vo, Cloth, $3 00.

BALDWIN'S PRE-HISTORIC NATIONS. Pre-Historic Nations; or, In-quiries concerning some of the Great Peoples and Civilizations of An-tiquity, and their Probable Relation to a still Older Civilization of the Ethiopians or Cushites of Arabia. By JOHN D. BALDWIN, Member of the American Oriental Society. 12mo, Cloth, $1 75.

BARTH'S NORTH AND CENTRAL AFRICA. Travels and Discoveries in North and Central Africa: being a Journal of an Expedition under-taken under the Auspices of H. B. M.'s Government, in the Years 1849-1855. By HENRY BARTH, Ph.D., D.C.L. Illustrated. 3 vols., 8vo, Cloth, $12 00.

HENRY WARD BEECHER'S SERMONS. Sermons by HENRY WARD BEECH-ER, Plymouth Church, Brooklyn. Selected from Published and Unpub-lished Discourses, and Revised by their Author. With Steel Portrait. Complete in 2 vols., 8vo, Cloth, $5 00.

LYMAN BEECHER'S AUTOBIOGRAPHY, &c. Autobiography, Corre-spondence, &c., of Lyman Beecher, D.D. Edited by his Son, CHARLES BEECHER. With Three Steel Portraits, and Engravings on Wood. In 2 vols., 12mo, Cloth, $5 00.

BELLOWS'S OLD WORLD. The Old World in its New Face: Impressions of Europe in 1867-1868. By HENRY W. BELLOWS. 2 vols., 12mo, Cloth, $3 50.

BOSWELL'S JOHNSON. The Life of Samuel Johnson, LL.D. Including a Journey to the Hebrides. By JAMES BOSWELL, Esq. A New Edition, with numerous Additions and Notes. By JOHN WILSON CROKER, LL.D., F.R.S. Portrait of Boswell. 2 vols., 8vo, Cloth, $4 00.

BRODHEAD'S HISTORY OF NEW YORK. History of the State of New York. By JOHN ROMEYN BRODHEAD. 1609-1691. 2 vols. 8vo, Cloth, $3 00 each.

BULWER'S PROSE WORKS. Miscellaneous Prose Works of Edward Bul-wer, Lord Lytton. 2 vols., 12mo, Cloth, $3 50.

BURNS'S LIFE AND WORKS. The Life and Works of Robert Burns. Edited by ROBERT CHAMBERS. 4 vols., 12mo, Cloth, $6 00.

CARLYLE'S FREDERICK THE GREAT. History of Friedrich II., called Frederick the Great. By THOMAS CARLYLE. Portraits, Maps, Plans, &c. 6 vols., 12mo, Cloth, $12 00.

CARLYLE'S FRENCH REVOLUTION. History of the French Revolution. Newly Revised by the Author, with Index, &c. 2 vols., 12mo, Cloth, $3 50.

CARLYLE'S OLIVER CROMWELL. Letters and Speeches of Oliver Crom-well. With Elucidations and Connecting Narrative. 2 vols., 12mo, Cloth, $3 50.

CHALMERS'S POSTHUMOUS WORKS. The Posthumous Works of Dr Chalmers. Edited by his Son-in-Law, Rev. WILLIAM HANNA, LL.D. Complete in 9 vols., 12mo, Cloth, $13 50.

COLERIDGE'S COMPLETE WORKS. The Complete Works of Samuel Taylor Coleridge. With an Introductory Essay upon his Philosophical and Theological Opinions. Edited by Professor SHEDD. Complete in Seven Vols. With a fine Portrait. Small 8vo, Cloth, $10 50.

CURTIS'S HISTORY OF THE CONSTITUTION. History of the Origin, Formation, and Adoption of the Constitution of the United States. By GEORGE TICKNOR CURTIS. 2 vols., 8vo, Cloth, $6 00.

DAVIS'S CARTHAGE. Carthage and her Remains: being an Account of the Excavations and Researches on the Site of the Phœnician Metropolis in Africa and other adjacent Places. Conducted under the Auspices of Her Majesty's Government. By Dr. DAVIS, F.R.G.S. Profusely Illus-trated with Maps, Woodcuts, Chromo-Lithographs, &c. 8vo, Cloth, $4 00.

DRAPER'S CIVIL WAR. History of the American Civil War. By JOHN W. DRAPER, M.D., LL.D., Professor of Chemistry and Physiology in the University of New York. In Three Vols. 8vo, Cloth, $3 50 per vol.

DRAPER'S INTELLECTUAL DEVELOPMENT OF EUROPE. A History of the Intellectual Development of Europe. By JOHN W. DRAPER, M.D., LL.D., Professor of Chemistry and Physiology in the University of New York. 8vo, Cloth, $5 00.

DRAPER'S AMERICAN CIVIL POLICY. Thoughts on the Future Civil Policy of America. By JOHN W. DRAPER, M.D., LL.D., Professor of Chemistry and Physiology in the University of New York. Crown 8vo, Cloth, $2 50.

DU CHAILLU'S AFRICA. Explorations and Adventures in Equatorial Africa: with Accounts of the Manners and Customs of the People, and of the Chase of the Gorilla, the Crocodile, Leopard, Elephant, Hippopotamus, and other Animals. By PAUL B. DU CHAILLU. Numerous Illustrations. 8vo, Cloth, $5 00.

DU CHAILLU'S ASHANGO LAND. A Journey to Ashango Land: and Further Penetration into Equatorial Africa. By PAUL B. DU CHAILLU. New Edition. Handsomely Illustrated. 8vo, Cloth, $5 00.

DOOLITTLE'S CHINA. Social Life of the Chinese: with some Account of their Religious, Governmental, Educational, and Business Customs and Opinions. With special but not exclusive Reference to Fuhchau. By Rev. JUSTUS DOOLITTLE, Fourteen Years Member of the Fuhchau Mission of the American Board. Illustrated with more than 150 characteristic Engravings on Wood. 2 vols., 12mo, Cloth, $5 00.

EDGEWORTH'S (MISS) NOVELS. With Engravings. 10 vols., 12mo, Cloth, $15 00.

GIBBON'S ROME. History of the Decline and Fall of the Roman Empire. By EDWARD GIBBON. With Notes by Rev. H. H. MILMAN and M. GUIZOT. A new cheap Edition. To which is added a complete Index of the whole Work, and a Portrait of the Author. 6 vols., 12mo, Cloth, $9 00.

GROTE'S HISTORY OF GREECE. 12 vols., 12mo, Cloth, $18 00.

HALE'S (MRS.) WOMAN'S RECORD. Woman's Record; or, Biographical Sketches of all Distinguished Women, from the Creation to the Present Time. Arranged in Four Eras, with Selections from Female Writers of each Era. By Mrs. SARAH JOSEPHA HALE. Illustrated with more than 200 Portraits. 8vo, Cloth, $5 00.

HALL'S ARCTIC RESEARCHES. Arctic Researches and Life among the Esquimaux: being the Narrative of an Expedition in Search of Sir John Franklin, in the Years 1860, 1861, and 1862. By CHARLES FRANCIS HALL. With Maps and 100 Illustrations. The Illustrations are from Original Drawings by Charles Parsons, Henry L. Stephens, Solomon Eytinge, W. S. L. Jewett, and Granville Perkins, after Sketches by Captain Hall. 8vo, Cloth, $5 00.

HALLAM'S CONSTITUTIONAL HISTORY OF ENGLAND, from the Accession of Henry VII. to the Death of George II. 8vo, Cloth, $2 00.

HALLAM'S LITERATURE. Introduction to the Literature of Europe during the Fifteenth, Sixteenth, and Seventeenth Centuries. By HENRY HALLAM. 2 vols., 8vo, Cloth, $4 00.

HALLAM'S MIDDLE AGES. State of Europe during the Middle Ages. By HENRY HALLAM. 8vo, Cloth, $2 00.

HILDRETH'S HISTORY OF THE UNITED STATES. FIRST SERIES: From the First Settlement of the Country to the Adoption of the Federal Constitution. SECOND SERIES: From the Adoption of the Federal Constitution to the End of the Sixteenth Congress. 6 vols., 8vo, Cloth, $18 00.

HARPER'S PICTORIAL HISTORY OF THE REBELLION. Harper's Pictorial History of the Great Rebellion in the United States. With nearly 1000 Illustrations. In Two Vols., 4to. Price $6 00 per vol.

HARPER'S NEW CLASSICAL LIBRARY. Literal Translations. The following Volumes are now ready. Portraits. 12mo, Cloth, $1 50 each.
CÆSAR. —VIRGIL. — SALLUST. — HORACE.— CICERO'S ORATIONS.—CICERO'S OFFICES, &c.—CICERO ON ORATORY AND ORATORS.—TACITUS (2 vols.). —TERENCE.—SOPHOCLES.—JUVENAL.—XENOPHON.—HOMER'S ILIAD.— HOMER'S ODYSSEY. — HERODOTUS. — DEMOSTHENES. — THUCYDIDES. — ÆSCHYLUS.—EURIPIDES (2 vols.).—LIVY (2 vols.).

HELPS'S SPANISH CONQUEST. The Spanish Conquest in America, and its Relation to the History of Slavery and to the Government of Colonies. By ARTHUR HELPS. 4 vols., 12mo, Cloth, $6 00.

HUME'S HISTORY OF ENGLAND. History of England, from the Invasion of Julius Cæsar to the Abdication of James II., 1688. By DAVID HUME. A new Edition, with the Author's last Corrections and Improvements. To which is Prefixed a short Account of his Life, written by Himself. With a Portrait of the Author. 6 vols., 12mo, Cloth, $9 00.

JAY'S WORKS. Complete Works of Rev. William Jay: comprising his Sermons, Family Discourses, Morning and Evening Exercises for every Day in the Year, Family Prayers, &c. Author's enlarged Edition, revised. 3 vols., 8vo, Cloth, $6 00.

JOHNSON'S COMPLETE WORKS. The Works of Samuel Johnson, LL.D. With an Essay on his Life and Genius, by ARTHUR MURPHY, Esq. Portrait of Johnson. 2 vols., 8vo, Cloth, $4 00.

KINGLAKE'S CRIMEAN WAR. The Invasion of the Crimea, and an Account of its Progress down to the Death of Lord Raglan. By ALEXANDER WILLIAM KINGLAKE. With Maps and Plans. Two Vols. ready. 12mo, Cloth, $2 00 per vol.

KRUMMACHER'S DAVID, KING OF ISRAEL. David, the King of Israel: a Portrait drawn from Bible History and the Book of Psalms. By FREDERICK WILLIAM KRUMMACHER, D.D., Author of "Elijah the Tishbite," &c. Translated under the express Sanction of the Author by the Rev. M. G. EASTON, M.A. With a Letter from Dr. Krummacher to his American Readers, and a Portrait. 12mo, Cloth, $1 75.

LAMB'S **COMPLETE** WORKS. The Works of Charles Lamb. Comprising his **Letters, Poems,** Essays of Elia, Essays upon Shakspeare, Hogarth, &c., **and a Sketch of** his Life, **with** the Final Memorials, by T. NOON TALFOURD. Portrait. 2 vols., 12mo, Cloth, $3 00.

LIVINGSTONE'S SOUTH AFRICA. Missionary Travels and Researches in South Africa; including a Sketch of Sixteen Years' Residence in the Interior of Africa, and a Journey from the Cape of Good Hope to Loando on the West Coast; thence across the Continent, down the River Zambesi, to the Eastern Ocean. By DAVID LIVINGSTONE, LL.D., D.C.L. With Portrait, Maps by Arrowsmith, and numerous Illustrations. 8vo, Cloth, $4 50.

LIVINGSTONE'S ZAMBESI. Narrative of an Expedition to the Zambesi and its Tributaries, and of the Discovery of the Lakes Shirwa and Nyassa. 1858–1864. By DAVID and CHARLES LIVINGSTONE. With Map and Illustrations. 8vo, Cloth, $5 00.

MARCY'S ARMY LIFE ON THE BORDER. Thirty Years of Army Life on the Border. Comprising Descriptions of the Indian Nomads of the Plains; Explorations of New Territory; a Trip across the Rocky Mountains in the Winter; Descriptions of the Habits of Different Animals found in the West, and the Methods of Hunting them; with Incidents in the Life of Different Frontier Men, &c., &c. By Brevet Brigadier-General R. B. MARCY, U.S.A., Author of "The Prairie Traveller." With numerous Illustrations. 8vo, Cloth, Beveled Edges, $3 00.

M'CLINTOCK & STRONG'S CYCLOPÆDIA. Cyclopædia of Biblical, Theological, and Ecclesiastical Literature. Prepared by the Rev. John M'Clintock, D.D., and James Strong, S.T.D. 3 *vols. now ready.* Royal 8vo. Price per vol., Cloth, $5 00; Sheep, $6 00; Half Morocco, $8 00.

MACAULAY'S HISTORY OF ENGLAND. The History of England from the Accession of James II. By Thomas Babington Macaulay. With an Original Portrait of the Author. 5 vols., 8vo, Cloth, $10 00; 12mo, Cloth, $7 50.

MOSHEIM'S ECCLESIASTICAL HISTORY, Ancient and Modern; In which the Rise, Progress, and Variation of Church Power are considered in their Connection with the State of Learning and Philosophy, and the Political History of Europe during that Period. Translated, with Notes, &c., by A. Maclaine, D.D. A new Edition, continued to 1826, by C. Coote, LL.D. 2 vols., 8vo, Cloth, $4 00.

NEVIUS'S CHINA. China and the Chinese: a General Description of the Country and its Inhabitants; its Civilization and Form of Government; its Religious and Social Institutions; its Intercourse with other Nations; and its Present Condition and Prospects. By the Rev. John L. Nevius, Ten Years a Missionary in China. With a Map and Illustrations. 12mo, Cloth, $1 75.

OLIN'S (Dr.) LIFE AND LETTERS. 2 vols., 12mo, Cloth, $3 00.

OLIN'S (Dr.) TRAVELS. Travels in Egypt, Arabia Petræa, and the Holy Land. Engravings. 2 vols., 8vo, Cloth, $3 00.

OLIN'S (Dr.) WORKS. The Works of Stephen Olin, D.D., late President of the Wesleyan University. 2 vols., 12mo, Cloth, $3 00.

OLIPHANT'S **CHINA** AND JAPAN. Narrative of the Earl of Elgin's Mission to China and Japan, in the Years 1857, '58, '59. By Laurence Oliphant, Private Secretary to Lord Elgin. Illustrations. 8vo, Cloth, $3 50.

OLIPHANT'S (Mrs.) LIFE OF EDWARD IRVING. The Life of Edward Irving, Minister of the National Scotch Church, London. Illustrated by his Journals and Correspondence. By Mrs. Oliphant. Portrait. 8vo, Cloth, $3 50.

PAGE'S **LA PLATA.** La Plata: the Argentine Confederation **and Paraguay.** Being a Narrative of the Exploration of the Tributaries of **the River La** Plata and Adjacent Countries, during the Years 1853, '54, '55, and '56, under the Orders of the United States Government. New Edition, containing Farther Explorations in La Plata, during 1859 and '60. By Thomas J. Page, U.S.N., Commander of the Expeditions. With Map and numerous Engravings. 8vo, Cloth, **$5** 00.

POETS **OF** THE NINETEENTH CENTURY. The Poets of the Nineteenth Century. Selected and Edited by the Rev. Robert Aris Willmott. With English and American Additions, arranged by **Evert A.** Duyckinck, Editor of "Cyclopædia of American Literature." Comprising Selections from the Greatest Authors of the Age. Superbly Illustrated with **132** Engravings from Designs by the most Eminent Artists. In **elegant** small 4to form, printed on Superfine Tinted Paper, richly bound in **extra** Cloth, Beveled, Gilt Edges, $6 00; Half Calf, $6 00; Full Turkey Morocco, $10 00.

PRIME'S COINS, MEDALS, AND SEALS. Coins, Medals, **and** Seals, Ancient and Modern. Illustrated and Described. With **a** Sketch of the History of Coins and Coinage, Instructions for Young Collectors, Tables of Comparative Rarity, Price-Lists of English and American Coins, Medals, and Tokens, &c., &c. Edited by W. C. Prime, Author of "Boat Life in Egypt and Nubia," "Tent Life in the Holy Land," **&c.**, &c. 8vo, Cloth, $3 50.

SPRING'S SERMONS. Pulpit Ministrations; or, Sabbath Readings. A Series of Discourses on Christian Doctrine and Duty. By Rev. Gardiner Spring, D.D., Pastor of the Brick Presbyterian Church in the City of New York. Portrait on Steel. 2 vols., 8vo, Cloth, $6 00.

SHAKSPEARE. The Dramatic Works of William Shakspeare, with the Corrections and Illustrations of Dr. JOHNSON, G. STEEVENS, and others. Revised by ISAAC REED. Engravings. 6 vols., Royal 12mo, Cloth, $9 00.

SMILES'S LIFE OF THE STEPHENSONS. The Life of George Stephenson, and of his Son, Robert Stephenson; comprising, also, a History of the Invention and Introduction of the Railway Locomotive. By SAMUEL SMILES, Author of "Self-Help," &c. With Steel Portraits and numerous Illustrations. 8vo, Cloth, $3 00.

SMILES'S HISTORY OF THE HUGUENOTS. The Huguenots: their Settlements, Churches, and Industries in England and Ireland. By SAMUEL SMILES. With an Appendix relating to the Huguenots in America. Crown 8vo, Cloth, Beveled, $1 75.

SMILES'S SELF-HELP. Self-Help; with Illustrations of Character, Conduct, and Perseverance. By SAMUEL SMILES. New Edition, Revised and Enlarged. 12mo, Cloth, $1 00.

SPEKE'S AFRICA. Journal of the Discovery of the Source of the Nile. By Captain JOHN HANNING SPEKE, Captain H. M. Indian Army, Fellow and Gold Medalist of the Royal Geographical Society, Hon. Corresponding Member and Gold Medalist of the French Geographical Society, &c. With Maps and Portraits and numerous Illustrations, chiefly from Drawings by Captain GRANT. 8vo, Cloth, uniform with Livingstone, Barth, Burton, &c., $4 00.

STRICKLAND'S (MISS) **QUEENS OF SCOTLAND.** Lives of the Queens of Scotland and English Princesses connected with the Regal Succession of Great Britain. By AGNES STRICKLAND. 8 vols., 12mo, Cloth, $12 00.

THE STUDENT'S HISTORIES.
France. Engravings. 12mo, Cloth, $2 00.
Gibbon. Engravings. 12mo, Cloth, $2 00.
Greece. Engravings. 12mo, Cloth, $2 00.
Hume. Engravings. 12mo, Cloth, $2 00.
Rome. By Liddell. Engravings. 12mo, Cloth, $2 00.
Old Testament History. Engravings. 12mo, Cloth, $2 00.
New Testament History. Engravings. 12mo, Cloth, $2 00.
Strickland's Queens of England. Abridged. Engravings. 12mo, Cloth, $2 00.

TENNYSON'S COMPLETE POEMS. The Complete Poems of Alfred Tennyson, Poet Laureate. With numerous Illustrations by Eminent Artists, and Three Characteristic Portraits. 8vo, Paper, 75 cts.; Cloth, $1 25.

THOMSON'S LAND AND THE BOOK. The Land and the Book; or, Biblical Illustrations drawn from the Manners and Customs, the Scenes and the Scenery of the Holy Land. By W. M. THOMSON, D.D., Twenty-five Years a Missionary of the A.B.C.F.M. in Syria and Palestine. With two elaborate Maps of Palestine, an accurate Plan of Jerusalem, and several hundred Engravings, representing the Scenery, Topography, and Productions of the Holy Land, and the Costumes, Manners, and Habits of the People. 2 large 12mo vols., Cloth, $5 00.

TICKNOR'S HISTORY OF SPANISH LITERATURE. With Criticisms on the particular Works, and Biographical Notices of Prominent Writers. 3 vols., 8vo, Cloth, $5 00.

VÁMBÉRY'S CENTRAL ASIA. Travels in Central Asia. Being the Account of a Journey from Teheran across the Turkoman Desert, on the Eastern Shore of the Caspian, to Khiva, Bokhara, and Samarcand, performed in the Year 1863. By ARMINIUS VÁMBÉRY, Member of the Hungarian Academy of Pesth, by whom he was sent on this Scientific Mission. With Map and Woodcuts. 8vo, Cloth, $4 50.

ENGLISHMAN'S GREEK CONCORDANCE. The Englishman's Greek Concordance of the New Testament: being an Attempt at a Verbal Connection between the Greek and the English Texts; including a Concordance to the Proper Names, with Indexes, Greek-English and English-Greek. 8vo, Cloth, $5 00.

WOOD'S HOMES WITHOUT HANDS. Homes Without Hands: being a Description of the Habitations of Animals, classed according to their Principle of Construction. By J. G. Wood, M.A., F.L.S., Author of "Illustrated Natural History." With about 140 Illustrations, engraved by G. Pearson, from Original Designs made by F. W. Keyl and E. A. Smith, under the Author's Superintendence. 8vo, Cloth, Beveled Edges, $4 50.

WILKINSON'S ANCIENT EGYPTIANS. A Popular Account of their Manners and Customs, condensed from his larger Work, with some New Matter. Illustrated with 500 Woodcuts. 2 vols., 12mo, Cloth, $3 50.

MAURY'S (M. F.) PHYSICAL GEOGRAPHY OF THE SEA. The Physical Geography of the Sea, and its Meteorology. By M. F. Maury, LL.D., late U.S.N. The Eighth Edition, Revised and greatly Enlarged. 8vo, Cloth, $4 00.

ANTHON'S SMITH'S DICTIONARY OF ANTIQUITIES. A Dictionary of Greek and Roman Antiquities. Edited by William Smith, LL.D., and Illustrated by numerous Engravings on Wood. Third American Edition, carefully Revised, and containing, also, numerous additional Articles relative to the Botany, Mineralogy, and Zoology of the Ancients. By Charles Anthon, LL.D. Royal 8vo, Sheep extra, $6 00.

ANTHON'S CLASSICAL DICTIONARY. Containing an Account of the principal Proper Names mentioned in Ancient Authors, and intended to elucidate all the important Points connected with the Geography, History, Biography, Mythology, and Fine Arts of the Greeks and Romans; together with an Account of the Coins, Weights, and Measures of the Ancients, with Tabular Values of the same. Royal 8vo, Sheep extra, $6 00.

DWIGHT'S (Rev. Dr.) THEOLOGY. Theology Explained and Defended, in a Series of Sermons. By Timothy Dwight, S.T.D., LL.D. With a Memoir of the Life of the Author. Portrait. 4 vols., 8vo, Cloth, $8 00.

FOWLER'S ENGLISH LANGUAGE. The English Language in its Elements and Forms. With a History of its Origin and Development, and a full Grammar. Designed for Use in Colleges and Schools. Revised and Enlarged. By William C Fowler, LL.D., late Professor in Amherst College. 8vo, Cloth, $2 50.

GIESELER'S ECCLESIASTICAL HISTORY. A Text-Book of Church History. By Dr. John C. L. Gieseler. Translated from the Fourth Revised German Edition by Samuel Davidson, LL.D., and Rev. John Winstanley Hull, M.A. A New American Edition, Revised and Edited by Rev. Henry B. Smith, D.D., Professor in the Union Theological Seminary, New York. Four Volumes ready. (*Vol. V. in Press.*) 8vo, Cloth, $2 25 per vol.

GODWIN'S (PARKE) HISTORY OF FRANCE. The History of France. From the Earliest Times to the French Revolution of 1789. By Parke Godwin. Vol. I. (Ancient Gaul). 8vo, Cloth, $3 00.

HALL'S (ROBERT) WORKS. The Complete Works of Robert Hall; with a brief Memoir of his Life, by Dr. Gregory, and Observations on his Character as a Preacher, by Rev. John Foster. Edited by Olinthus Gregory, LL.D., and Rev. Joseph Belcher. Portrait. 4 vols., 8vo, Cloth, $8 00.

HAMILTON'S (Sir WILLIAM) WORKS. Discussions on Philosophy and Literature, Education and University Reform. Chiefly from the *Edinburgh Review.* Corrected, Vindicated, and Enlarged, in Notes and Appendices. By Sir William Hamilton, Bart. With an Introductory Essay, by Rev. Robert Turnbull, D.D. 8vo, Cloth, $3 00.

HUMBOLDT'S COSMOS. Cosmos: a Sketch of a Physical Description of the Universe. By Alexander Von Humboldt. Translated from the German, by E. C. Otté. 5 vols., 12mo, Cloth, $6 25.

ROBINSON'S GREEK LEXICON OF THE TESTAMENT. A Greek and English Lexicon of the New Testament. By Edward Robinson, D.D., LL.D., late Professor of Biblical Literature in the Union Theological Seminary, New York. A New Edition, Revised, and in great part Rewritten. Royal 8vo, Cloth, $6 00.

www.ingramcontent.com/pod-product-compliance
Lightning Source LLC
Chambersburg PA
CBHW022027110726
47901CB00006B/1676